CLASSIC AMERICAN
WOMEN WRITERS

CLASSIC AMERICAN WOMEN WRITERS

EDITED WITH AN INTRODUCTION, CHRONOLOGIES AND BIBLIOGRAPHIES

CYNTHIA GRIFFIN WOLFF

SARAH ORNE JEWETT

KATE CHOPIN

EDITH WHARTON

WILLA CATHER

PERENNIAL LIBRARY
HARPER & ROW, PUBLISHERS
New York, Cambridge, Hagerstown, Philadelphia, San Francisco, London, Mexico City, São Paulo, Sydney

Grateful acknowledgement is made for permission to reprint:

"Désirée's Baby," "La Belle Zoraïde," "Athénaïse," "The Story of an Hour," "At the 'Cadian Ball," "The Storm," and "At Chênière Caminada" by Kate Chopin. Reprinted by permission of Louisiana State University Press from *The Complete Works of Kate Chopin*, Volume II, edited by Per Seyersted. Copyright © 1969 by Louisiana State University Press.

"The Muse's Tragedy," "The Souls Belated," and "The Other Two" by Edith Wharton. Reprinted with the permission of Charles Scribner's Sons.

"Roman Fever" by Edith Wharton. Reprinted with the permission of Charles Scribner's Sons from *The World Over* by Edith Wharton. Copyright 1934 by *Liberty* Magazine. Copyright renewed 1962 by William R. Tyler.

"Paul's Case," "The Sculptor's Funeral," and "A Wagner Matinee" by Willa Cather. Reprinted from *Youth and the Bright Medusa* by Willa Cather, by courtesy of Alfred A. Knopf, Inc.

"The Best Years" by Willa Cather. Reprinted from *Five Stories* by Willa Cather, by permission of Alfred A. Knopf, Inc. Copyright 1948 by Alfred A. Knopf, Inc.

 For information address Harper & Row, Publishers, Inc., 10 East 53rd Street, New York, N.Y. 10022. Published simultaneously in Canada by Fitzhenry & Whiteside Limited, Toronto.

FIRST EDITION

Designer: Janice Stern

Library of Congress Cataloging in Publication Data
Main entry under title:

Classic American women writers.

(Perennial library; P/502)
1. Short stories, American—Women authors.
I. Wolff, Cynthia Griffin.
PZ1.C5635. [PS647.W6] 813'.01 79-2743'
ISBN 0-06-080502-1

80 81 82 83 84 10 9 8 7 6 5 4 3 2 1

Contents

Introduction, by Cynthia Griffin Wolff 1

SARAH ORNE JEWETT

A White Heron 15
The Only Rose 30
The Hiltons' Holiday 51

KATE CHOPIN

Désirée's Baby 77
La Belle Zoraïde 85
Athénaïse 93
The Story of an Hour 139
At the 'Cadian Ball 143
The Storm 157
At Chênière Caminada 165

EDITH WHARTON

The Muse's Tragedy 183
Souls Belated 204
The Other Two 243
Roman Fever 272

WILLA CATHER

Paul's Case 293
The Sculptor's Funeral 323
A Wagner Matinee 344
The Best Years 356

Chronologies and Bibliographies 401

CLASSIC AMERICAN WOMEN WRITERS

Introduction

Until a very short time ago, teachers and scholars of American literature paid scant attention to the large body of excellent fiction written by women: someone who went to college or graduate school as recently as the 1960s or early 1970s might take the entire range of courses in American literature without being assigned a single substantial work by an American woman writer. The "canon" was assumed to consist of the works of Hawthorne, Twain, James, Hemingway, and the like; and if their female contemporaries were mentioned at all, they were alluded to only as interesting minor figures—imitators, perhaps, of the male masters. In recent years, this distortion of our literary heritage has been largely rectified; our canon is being reexamined and redefined, and fiction written by women is at last being taken seriously on its own merits. In almost every case, the dismissive attitude of benevolent neglect which prevailed for so long has been exposed as unjust; and while the work of Harriet Beecher Stowe or

Sarah Orne Jewett may still take second place beside that of Hawthorne or Melville, the work of Edith Wharton and Willa Cather can now be seen as fully qualified to stand beside that of Henry James and Ernest Hemingway. In the end we have lost nothing, for the works of the male writers remain untouched; instead we have been immeasurably enriched as our definition of American literature has expanded to include the work of those women writers we have so long neglected.

The writers whose stories are collected here represent the beginning of this tradition of great fiction by American women. (One would have to add the name of Harriet Beecher Stowe to make the list genuinely complete; however, her full-length works are so much better than her short stories—none of which gives hint of her genuine power—that her short fictions are not represented here.) Jewett, Chopin, Wharton, Cather—they seem at first glance a diverse group. Yet their short stories share certain curious traits.

Most strikingly, their focus is intensive rather than extensive. The plots of their stories do not include adventurous exploits into an American wilderness or daring business ventures or even an examination of current social problems. Kate Chopin asserted that the only true subject for great fiction is "human existence in its subtle, complex, true meaning, stripped of the veil with which ethical and conventional standards have draped it"; and this is a statement with which all of the authors included here would agree. As a result, their fiction has a timeless quality; if its superficial qualities seem quaint or dated, its essential subject retains an inexhaustible interest. As one might expect, these authors are more interested than their male counterparts in exploring human existence as it is experienced by women; yet, although every one of them experienced professional difficulties that grew directly out of the constraints that society places upon women, none of them is a polemicist. They shared the conviction that life's experiences are mixed and complex—far too complex for easy solutions or glib slogans. All would agree that the author's highest duty is to communicate a compassionate understanding of this poignant complexity, and it is the triumph of each that she has, in her own way, managed to do so.

Sarah Orne Jewett was born in Maine in 1849; she died there in 1909 and spent most of her life among the people whose lives she observed with such sympathy. The granddaughter of a whaling captain and the daughter of a country doctor (she longed to follow her father's profession, but—as a girl—was not encouraged to do so), Jewett had deep roots in the culture of northern New England. Her ear for native dialect was acute, and her eye for regional detail—her sense of custom and tradition—gave her stories so distinctly the flavor of the region which was her home that for many years she was known only as one of America's most skilled practitioners of "local color" fiction. Having been categorized as a regionalist writer, she was dismissed from the mainstream of American fiction.

Jewett herself never intended her fiction to be read so narrowly. To a large extent, the character of the people of Maine serves to represent what is best in America as a whole, most distinctive of our culture: independence, a sense of duty and courage, the capacity for hard work, and above all, integrity. These traits constitute a large portion of our national heritage. Indeed, Jewett saw a westward movement of the New England "type," and it was her conviction that just as the residents of Maine typified America in her time, so the Midwesterners of the future would play that same role. This prophetic vision was later confirmed by Cather, whose stories of the Great Plains treat characters with many of the same traits that had been found earlier in Jewett's New Englanders.

However, the dilemmas around which Jewett's sketches are built go beyond even the boundaries of her native America. They are tales of the human condition. Perhaps no other of her stories so successfully transcends time and place as "A White Heron." Several forces are at work on Sylvia, the girl-heroine: The indefinable enchantment of the stranger—a muted sexual appeal combined with a mysterious sense of "civilization," the city with all of its vague pleasures; the desire merely to be distinguished or heroic in successful pursuit of the bird, not a blandishment easily resisted by this girl who has always been so otherwise undistinguished; and finally, the majestic power of the heron itself—a life force or perhaps the force of timeless beauty and grandeur. It is Jewett's achievement here that the subtle complexity of these themes does not intrude upon the reader. It is an apparently simple story, simply (and exquisitely) told—its subject merely life.

The other two Jewett stories have this same

quality of deceptive simplicity. "The Only Rose" begins with an old woman's trivial problem and follows the crooked, repetitive pathways of her wandering thoughts. There is a social dilemma behind the situation: women who did not have independent means could often not afford to remain single or, if they were widowed, not to remarry. This rather topical dilemma drifts into the reader's vision (though never explicitly into the widow's) and yet fades as principal subject in the light of a more general question. Three kinds of love, three different relationships—each honorable, each sufficient to sustain a marriage. Which was best, after all? A similar question of relative values informs Jewett's own favorite among her short stories, "The Hiltons' Holiday," a work whose central concern is echoed movingly in Cather's much later work, "The Best Years."

Like Jewett, Kate Chopin was for many years dismissed as no more than a deft regional writer. Born in St. Louis in 1851, Kate O'Flaherty married Oscar Chopin in 1870 and moved with him to his native New Orleans. The couple lived there for nine years, and then for the next five years took residence in Cloutierville, a tiny rural village in northwestern Louisiana. By every account, Kate Chopin was deeply in love with her husband; and when he died suddenly in 1883 (leaving her with six children), she returned, utterly grief-stricken, to St. Louis, where she lived until her death. Chopin did not begin to write until after her husband's death, and at first the occupation was undertaken almost as a form of therapy to absorb some of the misery of her loneliness. She had always had a keen eye for detail and an equally sharp ear for nuances of speech (as a young woman she had entertained her appreciative friends with amusing mimicry), and it is perhaps not surprising that her earliest fictions should have been light sketches designed to capture the life and manners of New Orleans and rural Louisiana. Very soon, however, influenced by the example of the French novelist Guy de Maupassant, her work took a more serious turn.

Chopin saw life as a precarious state: always—even at our apparently most secure moments—circumstances may shift and our emotional stability collapse. The forces which act upon us may come from without (a financial reverse, a death) or from within (the flash of uncontrollable rage or the swift lightning of sexual passion); and the central dilemma of all human beings is to maintain equilibrium in the midst of such potential turmoil.

Almost all of Chopin's best work focuses upon these problems as they occur in marriage and motherhood, for despite her own quite happy marriage and her ardent devotion to her children, she perceived the complexity of emotions that can attend these deepest of ties. "Désirée's Baby," for example, captures the fine line between a husband's sexual passion and the conversion of this passion into blind, destructive rage. "La Belle Zoraïde" traces the separation of slave mother and child and the gradual descent into madness that is precipitated by this separation. "Athénaïse," one of the longest and most subtle of Chopin's short stories, treats the full complement of emotions that attend an adolescent girl's maturing into marriage and motherhood: the resentment at confinement, the rebellion at trivial adjustments demanded by intimate life with another, the reluctance to relinquish fantasies of romantic love, the first stirrings of genuine feminine sexuality. All of this is told with exquisite discretion and amazing candor. "The Story of an Hour" looks to another side of marriage—marriage as that which may imprison even though it binds with ties of love.

As Chopin became more proficient in her artistry, her treatment of these themes became more direct and frank. (A comparison of "At the 'Cadian Ball," one of Chopin's early sketches, with its sequel "The Storm," a late story never published in her lifetime, gives some sense of the direction her talent was taking.) In 1899 she published her greatest work, *The Awakening*, a sensitive account of a vulnerable woman feeling for the first time the full force of her most intimate passions. The novel is set in the sensuous climate of Grande Isle (the setting for the short story "At Chênière Caminade"); and the evocation of this caressing climate combines with a vividness of emotion to make *The Awakening* one of the three or four great novels of the American nineteenth century.

Unfortunately, Chopin's genius was in advance of its time. The novel was banned fewer than two weeks after publication, and Chopin, deeply disappointed, wrote very little more. She died in 1904, and her work fell almost immediately from public attention. Only in the last ten years has she received the full acclaim that eluded her during her lifetime.

Edith Wharton, the first woman to win the

Pulitzer Prize in literature, never suffered from the obscurity that haunted Chopin's work for so many years; however, Wharton endured a different sort of indignity—a repressive upbringing that almost succeeded in preventing her from writing at all. Born in New York City in 1862, the child of prosperous and socially prominent parents, Edith Wharton suffered from the full force of American Victorianism. Although she married at twenty-three, it was only ten days after her marriage (so she confessed autobiographically) that she fully understood where babies came from. Her marriage was comfortable, but never passionate; eventually she and her husband were divorced, and only when she was in her mid-forties did she discover passionate sexual fulfillment in a protracted love affair with Morton Fullerton, a protégé of Henry James.

Sexual prohibitions were coupled in her upbringing with absolute prohibitions against a woman's having any sort of occupation or profession save that of wife and mother. For many years Wharton longed to write, but the combination of social disapproval and personal guilt blocked her efforts. Eventually, she became one of America's most prolific great novelists, but the outpouring of creativity did not really begin until after she was forty.

The first three stories included here are all early efforts (for the most part, Wharton's early short stories—those that came before her novel-writing—are the best). The first, "The Muse's Tragedy," is especially poignant, for there is really a double subject. The first—quite explicit in the story—is Silvia Anerton's pain at never achieving authentic affection because her status as the "beautiful object' who was her beloved's "inspiration" did not allow it. The second is more subtle; it does not emerge explicitly in the story at all. Yet, given that the author of this tale is a woman, a perceptive reader may see the further problem: what is woman's role in the creative process? Is she to be the maker of beauty (an active artist herself), or only the passive object of some man's aesthetic contemplation?

"Souls Belated" and "The Other Two" take diametrically opposite positions from which to examine the complexity of passions that may combine to make a marriage. In "Souls Belated" the lovers have flaunted custom and convention and have run away to find their happiness somewhere that is utterly independent of the rest of the world. Marriage, they like to think, is not necessary. The question raised by the story is whether mere passion is enough. In "The Other Two" the accommodating Alice Waythorn is examined as we are introduced bit by bit to each of her three husbands (this story compares interestingly with Jewett's "The Only Rose"). The wife's role—it is her husband's expectation and right (the fiction makes that fact ironically clear)—is to adjust to her husband, to give up assertions of self and instead to adapt herself to *his* life. After she has done so and done so successfully, what can then be said to be left of the wife's *own* personality? Who is she, finally? The horrifying portrait of Alice Waythorn gives a grisly answer.

"Roman Fever" is one of Wharton's strongest

late stories (the title has a double meaning: it identifies the typhoid fever which threatened Roman tourists in the nineteenth century; it also identifies that particular fever or passion that characterizes impetuous, youthful love). Edith Wharton never had children; in the end, it was perhaps the greatest tragedy of her life—certainly she felt it as such. Perhaps by way of compensation, all of the best late works—both novels and short stories—treat the subject of parent and child. As a middle-aged woman and then as an elderly woman, Wharton recognized one of life's wry truths: all human beings make painful sacrifices—relinquish opportunities that can never be reclaimed; but there is compensation. To some degree, children may enjoy the things that their parents have lost, and in generously freeing their children to reclaim what they have lost, the parents, too, may finally savor some of the happiness that they have given over to the next generation.

Willa Cather is the most modern of our authors, for although she was born fewer than ten years after the end of the Civil War, she did not die until 1947—living to see not one but two global wars. Paradoxically, her work little reflects the vast changes that took place in America during her lifetime. She once remarked that her only meaningful and lasting impressions (that is, those which shaped her fictions) had all occurred before she was twenty. Influenced by Sarah Orne Jewett whom she met in the last years of that author's life, she was driven to discover that which was essential to the human experience—and especially that which was essential to the pioneering experience of this country. There is in all of her best work the muted force of some deeply primitive power.

Although she was born in Virginia, Cather moved with her family to the arid, harsh plains of frontier Nebraska when she was but nine years old. A sensitive child, she was oppressed and often horrified by the sea of grass scarcely touched by human habitation, by the force of a rude and cruel nature which brought blazing summers and arctic winters, and most of all by the numbing, stupifying dullness that threatened always to engulf her life. Her answer was to rebel.

As an adolescent, her rebellion took the form of tomboyish behavior: cutting her hair short, wearing boy's clothing, and studying science. Later, she went to the State University of Lincoln—more conventional now but still stubbornly resistant to the forces of conformity. Her long story, "Paul's Case," is almost certainly autobiographical in the sense that it captures the intensity of longing that Cather herself felt to transcend the givens of a trite world. Paul, however, is doomed from the beginning by his own febrile nature; Willa Cather was made of sturdier material.

After graduation from college, she served a long apprenticeship in the literary world, working in editorial positions for a number of magazines. Even in her first collection of short stories, which she did not publish until she was thirty-two, one can begin to hear the quintessential cadence of Cather's fiction. The subject of "The Sculptor's Funeral" and "A Wagner Matinee" is an uncultured, harsh land and its people—the Kansas natives who await the sculptor's coffin in a bleak railroad yard or the pathetic and poignant figure of Aunt Georgiana, who brings a lifetime of innocence to the Wagner matinee. Usually our impression of these people is filtered through the more sophisticated consciousness of an outsider, a city-dweller who becomes gradually appalled at the terms of existence implied by the lives of such people. And underlying all, there is, in the end, an uncertain question. Can it be that the privation, the intimate contact with brute nature, kindles an intenser flame of heroism than the apparently more admirable life of a cultured urban dweller? In the earlier stories—"The Sculptor's Funeral" and "A Wagner Matinée"—the verdict seems to come against that harsh pioneer life; however, in her later work—in the novels and in such shorter fictions as "The Best Years"—the uncompromising presence of Nature felt at first hand (rain heard directly overhead as it strikes the roof of an attic bedroom) seems the necessary condition for a full heroic development of individual identity. When you look back to draw your final conclusions, the story seems to say to the reader, what will have been *your* best years?

None of these American women writers suggests ready or tidy solutions. For each, life was a complex skein of problems—of deprivations and compensations. Each saw fiction as an ideal mode through which one might explore this complexity. None offers easy answers to the reader; each, however, sought to raise the fundamental questions.

Cynthia Griffin Wolff

SARAH ORNE JEWETT

A White Heron

I

The woods were already filled with shadows one June evening, just before eight o'clock, though a bright sunset still glimmered faintly among the trunks of the trees. A little girl was driving home her cow, a plodding, dilatory, provoking creature in her behavior, but a valued companion for all that. They were going away from the western light, and striking deep into the dark woods, but their feet were familiar with the path, and it was no matter whether their eyes could see it or not.

There was hardly a night the summer through when the old cow could be found waiting at the pasture bars; on the contrary, it was her greatest pleasure to hide herself away among the high huckleberry bushes, and though she wore a loud bell she had made the discovery that if one stood perfectly still it would not ring. So Sylvia had to hunt for her until she found her, and call Co'! Co'! with never an answering Moo, until her childish patience was quite spent. If the creature had not given good milk and plenty of it, the case would have seemed very different to her owners. Besides, Sylvia had all the time there was, and very little use to make of it. Sometimes in pleasant weather it was a consolation to look upon the cow's pranks as an intelligent attempt to play hide and seek, and as the child had no playmates she lent herself to this amusement with a good deal of zest. Though this chase had been so long that the wary animal herself had given an unusual signal of her whereabouts, Sylvia had only laughed when she came upon Mistress Moolly at the swamp side, and urged her affectionately homeward with a twig of birch leaves. The old cow was not inclined to wander farther, she even turned in the right direction for once as they left the pasture, and stepped along the road at a good pace. She was quite ready to be milked now, and seldom stopped to browse.

Sylvia wondered what her grandmother would say because they were so late. It was a great while since she had left home at half past five o'clock, but everybody knew the difficulty of making this errand a short one. Mrs. Tilley had chased the hornéd torment too many summer evenings herself to blame any one else for lingering, and was only thankful as she waited that she had Sylvia, nowadays, to give such valuable assistance. The good woman suspected that Sylvia loitered occasionally on her own account; there never was such a child for straying about out of doors since the world was made! Everybody said that it was a good change for a little maid who had tried to grow for eight years in a crowded manufacturing town, but, as for

Sylvia herself, it seemed as if she never had been alive at all before she came to live at the farm. She thought often with wistful compassion of a wretched dry geranium that belonged to a town neighbor.

" 'Afraid of folks,' " old Mrs. Tilley said to herself, with a smile, after she had made the unlikely choice of Sylvia from her daughter's houseful of children, and was returning to the farm. " 'Afraid of folks,' they said! I guess she won't be troubled no great with 'em up to the old place!" When they reached the door of the lonely house and stopped to unlock it, and the cat came to purr loudly, and rub against them, a deserted pussy, indeed, but fat with young robins, Sylvia whispered that this was a beautiful place to live in, and she never should wish to go home.

The companions followed the shady woodroad, the cow taking slow steps, and the child very fast ones. The cow stopped long at the brook to drink, as if the pasture were not half a swamp, and Sylvia stood still and waited, letting her bare feet cool themselves in the shoal water, while the great twilight moths struck softly against her. She waded on through the brook as the cow moved away, and listened to the thrushes with a heart that beat fast with pleasure. There was a stirring in the great boughs overhead. They were full of little birds and beasts that seemed to be wide-awake, and going about their world, or else saying goodnight to each other in sleepy twitters. Sylvia herself felt sleepy as she walked along. However, it was not much farther to the house, and the air was soft and sweet. She was not often in the woods so late as this, and it made her feel as if she were a part of the gray shadows and the moving leaves. She was just thinking how long it seemed since she first came to the farm a year ago, and wondering if everything went on in the noisy town just the same as when she was there; the thought of the great red-faced boy who used to chase and frighten her made her hurry along the path to escape from the shadow of the trees.

Suddenly this little woods girl is horror stricken to hear a clear whistle not very far away. Not a bird's whistle, which would have a sort of friendliness, but a boy's whistle, determined, and somewhat aggressive. Sylvia left the cow to whatever sad fate might await her, and stepped discreetly aside into the bushes, but she was just too late. The enemy had discovered her, and called out in a very cheerful and persuasive tone, "Halloa, little girl, how far is it to the road?" and trembling Sylvia answered almost inaudibly, "A good ways."

She did not dare to look boldly at the tall young man, who carried a gun over his shoulder, but she came out of her bush and again followed the cow, while he walked alongside.

"I have been hunting for some birds," the stranger said kindly, "and I have lost my way, and need a friend very much. Don't be afraid," he added gallantly. "Speak up and tell me what your name is, and whether you think I can spend the night at your house, and go out gunning early in the morning."

Sylvia was more alarmed than before. Would not her grandmother consider her much to blame? But who could have foreseen such an accident as this? It did not appear to be her fault and she hung her head as if the stem of it were broken, but managed to answer "Sylvy," with much effort when her companion again asked her name.

Mrs. Tilley was standing in the doorway when the trio came into view. The cow gave a loud moo by way of explanation.

"Yes, you'd better speak up for yourself, you old trial! Where'd she tuck herself away this time, Sylvy?" Sylvia kept an awed silence; she knew by instinct that her grandmother did not comprehend the gravity of the situation. She must be mistaking the stranger for one of the farmer lads of the region.

The young man stood his gun beside the door, and dropped a heavy game-bag beside it; then he bade Mrs. Tilley good-evening, and repeated his wayfarer's story, and asked if he could have a night's lodging.

"Put me anywhere you like," he said. "I must be off early in the morning, before day; but I am very hungry, indeed. You can give me some milk at any rate, that's plain."

"Dear sakes, yes," responded the hostess, whose long slumbering hospitality seemed to be easily awakened. "You might fare better if you went out on the main road a mile or so, but you're welcome to what we've got. I'll milk right off, and you make yourself at home. You can sleep on husks or feathers," she proffered graciously. "I raised them all myself. There's good pasturing for geese just below here towards the ma'sh. Now step round and set a plate for the gentleman, Sylvy!" And Sylvia promptly stepped. She was glad to have something to do, and she was hungry herself.

It was a surprise to find so clean and comfortable

a little dwelling in this New England wilderness. The young man had known the horrors of its most primitive housekeeping, and the dreary squalor of that level of society which does not rebel at the companionship of hens. This was the best thrift of an old-fashioned farmstead, though on such a small scale that it seemed like a hermitage. He listened eagerly to the old woman's quaint talk, he watched Sylvia's pale face and shining gray eyes with ever growing enthusiasm, and insisted that this was the best supper he had eaten for a month; then, afterward, the new-made friends sat down in the doorway together while the moon came up.

Soon it would be berry time, and Sylvia was a great help at picking. The cow was a good milker, though a plaguy thing to keep track of, the hostess gossiped frankly, adding presently that she had buried four children, so that Sylvia's mother, and a son (who might be dead) in California were all the children she had left. "Dan, my boy, was a great hand to go gunning," she explained sadly. "I never wanted for pa'tridges or gray squer'ls while he was to home. He's been a great wand'rer, I expect, and he's no hand to write letters. There, I don't blame him, I'd ha' seen the world myself if it had been so I could.

"Sylvia takes after him," the grandmother continued affectionately, after a minute's pause. "There ain't a foot o' ground she don't know her way over, and the wild creatur's counts her one o' themselves. Squer'ls she'll tame to come an' feed right out o' her hands, and all sorts o' birds. Last winter she got the jay birds to bangeing here, and I believe she'd 'a' scanted herself of her own meals to have plenty to throw out amongst 'em, if I hadn't kep' watch. Anything but crows, I tell her, I'm willin' to help support,—though Dan he went an' tamed one o' them that did seem to have reason same as folks. It was round here a good spell after he went away. Dan an' his father they didn't hitch,—but he never held up his head ag'in after Dan had dared him an' gone off."

The guest did not notice this hint of family sorrows in his eager interest in something else.

"So Sylvy knows all about birds, does she?" he exclaimed, as he looked round at the little girl who sat, very demure but increasingly sleepy, in the moonlight. "I am making a collection of birds myself. I have been at it ever since I was a boy." (Mrs. Tilley smiled.) "There are two or three very rare ones I have been hunting for these five years. I mean to get them on my own ground if they can be found."

"Do you cage 'em up?" asked Mrs. Tilley doubtfully, in response to this enthusiastic announcement.

"Oh, no, they're stuffed and preserved, dozens and dozens of them," said the ornithologist, "and I have shot or snared every one myself. I caught a glimpse of a white heron three miles from here on Saturday, and I have followed it in this direction. They have never been found in this district at all. The little white heron, it is," and he turned again to look at Sylvia with the hope of discovering that the rare bird was one of her acquaintances.

But Sylvia was watching a hop toad in the narrow footpath.

"You would know the heron if you saw it," the

stranger continued eagerly. "A queer tall white bird with soft feathers and long thin legs. And it would have a nest perhaps in the top of a high tree, made of sticks, something like a hawk's nest."

Sylvia's heart gave a wild beat; she knew that strange white bird, and had once stolen softly near where it stood in some bright green swamp grass, away over at the other side of the woods. There was an open place where the sunshine always seemed strangely yellow and hot, where tall, nodding rushes grew, and her grandmother had warned her that she might sink in the soft black mud underneath and never be heard of more. Not far beyond were the salt marshes and beyond those was the sea, the sea which Sylvia wondered and dreamed about, but never had looked upon, though its great voice could often be heard above the noise of the woods on stormy nights.

"I can't think of anything I should like so much as to find that heron's nest," the handsome stranger was saying. "I would give ten dollars to anybody who could show it to me," he added desperately, "and I mean to spend my whole vacation hunting for it if need be. Perhaps it was only migrating, or had been chased out of its own region by some bird of prey."

Mrs. Tilley gave amazed attention to all this, but Sylvia still watched the toad, not divining, as she might have done at some calmer time, that the creature wished to get to its hole under the doorstep, and was much hindered by the unusual spectators at that hour of the evening. No amount of thought, that night, could decide how many wished-for treasures the ten dollars, so lightly spoken of, would buy.

The next day the young sportsman hovered about the woods, and Sylvia kept him company, having lost her first fear of the friendly lad, who proved to be most kind and sympathetic. He told her many things about the birds and what they knew and where they lived and what they did with themselves. And he gave her a jackknife, which she thought as great a treasure as if she were a desert islander. All day long he did not once make her troubled or afraid except when he brought down some unsuspecting singing creature from its bough. Sylvia would have liked him vastly better without his gun; she could not understand why he killed the very birds he seemed to like so much. But as the day waned, Sylvia watched the young man with loving admiration. She had never seen anybody so charming and delightful; the woman's heart, asleep in the child, was vaguely thrilled by a dream of love. Some premonition of that great power stirred and swayed these young foresters who traversed the solemn woodlands with soft-footed silent care. They stopped to listen to a bird's song; they pressed forward again eagerly, parting the branches,—speaking to each other rarely and in whispers; the young man going first and Sylvia following, fascinated, a few steps behind, with her gray eyes dark with excitement.

She grieved because the longed-for white heron was elusive, but she did not lead the guest, she only followed, and there was no such thing as speaking first. The sound of her own unquestioned voice would have terrified her,—it was hard enough to answer yes or no when there was need of that. At last evening began to fall, and they drove the cow together, and Sylvia smiled with pleasure when they came to the place where she heard the whistle and was afraid only the night before.

II

Half a mile from home, at the farther edge of the woods, where the land was highest, a great pine tree stood, the last of its generation. Whether it was left for a boundary mark, or for what reason, no one could say; the woodchoppers who had felled its mates were dead and gone long ago, and a whole forest of sturdy trees, pines and oaks and maples, had grown again. But the stately head of this old pine towered above them all and made a landmark for sea and shore miles and miles away. Sylvia knew it well. She had always believed that whoever climbed to the top of it could see the ocean; and the little girl had often laid her hand on the great rough trunk and looked up wistfully at those dark boughs that the wind always stirred, no matter how hot and still the air might be below. Now she thought of the tree with a new excitement, for why, if one climbed it at break of day, could not one see all the world, and easily discover whence the white heron flew, and mark the place, and find the hidden nest?

What a spirit of adventure, what wild ambition! What fancied triumph and delight and glory for the later morning when she could make known the secret! It was almost too real and too great for the childish heart to bear.

All night the door of the little house stood open, and the whippoorwills came and sang upon the very step. The young sportsman and his old hostess were sound asleep, but Sylvia's great design kept her broad awake and watching. She forgot to think of sleep. The short summer night seemed as long as the winter darkness, and at last when the whippoorwills ceased, and she was afraid the morning would after all come too soon, she stole out of the house and followed the pasture path through the woods, hastening toward the open ground beyond, listening with a sense of comfort and companionship to the drowsy twitter of a half-awakened bird, whose perch she had jarred in passing. Alas, if the great wave of human interest which flooded for the first time this dull little life should sweep away the satisfactions of an existence heart to heart with nature and the dumb life of the forest!

There was the huge tree asleep yet in the paling moonlight, and small and hopeful Sylvia began with utmost bravery to mount to the top of it, with tingling, eager blood coursing the channels of her whole frame, with her bare feet and fingers, that pinched and held like bird's claws to the monstrous ladder reaching up, up, almost to the sky itself. First she must mount the white oak tree that grew alongside, where she was almost lost among the dark branches and the green leaves heavy and wet with dew; a bird fluttered off its nest, and a red squirrel ran to and fro and scolded pettishly at the harmless housebreaker. Sylvia felt her way easily. She had often climbed there, and knew that higher still one of the oak's upper branches chafed against the pine trunk, just where its lower boughs were set close together. There, when she made the dangerous pass from one tree to the other, the great enterprise would really begin.

She crept out along the swaying oak limb at last, and took the daring step across into the old pine tree. The way was harder than she thought; she must reach far and hold fast, the sharp dry twigs caught and held her and scratched her like angry talons, the pitch made her thin little fingers clumsy and stiff as she went round and round the tree's great stem, higher and higher upward. The sparrows and robins in the woods below were beginning to wake and twitter to the dawn, yet it seemed much lighter there aloft in the pine tree, and the child knew that she must hurry if her project were to be of any use.

The tree seemed to lengthen itself out as she went up, and to reach farther and farther upward. It was like a great mainmast to the voyaging earth; it must truly have been amazed that morning through all its ponderous frame as it felt this determined spark of human spirit creeping and climbing from higher branch to branch. Who knows how steadily the least twigs held themselves to advantage this light, weak creature on her way! The old pine must have loved his new dependent. More than all the hawks, and bats, and moths, and even the sweet-voiced thrushes, was the brave, beating heart of the solitary gray-eyed child. And the tree stood still and held away the winds that June morning while the dawn grew bright in the east.

Sylvia's face was like a pale star, if one had seen it from the ground, when the last thorny bough was past, and she stood trembling and tired but wholly triumphant, high in the treetop. Yes, there was the sea with the dawning sun making a golden dazzle over it, and toward that glorious east flew two hawks with slow-moving pinions. How low they looked in the air from that height when before one had only seen them far up, and dark against the blue sky. Their gray feathers were as soft as moths; they seemed only a little way from the tree, and Sylvia felt as if she too could go flying away among the clouds. Westward, the woodlands and farms reached miles and miles into the distance; here and there were church steeples, and white villages; truly it was a vast and awesome world.

The birds sang louder and louder. At last the sun came up bewilderingly bright. Sylvia could see the white sails of ships out at sea, and the clouds that were purple and rose-colored and yellow at first began to fade away. Where was the white heron's nest in the sea of green branches, and was this wonderful sight and pageant of the world the only reward for having climbed to such a giddy height? Now look down again, Sylvia, where the green marsh is set among the shining birches and dark hemlocks; there where you saw the white heron once you will see him again; look, look! a white spot of him like a single floating feather comes up from the dead hemlock and grows larger, and rises, and comes close at last, and goes by the landmark pine with steady sweep of wing and outstretched slender neck and crested head. And wait! wait! do not move a foot or a finger, little girl, do not send an arrow of light and consciousness from your two eager eyes, for the heron has perched on a pine bough not far beyond yours, and cries back to his mate on the nest, and plumes his feathers for the new day!

The child gives a long sigh a minute later when a

company of shouting catbirds comes also to the tree, and vexed by their fluttering and lawlessness the solemn heron goes away. She knows his secret now, the wild, light, slender bird that floats and wavers, and goes back like an arrow presently to his home in the green world beneath. Then Sylvia, well satisfied, makes her perilous way down again, not daring to look far below the branch she stands on, ready to cry sometimes because her fingers ache and her lamed feet slip. Wondering over and over again what the stranger would say to her, and what he would think when she told him how to find his way straight to the heron's nest.

"Sylvy, Sylvy!" called the busy old grandmother again and again, but nobody answered, and the small husk bed was empty, and Sylvia had disappeared.

The guest waked from a dream, and remembering his day's pleasure hurried to dress himself that it might sooner begin. He was sure from the way the shy little girl looked once or twice yesterday that she had at least seen the white heron, and now she must really be persuaded to tell. Here she comes now, paler than ever, and her worn old frock is torn and tattered, and smeared with pine pitch. The grandmother and the sportsman stand in the door together and question her, and the splendid moment has come to speak of the dead hemlock tree by the green marsh.

But Sylvia does not speak after all, though the old grandmother fretfully rebukes her, and the young man's kind appealing eyes are looking straight in her own. He can make them rich with money; he has promised it, and they are poor now.

He is so well worth making happy, and he waits to hear the story she can tell.

No, she must keep silence! What is it that suddenly forbids her and makes her dumb? Has she been nine years growing, and now, when the great world for the first time puts out a hand to her, must she thrust it aside for a bird's sake? The murmur of the pine's green branches is in her ears, she remembers how the white heron came flying through the golden air and how they watched the sea and the morning together, and Sylvia cannot speak; she cannot tell the heron's secret and give its life away.

Dear loyalty, that suffered a sharp pang as the guest went away disappointed later in the day, that could have served and followed him and loved him as a dog loves! Many a night Sylvia heard the echo of his whistle haunting the pasture path as she came home with the loitering cow. She forgot even her sorrow at the sharp report of his gun and the piteous sight of thrushes and sparrows dropping silent to the ground, their songs hushed and their pretty feathers stained and wet with blood. Were the birds better friends than their hunter might have been,—who can tell? Whatever treasures were lost to her, woodlands and summer time, remember! Bring your gifts and graces and tell your secrets to this lonely country child!

The Only Rose

I

Just where the village abruptly ended, and the green mowing fields began, stood Mrs. Bickford's house, looking down the road with all its windows, and topped by two prim chimneys that stood up like ears. It was placed with an end to the road, and fronted southward; you could follow a straight path from the gate past the front door and find Mrs. Bickford sitting by the last window of all in the kitchen, unless she were solemnly stepping about, prolonging the stern duties of her solitary housekeeping.

One day in early summer, when almost every one else in Fairfield had put her house plants out of doors, there were still three flower pots on a kitchen window sill. Mrs. Bickford spent but little time over her rose and geranium and Jerusalem cherry-tree, although they had gained a kind of personality born of long association. They rarely undertook to bloom, but had most courageously maintained life in spite of their owner's unsympathetic but conscientious care. Later in the season she would carry them out of doors, and leave them, until the time of frosts, under the shade of a great apple-tree, where they might make the best of what the summer had to give.

The afternoon sun was pouring in, the Jerusalem cherry-tree drooped its leaves in the heat and looked pale, when a neighbor, Miss Pendexter, came in from the next house but one to make a friendly call. As she passed the parlor with its shut blinds, and the sitting-room, also shaded carefully from the light, she wished, as she had done many times before, that somebody beside the owner might have the pleasure of living in and using so good and pleasant a house. Mrs. Bickford always complained of having so much care, even while she valued herself intelligently upon having the right to do as she pleased with one of the best houses in Fairfield. Miss Pendexter was a cheerful, even gay little person, who always brought a pleasant flurry of excitement, and usually had a genuine though small piece of news to tell, or some new aspect of already received information.

Mrs. Bickford smiled as she looked up to see this sprightly neighbor coming. She had no gift at entertaining herself, and was always glad, as one might say, to be taken off her own hands.

Miss Pendexter smiled back, as if she felt herself to be equal to the occasion.

"How be you to-day?" the guest asked kindly, as she entered the kitchen. "Why, what a sight o' flowers, Mis' Bickford! What be you goin' to do with 'em all?"

Mrs. Bickford wore a grave expression as she glanced over her spectacles. "My sister's boy fetched 'em over," she answered. "You know my sister Parsons's a great hand to raise flowers, an' this boy takes after her. He said his mother thought the gardin never looked handsomer, and she picked me these to send over. They was sendin' a team to Westbury for some fertilizer to put on the land, an' he come with the men, an' stopped to eat his dinner 'long o' me. He's been growin' fast, and looks peakëd. I expect sister 'Liza thought the ride, this pleasant day, would do him good. 'Liza sent word for me to come over and pass some days next week, but it ain't so that I can."

"Why, it's a pretty time of year to go off and make a little visit," suggested the neighbor encouragingly.

"I ain't got my sitting-room chamber carpet taken up yet," sighed Mrs. Bickford. "I do feel condemned. I might have done it to-day, but't was all at end when I saw Tommy coming. There, he's a likely boy, an' so relished his dinner; I happened to be well prepared. I don't know but he's my favorite o' that family. Only I've been sittin' here thinkin', since he went, an' I can't remember that I ever was so belated with my spring cleaning."

"'Twas owin' to the weather," explained Miss Pendexter. "None of us could be so smart as common this year, not even the lazy ones that always get one room done the first o' March, and brag of it to others' shame, and then never let on when they do the rest."

The two women laughed together cheerfully. Mrs. Bickford had put up the wide leaf of her large table between the windows and spread out the flowers. She was sorting them slowly into three heaps.

"Why, I do declare if you haven't got a rose in bloom yourself!" exclaimed Miss Pendexter abruptly, as if the bud had not been announced weeks before, and its progress regularly commented upon. "Ain't it a lovely rose? Why, Mis' Bickford!"

"Yes'm, it's out to-day," said Mrs. Bickford, with a somewhat plaintive air. "I'm glad you come in so as to see it."

The bright flower was like a face. Somehow, the beauty and life of it were surprising in the plain room, like a gay little child who might suddenly appear in a doorway. Miss Pendexter forgot herself and her hostess and the tangled mass of garden flowers in looking at the red rose. She even forgot that it was incumbent upon her to carry forward the conversation. Mrs. Bickford was subject to fits of untimely silence which made her friends anxiously sweep the corners of their minds in search of something to say, but any one who looked at her now could easily see that it was not poverty of thought that made her speechless, but an overburdening sense of the inexpressible.

"Goin' to make up all your flowers into bo'quets? I think the short-stemmed kinds is often pretty in a dish," suggested Miss Pendexter compassionately.

"I thought I should make them into three bo'quets. I wish there wa'n't quite so many. Sister Eliza's very lavish with her flowers; she's always been a kind sister, too," said Mrs. Bickford vaguely. She was not apt to speak with so much sentiment, and as her neighbor looked at her narrowly she detected unusual signs of emotion. It suddenly became evident that the three nosegays were connected in her mind with her bereavement of three husbands, and Miss Pendexter's easily roused curiosity was quieted by the discovery that her friend was bent upon a visit to the burying-ground. It was the time of year when she was pretty sure to spend an afternoon there, and sometimes they had taken the walk in company. Miss Pendexter expected to receive the usual invitation, but there was nothing further said at the moment, and she looked again at the pretty rose.

Mrs. Bickford aimlessly handled the syringas and flowering almond sprays, choosing them out of the fragrant heap only to lay them down again. She glanced out of the window; then gave Miss Pendexter a long expressive look.

"I expect you're going to carry 'em over to the burying-ground?" inquired the guest, in a sympathetic tone.

"Yes'm," said the hostess, now well started in conversation and in quite her every-day manner. "You see I was goin' over to my brother's folks to-morrow in South Fairfield, to pass the day; they said they were goin' to send over to-morrow to leave a wagon at the blacksmith's, and they'd hitch that to their best chaise, so I could ride back very comfortable. You know I have to avoid bein' out in the mornin' sun?"

Miss Pendexter smiled to herself at this moment; she was obliged to move from her chair at the window, the May sun was so hot on her back, for Mrs. Bickford always kept the curtains rolled high up, out of the way, for fear of fading and dust. The kitchen was a blaze of light. As for the Sunday chaise being sent, it was well known that Mrs. Bickford's married brothers and sisters comprehended the truth that she was a woman of property, and had neither chick nor child.

"So I thought't was a good opportunity to just stop an' see if the lot was in good order,—last spring Mr. Wallis's stone hove with the frost; an' so I could take these flowers." She gave a sigh. "I ain't one that can bear flowers in a close room,—they bring on a headache; but I enjoy 'em as much as anybody to look at, only you never know what to put 'em in. If I could be out in the mornin' sun, as some do, and keep flowers in the house, I should have me a gardin, certain," and she sighed again.

"A garden's a sight o' care, but I don't begrudge none o' the care I give to mine. I have to scant on flowers so's to make room for pole beans," said Miss Pendexter gayly. She had only a tiny strip of land behind her house, but she always had something to give away, and made riches out of her narrow poverty. "A few flowers gives me just as much pleasure as more would," she added. "You get acquainted with things when you've only got one or two roots. My sweet-williams is just like folks."

"Mr. Bickford was partial to sweet-williams," said Mrs. Bickford. "I never knew him to take notice of no other sort of flowers. When we'd be over to Eliza's, he'd walk down her gardin, an' he'd never make no comments until he come to them, and then he'd say, 'Those is sweet-williams.' How many times I've heard him!"

"You ought to have a sprig of 'em for his bo'quet," suggested Miss Pendexter.

"Yes, I've put a sprig in," said her companion.

At this moment Miss Pendexter took a good look at the bouquets, and found that they were as nearly alike as careful hands could make them. Mrs. Bickford was evidently trying to reach absolute impartiality.

"I don't know but you think it's foolish to tie 'em up this afternoon," she said presently, as she wound the first with a stout string. "I thought I could put 'em in a bucket o' water out in the shed, where there's a draught o' air, and then I should have all my time in the morning. I shall have a good deal to do before I go. I always sweep the setting-room and front entry Wednesdays. I want to leave everything nice, goin' away for all day so. So I meant to get the flowers out o' the way this afternoon. Why, it's most half past four, ain't it? But I sha'n't pick the rose till mornin'; 't will be blowed out better then."

"The rose?" questioned Miss Pendexter. "Why, are you goin' to pick that, too?"

"Yes, I be. I never like to let 'em fade on the bush. There, that's just what's a-troublin' me," and she turned to give a long, imploring look at the friend who sat beside her. Miss Pendexter had moved her chair before the table in order to be out of the way of the sun. "I don't seem to know which of 'em ought to have it," said Mrs. Bickford despondently. "I do so hate to make a choice between 'em; they all had their good points, especially Mr. Bickford, and I respected 'em all. I don't know but what I think of one on 'em 'most as much as I do of the other."

"Why, 'tis difficult for you, ain't it?" responded Miss Pendexter. "I don't know's I can offer advice."

"No, I s'pose not," answered her friend slowly, with a shadow of disappointment coming over her calm face. "I feel sure you would if you could, Abby."

Both of the women felt as if they were powerless before a great emergency.

"There's one thing,—they're all in a better world now," said Miss Pendexter, in a self-conscious and constrained voice; "they can't feel such little things or take note o' slights same's we can."

"No; I suppose 'tis myself that wants to be just," answered Mrs. Bickford. "I feel under obligations to my last husband when I look about and see how comfortable he left me. Poor Mr. Wallis had his great projects, an' perhaps if he'd lived longer he'd have made a record; but when he died he'd failed all up, owing to that patent corn-sheller he'd put everything into, and, as you know, I had to get along 'most any way I could for the next few years. Life was very disappointing with Mr. Wallis, but he meant well, an' used to be an amiable person to dwell with, until his temper got spoilt makin' so many hopes an' havin' 'em turn out failures. He had consider'ble of an air, an' dressed very handsome when I was first acquainted with him, Mr. Wallis did. I don't know's you ever knew Mr. Wallis in his prime?''

''He died the year I moved over here from North Denfield,'' said Miss Pendexter, in a tone of sympathy. ''I just knew him by sight. I was to his funeral. You know you lived in what we call the Wells house then, and I felt it wouldn't be an intrusion, we was such near neighbors. The first time I ever was in your house was just before that, when he was sick, an' Mary 'Becca Wade an' I called to see if there was anything we could do.''

''They used to say about town that Mr. Wallis went to an' fro like a mail-coach an' brought nothin' to pass,'' announced Mrs. Bickford without bitterness. ''He ought to have had a better chance than he did in this little neighborhood. You see, he had excellent ideas, but he never'd learned the machinist's trade, and there was somethin' the matter with every model he contrived. I used to be real narrow-minded when he talked about moving 'way up to Lowell, or some o' them places; I hated to think of leaving my folks; and now I see that I never done right by him. His ideas was good. I know once he was on a jury, and there was a man stopping to the tavern where he was, near the court house, a man that traveled for a firm to Lowell; and they engaged in talk, an' Mr. Wallis let out some o' his notions an' contrivances, an' he said that man wouldn't hardly stop to eat, he was so interested, an' said he'd look for a chance for him up to Lowell. It all sounded so well that I kind of begun to think about goin' myself. Mr. Wallis said we'd close the house here, and go an' board through the winter. But he never heard a word from him, and the disappointment was one he never got over. I think of it now different from what I did then. I often used to be kind of disapproving to Mr. Wallis; but there, he used to be always tellin' over his great projects. Somebody told me once that a man by the same name of the one he met while he was to court had got some patents for the very things Mr. Wallis used to be workin' over; but't was after he died, an' I don't know's 't was in him to ever really set things up so other folks could ha' seen their value. His machines always used to work kind of rickety, but folks used to come from all round to see 'em; they was curiosities if they wa'n't nothin' else, an' gave him a name."

Mrs. Bickford paused a moment, with some geranium leaves in her hand, and seemed to suppress with difficulty a desire to speak even more freely.

"He was a dreadful notional man," she said at last, regretfully, and as if this fact were a poor substitute for what had just been in her mind. "I recollect one time he worked all through the early winter over my churn, an' got it so it would go three quarters of an hour all of itself if you wound it up; an' if you'll believe it, he went an' spent all that time for nothin' when the cow was dry, an' we was with difficulty borrowin' a pint o' milk a day somewheres in the neighborhood just to get along with." Mrs. Bickford flushed with displeasure, and turned to look at her visitor. "Now what do you think of such a man as that, Miss Pendexter?" she asked.

"Why, I don't know but 't was just as good for

an invention,'' answered Miss Pendexter timidly; but her friend looked doubtful, and did not appear to understand.

''Then I asked him where it was, one day that spring when I'd got tired to death churnin', an' the butter wouldn't come in a churn I'd had to borrow, and he'd gone an' took ours all to pieces to get the works to make some other useless contrivance with. He had no sort of a business turn, but he was well meanin', Mr. Wallis was, an' full o' divertin' talk; they used to call him very good company. I see now that he never had no proper chance. I've always regretted Mr. Wallis,'' said she who was now the widow Bickford.

''I'm sure you always speak well of him,'' said Miss Pendexter. '''Twas a pity he hadn't got among good business men, who could push his inventions an' do all the business part.''

''I was left very poor an' needy for them next few years,'' said Mrs. Bickford mournfully; ''but he never'd give up but what he should die worth his fifty thousand dollars. I don't see now how I ever did get along them next few years without him; but there, I always managed to keep a pig, an' sister Eliza gave me my potatoes, and I made out somehow. I could dig me a few greens, you know, in spring, and then't would come strawberry-time, and other berries a-followin' on. I was always decent to go to meetin' till within the last six months, an' then I went in bad weather, when folks wouldn't notice; but 't was a rainy summer, an' I managed to get considerable preachin' after all. My clothes looked proper enough when 't was a wet Sabbath. I often think o' them pinched days now, when I'm left so comfortable by Mr. Bickford."

"Yes'm, you've everything to be thankful for," said Miss Pendexter, who was as poor herself at that moment as her friend had ever been, and who could never dream of venturing upon the support and companionship of a pig. "Mr. Bickford was a very personable man," she hastened to say, the confidences were so intimate and interesting.

"Oh, very," replied Mrs. Bickford; "there was something about him that was very marked. Strangers would always ask who he was as he come into meetin'. His words counted; he never spoke except he had to. 'Twas a relief at first after Mr. Wallis's being so fluent; but Mr. Wallis was splendid company for winter evenings,—'t would be eight o'clock before you knew it. I didn't use to listen to it all, but he had a great deal of information. Mr. Bickford was dreadful dignified; I used to be sort of meechin' with him along at the first, for fear he'd disapprove of me; but I found out't wa'n't no need; he was always just that way, an' done everything by rule an' measure. He hadn't the mind of my other husbands, but he was a very dignified appearing man; he used 'most always to sleep in the evenin's, Mr. Bickford did."

"Them is lovely bo'quets, certain!" exclaimed Miss Pendexter. "Why, I couldn't tell 'em apart; the flowers are comin' out just right, aren't they?"

Mrs. Bickford nodded assent, and then, startled by sudden recollection, she cast a quick glance at the rose in the window.

"I always seem to forget about your first husband, Mr. Fraley," Miss Pendexter suggested bravely. "I've often heard you speak of him, too, but he'd passed away long before I ever knew you."

"He was but a boy," said Mrs. Bickford. "I thought the world was done for me when he died, but I've often thought since 't was a mercy for him. He come of a very melancholy family, and all his brothers an' sisters enjoyed poor health; it might have been his lot. Folks said we was as pretty a couple as ever come into church; we was both dark, with black eyes an' a good deal o' color,—you wouldn't expect it to see me now. Albert was one that held up his head, and looked as if he meant to own the town, an' he had a good word for everybody. I don't know what the years might have brought."

There was a long pause. Mrs. Bickford leaned over to pick up a heavy-headed Guelder-rose that had dropped on the floor.

"I expect 't was what they call fallin' in love," she added, in a different tone; "he wa'n't nothin' but a boy, an' I wa'n't nothin' but a girl, but we was dreadful happy. He didn't favor his folks,—they all had hay-colored hair and was faded-looking, except his mother; they was alike, and looked alike, an' set everything by each other. He was just the kind of strong, hearty young man that goes right off if they get a fever. We was just settled on a little farm, an' he'd have done well if he'd had time; as it was, he left debts. He had a hasty temper, that was his great fault, but Albert had a lovely voice to sing; they said there wa'n't no such tenor voice in this part o' the State. I could hear him singin' to himself right out in the field a-ploughin' or hoein', an' he didn't know it half o' the time, no more'n a common bird would. I don't know's I valued his gift as I ought to, but there was nothin' ever sounded so sweet to me. I ain't one that ever had much fancy, but I knowed Albert had a pretty voice."

Mrs. Bickford's own voice trembled a little, but she held up the last bouquet and examined it critically. "I must hurry now an' put these in water," she said, in a matter of fact tone. Little Miss Pendexter was so quiet and sympathetic that her hostess felt no more embarrassed than if she had been talking only to herself.

"Yes, they do seem to droop some; 'tis a little warm for them here in the sun," said Miss Pendexter; "but you'll find they'll all come up if you give them their fill o' water. They'll look very handsome to-morrow; folks'll notice them from the road. You've arranged them very tasty, Mis' Bickford."

"They do look pretty, don't they?" Mrs. Bickford regarded the three in turn. "I want to have them all pretty. You may deem it strange, Abby."

"Why, no, Mis' Bickford," said the guest sincerely, although a little perplexed by the solemnity of the occasion. "I know how 'tis with friends,—that having one don't keep you from wantin' another; 'tis just like havin' somethin' to eat, and then wantin' somethin' to drink just the same. I expect all friends find their places."

But Mrs. Bickford was not interested in this figure, and still looked vague and anxious as she began to brush the broken stems and wilted leaves into her wide calico apron. "I done the best I could while they was alive," she said, "and mourned 'em when I lost 'em, an' I feel grateful to be left so comfortable now when all is over. It seems foolish, but I'm still at a loss about that rose."

"Perhaps you'll feel sure when you first wake up in the morning," answered Miss Pendexter solicitously. "It's a case where I don't deem myself qualified to offer you any advice. But I'll say one thing, seeing's you've been so friendly spoken and confiding with me. I never was married myself, Mis' Bickford, because it wa'n't so that I could have the one I liked."

"I suppose he ain't livin', then? Why, I wan't never aware you had met with a disappointment, Abby," said Mrs. Bickford instantly. None of her neighbors had ever suspected little Miss Pendexter of a romance.

"Yes'm, he's livin'," replied Miss Pendexter humbly. "No'm, I never have heard that he died."

"I want to know!" exclaimed the woman of experience. "Well, I'll tell you this, Abby: you may have regretted your lot, and felt lonesome and hardshipped, but they all have their faults, and a single woman's got her liberty, if she ain't got other blessin's."

"'Twouldn't have been my choice to live alone," said Abby, meeker than before. "I feel very thankful for my blessin's, all the same. You've always been a kind neighbor, Mis' Bickford."

"Why can't you stop to tea?" asked the elder woman, with unusual cordiality; but Miss Pendexter remembered that her hostess often expressed a dislike for unexpected company, and promptly took her departure after she had risen to go, glancing up at the bright flower as she passed outside the window. It seemed to belong most to Albert, but she had not liked to say so. The sun was low; the green fields stretched away southward into the misty distance.

II

Mrs. Bickford's house appeared to watch her out of sight down the road, the next morning. She had lost all spirit for her holiday. Perhaps it was the unusual excitement of the afternoon's reminiscences, or it might have been simply the bright moonlight night which had kept her broad awake until dawn, thinking of the past, and more and more concerned about the rose. By this time it had ceased to be merely a flower, and had become a definite symbol and assertion of personal choice. She found it very difficult to decide. So much of her present comfort and well-being was due to Mr. Bickford; still, it was Mr. Wallis who had been most unfortunate, and to whom she had done least justice. If she owed recognition to Mr. Bickford, she certainly owed amends to Mr. Wallis. If she gave him the rose, it would be for the sake of affectionate apology. And then there was Albert, to whom she had no thought of being either indebted or forgiving. But she could not escape from the terrible feeling of indecision.

It was a beautiful morning for a drive, but Mrs. Bickford was kept waiting some time for the chaise. Her nephew, who was to be her escort, had found much social advantage at the blacksmith's shop, so that it was after ten when she finally started with the three large flat-backed bouquets, covered with a newspaper to protect them from the sun. The petals of the almond flowers were beginning to scatter, and now and then little streams of water leaked out of the newspaper and trickled down the steep slope of her best dress to the bottom of the chaise. Even yet she had not made up her mind; she had stopped trying to deal with such an evasive thing as decision, and leaned back and rested as best she could.

"What an old fool I be!" she rebuked herself from time to time, in so loud a whisper that her companion ventured a respectful "What, ma'am?" and was astonished that she made no reply. John was a handsome young man, but Mrs. Bickford could never cease thinking of him as a boy. He had always been her favorite among the younger members of the family, and now returned this affectionate feeling, being possessed of an instinctive confidence in the sincerities of his prosaic aunt.

As they drove along, there had seemed at first to be something unsympathetic and garish about the beauty of the summer day. After the shade and shelter of the house, Mrs. Bickford suffered even more from a contracted and assailed feeling out of doors. The very trees by the roadside had a curiously fateful, trying way of standing back to watch her, as she passed in the acute agony of indecision, and she was annoyed and startled by a bird that flew too near the chaise in a moment of surprise. She was conscious of a strange reluctance to the movement of the Sunday chaise, as if she were being conveyed against her will; but the companionship of her nephew John grew every moment to be more and more a reliance. It was very comfortable to sit by his side, even though he had nothing to say; he was manly and cheerful, and she began to feel protected.

"Aunt Bickford," he suddenly announced, "I may's well out with it! I've got a piece o' news to tell you, if you won't let on to nobody. I expect you'll laugh, but you know I've set everything by Mary Lizzie Gifford ever since I was a boy. Well, sir!"

"Well, sir!" exclaimed aunt Bickford in her turn, quickly roused into most comfortable self-forgetfulness. "I am really pleased. She'll make you a good, smart wife, John. Ain't all the folks pleased, both sides?"

"Yes, they be," answered John soberly, with a happy, important look that became him well.

"I guess I can make out to do something for you to help along, when the right time comes," said aunt Bickford impulsively, after a moment's reflection. "I've known what it is to be starting out in life with plenty o' hope. You ain't calculatin' on gettin' married before fall,—or be ye?"

"'Long in the fall," said John regretfully. "I wisht' we could set up for ourselves right away this summer. I ain't got much ahead, but I can work well as anybody, an' now I'm out o' my time."

"She's a nice, modest, pretty girl. I thought she liked you, John," said the old aunt. "I saw her over to your mother's, last day I was there. Well, I expect you'll be happy."

"Certain," said John, turning to look at her affectionately, surprised by this outspokenness and lack of embarrassment between them. "Thank you, aunt," he said simply; "you're a real good friend to me;" and he looked away again hastily, and blushed a fine scarlet over his sun-browned face. "She's coming over to spend the day with the girls," he added. "Mother thought of it. You don't get over to see us very often."

Mrs. Bickford smiled approvingly. John's mother looked for her good opinion, no doubt, but it was very proper for John to have told his prospects himself, and in such a pretty way. There was no shilly-shallying about the boy.

"My gracious!" said John suddenly. "I'd like to have drove right by the burying-ground. I forgot we wanted to stop."

Strange as it may appear, Mrs. Bickford herself had not noticed the burying-ground, either, in her excitement and pleasure; now she felt distressed and responsible again, and showed it in her face at once. The young man leaped lightly to the ground, and reached for the flowers.

"Here, you just let me run up with 'em," he said kindly. " 'Tis hot in the sun to-day, an' you'll mind it risin' the hill. We'll stop as I fetch you back to-night, and you can go up comfortable an' walk the yard after sundown when it's cool, an' stay as long as you're a mind to. You seem sort of tired, aunt."

"I don't know but what I will let you carry 'em," said Mrs. Bickford slowly.

To leave the matter of the rose in the hands of fate seemed weakness and cowardice, but there was not a moment for consideration. John was a smiling fate, and his proposition was a great relief. She watched him go away with a terrible inward shaking, and sinking of pride. She had held the flowers with so firm a grasp that her hands felt weak and numb, and as she leaned back and shut her eyes she was afraid to open them again at first for fear of knowing the bouquets apart even at that distance, and giving instructions which she might regret. With a sudden impulse she called John once or twice eagerly; but her voice had a thin and piping sound, and the meditative early crickets that chirped in the fresh summer grass probably sounded louder in John's ears. The bright light on the white stones dazzled Mrs. Bickford's eyes; and then all at once she felt light-hearted, and the sky seemed to lift itself higher and wider from the earth, and she gave a sigh of relief as her messenger came back along the path. "I know who I do hope's got the right one," she said to herself. "There, what a touse I be in! I don't see what I had to go and pick the old rose for, anyway."

"I declare, they did look real handsome, aunt," said John's hearty voice as he approached the chaise. "I set 'em up just as you told me. This one fell out, an' I kept it. I don't know's you'll care. I can give it to Lizzie."

He faced her now with a bright, boyish look. There was something gay in his buttonhole,—it was the red rose.

Aunt Bickford blushed like a girl. "Your choice is easy made," she faltered mysteriously, and then burst out laughing, there in front of the burying-ground. "Come, get right in, dear," she said.

"Well, well! I guess the rose was made for you; it looks very pretty in your coat, John."

She thought of Albert, and the next moment the tears came into her old eyes. John was a lover, too.

"My first husband was just such a tall, straight young man as you be," she said as they drove along. "The flower he first give me was a rose."

The Hiltons' Holiday

I

There was a bright, full moon in the clear sky, and the sunset was still shining faintly in the west. Dark woods stood all about the old Hilton farmhouse, save down the hill, westward, where lay the shadowy fields which John Hilton, and his father before him, had cleared and tilled with much toil,—the small fields to which they had given the industry and even affection of their honest lives.

John Hilton was sitting on the doorstep of his house. As he moved his head in and out of the shadows, turning now and then to speak to his wife, who sat just within the doorway, one could see his good face, rough and somewhat unkempt, as if he were indeed a creature of the shady woods and brown earth, instead of the noisy town. It was late in the long spring evening, and he had just come from the lower field as cheerful as a boy, proud of having finished the planting of his potatoes.

"I had to do my last row mostly by feelin'," he said to his wife. "I'm proper glad I pushed through, an' went back an' ended off after supper. 'Twould have taken me a good part o' to-morrow mornin', an' broke my day."

"'Tain't no use for ye to work yourself all to pieces, John," answered the woman quickly. "I declare it does seem harder than ever that we couldn't have kep' our boy; he'd been comin' fourteen years old this fall, most a grown man, and he'd work right 'longside of ye now the whole time."

"'Twas hard to lose him; I do seem to miss little John," said the father sadly. "I expect there was reasons why't was best. I feel able an' smart to work; my father was a girt strong man, an' a monstrous worker afore me. 'Tain't that; but I was thinkin' by myself to-day what a sight o' company the boy would ha' been. You know, small's he was, how I could trust to leave him anywheres with the team, and how he'd beseech to go with me wherever I was goin'; always right in my tracks I used to tell 'em. Poor little John, for all he was so young he had a great deal o' judgment; he'd ha' made a likely man."

The mother sighed heavily as she sat within the shadow.

"But then there's the little girls, a sight o' help an' company," urged the father eagerly, as if it were wrong to dwell upon sorrow and loss. "Katy, she's most as good as a boy, except that she ain't very rugged. She's a real little farmer, she's helped me a sight this spring; an' you've got Susan Ellen, that makes a complete little housekeeper for ye as far as she's learnt. I don't see but we're better off than most folks, each on us having a workmate."

"That's so, John," acknowledged Mrs. Hilton wistfully, beginning to rock steadily in her straight, splint-bottomed chair. It was always a good sign when she rocked.

"Where be the little girls so late?" asked their father. "'Tis gettin' long past eight o'clock. I don't know when we've all set up so late, but it's so kind o' summer-like an' pleasant. Why, where be they gone?"

"I've told ye; only over to Becker's folks," answered the mother. "I don't see myself what keeps 'em so late; they beseeched me after supper till I let 'em go. They're all in a dazzle with the new teacher; she asked 'em to come over. They say she's unusual smart with 'rethmetic, but she has a kind of a gorpen look to me. She's goin' to give Katy some pieces for her doll, but I told Katy she ought to be ashamed wantin' dolls' pieces, big as she's gettin' to be. I don't know's she ought, though; she ain't but nine this summer."

"Let her take her comfort," said the kind-hearted man. "Them things draws her to the teacher, an' makes them acquainted. Katy's shy with new folks, more so'n Susan Ellen, who's of the business kind. Katy's shy-feelin' and wishful."

"I don't know but she is," agreed the mother slowly. "Ain't it sing'lar how well acquainted you be with that one, an' I with Susan Ellen? 'Twas always so from the first. I'm doubtful sometimes our Katy ain't one that'll be like to get married—anyways not about here. She lives right with herself, but Susan Ellen ain't nothin' when she's alone, she's always after company; all the boys is waitin' on her a'ready. I ain't afraid but she'll take her pick when the time comes. I expect to see Susan Ellen well settled,—she feels grown up now,—but Katy don't care one mite 'bout none o' them things. She wants to be rovin' out o' doors. I do believe she'd stand an' hark to a bird the whole forenoon."

"Perhaps she'll grow up to be a teacher," suggested John Hilton. "She takes to her book more'n the other one. I should like one on 'em to be a teacher same's my mother was. They're good girls as anybody's got."

"So they be," said the mother, with unusual gentleness, and the creak of her rocking-chair was heard, regular as the ticking of a clock. The night breeze stirred in the great woods, and the sound of a brook that went falling down the hillside grew louder and louder. Now and then one could hear the plaintive chirp of a bird. The moon glittered with whiteness like a winter moon, and shone upon the low-roofed house until its small window-panes gleamed like silver, and one could almost see the colors of a blooming bush of lilac that grew in a sheltered angle by the kitchen door. There was an incessant sound of frogs in the lowlands.

"Be you sound asleep, John?" asked the wife presently.

"I don't know but what I was a'most," said the tired man, starting a little. "I should laugh if I was to fall sound asleep right here on the step; 'tis the bright night, I expect, makes my eyes feel heavy, an' 'tis so peaceful. I was up an' dressed a little past four an' out to work. Well, well!" and he laughed sleepily and rubbed his eyes. "Where's the little girls? I'd better step along an' meet 'em."

"I wouldn't just yet; they'll get home all right, but't is late for 'em certain. I don't want 'em keepin' Mis' Becker's folks up neither. There, le' 's wait a few minutes," urged Mrs. Hilton.

"I've be'n a-thinkin' all day I'd like to give the child'n some kind of a treat," said the father, wide awake now. "I hurried up my work 'cause I had it so in mind. They don't have the opportunities some do, an' I want 'em to know the world, an' not stay right here on the farm like a couple o' bushes."

"They're a sight better off not to be so full o' notions as some is," protested the mother suspiciously.

"Certain," answered the farmer; "but they're good, bright child'n, an' commencin' to take a sight o' notice. I want 'em to have all we can give 'em. I want 'em to see how other folks does things."

"Why, so do I,"—here the rocking-chair stopped ominously,—"but so long's they're contented"—

"Contented ain't all in this world; hopper-toads may have that quality an' spend all their time a-blinkin'. I don't know's bein' contented is all there is to look for in a child. Ambition's somethin' to me."

"Now you've got your mind on to some plot or other." (The rocking-chair began to move again.) "Why can't you talk right out?"

"'Tain't nothin' special," answered the good man, a little ruffled; he was never prepared for his wife's mysterious powers of divination. "Well there, you do find things out the master! I only thought perhaps I'd take 'em to-morrow, an' go off somewhere if't was a good day. I've been promisin' for a good while I'd take 'em to Topham Corners; they've never been there since they was very small."

"I believe you want a good time yourself. You ain't never got over bein' a boy." Mrs. Hilton seemed much amused. "There, go if you want to an' take 'em; they've got their summer hats an' new dresses. I don't know o' nothin' that stands in the way. I should sense it better if there was a circus or anythin' to go to. Why don't you wait an' let the girls pick 'em some strawberries or nice ros'berries, and then they could take an' sell 'em to the stores?"

John Hilton reflected deeply. "I should like to get me some good yellow-turnip seed to plant late. I ain't more'n satisfied with what I've been gettin' o' late years o' Ira Speed. An' I'm goin' to provide me with a good hoe; mine's gettin' wore out an' all shackly. I can't seem to fix it good."

"Them's excuses," observed Mrs. Hilton, with friendly tolerance. "You just cover up the hoe with somethin', if you get it—I would. Ira Speed's so jealous he'll remember it of you this twenty year, your goin' an' buyin' a new hoe o' anybody but him."

"I've always thought't was a free country," said John Hilton soberly. "I don't want to vex Ira neither; he favors us all he can in trade. 'Tis difficult for him to spare a cent, but he's as honest as daylight."

At this moment there was a sudden sound of

young voices, and a pair of young figures came out from the shadow of the woods into the moonlighted open space. An old cock crowed loudly from his perch in the shed, as if he were a herald of royalty. The little girls were hand in hand, and a brisk young dog capered about them as they came.

"Wa'n't it dark gittin' home through the woods this time o' night?" asked the mother hastily, and not without reproach.

"I don't love to have you gone so late; mother an' me was timid about ye, and you've kep' Mis' Becker's folks up, I expect," said their father regretfully. "I don't want to have it said that my little girls ain't got good manners."

"The teacher had a party," chirped Susan Ellen, the elder of the two children. "Goin' home from school she asked the Grover boys, an' Mary an' Sarah Speed. An' Mis' Becker was real pleasant to us: she passed round some cake, an' handed us sap sugar on one of her best plates, an' we played games an' sung some pieces too. Mis' Becker thought we did real well. I can pick out most of a tune on the cabinet organ; teacher says she'll give me lessons."

"I want to know, dear!" exclaimed John Hilton.

"Yes, an' we played Copenhagen, an' took sides spellin', an' Katy beat everybody spellin' there was there."

Katy had not spoken; she was not so strong as her sister, and while Susan Ellen stood a step or two away addressing her eager little audience, Katy had seated herself close to her father on the doorstep. He put his arm around her shoulders, and drew her close to his side, where she stayed.

"Ain't you got nothin' to tell, daughter?" he

asked, looking down fondly; and Katy gave a pleased little sigh for answer.

"Tell 'em what's goin' to be the last day o' school, and about our trimmin' the schoolhouse," she said; and Susan Ellen gave the programme in most spirited fashion.

"'Twill be a great time," said the mother, when she had finished. "I don't see why folks wants to go trapesin' off to strange places when such things is happenin' right about 'em." But the children did not observe her mysterious air. "Come, you must step yourselves right to bed!"

They all went into the dark, warm house; the bright moon shone upon it steadily all night, and the lilac flowers were shaken by no breath of wind until the early dawn.

II

The Hiltons always waked early. So did their neighbors, the crows and song-sparrows and robins, the light-footed foxes and squirrels in the woods. When John Hilton waked, before five o'clock, an hour later than usual because he had sat up so late, he opened the house door and came out into the yard, crossing the short green turf hurriedly as if the day were too far spent for any loitering. The magnitude of the plan for taking a whole day of pleasure confronted him seriously, but the weather was fair, and his wife, whose disapproval could not have been set aside, had accepted and even smiled upon the great project. It was inevitable now, that he and the children should go to Topham Corners. Mrs. Hilton had the pleasure of waking them, and telling the news.

In a few minutes they came frisking out to talk over the great plans. The cattle were already fed, and their father was milking. The only sign of high festivity was the wagon pulled out into the yard, with both seats put in as if it were Sunday; but Mr. Hilton still wore his every-day clothes, and Susan Ellen suffered instantly from disappointment.

"Ain't we goin', father?" she asked complainingly; but he nodded and smiled at her, even though the cow, impatient to get to pasture, kept whisking her rough tail across his face. He held his head down and spoke cheerfully, in spite of this vexation.

"Yes, sister, we're goin' certain', an' goin' to have a great time too." Susan Ellen thought that he seemed like a boy at that delightful moment, and felt new sympathy and pleasure at once. "You go an' help mother about breakfast an' them things; we want to get off quick's we can. You coax mother now, both on ye, an' see if she won't go with us."

"She said she wouldn't be hired to," responded Susan Ellen. "She says it's goin' to be hot, an' she's laid out to go over an' see how her aunt Tamsen Brooks is this afternoon."

The father gave a little sigh; then he took heart again. The truth was that his wife made light of the contemplated pleasure, and, much as he usually valued her companionship and approval, he was sure that they should have a better time without her. It was impossible, however, not to feel guilty of disloyalty at the thought. Even though she might be completely unconscious of his best ideals, he only loved her and the ideals the more, and bent his energies to satisfying her indefinite expectations. His wife still kept much of that youthful beauty which Susan Ellen seemed likely to reproduce.

An hour later the best wagon was ready, and the great expedition set forth. The little dog sat apart, and barked as if it fell entirely upon him to voice the general excitement. Both seats were in the wagon, but the empty place testified to Mrs. Hilton's unyielding disposition. She had wondered why one broad seat would not do, but John Hilton meekly suggested that the wagon looked better with both. The little girls sat on the back seat dressed alike in their Sunday hats of straw with blue ribbons, and their little plaïd shawls pinned neatly about their small shoulders. They wore gray thread gloves, and sat very straight. Susan Ellen was half a head the taller, but otherwise, from behind, they looked much alike. As for their father, he was in his Sunday best,—a plain black coat, and a winter hat of felt, which was heavy and rusty-looking for that warm early summer day. He had it in mind to buy a new straw hat at Topham, so that this with the turnip seed and the hoe made three important reasons for going.

"Remember an' lay off your shawls when you get there, an' carry them over your arms," said the mother, clucking like an excited hen to her chickens. "They'll do to keep the dust off your new dresses goin' an' comin'. An' when you eat your dinners don't get spots on you, an' don't point at folks as you ride by, an' stare, or they'll know you come from the country. An' John, you call into Cousin Ad'line Marlow's an' see how they all be, an' tell her I expect her over certain to stop awhile before hayin'. It always eases her phthisic to git up here on the high land, an' I've got a new notion about doin' over her best-room carpet sence I see her that'll save rippin' one breadth. An' don't come home all wore out; an', John, don't you go an' buy me no kickshaws to fetch home. I ain't a child, an' you ain't got no money to waste. I expect you'll go, like's not, an' buy you some kind of a foolish boy's hat; do look an' see if it's reasonable good straw, an' won't splinter all off round the edge. An' you mind, John''—

''Yes, yes, hold on!'' cried John impatiently; then he cast a last affectionate, reassuring look at her face, flushed with the hurry and responsibility of starting them off in proper shape. ''I wish you was goin' too,'' he said, smiling. ''I do so!'' Then the old horse started, and they went out at the bars, and began the careful long descent of the hill. The young dog, tethered to the lilac-bush, was frantic with piteous appeals; the little girls piped their eager good-bys again and again, and their father turned many times to look back and wave his hand. As for their mother, she stood alone and watched them out of sight.

There was one place far out on the highroad where she could catch a last glimpse of the wagon, and she waited what seemed a very long time until it appeared and then was lost to sight again behind a low hill. ''They're nothin' but a pack o' child'n together,'' she said aloud; and then felt lonelier than she expected. She even stooped and patted the unresigned little dog as she passed him, going into the house.

The occasion was so much more important than

any one had foreseen that both the little girls were speechless. It seemed at first like going to church in new clothes, or to a funeral; they hardly knew how to behave at the beginning of a whole day of pleasure. They made grave bows at such persons of their acquaintance as happened to be straying in the road. Once or twice they stopped before a farmhouse, while their father talked an inconsiderately long time with some one about the crops and the weather, and even dwelt upon town business and the doings of the selectmen, which might be talked of at any time. The explanations that he gave of their excursion seemed quite unnecessary. It was made entirely clear that he had a little business to do at Topham Corners, and thought he had better give the little girls a ride; they had been very steady at school, and he had finished planting, and could take the day as well as not. Soon, however, they all felt as if such an excursion were an everyday affair, and Susan Ellen began to ask eager questions, while Katy silently sat apart enjoying herself as she never had done before. She liked to see the strange houses, and the children who belonged to them; it was delightful to find flowers that she knew growing all along the road, no matter how far she went from home. Each small homestead looked its best and pleasantest, and shared the exquisite beauty that early summer made,—shared the luxury of greenness and floweriness that decked the rural world. There was an early peony or a late lilac in almost every dooryard.

It was seventeen miles to Topham. After a while they seemed very far from home, having left the hills far behind, and descended to a great level country with fewer tracts of woodland, and wider fields where the crops were much more forward. The houses were all painted, and the roads were smoother and wider. It had been so pleasant driving along that Katy dreaded going into the strange town when she first caught sight of it, though Susan Ellen kept asking with bold fretfulness if they were not almost there. They counted the steeples of four churches, and their father presently showed them the Topham Academy, where their grandmother once went to school, and told them that perhaps some day they would go there too. Katy's heart gave a strange leap; it was such a tremendous thing to think of, but instantly the suggestion was transformed for her into one of the certainties of life. She looked with solemn awe at the tall belfry, and the long rows of windows in the front of the academy, there where it stood high and white among the clustering trees. She hoped that they were going to drive by, but something forbade her taking the responsibility of saying so.

Soon the children found themselves among the crowded village houses. Their father turned to look at them with affectionate solicitude.

"Now sit up straight and appear pretty," he whispered to them. "We're among the best people now, an' I want folks to think well of you."

"I guess we're as good as they be," remarked Susan Ellen, looking at some innocent passers-by with dark suspicion, but Katy tried indeed to sit straight, and folded her hands prettily in her lap, and wished with all her heart to be pleasing for her father's sake. Just then an elderly woman saw the wagon and the sedate party it carried, and smiled so kindly that it seemed to Katy as if Topham Corners had welcomed and received them. She smiled back again as if this hospitable person were an old friend, and entirely forgot that the eyes of all Topham had been upon her.

"There, now we're coming to an elegant house that I want you to see; you'll never forget it," said John Hilton. "It's where Judge Masterson lives, the great lawyer; the handsomest house in the county, everybody says."

"Do you know him, father?" asked Susan Ellen.

"I do," answered John Hilton proudly. "Him and my mother went to school together in their young days, and were always called the two best scholars of their time. The judge called to see her once; he stopped to our house to see her when I was a boy. An' then, some years ago—you've heard me tell how I was on the jury, an' when he heard my name spoken he looked at me sharp, and asked if I wa'n't the son of Catharine Winn, an' spoke most beautiful of your grandmother, an' how well he remembered their young days together."

"I like to hear about that," said Katy.

"She had it pretty hard, I'm afraid, up on the old farm. She was keepin' school in our district when father married her—that's the main reason I backed 'em down when they wanted to tear the old schoolhouse all to pieces," confided John Hilton, turning eagerly. "They all say she lived longer up here on the hill than she could anywhere, but she never had her health. I wa'n't but a boy when she died. Father an' me lived alone afterward till the time your mother come; 'twas a good while, too; I wa'n't married so young as some. 'Twas lonesome, I tell you; father was plumb discouraged losin' of his wife, an' her long sickness an' all set him back, an' we'd work all day on the land an' never say a word. I s'pose 't is bein' so lonesome early in life that makes me so pleased to have some nice girls growin' up round me now."

There was a tone in her father's voice that drew Katy's heart toward him with new affection. She dimly understood, but Susan Ellen was less interested. They had often heard this story before, but to one child it was always new and to the other old. Susan Ellen was apt to think it tiresome to hear about her grandmother, who, being dead, was hardly worth talking about.

"There's Judge Masterson's place," said their father in an every-day manner, as they turned a corner, and came into full view of the beautiful old white house standing behind its green trees and terraces and lawns. The children had never imagined anything so stately and fine, and even Susan Ellen exclaimed with pleasure. At that moment they saw an old gentleman, who carried himself with great dignity, coming slowly down the wide box-bordered path toward the gate.

"There he is now, there's the judge!" whispered John Hilton excitedly, reining his horse quickly to the green roadside. "He's goin' down-town to his office; we can wait right here an' see him. I can't expect him to remember me; it's been a good many years. Now you are goin' to see the great Judge Masterson!"

There was a quiver of expectation in their hearts. The judge stopped at his gate, hesitating a moment before he lifted the latch, and glanced up the street at the country wagon with its two prim little girls on the back seat, and the eager man who drove. They seemed to be waiting for something; the old horse was nibbling at the fresh roadside grass. The judge was used to being looked at with interest, and responded now with a smile as he came out to the sidewalk, and unexpectedly turned their way. Then he suddenly lifted his hat with grave politeness, and came directly toward them.

"Good-morning, Mr. Hilton," he said. "I am very glad to see you, sir;" and Mr. Hilton, the little girls' own father, took off his hat with equal courtesy, and bent forward to shake hands.

Susan Ellen cowered and wished herself away, but little Katy sat straighter than ever, with joy in her father's pride and pleasure shining in her pale, flower-like little face.

"These are your daughters, I am sure," said the old gentleman kindly, taking Susan Ellen's limp and reluctant hand; but when he looked at Katy, his face brightened. "How she recalls your mother!" he said with great feeling. "I am glad to see this dear child. You must come to see me with your father, my dear," he added, still looking at her. "Bring both the little girls, and let them run about the old garden; the cherries are just getting ripe," said Judge Masterson hospitably. "Perhaps you will have time to stop this afternoon as you go home?"

"I should call it a great pleasure if you would come and see us again some time. You may be driving our way, sir," said John Hilton.

"Not very often in these days," answered the

old judge. "I thank you for the kind invitation. I should like to see the fine view again from your hill westward. Can I serve you in any way while you are in town? Good-by, my little friends!"

Then they parted, but not before Katy, the shy Katy, whose hand the judge still held unconsciously while he spoke, had reached forward as he said good-by, and lifted her face to kiss him. She could not have told why, except that she felt drawn to something in the serious, worn face. For the first time in her life the child had felt the charm of manners; perhaps she owned a kinship between that which made him what he was, and the spark of nobleness and purity in her own simple soul. She turned again and again to look back at him as they drove away.

"Now you have seen one of the first gentlemen in the country," said their father. "It was worth comin' twice as far"—but he did not say any more, nor turn as usual to look in the children's faces.

In the chief business street of Topham a great many country wagons like the Hiltons' were fastened to the posts, and there seemed to our holiday-makers to be a great deal of noise and excitement.

"Now I've got to do my errands, and we can let the horse rest and feed," said John Hilton. "I'll slip his headstall right off, an' put on his halter. I'm goin' to buy him a real good treat o' oats. First we'll go an' buy me my straw hat; I feel as if this one looked a little past to wear in Topham. We'll buy the things we want, an' then we'll walk all along the street, so you can look in the windows an' see the han'some things, same's your mother likes to. What was it mother told you about your shawls?"

"To take 'em off an' carry 'em over our arms," piped Susan Ellen, without comment, but in the interest of alighting and finding themselves afoot upon the pavement the shawls were forgotten. The children stood at the doorway of a shop while their father went inside, and they tried to see what the Topham shapes of bonnets were like, as their mother had advised them; but everything was exciting and confusing, and they could arrive at no decision. When Mr. Hilton came out with a hat in his hand to be seen in a better light, Katy whispered that she wished he would buy a shiny one like Judge Masterson's; but her father only smiled and shook his head, and said that they were plain folks, he and Katy. There were dry-goods for sale in the same shop, and a young clerk who was measuring linen kindly pulled off some pretty labels with gilded edges and gay pictures, and gave them to the little girls, to their exceeding joy. He may have had small sisters at home, this friendly lad, for he took pains to find two pretty blue boxes besides, and was rewarded by their beaming gratitude.

It was a famous day; they even became used to seeing so many people pass. The village was full of its morning activity, and Susan Ellen gained a new respect for her father, and an increased sense of her own consequence, because even in Topham several persons knew him and called him familiarly by name. The meeting with an old man who had once been a neighbor seemed to give Mr. Hilton the greatest pleasure. The old man called to them from a house doorway as they were passing, and they all went in. The children seated themselves wearily on the wooden step, but their father shook his old friend eagerly by the hand, and declared that he was delighted to see him so well and enjoying the fine weather.

"Oh, yes," said the old man, in a feeble, quavering voice, "I'm astonishin' well for my age. I don't complain, John, I don't complain."

They talked long together of people whom they had known in the past, and Katy, being a little tired, was glad to rest, and sat still with her hands folded, looking about the front yard. There were some kinds of flowers that she never had seen before.

"This is the one that looks like my mother," her father said, and touched Katy's shoulder to remind her to stand up and let herself be seen. "Judge Masterson saw the resemblance; we met him at his gate this morning."

"Yes, she certain does look like your mother, John," said the old man, looking pleasantly at Katy, who found that she liked him better than at first. "She does, certain; the best of young folks is, they remind us of the old ones. 'Tis nateral to cling to life, folks say, but for me, I git impatient at times. Most everybody's gone now, an' I want to be goin'. 'Tis somethin' before me, an' I want to have it over with. I want to be there 'long o' the rest o' the folks. I expect to last quite a while though; I may see ye couple o' times more, John."

John Hilton responded cheerfully, and the children were urged to pick some flowers. The old man awed them with his impatience to be gone. There was such a townful of people about him, and he seemed as lonely as if he were the last survivor of a former world. Until that moment they had felt as if everything were just beginning.

"Now I want to buy somethin' pretty for your mother," said Mr. Hilton, as they went soberly away down the street, the children keeping fast hold of his hands. "By now the old horse will have eat his dinner and had a good rest, so pretty soon we can jog along home. I'm goin' to take you round by the academy, and the old North Meetinghouse where Dr. Barstow used to preach. Can't you think o' somethin' that your mother'd want?" he asked suddenly, confronted by a man's difficulty of choice.

"She was talkin' about wantin' a new pepper-box, one day; the top o' the old one won't stay on," suggested Susan Ellen, with delightful readiness. "Can't we have some candy, father?"

"Yes, ma'am," said John Hilton, smiling and swinging her hand to and fro as they walked. "I feel as if some would be good myself. What's all this?" They were passing a photographer's doorway with its enticing array of portraits. "I do declare!" he exclaimed excitedly, "I'm goin' to have our pictures taken; 'twill please your mother more 'n a little."

This was, perhaps, the greatest triumph of the day, except the delightful meeting with the judge; they sat in a row, with the father in the middle, and there was no doubt as to the excellence of the likeness. The best hats had to be taken off because they cast a shadow, but they were not missed, as their owners had feared. Both Susan Ellen and Katy looked their brightest and best; their eager young faces would forever shine there; the joy of the holiday was mirrored in the little picture. They did not know why their father was so pleased with it; they would not know until age had dowered them with the riches of association and remembrance.

Just at nightfall the Hiltons reached home again, tired out and happy. Katy had climbed over into the front seat beside her father, because that was always her place when they went to church on Sundays. It was a cool evening, there was a fresh sea wind that brought a light mist with it, and the sky was fast growing cloudy. Somehow the children looked different; it seemed to their mother as if they had grown older and taller since they went away in the morning, and as if they belonged to the town now as much as to the country. The greatness of their day's experience had left her far behind; the day had been silent and lonely without them, and she had had their supper ready, and been watching anxiously, ever since five o'clock. As for the children themselves they had little to say at first—they had eaten their luncheon early on the way to Topham. Susan Ellen was childishly cross, but Katy was pathetic and wan. They could hardly wait to show the picture, and their mother was as much pleased as everybody had expected.

"There, what did make you wear your shawls?" she exclaimed a moment afterward, reproachfully. "You ain't been an' wore 'em all day long? I wanted folks to see how pretty your new dresses was, if I did make 'em. Well, well! I wish more'n ever now I'd gone an' seen to ye!"

"An' here's the pepper-box!" said Katy, in a pleased, unconscious tone.

"That really is what I call beautiful," said Mrs. Hilton, after a long and doubtful look. "Our other one was only tin. I never did look so high as a chiny one with flowers, but I can get us another any time for every day. That's a proper hat, as good as you could have got, John. Where's your new hoe?" she asked as he came toward her from the barn, smiling with satisfaction.

"I declare to Moses if I didn't forget all about it," meekly acknowledged the leader of the great excursion. "That an' my yellow turnip seed, too; they went clean out o' my head, there was so many other things to think of. But 't ain't no sort o' matter; I can get a hoe just as well to Ira Speed's."

His wife could not help laughing. "You an' the little girls have had a great time. They was full o' wonder to me about everything, and I expect they'll talk about it for a week. I guess we was right about havin' 'em see somethin' more o' the world."

"Yes," answered John Hilton, with humility, "yes, we did have a beautiful day. I didn't expect so much. They looked as nice as anybody, and appeared so modest an' pretty. The little girls will remember it perhaps by an' by. I guess they won't never forget this day they had 'long o' father."

It was evening again, the frogs were piping in the lower meadows, and in the woods, higher up the great hill, a little owl began to hoot. The sea air, salt and heavy, was blowing in over the country at the end of the hot bright day. A lamp was lighted in the house, the happy children were talking together, and supper was waiting. The father and mother lingered for a moment outside and looked down over the shadowy fields; then they went in, without speaking. The great day was over, and they shut the door.

KATE CHOPIN

Désirée's Baby

As the day was pleasant, Madame Valmondé drove over to L'Abri to see Désirée and the baby.

It made her laugh to think of Désirée with a baby. Why, it seemed but yesterday that Désirée was little more than a baby herself; when Monsieur in riding through the gateway of Valmondé had found her lying asleep in the shadow of the big stone pillar.

The little one awoke in his arms and began to cry for "Dada." That was as much as she could do or say. Some people thought she might have strayed there of her own accord, for she was of the toddling age. The prevailing belief was that she had been purposely left by a party of Texans, whose canvas-covered wagon, late in the day, had crossed the ferry that Coton Maïs kept, just below the plantation. In time Madame Valmondé abandoned every speculation but the one that Désirée had been sent to her by a beneficent Providence to be the child of her affection, seeing that she was without child of the flesh. For the girl grew to be beautiful and gentle, affectionate and sincere,—the idol of Valmondé.

It was no wonder, when she stood one day against the stone pillar in whose shadow she had lain asleep, eighteen years before, that Armand Aubigny riding by and seeing her there, had fallen in love with her. That was the way all the Aubignys fell in love, as if struck by a pistol shot. The wonder was that he had not loved her before; for he had known her since his father brought him home from Paris, a boy of eight, after his mother died there. The passion that awoke in him that day, when he saw her at the gate, swept along like an avalanche, or like a prairie fire, or like anything that drives headlong over all obstacles.

Monsieur Valmondé grew practical and wanted things well considered: that is, the girl's obscure origin. Armand looked into her eyes and did not care. He was reminded that she was nameless. What did it matter about a name when he could give her one of the oldest and proudest in Louisiana? He ordered the *corbeille* from Paris, and contained himself with what patience he could until it arrived; then they were married.

Madame Valmondé had not seen Désirée and the baby for four weeks. When she reached L'Abri she shuddered at the first sight of it, as she always did. It was a sad looking place, which for many years had not known the gentle presence of a mistress, old Monsieur Aubigny having married and buried his wife in France, and she having loved her own land too well ever to leave it. The roof came down steep and black like a cowl, reaching out beyond the wide galleries that encircled the yellow stuccoed house. Big solemn oaks grew close to it, and their thick-leaved, far-reaching branches shadowed it like a pall. Young Aubigny's rule was a strict one, too, and under it his negroes had forgotten how to be gay, as they had been during the old master's easy-going and indulgent lifetime.

The young mother was recovering slowly, and lay full length, in her soft white muslins and laces, upon a couch. The baby was beside her, upon her arm, where he had fallen asleep, at her breast. The yellow nurse woman sat beside a window fanning herself.

Madame Valmondé bent her portly figure over Désirée and kissed her, holding her an instant tenderly in her arms. Then she turned to the child.

"This is not the baby!" she exclaimed, in startled tones. French was the language spoken at Valmondé in those days.

"I knew you would be astonished," laughed Désirée, "at the way he has grown. The little *cochon de lait!* Look at his legs, mamma, and his hands and fingernails,—real finger-nails. Zandrine had to cut them this morning. Isn't it true, Zandrine?"

The woman bowed her turbaned head majestically, "Mais si, Madame."

"And the way he cries," went on Désirée, "is deafening. Armand heard him the other day as far away as La Blanche's cabin."

Madame Valmondé had never removed her eyes from the child. She lifted it and walked with it over to the window that was lightest. She scanned the baby narrowly, then looked as searchingly at Zandrine, whose face was turned to gaze across the fields.

"Yes, the child has grown, has changed," said Madame Valmondé, slowly, as she replaced it beside its mother. "What does Armand say?"

Désirée's face became suffused with a glow that was happiness itself.

"Oh, Armand is the proudest father in the parish, I believe, chiefly because it is a boy, to bear his name; though he says not,—that he would have loved a girl as well. But I know it isn't true. I know he says that to please me. And mamma," she added, drawing Madame Valmondé's head down to her, and speaking in a whisper, "he hasn't punished one of them—not one of them—since baby is born. Even Négrillon, who pretended to have burnt his leg that he might rest from work—he only laughed, and said Négrillon was a great scamp. Oh, mamma, I'm so happy; it frightens me."

What Désirée said was true. Marriage, and later the birth of his son had softened Armand Aubigny's imperious and exacting nature greatly. This was what made the gentle Désirée so happy, for she loved him desperately. When he frowned she trembled, but loved him. When he smiled, she asked no greater blessing of God. But Armand's dark, handsome face had not often been disfigured by frowns since the day he fell in love with her.

When the baby was about three months old, Désirée awoke one day to the conviction that there was something in the air menacing her peace. It was at first too subtle to grasp. It had only been a disquieting suggestion; an air of mystery among the blacks; unexpected visits from far-off neighbors who could hardly account for their coming. Then a strange, an awful change in her husband's manner, which she dared not ask him to explain.

When he spoke to her, it was with averted eyes, from which the old love-light seemed to have gone out. He absented himself from home; and when there, avoided her presence and that of her child, without excuse. And the very spirit of Satan seemed suddenly to take hold of him in his dealings with the slaves. Désirée was miserable enough to die.

She sat in her room, one hot afternoon, in her *peignoir,* listlessly drawing through her fingers the strands of her long, silky brown hair that hung about her shoulders. The baby, half naked, lay asleep upon her own great mahogany bed, that was like a sumptuous throne, with its satin-lined half-canopy. One of La Blanche's little quadroon boys—half naked too—stood fanning the child slowly with a fan of peacock feathers. Désirée's eyes had been fixed absently and sadly upon the baby, while she was striving to penetrate the threatening mist that she felt closing about her. She looked from her child to the boy who stood beside him, and back again; over and over. "Ah!" It was a cry that she could not help; which she was not conscious of having uttered. The blood turned like ice in her veins, and a clammy moisture gathered upon her face.

She tried to speak to the little quadroon boy; but no sound would come, at first. When he heard his name uttered, he looked up, and his mistress was pointing to the door. He laid aside the great, soft fan, and obediently stole away, over the polished floor, on his bare tiptoes.

She stayed motionless, with gaze riveted upon her child, and her face the picture of fright.

Presently her husband entered the room, and

without noticing her, went to a table and began to search among some papers which covered it.

"Armand," she called to him, in a voice which must have stabbed him, if he was human. But he did not notice. "Armand," she said again. Then she rose and tottered towards him. "Armand," she panted once more, clutching his arm, "look at our child. What does it mean? tell me."

He coldly but gently loosened her fingers from about his arm and thrust the hand away from him. "Tell me what it means!" she cried despairingly.

"It means," he answered lightly, "that the child is not white; it means that you are not white."

A quick conception of all that this accusation meant for her nerved her with unwonted courage to deny it. "It is a lie; it is not true, I am white! Look at my hair, it is brown; and my eyes are gray, Armand, you know they are gray. And my skin is fair," seizing his wrist. "Look at my hand; whiter than yours, Armand," she laughed hysterically.

"As white as La Blanche's," he returned cruelly; and went away leaving her alone with their child.

When she could hold a pen in her hand, she sent a despairing letter to Madame Valmondé.

"My mother, they tell me I am not white. Armand has told me I am not white. For God's sake tell them it is not true. You must know it is not true. I shall die. I must die. I cannot be so unhappy, and live."

The answer that came was as brief:

"My own Désirée: Come home to Valmondé; back to your mother who loves you. Come with your child."

When the letter reached Désirée she went with it

to her husband's study, and laid it open upon the desk before which he sat. She was like a stone image: silent, white, motionless after she placed it there.

In silence he ran his cold eyes over the written words. He said nothing. "Shall I go, Armand?" she asked in tones sharp with agonized suspense.

"Yes, go."

"Do you want me to go?"

"Yes, I want you to go."

He thought Almighty God had dealt cruelly and unjustly with him; and felt, somehow, that he was paying Him back in kind when he stabbed thus into his wife's soul. Moreover he no longer loved her, because of the unconscious injury she had brought upon his home and his name.

She turned away like one stunned by a blow, and walked slowly towards the door, hoping he would call her back.

"Good-by, Armand," she moaned.

He did not answer her. That was his last blow at fate.

Désirée went in search of her child. Zandrine was pacing the sombre gallery with it. She took the little one from the nurse's arms with no word of explanation, and descending the steps, walked away, under the live-oak branches.

It was an October afternoon; the sun was just sinking. Out in the still fields the negroes were picking cotton.

Désirée had not changed the thin white garment nor the slippers which she wore. Her hair was uncovered and the sun's rays brought a golden gleam from its brown meshes. She did not take the broad, beaten road which led to the far-off plantation of Valmondé. She walked across a deserted field, where the stubble bruised her tender feet, so delicately shod, and tore her thin gown to shreds.

She disappeared among the reeds and willows that grew thick along the banks of the deep, sluggish bayou; and she did not come back again.

Some weeks later there was a curious scene enacted at L'Abri. In the centre of the smoothly swept back yard was a great bonfire. Armand Aubigny sat in the wide hallway that commanded a view of the spectacle; and it was he who dealt out to a half dozen negroes the material which kept this fire ablaze.

A graceful cradle of willow, with all its dainty furbishings, was laid upon the pyre, which had already been fed with the richness of a priceless *layette*. Then there were silk gowns, and velvet and satin ones added to these; laces, too, and embroideries; bonnets and gloves; for the *corbeille* had been of rare quality.

The last thing to go was a tiny bundle of letters; innocent little scribblings that Désirée had sent to him during the days of their espousal. There was the remnant of one back in the drawer from which he took them. But it was not Désirée's; it was part of an old letter from his mother to his father. He read it. She was thanking God for the blessing of her husband's love:—

"But, above all," she wrote, "night and day, I thank the good God for having so arranged our lives that our dear Armand will never know that his mother, who adores him, belongs to the race that is cursed with the brand of slavery."

La Belle Zoraïde

The summer night was hot and still; not a ripple of air swept over the *marais*. Yonder, across Bayou St. John, lights twinkled here and there in the darkness, and in the dark sky above a few stars were blinking. A lugger that had come out of the lake was moving with slow, lazy motion down the bayou. A man in the boat was singing a song.

The notes of the song came faintly to the ears of old Manna-Loulou, herself as black as the night, who had gone out upon the gallery to open the shutters wide.

Something in the refrain reminded the woman of an old, half-forgotten Creole romance, and she began to sing it low to herself while she threw the shutters open:—

> "Lisett' to kité la plaine,
> Mo perdi bonhair à moué;
> Ziés à moué semblé fontaine,
> Dépi mo pa miré toué."

And then this old song, a lover's lament for the loss of his mistress, floating into her memory, brought with it the story she would tell to Madame, who lay in her sumptuous mahogany bed, waiting to be fanned and put to sleep to the sound of one of Manna-Loulou's stories. The old negress had already bathed her mistress's pretty white feet and kissed them lovingly, one, then the other. She had brushed her mistress's beautiful hair, that was as soft and shining as satin, and was the color of Madame's wedding-ring. Now, when she reëntered the room, she moved softly toward the bed, and seating herself there began gently to fan Madame Delisle.

Manna-Loulou was not always ready with her story, for Madame would hear none but those which were true. But to-night the story was all there in Manna-Loulou's head—the story of la belle Zoraïde—and she told it to her mistress in the soft Creole patois, whose music and charm no English words can convey.

"La belle Zoraïde had eyes that were so dusky, so beautiful, that any man who gazed too long into their depths was sure to lose his head, and even his heart sometimes. Her soft, smooth skin was the color of *café-au-lait*. As for her elegant manners, her *svelte* and graceful figure, they were the envy of half the ladies who visited her mistress, Madame Delarivière.

"No wonder Zoraïde was as charming and as dainty as the finest lady of la rue Royale: from a toddling thing she had been brought up at her mistress's side; her fingers had never done rougher work than sewing a fine muslin seam; and she even had her own little black servant to wait upon her. Madame, who was her godmother as well as her mistress, would often say to her:—

" 'Remember, Zoraïde, when you are ready to marry, it must be in a way to do honor to your bringing up. It will be at the Cathedral. Your wedding gown, your *corbeille*, all will be of the best; I shall see to that myself. You know, M'sieur Ambroise is ready whenever you say the word; and his master is willing to do as much for him as I shall do for you. It is a union that will please me in every way.'

"M'sieur Ambroise was then the body servant of Doctor Langlé. La belle Zoraïde detested the little mulatto, with his shining whiskers like a white man's, and his small eyes, that were cruel and false as a snake's. She would cast down her own mischievous eyes, and say:—

" 'Ah, nénaine, I am so happy, so contented here at your side just as I am. I don't want to marry now; next year, perhaps, or the next.' And Madame would smile indulgently and remind Zoraïde that a woman's charms are not everlasting.

"But the truth of the matter was, Zoraïde had seen le beau Mézor dance the Bamboula in Congo Square. That was a sight to hold one rooted to the ground. Mézor was as straight as a cypress-tree and as proud looking as a king. His body, bare to the waist, was like a column of ebony and it glistened like oil.

"Poor Zoraïde's heart grew sick in her bosom with love for le beau Mézor from the moment she saw the fierce gleam of his eye, lighted by the inspiring strains of the Bamboula, and beheld the stately movements of his splendid body swaying and quivering through the figures of the dance.

"But when she knew him later, and he came near her to speak with her, all the fierceness was gone out of his eyes, and she saw only kindness in them and heard only gentleness in his voice; for love had taken possession of him also, and Zoraïde was more distracted than ever. When Mézor was not dancing Bamboula in Congo Square, he was hoeing sugar-cane, barefooted and half naked, in his master's field outside of the city. Doctor Langlé was his master as well as M'sieur Ambroise's.

"One day, when Zoraïde kneeled before her mistress, drawing on Madame's silken stockings, that were of the finest, she said:

" 'Nénaine, you have spoken to me often of marrying. Now, at last, I have chosen a husband, but it is not M'sieur Ambroise; it is le beau Mézor that I want and no other.' And Zoraïde hid her face in her hands when she had said that, for she guessed, rightly enough, that her mistress would be very angry. And, indeed, Madame Delarivière was at first speechless with rage. When she finally spoke it was only to gasp out, exasperated:—

" 'That negro! that negro! Bon Dieu Seigneur, but this is too much!'

" 'Am I white, nénaine?' pleaded Zoraïde.

" 'You white! *Malheureuse!* You deserve to have the lash laid upon you like any other slave; you have proven yourself no better than the worst.'

" 'I am not white,' persisted Zoraïde, respectfully and gently. 'Doctor Langlé gives me his slave to marry, but he would not give me his son. Then, since I am not white, let me have from out of my own race the one whom my heart has chosen.'

"However, you may well believe that Madame would not hear to that. Zoraïde was forbidden to speak to Mézor, and Mézor was cautioned against seeing Zoraïde again. But you know how the negroes are, Ma'zélle Titite," added Manna-Loulou, smiling a little sadly. "There is no mistress, no master, no king nor priest who can hinder them from loving when they will. And these two found ways and means.

"When months had passed by, Zoraïde, who had grown unlike herself,—sober and preoccupied,—said again to her mistress:—

" 'Nénaine, you would not let me have Mézor for my husband; but I have disobeyed you, I have sinned. Kill me if you wish, nénaine: forgive me if you will; but when I heard le beau Mézor say to me, "Zoraïde, mo l'aime toi," I could have died, but I could not have helped loving him.'

"This time Madame Delarivière was so actually pained, so wounded at hearing Zoraïde's confession, that there was no place left in her heart for anger. She could utter only confused reproaches. But she was a woman of action rather than of words, and she acted promptly. Her first step was to induce Doctor Langlé to sell Mézor. Doctor Langlé, who was a widower, had long wanted to marry Madame Delarivière, and he would willingly have walked on all fours at noon through the Place d'Armes if she wanted him to. Naturally he lost no time in disposing of le beau Mézor, who was sold away into Georgia, or the Carolinas, or one of those distant countries far away, where he would no longer hear his Creole tongue spoken, nor dance Calinda, nor hold la belle Zoraïde in his arms.

"The poor thing was heartbroken when Mézor was sent away from her, but she took comfort and hope in the thought of her baby that she would soon be able to clasp to her breast.

"La belle Zoraïde's sorrows had now begun in earnest. Not only sorrows but sufferings, and with the anguish of maternity came the shadow of death. But there is no agony that a mother will not forget when she holds her first-born to her heart, and presses her lips upon the baby flesh that is her own, yet far more precious than her own.

"So, instinctively, when Zoraïde came out of the awful shadow she gazed questioningly about her and felt with her trembling hands upon either side of her. 'Où li, mo piti a moin? (Where is my little one?)' she asked imploringly. Madame who was there and the nurse who was there both told her in turn, 'To piti à toi, li mouri' ('Your little one is dead'), which was a wicked falsehood that must have caused the angels in heaven to weep. For the baby was living and well and strong. It had at once been removed from its mother's side, to be sent away to Madame's plantation, far up the coast. Zoraïde could only moan in reply, 'Li mouri, li mouri,' and she turned her face to the wall.

"Madame had hoped, in thus depriving Zoraïde of her child, to have her young waiting-maid again at her side free, happy, and beautiful as of old. But there was a more powerful will than Madame's at work—the will of the good God, who had already designed that Zoraïde should grieve with a sorrow that was never more to be lifted in this world. La belle Zoraïde was no more. In her stead was a sad-eyed woman who mourned night and day for her baby. 'Li mouri, li mouri,' she would sigh over and over again to those about her, and to herself when others grew weary of her complaint.

"Yet, in spite of all, M'sieur Ambroise was still in the notion to marry her. A sad wife or a merry one was all the same to him so long as that wife was Zoraïde. And she seemed to consent, or rather submit, to the approaching marriage as though nothing mattered any longer in this world.

"One day, a black servant entered a little noisily the room in which Zoraïde sat sewing. With a look of strange and vacuous happiness upon her face, Zoraïde arose hastily. 'Hush, hush,' she whispered, lifting a warning finger, 'my little one is asleep; you must not awaken her.'

"Upon the bed was a senseless bundle of rags shaped like an infant in swaddling clothes. Over this dummy the woman had drawn the mosquito bar, and she was sitting contentedly beside it. In short, from that day Zoraïde was demented. Night nor day did she lose sight of the doll that lay in her bed or in her arms.

"And now was Madame stung with sorrow and remorse at seeing this terrible affliction that had befallen her dear Zoraïde. Consulting with Doctor Langlé, they decided to bring back to the mother the real baby of flesh and blood that was now toddling about, and kicking its heels in the dust yonder upon the plantation.

"It was Madame herself who led the pretty, tiny little "griffe" girl to her mother. Zoraïde was sitting upon a stone bench in the courtyard, listening to the soft splashing of the fountain, and watching the fitful shadows of the palm leaves upon the broad, white flagging.

" 'Here,' said Madame, approaching, 'here, my poor dear Zoraïde, is your own little child. Keep her; she is yours. No one will ever take her from you again.'

"Zoraïde looked with sullen suspicion upon her mistress and the child before her. Reaching out a hand she thrust the little one mistrustfully away from her. With the other hand she clasped the rag bundle fiercely to her breast; for she suspected a plot to deprive her of it.

"Nor could she ever be induced to let her own child approach her; and finally the little one was sent back to the plantation, where she was never to know the love of mother or father.

"And now this is the end of Zoraïde's story. She was never known again as la belle Zoraïde, but ever after as Zoraïde la folle, whom no one ever wanted to marry—not even M'sieur Ambroise. She lived to be an old woman, whom some people pitied and others laughed at—always clasping her bundle of rags—her 'piti.'

"Are you asleep, Ma'zélle Titite?"

"No, I am not asleep; I was thinking. Ah, the poor little one, Man Loulou, the poor little one! better had she died!"

But this is the way Madame Delisle and Manna-Loulou really talked to each other:—

"Vou pré droumi, Ma'zélle Titite?"

"Non, pa pré droumi; mo yapré zongler. Ah, la pauv' piti, Man Loulou. La pauv' piti! Mieux li mouri!"

Athénaïse

I

Athénaïse went away in the morning to make a visit to her parents, ten miles back on rigolet de Bon Dieu. She did not return in the evening, and Cazeau, her husband, fretted not a little. He did not worry much about Athénaïse, who, he suspected, was resting only too content in the bosom of her family; his chief solicitude was manifestly for the pony she had ridden. He felt sure those "lazy pigs," her brothers, were capable of neglecting it seriously. This misgiving Cazeau communicated to his servant, old Félicité, who waited upon him at supper.

His voice was low pitched, and even softer than Félicité's. He was tall, sinewy, swarthy, and altogether severe looking. His thick black hair waved, and it gleamed like the breast of a crow. The sweep of his mustache, which was not so black, outlined the broad contour of the mouth. Beneath the under lip grew a small tuft which he was much given to twisting, and which he permitted to grow, apparently for no other purpose. Cazeau's eyes were dark blue, narrow and overshadowed. His hands were coarse and stiff from close acquaintance with farming tools and implements, and he handled his fork and knife clumsily. But he was distinguished looking, and succeeded in commanding a good deal of respect, and even fear sometimes.

He ate his supper alone, by the light of a single coal-oil lamp that but faintly illuminated the big room, with its bare floor and huge rafters, and its heavy pieces of furniture that loomed dimly in the gloom of the apartment. Félicité, ministering to his wants, hovered about the table like a little, bent, restless shadow.

She served him with a dish of sunfish fried crisp and brown. There was nothing else set before him beside the bread and butter and the bottle of red wine which she locked carefully in the buffet after he had poured his second glass. She was occupied with her mistress's absence, and kept reverting to it after he had expressed his solicitude about the pony.

"Dat beat me! on'y marry two mont', an' got de head turn' a'ready to go 'broad. C'est pas Chrétien, tenez!"

Cazeau shrugged his shoulders for answer, after he had drained his glass and pushed aside his plate. Félicité's opinion of the unchristianlike behavior of his wife in leaving him thus alone after two months of marriage weighed little with him. He was used to solitude, and did not mind a day or a night or two of it. He had lived alone ten years, since his first wife died, and Félicité might have known better than to suppose that he cared. He told her she was a fool. It sounded like a compliment in his modulated, caressing voice. She grumbled to herself as she set about clearing the table, and Cazeau arose and walked outside on the gallery; his spur, which he had not removed upon entering the house, jangled at every step.

The night was beginning to deepen, and to gather black about the clusters of trees and shrubs that were grouped in the yard. In the beam of light from the open kitchen door a black boy stood feeding a brace of snarling, hungry dogs; further away, on the steps of a cabin, some one was playing the accordion; and in still another direction a little negro baby was crying lustily. Cazeau walked around to the front of the house, which was square, squat and one-story.

A belated wagon was driving in at the gate, and the impatient driver was swearing hoarsely at his jaded oxen. Félicité stepped out on the gallery, glass and polishing towel in hand, to investigate, and to wonder, too, who could be singing out on the river. It was a party of young people paddling around, waiting for the moon to rise, and they were singing Juanita, their voices coming tempered and melodious through the distance and the night.

Cazeau's horse was waiting, saddled, ready to be mounted, for Cazeau had many things to attend to before bed-time; so many things that there was not left to him a moment in which to think of Athénaïse. He felt her absence, though, like a dull, insistent pain.

However, before he slept that night he was visited by the thought of her, and by a vision of her fair young face with its drooping lips and sullen and averted eyes. The marriage had been a blunder; he had only to look into her eyes to feel that, to discover her growing aversion. But it was a thing not by any possibility to be undone. He was quite prepared to make the best of it, and expected no less than a like effort on her part. The less she revisited the rigolet, the better. He would find means to keep her at home hereafter.

These unpleasant reflections kept Cazeau awake far into the night, notwithstanding the craving of his whole body for rest and sleep. The moon was shining, and its pale effulgence reached dimly into the room, and with it a touch of the cool breath of the spring night. There was an unusual stillness abroad; no sound to be heard save the distant, tireless, plaintive notes of the accordion.

II

Athénaïse did not return the following day, even though her husband sent her word to do so by her brother, Montéclin, who passed on his way to the village early in the morning.

On the third day Cazeau saddled his horse and went himself in search of her. She had sent no word, no message, explaining her absence, and he felt that he had good cause to be offended. It was rather awkward to have to leave his work, even though late in the afternoon,—Cazeau had always so much to do; but among the many urgent calls upon him, the task of bringing his wife back to a sense of her duty seemed to him for the moment paramount.

The Michés, Athénaïse's parents, lived on the old Gotrain place. It did not belong to them; they were "running" it for a merchant in Alexandria. The house was far too big for their use. One of the lower rooms served for the storing of wood and tools; the person "occupying" the place before Miché having pulled up the flooring in despair of being able to patch it. Upstairs, the rooms were so large, so bare, that they offered a constant temptation to lovers of the dance, whose importunities Madame Miché was accustomed to meet with amiable indulgence. A dance at Miché's and a plate of Madame Miché's gumbo filé at midnight were pleasures not to be neglected or despised, unless by such serious souls as Cazeau.

Long before Cazeau reached the house his approach had been observed, for there was nothing to obstruct the view of the outer road; vegetation was not yet abundantly advanced, and there was but a patchy, straggling stand of cotton and corn in Miché's field.

Madame Miché, who had been seated on the gallery in a rocking-chair, stood up to greet him as he drew near. She was short and fat, and wore a black skirt and loose muslin sack fastened at the throat with a hair brooch. Her own hair, brown and glossy, showed but a few threads of silver. Her round pink face was cheery, and her eyes were bright and good humored. But she was plainly perturbed and ill at ease as Cazeau advanced.

Montéclin, who was there too, was not ill at ease, and made no attempt to disguise the dislike with which his brother-in-law inspired him. He was a slim, wiry fellow of twenty-five, short of stature like his mother, and resembling her in feature. He was in shirt-sleeves, half leaning, half sitting, on the insecure railing of the gallery, and fanning himself with his broad-rimmed felt hat.

"Cochon!" he muttered under his breath as Cazeau mounted the stairs,—"sacré cochon!"

"Cochon" had sufficiently characterized the man who had once on a time declined to lend Montéclin money. But when this same man had had the presumption to propose marriage to his well-beloved sister, Athénaïse, and the honor to be accepted by her, Montéclin felt that a qualifying epithet was needed fully to express his estimate of Cazeau.

Miché and his oldest son were absent. They both esteemed Cazeau highly, and talked much of his qualities of head and heart, and thought much of his excellent standing with city merchants.

Athénaïse had shut herself up in her room. Cazeau had seen her rise and enter the house at perceiving him. He was a good deal mystified, but no one could have guessed it when he shook hands with Madame Miché. He had only nodded to Montéclin, with a muttered "Comment ça va?"

"Tiens! something tole me you were coming today!" exclaimed Madame Miché, with a little blustering appearance of being cordial and at ease, as she offered Cazeau a chair.

He ventured a short laugh as he seated himself.

"You know, nothing would do," she went on, with much gesture of her small, plump hands, "nothing would do but Athénaïse mus' stay las' night fo' a li'le dance. The boys wouldn' year to their sister leaving."

Cazeau shrugged his shoulders significantly, telling as plainly as words that he knew nothing about it.

"Comment! Montéclin didn' tell you we were going to keep Athénaïse?" Montéclin had evidently told nothing.

"An' how about the night befo'," questioned Cazeau, "an' las' night? It isn't possible you dance every night out yere on the Bon Dieu!"

Madame Miché laughed, with amiable appreciation of the sarcasm; and turning to her son, "Montéclin, my boy, go tell yo' sister that Monsieur Cazeau is yere."

Montéclin did not stir except to shift his position and settle himself more securely on the railing.

"Did you year me, Montéclin?"

"Oh yes, I yeard you plain enough," responded her son, "but you know as well as me it's no use to tell 'Thénaïse anything. You been talkin' to her yo'se'f since Monday; an' pa's preached himse'f hoa'se on the subject; an' you even had uncle Achille down yere yesterday to reason with her. W'en 'Thénaïse said she wasn' goin' to set her foot back in Cazeau's house, she meant it."

This speech, which Montéclin delivered with thorough unconcern, threw his mother into a condition of painful but dumb embarrassment. It brought two fiery red spots to Cazeau's cheeks, and for the space of a moment he looked wicked.

What Montéclin had spoken was quite true, though his taste in the manner and choice of time and place in saying it were not of the best. Athénaïse, upon the first day of her arrival, had announced that she came to stay, having no intention of returning under Cazeau's roof. The announcement had scattered consternation, as she knew it would. She had been implored, scolded, entreated, stormed at, until she felt herself like a dragging sail that all the winds of heaven had beaten upon. Why in the name of God had she married Cazeau? Her father had lashed her with the question a dozen times. Why indeed? It was difficult now for her to understand why, unless because she supposed it was customary for girls to marry when the right opportunity came. Cazeau, she knew, would make life more comfortable for her; and again, she had liked him, and had even been rather flustered when he pressed her hands and kissed them, and kissed her lips and cheeks and eyes, when she accepted him.

Montéclin himself had taken her aside to talk the thing over. The turn of affairs was delighting him.

"Come, now, 'Thénaïse, you mus' explain to me all about it, so we can settle on a good cause, an' secu' a separation fo' you. Has he been mistreating an' abusing you, the sacré cochon?" They were alone together in her room, whither she had taken refuge from the angry domestic elements.

"You please to reserve yo' disgusting expressions, Montéclin. No, he has not abused me in any way that I can think."

"Does he drink? Come 'Thénaïse, think well over it. Does he ever get drunk?"

"Drunk! Oh, mercy, no,—Cazeau never gets drunk."

"I see; it's jus' simply you feel like me; you hate him."

"No, I don't hate him," she returned reflectively; adding with a sudden impulse, "It's jus' being married that I detes' an' despise. I hate being Mrs. Cazeau, an' would want to be Athénaïse Miché again. I can't stan' to live with a man; to have him always there; his coats an' pantaloons hanging in my room; his ugly bare feet—washing them in my tub, befo' my very eyes, ugh!" She shuddered with recollections, and resumed, with a sigh that was almost a sob: "Mon Dieu, mon Dieu! Sister Marie Angélique knew w'at she was saying; she knew me better than myse'f w'en she said God had sent me a vocation an' I was turning deaf ears. W'en I think of a blessed life in the convent, at peace! Oh, w'at was I dreaming of!" and then the tears came.

Montéclin felt disconcerted and greatly disappointed at having obtained evidence that would carry no weight with a court of justice. The day had not come when a young woman might ask the court's permission to return to her mamma on the sweeping ground of a constitutional disinclination for marriage. But if there was no way of untying this Gordian knot of marriage, there was surely a way of cutting it.

"Well, 'Thénaïse, I'm mighty durn sorry you got no better groun's 'an w'at you say. But you can count on me to stan' by you w'atever you do. God knows I don' blame you fo' not wantin' to live with Cazeau."

And now there was Cazeau himself, with the red spots flaming in his swarthy cheeks, looking and feeling as if he wanted to thrash Montéclin into some semblance of decency. He arose abruptly, and approaching the room which he had seen his wife enter, thrust open the door after a hasty preliminary knock. Athénaïse, who was standing erect at a far window, turned at his entrance.

She appeared neither angry nor frightened, but thoroughly unhappy, with an appeal in her soft dark eyes and a tremor on her lips that seemed to him expressions of unjust reproach, that wounded and maddened him at once. But whatever he might feel, Cazeau knew only one way to act toward a woman.

"Athénaïse, you are not ready?" he asked in his quiet tones. "It's getting late; we havn' any time to lose."

She knew that Montéclin had spoken out, and she had hoped for a wordy interview, a stormy scene, in which she might have held her own as she had held it for the past three days against her family, with Montéclin's aid. But she had no weapon with which to combat subtlety. Her husband's looks, his tones, his mere presence, brought to her a sudden sense of hopelessness, an instinctive realization of the futility of rebellion against a social and sacred institution.

Cazeau said nothing further, but stood waiting in the doorway. Madame Miché had walked to the far end of the gallery, and pretended to be occupied with having a chicken driven from her parterre. Montéclin stood by, exasperated, fuming, ready to burst out.

Athénaïse went and reached for her riding skirt that hung against the wall. She was rather tall, with a figure which, though not robust, seemed perfect in its fine proportions. "La fille de son père," she was often called, which was a great compliment to Miché. Her brown hair was brushed all fluffily back from her temples and low forehead, and about her features and expression lurked a softness, a prettiness, a dewiness, that were perhaps too childlike, that savored of immaturity.

She slipped the riding-skirt, which was of black alpaca, over her head, and with impatient fingers hooked it at the waist over her pink linen-lawn. Then she fastened on her white sunbonnet and reached for her gloves on the mantelpiece.

"If you don' wan' to go, you know w'at you got to do, 'Thénaïse," fumed Montéclin. "You don' set yo' feet back on Cane River, by God, unless you want to,—not w'ile I'm alive."

Cazeau looked at him as if he were a monkey whose antics fell short of being amusing.

Athénaïse still made no reply, said not a word. She walked rapidly past her husband, past her brother; bidding good-bye to no one, not even to her mother. She descended the stairs, and without assistance from any one mounted the pony, which Cazeau had ordered to be saddled upon his arrival. In this way she obtained a fair start of her husband, whose departure was far more leisurely, and for the greater part of the way she managed to keep an appreciable gap between them. She rode almost madly at first, with the wind inflating her skirt balloonlike about her knees, and her sunbonnet falling back between her shoulders.

At no time did Cazeau make an effort to overtake her until traversing an old fallow meadow that was level and hard as a table. The sight of a great solitary oak-tree, with its seemingly immutable outlines, that had been a landmark for ages—or was it the odor of elderberry stealing up from the gully to the south? or what was it that brought vividly back to Cazeau, by some association of ideas, a scene of many years ago? He had passed that old live-oak hundreds of times, but it was only now that the memory of one day came back to him. He was a very small boy that day, seated before his father on horse-back. They were proceeding slowly, and Black Gabe was moving on before them at a little dog-trot. Black Gabe had run away, and had been discovered back in the Gotrain swamp. They had halted beneath this big oak to enable the negro to take breath; for Cazeau's father was a kind and considerate master, and every one had agreed at the time that Black Gabe was a fool, a great idiot indeed, for wanting to run away from him.

The whole impression was for some reason hideous, and to dispel it Cazeau spurred his horse to a swift gallop. Overtaking his wife, he rode the remainder of the way at her side in silence.

It was late when they reached home. Félicité was standing on the grassy edge of the road, in the moonlight, waiting for them.

Cazeau once more ate his supper alone; for Athénaïse went to her room, and there she was crying again.

III

Athénaïse was not one to accept the inevitable with patient resignation, a talent born in the souls of many women; neither was she the one to accept it with philosophical resignation, like her husband. Her sensibilities were alive and keen and responsive. She met the pleasurable things of life with frank, open appreciation, and against distasteful conditions she rebelled. Dissimulation was as foreign to her nature as guile to the breast of a babe, and her rebellious outbreaks, by no means rare, had hitherto been quite open and aboveboard. People often said that Athénaïse would know her own mind some day, which was equivalent to saying that she was at present unacquainted with it. If she ever came to such knowledge, it would be by no intellectual research, by no subtle analyses or tracing the motives of actions to their source. It would come to her as the song to the bird, the perfume and color to the flower.

Her parents had hoped—not without reason and justice—that marriage would bring the poise, the desirable pose, so glaringly lacking in Athénaïse's character. Marriage they knew to be a wonderful and powerful agent in the development and formation of a woman's character; they had seen its effect too often to doubt it.

"And if this marriage does nothing else," exclaimed Miché in an outburst of sudden exasperation, "it will rid us of Athénaïse; for I am at the end of my patience with her! You have never had the firmness to manage her,"—he was speaking to his wife,—"I have not had the time, the leisure, to devote to her training; and what good we might have accomplished, that maudit Montéclin—Well, Cazeau is the one! It takes just such a steady hand to guide a disposition like Athénaïse's, a master hand, a strong will that compels obedience."

And now, when they had hoped for so much,

here was Athénaïse, with gathered and fierce vehemence, beside which her former outbursts appeared mild, declaring that she would not, and she would not, and she would not continue to enact the role of wife to Cazeau. If she had had a reason! as Madame Miché lamented; but it could not be discovered that she had any sane one. He had never scolded, or called names, or deprived her of comforts, or been guilty of any of the many reprehensible acts commonly attributed to objectionable husbands. He did not slight nor neglect her. Indeed, Cazeau's chief offense seemed to be that he loved her, and Athénaïse was not the woman to be loved against her will. She called marriage a trap set for the feet of unwary and unsuspecting girls, and in round, unmeasured terms reproached her mother with treachery and deceit.

"I told you Cazeau was the man," chuckled Miché, when his wife had related the scene that had accompanied and influenced Athénaïse's departure.

Athénaïse again hoped, in the morning, that Cazeau would scold or make some sort of a scene, but he apparently did not dream of it. It was exasperating that he should take her acquiescence so for granted. It is true he had been up and over the fields and across the river and back long before she was out of bed, and he may have been thinking of something else, which was no excuse, which was even in some sense an aggravation. But he did say to her at breakfast, "That brother of yo's, that Montéclin, is unbearable."

"Montéclin? Par exemple!"

Athénaïse, seated opposite to her husband, was attired in a white morning wrapper. She wore a somewhat abused, long face, it is true,—an expression of countenance familiar to some husbands,—but the expression was not sufficiently pronounced to mar the charm of her youthful freshness. She had little heart to eat, only playing with the food before her, and she felt a pang of resentment at her husband's healthy appetite.

"Yes, Montéclin," he reasserted. "He's developed into a firs'-class nuisance; an' you better tell him, Athénaïse,—unless you want me to tell him,—to confine his energies after this to matters that concern him. I have no use fo' him or fo' his interference in w'at regards you an' me alone."

This was said with unusual asperity. It was the little breach that Athénaïse had been watching for, and she charged rapidly: "It's strange, if you detes' Montéclin so heartily, that you would desire to marry his sister." She knew it was a silly thing to say, and was not surprised when he told her so. It gave her a little foothold for further attack, however. "I don't see, anyhow, w'at reason you had to marry me, w'en there were so many others," she complained, as if accusing him of persecution and injury. "There was Marianne running after you fo' the las' five years till it was disgraceful; an' any one of the Dortrand girls would have been glad to marry you. But no, nothing would do; you mus' come out on the rigolet fo' me." Her complaint was pathetic, and at the same time so amusing that Cazeau was forced to smile.

"I can't see w'at the Dortrand girls or Marianne

have to do with it,'' he rejoined; adding, with no trace of amusement, ''I married you because I loved you; because you were the woman I wanted to marry, an' the only one. I reckon I tole you that befo'. I thought—of co'se I was a fool fo' taking things fo' granted—but I did think that I might make you happy in making things easier an' mo' comfortable fo' you. I expected—I was even that big a fool—I believed that yo' coming yere to me would be like the sun shining out of the clouds, an' that our days would be like w'at the story-books promise after the wedding. I was mistaken. But I can't imagine w'at induced you to marry me. W'atever it was, I reckon you foun' out you made a mistake, too. I don' see anything to do but make the best of a bad bargain, an' shake han's over it.''

He had arisen from the table, and, approaching, held out his hand to her. What he had said was commonplace enough, but it was significant, coming from Cazeau, who was not often so unreserved in expressing himself.

Athénaïse ignored the hand held out to her. She was resting her chin in her palm, and kept her eyes fixed moodily upon the table. He rested his hand, that she would not touch, upon her head for an instant, and walked away out of the room.

She heard him giving orders to workmen who had been waiting for him out on the gallery, and she heard him mount his horse and ride away. A hundred things would distract him and engage his attention during the day. She felt that he had perhaps put her and her grievance from his thoughts when he crossed the threshold; whilst she—

Old Félicité was standing there holding a shining tin pail, asking for flour and lard and eggs from the storeroom, and meal for the chicks.

Athénaïse seized the bunch of keys which hung from her belt and flung them at Félicité's feet.

"Tiens! tu vas les garder comme tu as jadis fait. Je ne veux plus de ce train là, moi!"

The old woman stooped and picked up the keys from the floor. It was really all one to her that her mistress returned them to her keeping, and refused to take further account of the ménage.

IV

It seemed now to Athénaïse that Montéclin was the only friend left to her in the world. Her father and mother had turned from her in what appeared to be her hour of need. Her friends laughed at her, and refused to take seriously the hints which she threw out,—feeling her way to discover if marriage were as distasteful to other women as to herself. Montéclin alone understood her. He alone had always been ready to act for her and with her, to comfort and solace her with his sympathy and his support. Her only hope for rescue from her hateful surroundings lay in Montéclin. Of herself she felt powerless to plan, to act, even to conceive a way out of this pitfall into which the whole world seemed to have conspired to thrust her.

She had a great desire to see her brother, and wrote asking him to come to her. But it better suited Montéclin's spirit of adventure to appoint a meeting-place at the turn of the lane, where Athénaïse might appear to be walking leisurely for health and recreation, and where he might seem to be riding along, bent on some errand of business or pleasure.

There had been a shower, a sudden downpour, short as it was sudden, that had laid the dust in the road. It had freshened the pointed leaves of the live-oaks, and brightened up the big fields of cotton on either side of the lane till they seemed carpeted with green, glittering gems.

Athénaïse walked along the grassy edge of the road, lifting her crisp skirts with one hand, and with the other twirling a gay sunshade over her bare head. The scent of the fields after the rain was delicious. She inhaled long breaths of their freshness and perfume, that soothed and quieted her for the moment. There were birds splashing and spluttering in the pools, pluming themselves on the fence-rails, and sending out little sharp cries, twitters, and shrill rhapsodies of delight.

She saw Montéclin approaching from a great distance,—almost as far away as the turn of the woods. But she could not feel sure it was he; it appeared too tall for Montéclin, but that was because he was riding a large horse. She waved her parasol to him; she was so glad to see him. She had never been so glad to see Montéclin before; not even the day when he had taken her out of the convent, against her parents' wishes, because she had expressed a desire to remain there no longer. He seemed to her, as he drew near, the embodiment of kindness, of bravery, of chivalry, even of wisdom; for she had never known Montéclin at a loss to extricate himself from a disagreeable situation.

He dismounted, and, leading his horse by the bridle, started to walk beside her, after he had kissed her affectionately and asked her what she was crying about. She protested that she was not crying, for she was laughing, though drying her eyes at the same time on her handkerchief, rolled in a soft mop for the purpose.

She took Montéclin's arm, and they strolled slowly down the lane; they could not seat themselves for a comfortable chat, as they would have liked, with the grass all sparkling and bristling wet.

Yes, she was quite as wretched as ever, she told him. The week which had gone by since she saw him had in no wise lightened the burden of her discontent. There had even been some additional provocations laid upon her, and she told Montéclin all about them,—about the keys, for instance, which in a fit of temper she had returned to Félicité's keeping; and she told how Cazeau had brought them back to her as if they were something she had accidentally lost, and he had recovered; and how he had said, in that aggravating tone of his, that it was not the custom on Cane river for the negro servants to carry the keys, when there was a mistress at the head of the household.

But Athénaïse could not tell Montéclin anything to increase the disrespect which he already entertained for his brother-in-law; and it was then he unfolded to her a plan which he had conceived and worked out for her deliverance from this galling matrimonial yoke.

It was not a plan which met with instant favor, which she was at once ready to accept, for it involved secrecy and dissimulation, hateful alternatives, both of them. But she was filled with admiration for Montéclin's resources and wonderful talent for contrivance. She accepted the plan; not with the immediate determination to act upon it, rather with the intention to sleep and to dream upon it.

Three days later she wrote to Montéclin that she had abandoned herself to his counsel. Displeasing as it might be to her sense of honesty, it would yet be less trying than to live on with a soul full of bitterness and revolt, as she had done for the past two months.

V

When Cazeau awoke, one morning at his usual very early hour, it was to find the place at his side vacant. This did not surprise him until he discovered that Athénaïse was not in the adjoining room, where he had often found her sleeping in the morning on the lounge. She had perhaps gone out for an early stroll, he reflected, for her jacket and hat were not on the rack where she had hung them the night before. But there were other things absent,—a gown or two from the armoire; and there was a great gap in the piles of lingerie on the shelf; and her traveling-bag was missing, and so were her bits of jewelry from the toilet tray—and Athénaïse was gone!

But the absurdity of going during the night, as if she had been a prisoner, and he the keeper of a dungeon! So much secrecy and mystery, to go sojourning out on the Bon Dieu! Well, the Michés might keep their daughter after this. For the companionship of no woman on earth would he again undergo the humiliating sensation of baseness that had overtaken him in passing the old oak-tree in the fallow meadow.

But a terrible sense of loss overwhelmed Cazeau. It was not new or sudden; he had felt it for weeks growing upon him, and it seemed to culminate with Athénaïse's flight from home. He knew that he could again compel her return as he had done once before,—compel her to return to the shelter of his roof, compel her cold and unwilling submission to his love and passionate transports; but the loss of self-respect seemed to him too dear a price to pay for a wife.

He could not comprehend why she had seemed to prefer him above others; why she had attracted him with eyes, with voice, with a hundred womanly ways, and finally distracted him with love which she seemed, in her timid, maidenly fashion, to return. The great sense of loss came from the realization of having missed a chance for happiness,—a chance that would come his way again only through a miracle. He could not think of himself loving any other woman, and could not think of Athénaïse ever—even at some remote date—caring for him.

He wrote her a letter, in which he disclaimed any further intention of forcing his commands upon her. He did not desire her presence ever again in his home unless she came of her free will, uninfluenced by family or friends; unless she could be the companion he had hoped for in marrying her, and in some measure return affection and respect for the love which he continued and would always continue to feel for her. This letter he sent out to the rigolet by a messenger early in the day. But she was not out on the rigolet, and had not been there.

The family turned instinctively to Montéclin, and almost literally fell upon him for an explanation; he had been absent from home all night. There was much mystification in his answers, and a plain desire to mislead in his assurances of ignorance and innocence.

But with Cazeau there was no doubt or speculation when he accosted the young fellow. "Montéclin, w'at have you done with Athénaïse?" he questioned bluntly. They had met in the open road on horseback, just as Cazeau ascended the river bank before his house.

"W'at have you done to Athénaïse?" returned Montéclin for answer.

"I don't reckon you've considered yo' conduct by any light of decency an' propriety in encouraging yo' sister to such an action, but let me tell you"—

"Voyons! you can let me alone with yo' decency an' morality an' fiddlesticks. I know you mus' 'a' done Athénaïse pretty mean that she can't live with you; an' fo' my part, I'm mighty durn glad she had the spirit to quit you."

"I ain't in the humor to take any notice of yo' impertinence, Montéclin; but let me remine you that Athénaïse is nothing but a chile in character; besides that, she's my wife, an' I hole you responsible fo' her safety an' welfare. If any harm of any description happens to her, I'll strangle you, by God, like a rat, and fling you in Cane river, if I have to hang fo' it!" He had not lifted his voice. The only sign of anger was a savage gleam in his eyes.

"I reckon you better keep yo' big talk fo' the women, Cazeau," replied Montéclin, riding away.

But he went doubly armed after that, and intimated that the precaution was not needless, in view of the threats and menaces that were abroad touching his personal safety.

VI

Athénaïse reached her destination sound of skin and limb, but a good deal flustered, a little frightened, and altogether excited and interested by her unusual experiences.

Her destination was the house of Sylvie, on Dauphine Street, in New Orleans,—a three-story gray brick, standing directly on the banquette, with three broad stone steps leading to the deep front entrance. From the second-story balcony swung a small sign, conveying to passers-by the intelligence that within were *"chambres garnies."*

It was one morning in the last week of April that Athénaïse presented herself at the Dauphine Street house. Sylvie was expecting her, and introduced her at once to her apartment, which was in the second story of the back ell, and accessible by an open, outside gallery. There was a yard below, paved with broad stone flagging; many fragrant flowering shrubs and plants grew in a bed along the side of the opposite wall, and others were distributed about in tubs and green boxes.

It was a plain but large enough room into which

Athénaïse was ushered, with matting on the floor, green shades and Nottingham-lace curtains at the windows that looked out on the gallery, and furnished with a cheap walnut suit. But everything looked exquisitely clean, and the whole place smelled of cleanliness.

Athénaïse at once fell into the rocking-chair, with the air of exhaustion and intense relief of one who has come to the end of her troubles. Sylvie, entering behind her, laid the big traveling-bag on the floor and deposited the jacket on the bed.

She was a portly quadroon of fifty or thereabout, clad in an ample *volante* of the old-fashioned purple calico so much affected by her class. She wore large golden hoop-earrings, and her hair was combed plainly, with every appearance of effort to smooth out the kinks. She had broad, coarse features, with a nose that turned up, exposing the wide nostrils, and that seemed to emphasize the loftiness and command of her bearing,—a dignity that in the presence of white people assumed a character of respectfulness, but never of obsequiousness. Sylvie believed firmly in maintaining the color line, and would not suffer a white person, even a child, to call her "Madame Sylvie,"—a title which she exacted religiously, however, from those of her own race.

"I hope you be please' wid yo' room, madame," she observed amiably. "Dat's de same room w'at yo' brother, M'sieur Miché, all time like w'en he come to New Orlean'. He well, M'sieur Miché? I receive' his letter las' week, an' dat same day a gent'man want I give 'im dat room. I say, 'No, dat room already ingage'.' Ev-body like dat room on 'count it so quite (quiet). M'sieur Gouvernail, dere in nax' room, you can't pay 'im! He been stay t'ree year' in dat room; but all fix' up fine wid his own furn'ture an' books, 'tel you can't see! I say to 'im plenty time', M'sieur Gouvernail, w'y you don't take dat t'ree-story front, now, long it's empty?' He tells me, 'Leave me 'lone, Sylvie; I know a good room w'en I fine it, me.' "

She had been moving slowly and majestically about the apartment, straightening and smoothing down bed and pillows, peering into ewer and basin, evidently casting an eye around to make sure that everything was as it should be.

"I sen' you some fresh water, madame," she offered upon retiring from the room. "An' w'en you want an't'ing, you jus' go out on de gall'ry an' call Pousette: she year you plain,—she right down dere in de kitchen."

Athénaïse was really not so exhausted as she had every reason to be after that interminable and circuitous way by which Montéclin had seen fit to have her conveyed to the city.

Would she ever forget that dark and truly dangerous midnight ride along the "coast" to the mouth of Cane river! There Montéclin had parted with her, after seeing her aboard the St. Louis and Shreveport packet which he knew would pass there before dawn. She had received instructions to disembark at the mouth of Red river, and there transfer to the first south-bound steamer for New Orleans; all of which instructions she had followed implicitly, even to making her way at once to Sylvie's upon her arrival in the city. Montéclin had enjoined secrecy and much caution; the clandestine nature of the affair gave it a savor of adventure which was highly pleasing to him. Eloping with his sister was only a little less engaging than eloping with some one else's sister.

But Montéclin did not do the *grand seigneur* by halves. He had paid Sylvie a whole month in advance for Athénaïse's board and lodging. Part of the sum he had been forced to borrow, it is true, but he was not niggardly.

Athénaïse was to take her meals in the house, which none of the other lodgers did; the one exception being that Mr. Gouvernail was served with breakfast on Sunday mornings.

Sylvie's clientèle came chiefly from the southern parishes; for the most part, people spending but a few days in the city. She prided herself upon the quality and highly respectable character of her patrons, who came and went unobtrusively.

The large parlor opening upon the front balcony was seldom used. Her guests were permitted to entertain in this sanctuary of elegance,—but they never did. She often rented it for the night to parties of respectable and discreet gentlemen desiring to enjoy a quiet game of cards outside the bosom of their families. The second-story hall also led by a long window out on the balcony. And Sylvie advised Athénaïse, when she grew weary of her back room, to go and sit on the front balcony, which was shady in the afternoon, and where she might find diversion in the sounds and sights of the street below.

Athénaïse refreshed herself with a bath, and was soon unpacking her few belongings, which she ranged neatly away in the bureau drawers and the armoire.

She had revolved certain plans in her mind during the past hour or so. Her present intention was to live on indefinitely in this big, cool, clean back room on Dauphine street. She had thought seriously, for moments, of the convent, with all readiness to embrace the vows of poverty and chastity; but what about obedience? Later, she intended, in some round-about way, to give her parents and her husband the assurance of her safety and welfare; reserving the right to remain unmolested and lost to them. To live on at the expense of Montéclin's generosity was wholly out of the question, and Athénaïse meant to look about for some suitable and agreeable employment.

The imperative thing to be done at present, however, was to go out in search of material for an inexpensive gown or two; for she found herself in the painful predicament of a young woman having almost literally nothing to wear. She decided upon pure white for one, and some sort of a sprigged muslin for the other.

VII

On Sunday morning, two days after Athénaïse's arrival in the city, she went in to breakfast somewhat later than usual, to find two covers laid at table instead of the one to which she was accustomed. She had been to mass, and did not remove her hat, but put her fan, parasol, and prayerbook aside. The dining-room was situated just beneath her own apartment, and, like all rooms of the house, was large and airy; the floor was covered with a glistening oil-cloth.

The small, round table, immaculately set, was drawn near the open window. There were some tall plants in boxes on the gallery outside; and Pousette, a little, old, intensely black woman, was splashing and dashing buckets of water on the flagging, and talking loud in her Creole patois to no one in particular.

A dish piled with delicate river-shrimps and crushed ice was on the table; a caraffe of crystal-clear water, a few *hors d'œuvres,* beside a small golden-brown crusty loaf of French bread at each plate. A half-bottle of wine and the morning paper were set at the place opposite Athénaïse.

She had almost completed her breakfast when Gouvernail came in and seated himself at table. He felt annoyed at finding his cherished privacy invaded. Sylvie was removing the remains of a mutton-chop from before Athénaïse, and serving her with a cup of café au lait.

"M'sieur Gouvernail," offered Sylvie in her most insinuating and impressive manner, "you please leave me make you acquaint' wid Madame Cazeau. Dat's M'sieur Miché's sister; you meet 'im two t'ree time', you rec'lec', an' been one day to de race wid 'im. Madame Cazeau, you please leave me make you acquaint' wid M'sieur Gouvernail."

Gouvernail expressed himself greatly pleased to meet the sister of Monsieur Miché, of whom he had not the slightest recollection. He inquired after Monsieur Miché's health, and politely offered

Athénaïse a part of his newspaper,—the part which contained the Woman's Page and the social gossip.

Athénaïse faintly remembered that Sylvie had spoken of a Monsieur Gouvernail occupying the room adjoining hers, living amid luxurious surroundings and a multitude of books. She had not thought of him further than to picture him a stout, middle-aged gentleman, with a bushy beard turning gray, wearing large gold-rimmed spectacles, and stooping somewhat from much bending over books and writing material. She had confused him in her mind with the likeness of some literary celebrity that she had run across in the advertising pages of a magazine.

Gouvernail's appearance was, in truth, in no sense striking. He looked older than thirty and younger than forty, was of medium height and weight, with a quiet, unobtrusive manner which seemed to ask that he be let alone. His hair was light brown, brushed carefully and parted in the middle. His mustache was brown, and so were his eyes, which had a mild, penetrating quality. He was neatly dressed in the fashion of the day; and his hands seemed to Athénaïse remarkably white and soft for a man's.

He had been buried in the contents of his newspaper, when he suddenly realized that some further little attention might be due to Miché's sister. He started to offer her a glass of wine, when he was surprised and relieved to find that she had quietly slipped away while he was absorbed in his own editorial on Corrupt Legislation.

Gouvernail finished his paper and smoked his

cigar out on the gallery. He lounged about, gathered a rose for his buttonhole, and had his regular Sunday-morning confab with Pousette, to whom he paid a weekly stipend for brushing his shoes and clothing. He made a great pretense of haggling over the transaction, only to enjoy her uneasiness and garrulous excitement.

He worked or read in his room for a few hours, and when he quitted the house, at three in the afternoon, it was to return no more till late at night. It was his almost invariable custom to spend Sunday evenings out in the American quarter, among a congenial set of men and women,—*des esprits forts,* all of them, whose lives were irreproachable, yet whose opinions would startle even the traditional "sapeur," for whom "nothing is sacred." But for all his "advanced" opinions, Gouvernail was a liberal-minded fellow; a man or woman lost nothing of his respect by being married.

When he left the house in the afternoon, Athénaïse had already ensconced herself on the front balcony. He could see her through the jalousies when he passed on his way to the front entrance. She had not yet grown lonesome or homesick; the newness of her surroundings made them sufficiently entertaining. She found it diverting to sit there on the front balcony watching people pass by, even though there was no one to talk to. And then the comforting, comfortable sense of not being married!

She watched Gouvernail walk down the street, and could find no fault with his bearing. He could hear the sound of her rockers for some little distance. He wondered what the "poor little thing" was doing in the city, and meant to ask Sylvie about her when he should happen to think of it.

VIII

The following morning, towards noon, when Gouvernail quitted his room, he was confronted by Athénaïse, exhibiting some confusion and trepidation at being forced to request a favor of him at so early a stage of their acquaintance. She stood in her doorway, and had evidently been sewing, as the thimble on her finger testified, as well as a long-threaded needle thrust in the bosom of her gown. She held a stamped but unaddressed letter in her hand.

And would Mr. Gouvernail be so kind as to address the letter to her brother, Mr. Montéclin Miché? She would hate to detain him with explanations this morning,—another time, perhaps,—but now she begged that he would give himself the trouble.

He assured her that it made no difference, that it was no trouble whatever; and he drew a fountain pen from his pocket and addressed the letter at her dictation, resting it on the inverted rim of his straw hat. She wondered a little at a man of his supposed erudition stumbling over the spelling of "Montéclin" and "Miché."

She demurred at overwhelming him with the additional trouble of posting it, but he succeeded in convincing her that so simple a task as the posting of a letter would not add an iota to the burden of the day. Moreover, he promised to carry it in his hand, and thus avoid any possible risk of forgetting it in his pocket.

After that, and after a second repetition of the favor, when she had told him that she had had a letter from Montéclin, and looked as if she wanted to tell him more, he felt that he knew her better. He felt that he knew her well enough to join her out on the balcony, one night, when he found her sitting there alone. He was not one who deliberately sought the society of women, but he was not wholly a bear. A little commiseration for Athénaïse's aloneness, perhaps some curiosity to know further what manner of woman she was, and the natural influence of her feminine charm were equal unconfessed factors in turning his steps towards the balcony when he discovered the shimmer of her white gown through the open hall window.

It was already quite late, but the day had been intensely hot, and neighboring balconies and doorways were occupied by chattering groups of humanity, loath to abandon the grateful freshness of the outer air. The voices about her served to reveal to Athénaïse the feeling of loneliness that was gradually coming over her. Notwithstanding certain dormant impulses, she craved human sympathy and companionship.

She shook hands impulsively with Gouvernail, and told him how glad she was to see him. He was not prepared for such an admission, but it pleased him immensely, detecting as he did that the expression was as sincere as it was outspoken. He drew a chair up within comfortable conversational distance of Athénaïse, though he had no intention of talking more than was barely necessary to encourage Madame—He had actually forgotten her name!

He leaned an elbow on the balcony rail, and would have offered an opening remark about the oppressive heat of the day, but Athénaïse did not give him the opportunity. How glad she was to talk to some one, and how she talked!

An hour later she had gone to her room, and Gouvernail stayed smoking on the balcony. He knew her quite well after that hour's talk. It was not so much what she had said as what her half saying had revealed to his quick intelligence. He knew that she adored Montéclin, and he suspected that she adored Cazeau without being herself aware of it. He had gathered that she was self-willed, impulsive, innocent, ignorant, unsatisfied, dissatisfied; for had she not complained that things seemed all wrongly arranged in this world, and no one was permitted to be happy in his own way? And he told her he was sorry she had discovered that primordial fact of existence so early in life.

He commiserated her loneliness, and scanned his bookshelves next morning for something to lend her to read, rejecting everything that offered itself to his view. Philosophy was out of the question, and so was poetry; that is, such poetry as he possessed. He had not sounded her literary tastes, and strongly suspected she had none; that she would have rejected The Duchess as readily as Mrs. Humphry Ward. He compromised on a magazine.

It had entertained her passably, she admitted, upon returning it. A New England story had puzzled her, it was true, and a Creole tale had offended her, but the pictures had pleased her greatly, especially one which had reminded her so strongly of Montéclin after a hard day's ride that she was loath to give it up. It was one of Remington's Cowboys, and Gouvernail insisted upon her keeping it,—keeping the magazine.

He spoke to her daily after that, and was always eager to render her some service or to do something towards her entertainment.

One afternoon he took her out to the lake end. She had been there once, some years before, but in winter, so the trip was comparatively new and strange to her. The large expanse of water studded with pleasure-boats, the sight of children playing merrily along the grassy palisades, the music, all enchanted her. Gouvernail thought her the most beautiful woman he had ever seen. Even her gown—the sprigged muslin—appeared to him the most charming one imaginable. Nor could anything be more beçoming than the arrangement of her brown hair under the white sailor hat, all rolled back in a soft puff from her radiant face. And she carried her parasol and lifted her skirts and used her fan in ways that seemed quite unique and peculiar to herself, and which he considered almost worthy of study and imitation.

They did not dine out there at the water's edge, as they might have done, but returned early to the city to avoid the crowd. Athénaïse wanted to go home, for she said Sylvie would have dinner prepared and would be expecting her. But it was not difficult to persuade her to dine instead in the quiet little restaurant that he knew and liked, with its sanded floor, its secluded atmosphere, its delicious menu, and its obsequious waiter wanting to know what he might have the honor of serving to "monsieur et madame." No wonder he made the mistake, with Gouvernail assuming such an air of proprietorship! But Athénaïse was very tired after it all; the sparkle went out of her face, and she hung draggingly on his arm in walking home.

He was reluctant to part from her when she bade him good-night at her door and thanked him for the agreeable evening. He had hoped she would sit outside until it was time for him to regain the newspaper office. He knew that she would undress and get into her peignoir and lie upon her bed; and what he wanted to do, what he would have given much to do, was to go and sit beside her, read to her something restful, soothe her, do her bidding, whatever it might be. Of course there was no use in thinking of that. But he was surprised at his growing desire to be serving her. She gave him an opportunity sooner than he looked for.

"Mr. Gouvernail," she called from her room, "will you be so kine as to call Pousette an' tell her she fo'got to bring my ice-water?"

He was indignant at Pousette's negligence, and called severely to her over the banisters. He was sitting before his own door, smoking. He knew that Athénaïse had gone to bed, for her room was dark, and she had opened the slats of the door and windows. Her bed was near a window.

Pousette came flopping up with the ice-water, and with a hundred excuses: "Mo pa oua vou à tab c'te lanuite, mo cri vou pé gagni déja là-bas; parole! Vou pas cri conté ça Madame Sylvie?" She had not seen Athénaïse at table, and thought she was gone. She swore to this, and hoped Madame Sylvie would not be informed of her remissness.

A little later Athénaïse lifted her voice again: "Mr. Gouvernail, did you remark that young man sitting on the opposite side from us, coming in, with a gray coat an' a blue ban' aroun' his hat?"

Of course Gouvernail had not noticed any such individual, but he assured Athénaïse that he had observed the young fellow particularly.

"Don't you think he looked something,—not very much, of co'se,—but don't you think he had a little faux-air of Montéclin?"

"I think he looked strikingly like Montéclin," asserted Gouvernail, with the one idea of prolonging the conversation. "I meant to call your attention to the resemblance, and something drove it out of my head."

"The same with me," returned Athénaïse. "Ah, my dear Montéclin! I wonder w'at he is doing now?"

"Did you receive any news, any letter from him to-day?" asked Gouvernail, determined that if the conversation ceased it should not be through lack of effort on his part to sustain it.

"Not to-day, but yesterday. He tells me that maman was so distracted with uneasiness that finally, to pacify her, he was fo'ced to confess that he knew w'ere I was, but that he was boun' by a vow of secrecy not to reveal it. But Cazeau has not noticed him or spoken to him since he threaten' to throw po' Montéclin in Cane river. You know Cazeau wrote me a letter the morning I lef', thinking I had gone to the rigolet. An' maman opened it, an' said it was full of the mos' noble sentiments, an' she wanted Montéclin to sen' it to me; but Montéclin refuse' poin' blank, so he wrote to me."

Gouvernail preferred to talk of Montéclin. He pictured Cazeau as unbearable, and did not like to think of him.

A little later Athénaïse called out, "Good-night, Mr. Gouvernail."

"Good-night," he returned reluctantly. And when he thought that she was sleeping, he got up and went away to the midnight pandemonium of his newspaper office.

IX

Athénaïse could not have held out through the month had it not been for Gouvernail. With the need of caution and secrecy always uppermost in her mind, she made no new acquaintances, and she did not seek out persons already known to her; however, she knew so few, it required little effort to keep out of their way. As for Sylvie, almost every moment of her time was occupied in looking after her house; and, moreover, her deferential attitude towards her lodgers forbade anything like the gossipy chats in which Athénaïse might have condescended sometimes to indulge with her landlady. The transient lodgers, who came and went, she never had occasion to meet. Hence she was entirely dependent upon Gouvernail for company.

He appreciated the situation fully; and every moment that he could spare from his work he devoted to her entertainment. She liked to be out of doors, and they strolled together in the summer twilight through the mazes of the old French quarter. They went again to the lake end, and stayed for hours on the water; returning so late that the streets through which they passed were silent and deserted. On Sunday morning he arose at an unconscionable hour to take her to the French market, knowing that the sights and sounds there would interest her. And he did not join the intellectual coterie in the afternoon, as he usually did, but placed himself all day at the disposition and service of Athénaïse.

Notwithstanding all, his manner toward her was tactful, and evinced intelligence and a deep knowledge of her character, surprising upon so brief an acquaintance. For the time he was everything to her that she would have him; he replaced home and friends. Sometimes she wondered if he had ever loved a woman. She could not fancy him loving any one passionately, rudely, offensively, as Cazeau loved her. Once she was so naïve as to ask him outright if he had ever been in love, and he assured her promptly that he had not. She thought it an admirable trait in his character, and esteemed him greatly therefor.

He found her crying one night, not openly or violently. She was leaning over the gallery rail, watching the toads that hopped about in the moonlight, down on the damp flagstones of the courtyard. There was an oppressively sweet odor rising from the cape jessamine. Pousette was down there, mumbling and quarreling with someone, and seeming to be having it all her own way,—as well she might, when her companion was only a black cat that had come in from a neighboring yard to keep her company.

Athénaïse did admit feeling heart-sick, body-sick, when he questioned her; she supposed it was nothing but homesick. A letter from Montéclin had stirred her all up. She longed for her mother, for Montéclin; she was sick for a sight of the cotton-fields, the scent of the ploughed earth, for the dim, mysterious charm of the woods, and the old tumble-down home on the Bon Dieu.

As Gouvernail listened to her, a wave of pity and tenderness swept through him. He took her hands and pressed them against him. He wondered what would happen if he were to put his arms around her.

He was hardly prepared for what happened, but he stood it courageously. She twined her arms around his neck and wept outright on his shoulder; the hot tears scalding his cheek and neck, and her whole body shaken in his arms. The impulse was powerful to strain her to him; the temptation was fierce to seek her lips; but he did neither.

He understood a thousand times better than she herself understood it that he was acting as substitute for Montéclin. Bitter as the conviction was, he accepted it. He was patient; he could wait. He hoped some day to hold her with a lover's arms. That she was married made no particle of difference to Gouvernail. He could not conceive or dream of it making a difference. When the time came that she wanted him,—as he hoped and believed it would come,—he felt he would have a right to her. So long as she did not want him, he had no right to her,—no more than her husband had. It was very hard to feel her warm breath and tears upon his cheek, and her struggling bosom pressed against him and her soft arms clinging to him and his whole body and soul aching for her, and yet to make no sign.

He tried to think what Montéclin would have said and done, and to act accordingly. He stroked her hair, and held her in a gentle embrace, until the tears dried and the sobs ended. Before releasing herself she kissed him against the neck; she had to love somebody in her own way! Even that he endured like a stoic. But it was well he left her, to plunge into the thick of rapid, breathless, exacting work till nearly dawn.

Athénaïse was greatly soothed, and slept well. The touch of friendly hands and caressing arms had been very grateful. Henceforward she would not be lonely and unhappy, with Gouvernail there to comfort her.

X

The fourth week of Athénaïse's stay in the city was drawing to a close. Keeping in view the intention which she had of finding some suitable and agreeable employment, she had made a few tentatives in that direction. But with the exception of two little girls who had promised to take piano lessons at a price that would be embarrassing to mention, these attempts had been fruitless. Moreover, the homesickness kept coming back, and Gouvernail was not always there to drive it away.

She spent much of her time weeding and pottering among the flowers down in the courtyard. She tried to take an interest in the black cat, and a mockingbird that hung in a cage outside the kitchen door, and a disreputable parrot that belonged to the cook next door, and swore hoarsely all day long in bad French.

Beside, she was not well; she was not herself, as she told Sylvie. The climate of New Orleans did not agree with her. Sylvie was distressed to learn this, as she felt in some measure responsible for the health and well-being of Monsieur Miché's sister; and she made it her duty to inquire closely into the nature and character of Athénaïse's malaise.

Sylvie was very wise, and Athénaïse was very ignorant. The extent of her ignorance and the depth of her subsequent enlightenment were bewildering. She stayed a long, long time quite still, quite stunned, after her interview with Sylvie, except for the short, uneven breathing that ruffled her bosom. Her whole being was steeped in a wave of ecstasy. When she finally arose from the chair in which she had been seated, and looked at herself in the mirror, a face met hers which she seemed to see for the first time, so transfigured was it with wonder and rapture.

One mood quickly followed another, in this new turmoil of her senses, and the need of action became uppermost. Her mother must know at once, and her mother must tell Montéclin. And Cazeau must know. As she thought of him, the first purely sensuous tremor of her life swept over her. She half whispered his name, and the sound of it brought red blotches into her cheeks. She spoke it over and over, as if it were some new, sweet sound born out of darkness and confusion, and reaching her for the first time. She was impatient to be with him. Her whole passionate nature was aroused as if by a miracle.

She seated herself to write to her husband. The letter he would get in the morning, and she would be with him at night. What would he say? How would he act? She knew that he would forgive her, for had he not written a letter?—and a pang of resentment toward Montéclin shot through her. What did he mean by withholding that letter? How dared he not have sent it?

Athénaïse attired herself for the street, and went out to post the letter which she had penned with a single thought, a spontaneous impulse. It would have seemed incoherent to most people, but Cazeau would understand.

She walked along the street as if she had fallen heir to some magnificent inheritance. On her face was a look of pride and satisfaction that passersby noticed and admired. She wanted to talk to someone, to tell some person; and she stopped at the corner and told the oyster-woman, who was Irish, and who God-blessed her, and wished prosperity to the race of Cazeaus for generations to come. She held the oyster-woman's fat, dirty little baby in her arms and scanned it curiously and observingly, as if a baby were a phenomenon that she encountered for the first time in life. She even kissed it!

Then what a relief it was to Athénaïse to walk the streets without dread of being seen and recognized by some chance acquaintance from Red river! No one could have said now that she did not know her own mind.

She went directly from the oyster-woman's to the office of Harding & Offdean, her husband's merchants; and it was with such an air of partnership, almost proprietorship, that she demanded a sum of money on her husband's account, they gave it to her as unhesitatingly as they would have handed it over to Cazeau himself. When Mr. Harding, who knew her, asked politely after her health, she turned so rosy and looked so conscious, he thought it a great pity for so pretty a woman to be such a little goose.

Athénaïse entered a dry-goods store and bought all manner of things,—little presents for nearly everybody she knew. She bought whole bolts of sheerest, softest, downiest white stuff; and when the clerk, in trying to meet her wishes, asked if she intended it for infant's use, she could have sunk through the floor, and wondered how he might have suspected it.

As it was Montéclin who had taken her away from her husband, she wanted it to be Montéclin who should take her back to him. So she wrote him a very curt note,—in fact it was a postal card,—asking that he meet her at the train on the evening following. She felt convinced that after what had gone before, Cazeau would await her at their own home; and she preferred it so.

Then there was the agreeable excitement of getting ready to leave, of packing up her things. Pousette kept coming and going, coming and going; and each time that she quitted the room it was with something that Athénaïse had given her,—a handkerchief, a petticoat, a pair of stockings with two tiny holes at the toes, some broken prayer-beads, and finally a silver dollar.

Next it was Sylvie who came along bearing a gift of what she called "a set of pattern',"—things of complicated design which never could have been obtained in any new-fangled bazaar or pattern-store, that Sylvie had acquired of a foreign lady of distinction whom she had nursed years before at the St. Charles hotel. Athénaïse accepted and handled them with reverence, fully sensible of the great compliment and favor, and laid them religiously away in the trunk which she had lately acquired.

She was greatly fatigued after the day of unusual exertion, and went early to bed and to sleep. All day long she had not once thought of Gouvernail, and only did think of him when aroused for a brief instant by the sound of his foot-falls on the gallery, as he passed in going to his room. He had hoped to find her up, waiting for him.

But the next morning he knew. Some one must have told him. There was no subject known to her which Sylvie hesitated to discuss in detail with any man of suitable years and discretion.

Athénaïse found Gouvernail waiting with a carriage to convey her to the railway station. A momentary pang visited her for having forgotten him so completely, when he said to her, "Sylvie tells me you are going away this morning."

He was kind, attentive, and amiable, as usual, but respected to the utmost the new dignity and reserve that her manner had developed since yesterday. She kept looking from the carriage window, silent, and embarrassed as Eve after losing her ignorance. He talked of the muddy streets and the murky morning, and of Montéclin. He hoped she would find everything comfortable and pleasant in the country, and trusted she would inform him whenever she came to visit the city again. He talked as if afraid or mistrustful of silence and himself.

At the station she handed him her purse, and he bought her ticket, secured for her a comfortable section, checked her trunk, and got all the bundles and things safely aboard the train. She felt very grateful. He pressed her hand warmly, lifted his hat, and left her. He was a man of intelligence, and took defeat gracefully; that was all. But as he made his way back to the carriage, he was thinking, "By heaven, it hurts, it hurts!"

XI

Athénaïse spent a day of supreme happiness and expectancy. The fair sight of the country unfolding itself before her was balm to her vision and to her soul. She was charmed with the rather unfamiliar, broad, clean sweep of the sugar plantations, with their monster sugar-houses, their rows of neat cabins like little villages of a single street, and their impressive homes standing apart amid clusters of trees. There were sudden glimpses of a bayou curling between sunny, grassy banks, or creeping sluggishly out from a tangled growth of wood, and brush, and fern, and poison-vines, and palmettos. And passing through the long stretches of monotonous woodlands, she would close her eyes and taste in anticipation the moment of her meeting with Cazeau. She could think of nothing but him.

It was night when she reached her station. There was Montéclin, as she had expected, waiting for her with a two-seated buggy, to which he had hitched his own swift-footed, spirited pony. It was good, he felt, to have her back on any terms; and he had no fault to find since she came of her own choice. He more than suspected the cause of her coming; her eyes and her voice and her foolish little manner went far in revealing the secret that was brimming over in her heart. But after he had deposited her at her own gate, and as he continued his way toward the rigolet, he could not help feeling that the affair had taken a very disappointing, an ordinary, a most commonplace turn, after all. He left her in Cazeau's keeping.

Her husband lifted her out of the buggy, and neither said a word until they stood together within the shelter of the gallery. Even then they did not speak at first. But Athénaïse turned to him with an appealing gesture. As he clasped her in his arms, he felt the yielding of her whole body against him. He felt her lips for the first time respond to the passion of his own.

The country night was dark and warm and still, save for the distant notes of an accordion which some one was playing in a cabin away off. A little negro baby was crying somewhere. As Athénaïse withdrew from her husband's embrace, the sound arrested her.

"Listen, Cazeau! How Juliette's baby is crying! Pauvre ti chou, I wonder w'at is the matter with it?"

The Story of an Hour

Knowing that Mrs. Mallard was afflicted with a heart trouble, great care was taken to break to her as gently as possible the news of her husband's death.

It was her sister Josephine who told her, in broken sentences; veiled hints that revealed in half concealing. Her husband's friend Richards was there, too, near her. It was he who had been in the newspaper office when intelligence of the railroad disaster was received, with Brently Mallard's name leading the list of "killed." He had only taken the time to assure himself of its truth by a second telegram, and had hastened to forestall any less careful, less tender friend in bearing the sad message.

She did not hear the story as many women have heard the same, with a paralyzed inability to accept its significance. She wept at once, with sudden, wild abandonment, in her sister's arms. When the storm of grief had spent itself she went away to her room alone. She would have no one follow her.

There stood, facing the open window, a comfortable, roomy armchair. Into this she sank, pressed down by a physical exhaustion that haunted her body and seemed to reach into her soul.

She could see in the open square before her house the tops of trees that were all aquiver with the new spring life. The delicious breath of rain was in the air. In the street below a peddler was crying his wares. The notes of a distant song which some one was singing reached her faintly, and countless sparrows were twittering in the eaves.

There were patches of blue sky showing here and there through the clouds that had met and piled one above the other in the west facing her window.

She sat with her head thrown back upon the cushion of the chair, quite motionless, except when a sob came up into her throat and shook her, as a child who has cried itself to sleep continues to sob in its dreams.

She was young, with a fair, calm face, whose lines bespoke repression and even a certain strength. But now there was a dull stare in her eyes, whose gaze was fixed away off yonder on one of those patches of blue sky. It was not a glance of reflection, but rather indicated a suspension of intelligent thought.

There was something coming to her and she was waiting for it, fearfully. What was it? She did not know; it was too subtle and elusive to name. But she felt it, creeping out of the sky, reaching toward her through the sounds, the scents, the color that filled the air.

Now her bosom rose and fell tumultuously. She was beginning to recognize this thing that was approaching to possess her, and she was striving to beat it back with her will—as powerless as her two white slender hands would have been.

When she abandoned herself a little whispered word escaped her slightly parted lips. She said it over and over under her breath: "free, free, free!" The vacant stare and the look of terror that had followed it went from her eyes. They stayed keen and bright. Her pulses beat fast, and the coursing blood warmed and relaxed every inch of her body.

She did not stop to ask if it were or were not a monstrous joy that held her. A clear and exalted perception enabled her to dismiss the suggestion as trivial.

She knew that she would weep again when she saw the kind, tender hands folded in death; the face that had never looked save with love upon her, fixed and gray and dead. But she saw beyond that bitter moment a long procession of years to come that would belong to her absolutely. And she opened and spread her arms out to them in welcome.

There would be no one to live for her during those coming years; she would live for herself. There would be no powerful will bending hers in that blind persistence with which men and women believe they have a right to impose a private will upon a fellow-creature. A kind intention or a cruel intention made the act seem no less a crime as she looked upon it in that brief moment of illumination.

And yet she had loved him—sometimes. Often she had not. What did it matter! What could love, the unsolved mystery, count for in face of this possession of self-assertion which she suddenly recognized as the strongest impulse of her being!

"Free! Body and soul free!" she kept whispering.

Josephine was kneeling before the closed door with her lips to the keyhole, imploring for admission. "Louise, open the door! I beg; open the door—you will make yourself ill. What are you doing, Louise? For heaven's sake open the door."

"Go away. I am not making myself ill." No; she was drinking in a very elixir of life through that open window.

Her fancy was running riot along those days ahead of her. Spring days, and summer days, and all sorts of days that would be her own. She breathed a quick prayer that life might be long. It was only yesterday she had thought with a shudder that life might be long.

She arose at length and opened the door to her sister's importunities. There was a feverish triumph in her eyes, and she carried herself unwittingly like a goddess of Victory. She clasped her sister's waist, and together they descended the stairs. Richards stood waiting for them at the bottom.

Someone was opening the front door with a latchkey. It was Brently Mallard who entered, a little travel-stained, composedly carrying his gripsack and umbrella. He had been far from the scene of accident, and did not even know there had been one. He stood amazed at Josephine's piercing cry; at Richards' quick motion to screen him from the view of his wife.

But Richards was too late.

When the doctors came they said she had died of heart disease—of joy that kills.

At the 'Cadian Ball

Bobinôt, that big, brown, good-natured Bobinôt, had no intention of going to the ball, even though he knew Calixta would be there. For what came of those balls but heartache, and a sickening disinclination for work the whole week through, till Saturday night came again and his tortures began afresh? Why could he not love Ozéina, who would marry him tomorrow; or Fronie, or any one of a dozen others, rather than that little Spanish vixen? Calixta's slender foot had never touched Cuban soil; but her mother's had, and the Spanish was in her blood all the same. For that reason the prairie people forgave her much that they would not have overlooked in their own daughters or sisters.

Her eyes,—Bobinôt thought of her eyes, and weakened,—the bluest, the drowsiest, most tantalizing that ever looked into a man's; he thought of her flaxen hair that kinked worse than a mulatto's close to her head; that broad, smiling mouth and tiptilted nose, that full figure; that voice like a rich contralto song, with cadences in it that must have been taught by Satan, for there was no one else to teach her tricks on that 'Cadian prairie. Bobinôt thought of them all as he plowed his rows of cane.

There had even been a breath of scandal whispered about her a year ago, when she went to Assumption,—but why talk of it? No one did now. "C'est Espagnol, ça," most of them said with lenient shoulder-shrugs. "Bon chien tient de race," the old men mumbled over their pipes, stirred by recollections. Nothing was made of it, except that Fronie threw it up to Calixta when the two quarreled and fought on the church steps after mass one Sunday, about a lover. Calixta swore roundly in fine 'Cadian French and with true Spanish spirit, and slapped Fronie's face. Fronie had slapped her back; "Tiens, cocotte, va!" "Espèce de lionèse; prends ça, et ça!" till the curé himself was obliged to hasten and make peace between them. Bobinôt thought of it all, and would not go to the ball.

But in the afternoon, over at Friedheimer's store, where he was buying a trace-chain, he heard someone say that Alcée Laballière would be there. Then wild horses could not have kept him away. He knew how it would be—or rather he did not know how it would be—if the handsome young planter came over to the ball as he sometimes did. If Alcée happened to be in a serious mood, he might only go to the card-room and play a round or two; or he might stand out on the galleries talking crops and politics with the old people. But there was no telling. A drink or two could put the devil in his head,—that was what Bobinôt said to himself, as he wiped the sweat from his brow with his red bandanna; a gleam from Calixta's eyes, a flash of her ankle, a twirl of her skirts could do the same. Yes, Bobinôt would go to the ball.

That was the year Alcée Laballière put nine hundred acres in rice. It was putting a good deal of money into the ground, but the returns promised to be glorious. Old Madame Laballière, sailing about the spacious galleries in her white *volante,* figured it all out in her head. Clarisse, her goddaughter, helped her a little, and together they built more air-castles than enough. Alcée worked like a mule that time; and if he did not kill himself, it was because his constitution was an iron one. It was an every-day affair for him to come in from the field well-nigh exhausted, and wet to the waist. He did not mind if there were visitors; he left them to his mother and Clarisse. There were often guests: young men and women who came up from the city, which was but a few hours away, to visit his beautiful kinswoman. She was worth going a good deal farther than that to see. Dainty as a lily; hardy as a sunflower; slim, tall, graceful, like one of the reeds that grew in the marsh. Cold and kind and cruel by turn, and everything that was aggravating to Alcée.

He would have liked to sweep the place of those visitors, often. Of the men, above all, with their ways and their manners; their swaying of fans like women, and dandling about hammocks. He could have pitched them over the levee into the river, if it hadn't meant murder. That was Alcée. But he must have been crazy the day he came in from the rice-field, and, toil-stained as he was, clasped Clarisse by the arms and panted a volley of hot, blistering love-words into her face. No man had ever spoken love to her like that.

"Monsieur!" she exclaimed, looking him full in the eyes, without a quiver. Alcée's hands dropped and his glance wavered before the chill of her calm, clear eyes.

"Par exemple!" she muttered disdainfully, as she turned from him, deftly adjusting the careful toilet that he had so brutally disarranged.

That happened a day or two before the cyclone came that cut into the rice like fine steel. It was an awful thing, coming so swiftly, without a moment's warning in which to light a holy candle or set a piece of blessed palm burning. Old madame wept openly and said her beads, just as her son Didier, the New Orleans one, would have done. If such a thing had happened to Alphonse, the Laballière planting cotton up in Natchitoches, he would have raved and stormed like a second cyclone, and made his surroundings unbearable for a day or two. But Alcée took the misfortune differently. He looked ill and gray after it, and said nothing. His speechlessness was frightful. Clarisse's heart melted with tenderness; but when she offered her soft, purring words of condolence, he accepted them with mute indifference. Then she and her nénaine wept afresh in each other's arms.

A night or two later, when Clarisse went to her window to kneel there in the moonlight and say her prayers before retiring, she saw that Bruce, Alcée's negro servant, had led his master's saddle-horse noiselessly along the edge of the sward that bordered the gravel-path, and stood holding him near by. Presently, she heard Alcée quit his room, which was beneath her own, and traverse the lower portico. As he emerged from the shadow and crossed the strip of moonlight, she perceived that he carried a pair of well-filled saddle-bags which he at once flung across the animal's back. He then lost no time in mounting, and after a brief exchange of words with Bruce, went cantering away, taking no precaution to avoid the noisy gravel as the negro had done.

Clarisse had never suspected that it might be Alcée's custom to sally forth from the plantation secretly, and at such an hour; for it was nearly midnight. And had it not been for the telltale saddle-bags, she would only have crept to bed, to wonder, to fret and dream unpleasant dreams. But her impatience and anxiety would not be held in check. Hastily unbolting the shutters of her door that opened upon the gallery, she stepped outside and called softly to the old negro.

"Gre't Peter! Miss Clarisse. I was n' sho it was a ghos' o' w'at, stan'in' up dah, plumb in de night, dataway."

He mounted halfway up the long, broad flight of stairs. She was standing at the top.

"Bruce, w'ere has Monsieur Alcée gone?" she asked.

"W'y, he gone 'bout he business, I reckin," replied Bruce, striving to be non-committal at the outset.

"W'ere has Monsieur Alcée gone?" she reiterated, stamping her bare foot. "I won't stan' any nonsense or any lies; mine, Bruce."

"I don' ric'lic ez I eva tole you lie *yit,* Miss Clarisse. Mista Alcée, he all broke up, sho."

"W'ere—has—he gone? Ah, Sainte Vierge! faut de la patience! butor, va!"

"W'en I was in he room, a-breshin' off he clo'es to-day," the darkey began, settling himself against the stair-rail, "he look dat speechless an' down, I say, 'You 'pear to me like some pussun w'at gwine have a spell o' sickness, Mista Alcée.' He say, 'You reckin?' 'I dat he git up, go look hisse'f stiddy in de glass. Den he go to de chimbly an' jerk up de quinine bottle an' po' a gre't hoss-dose on to he han'. An' he swalla dat mess in a wink, an' wash hit down wid a big dram o' w'iskey w'at he keep in he room, aginst he come all soppin' wet outen de fiel'.

"He 'lows, 'No, I ain' gwine be sick, Bruce.' Den he square off. He say, 'I kin mak out to stan' up an' gi' an' take wid any man I knows, lessen hit's John L. Sulvun. But w'en God A'mighty an' a 'oman jines fo'ces agin me, dat's one too many fur me.' I tell 'im, 'Jis so,' whils' I 'se makin' out to bresh a spot off w'at ain' dah, on he coat colla. I tell 'im, 'You wants li'le res', suh.' He say, 'No, I wants li'le fling; dat w'at I wants; an' I gwine git it. Pitch me a fis'ful o' clo'es in dem 'ar saddle-bags.' Dat w'at he say. Don't you bodda, missy. He jis' gone a-caperin' yonda to de Cajun ball. Uh—uh—de skeeters is fair' a-swarmin' like bees roun' yo' foots!"

The mosquitoes were indeed attacking Clarisse's white feet savagely. She had unconsciously been alternately rubbing one foot over the other during the darkey's recital.

"The 'Cadian ball," she repeated contemptuously. "Humph! *Par exemple!* Nice conduc' for a

Laballière. An' he needs a saddle-bag, fill' with clothes, to go to the 'Cadian ball!"

"Oh, Miss Clarisse; you go on to bed, chile; git yo' soun' sleep. He 'low he come back in couple weeks o' so. I kiarn be repeatin' lot o' truck w'at young mans say, out heah face o' young gal."

Clarisse said no more, but turned and abruptly reëntered the house.

"You done talk too much wid yo' mouf a'ready, you ole fool nigga, you," muttered Bruce to himself as he walked away.

Alcée reached the ball very late, of course—too late for the chicken gumbo which had been served at midnight.

The big, low-ceiled room—they called it a hall—was packed with men and women dancing to the music of three fiddles. There were broad galleries all around it. There was a room at one side where sober-faced men were playing cards. Another, in which babies were sleeping, was called *le parc aux petits*. Any one who is white may go to a 'Cadian ball, but he must pay for his lemonade, his coffee and chicken gumbo. And he must behave himself like a 'Cadian. Grosbœuf was giving this ball. He had been giving them since he was a young man, and he was a middle-aged one, now. In that time he could recall but one disturbance, and that was caused by American railroaders, who were not in touch with their surroundings and had no business there. "Ces maudits gens du raiderode," Grosbœuf called them.

Alcée Laballière's presence at the ball caused a flutter even among the men, who could not but admire his "nerve" after such misfortune befalling him. To be sure, they knew the Laballières were rich—that there were resources East, and more again in the city. But they felt it took a *brave homme* to stand a blow like that philosophically. One old gentleman, who was in the habit of reading a Paris newspaper and knew things, chuckled gleefully to everybody that Alcée's conduct was altogether *chic, mais chic.* That he had more *panache* than Boulanger. Well, perhaps he had.

But what he did not show outwardly was that he was in a mood for ugly things to-night. Poor Bobinôt alone felt it vaguely. He discerned a gleam of it in Alcée's handsome eyes, as the young planter stood in the doorway, looking with rather feverish glance upon the assembly, while he laughed and talked with a 'Cadian farmer who was beside him.

Bobinôt himself was dull-looking and clumsy. Most of the men were. But the young women were very beautiful. The eyes that glanced into Alcée's as they passed him were big, dark, soft as those of the young heifers standing out in the cool prairie grass.

But the belle was Calixta. Her white dress was not nearly so handsome or well made as Fronie's (she and Fronie had quite forgotten the battle on the church steps, and were friends again), nor were her slippers so stylish as those of Ozéina; and she fanned herself with a handkerchief, since she had broken her red fan at the last ball, and her aunts and uncles were not willing to give her another. But all the men agreed she was at her best to-night. Such animation! and abandon! such flashes of wit!

"Hé, Bobinôt! *Mais* w'at's the matta? W'at you

standin' *planté là* like ole Ma'ame Tina's cow in the bog, you?"

That was good. That was an excellent thrust at Bobinôt, who had forgotten the figure of the dance with his mind bent on other things, and it started a clamor of laughter at his expense. He joined good-naturedly. It was better to receive even such notice as that from Calixta than none at all. But Madame Suzonne, sitting in a corner, whispered to her neighbor that if Ozéina were to conduct herself in a like manner, she should immediately be taken out to the mule-cart and driven home. The women did not always approve of Calixta.

Now and then were short lulls in the dance, when couples flocked out upon the galleries for a brief respite and fresh air. The moon had gone down pale in the west, and in the east was yet no promise of day. After such an interval, when the dancers again assembled to resume the interrupted quadrille, Calixta was not among them.

She was sitting upon a bench out in the shadow, with Alcée beside her. They were acting like fools. He had attempted to take a little gold ring from her finger; just for the fun of it, for there was nothing he could have done with the ring but replace it again. But she clinched her hand tight. He pretended that it was a very difficult matter to open it. Then he kept the hand in his. They seemed to forget about it. He played with her earring, a thin crescent of gold hanging from her small brown ear. He caught a wisp of the kinky hair that had escaped its fastening, and rubbed the ends of it against his shaven cheek.

"You know, last year in Assumption, Calixta?" They belonged to the younger generation, so preferred to speak English.

"Don't come say Assumption to me, M'sieur Alcée. I done yeard Assumption till I'm plumb sick."

"Yes, I know. The idiots! Because you were in Assumption, and I happened to go to Assumption, they must have it that we went together. But it was nice—*hein,* Calixta?—in Assumption?"

They saw Bobinôt emerge from the hall and stand a moment outside the lighted doorway, peering uneasily and searchingly into the darkness. He did not see them, and went slowly back.

"There is Bobinôt looking for you. You are going to set poor Bobinôt crazy. You'll marry him some day; *hein,* Calixta?"

"I don't say no, me," she replied, striving to withdraw her hand, which he held more firmly for the attempt.

"But come, Calixta; you know you said you would go back to Assumption, just to spite them."

"No, I neva said that, me. You mus' dreamt that."

"Oh, I thought you did. You know I'm going down to the city."

"W'en?"

"To-night."

"Betta make has'e, then; it's mos' day."

"Well, to-morrow'll do."

"W'at you goin' do, yonda?"

"I don't know. Drown myself in the lake, maybe; unless you go down there to visit your uncle."

Calixta's senses were reeling; and they well-nigh left her when she felt Alcée's lips brush her ear like the touch of a rose.

"Mista Alcée! Is dat Mista Alcée?" the thick voice of a negro was asking; he stood on the ground, holding to the banister-rails near which the couple sat.

"W'at do you want now?" cried Alcée impatiently. "Can't I have a moment of peace?"

"I ben huntin' you high an' low, suh," answered the man. "Dey—dey some one in de road, onda de mulbare-tree, want see you a minute."

"I wouldn't go out to the road to see the Angel Gabriel. And if you come back here with any more talk, I'll have to break your neck." The negro turned mumbling away.

Alcée and Calixta laughed softly about it. Her boisterousness was all gone. They talked low, and laughed softly, as lovers do.

"Alcée! Alcée Laballière!"

It was not the negro's voice this time; but one that went through Alcée's body like an electric shock, bringing him to his feet.

Clarisse was standing there in her riding-habit, where the negro had stood. For an instant confusion reigned in Alcée's thoughts, as with one who awakes suddenly from a dream. But he felt that something of serious import had brought his cousin to the ball in the dead of night.

"W'at does this mean, Clarisse?" he asked.

"It means something has happen' at home. You mus' come."

"Happened to maman?" he questioned, in alarm.

"No; nénaine is well, and asleep. It is something else. Not to frighten you. But you mus' come. Come with me, Alcée."

There was no need for the imploring note. He would have followed the voice anywhere.

She had now recognized the girl sitting back on the bench.

"Ah, c'est vous, Calixta? Comment ça va, mon enfant?"

"Tcha va b'en; et vous, mam'zélle?"

Alcée swung himself over the low rail and started to follow Clarisse, without a word, without a glance back at the girl. He had forgotten he was leaving her there. But Clarisse whispered something to him, and he turned back to say "Good-night, Calixta," and offer his hand to press through the railing. She pretended not to see it.

"How come that? You settin' yere by yo'se'f, Calixta?" It was Bobinôt who had found her there alone. The dancers had not yet come out. She looked ghastly in the faint, gray light struggling out of the east.

"Yes, that's me. Go yonda in the *parc aux petits* an' ask Aunt Olisse fu' my hat. She knows w'ere't is. I want to go home, me."

"How you came?"

"I come afoot, with the Cateaus. But I'm goin' now. I ent goin' wait fu' 'em. I'm plumb wo' out, me."

"Kin I go with you, Calixta?"

"I don' care."

They went together across the open prairie and

along the edge of the fields, stumbling in the uncertain light. He told her to lift her dress that was getting wet and bedraggled; for she was pulling at the weeds and grasses with her hands.

"I don' care; it's got to go in the tub, anyway. You been sayin' all along you want to marry me, Bobinôt. Well, if you want, yet, I don' care, me."

The glow of a sudden and overwhelming happiness shone in the brown, rugged face of the young Acadian. He could not speak, for very joy. It choked him.

"Oh well, if you don' want," snapped Calixta, flippantly, pretending to be piqued at his silence.

"*Bon Dieu!* You know that makes me crazy, w'at you sayin'. You mean that, Calixta? You ent goin' turn roun' agin?"

"I neva tole you that much *yet,* Bobinôt. I mean that. *Tiens,*" and she held out her hand in the business-like manner of a man who clinches a bargain with a hand-clasp. Bobinôt grew bold with happiness and asked Calixta to kiss him. She turned her face, that was almost ugly after the night's dissipation, and looked steadily into his.

"I don' want to kiss you, Bobinôt," she said, turning away again, "not to-day. Some other time. *Bonté divine!* ent you satisfy, *yet!*"

"Oh, I'm satisfy, Calixta," he said.

Riding through a patch of wood, Clarisse's saddle became ungirted, and she and Alcée dismounted to readjust it.

For the twentieth time he asked her what had happened at home.

"But, Clarisse, w'at is it? Is it a misfortune?"

"Ah Dieu sait! It's only something that happen' to me."

"To you!"

"I saw you go away las' night, Alcée, with those saddle-bags," she said, haltingly, striving to arrange something about the saddle, "an' I made Bruce tell me. He said you had gone to the ball, an' wouldn' be home for weeks an' weeks. I thought, Alcée—maybe you were going to—to Assumption. I got wild. An' then I knew if you didn't come back, *now,* to-night, I couldn't stan' it,—again."

She had her face hidden in her arm that she was resting against the saddle when she said that.

He began to wonder if this meant love. But she had to tell him so, before he believed it. And when she told him, he thought the face of the Universe was changed—just like Bobinôt. Was it last week the cyclone had well-nigh ruined him? The cyclone seemed a huge joke, now. It was he, then, who, an hour ago was kissing little Calixta's ear and whispering nonsense into it. Calixta was like a myth, now. The one, only, great reality in the world was Clarisse standing before him, telling him that she loved him.

In the distance they heard the rapid discharge of pistol-shots; but it did not disturb them. They knew it was only the negro musicians who had gone into the yard to fire their pistols into the air, as the custom is, and to announce "*le bal est fini.*"

The Storm
A Sequel to "The 'Cadian Ball"

I

The leaves were so still that even Bibi thought it was going to rain. Bobinôt, who was accustomed to converse on terms of perfect equality with his little son, called the child's attention to certain sombre clouds that were rolling with sinister intention from the west, accompanied by a sullen, threatening roar. They were at Friedheimer's store and decided to remain there till the storm had passed. They sat within the door on two empty kegs. Bibi was four years old and looked very wise.

"Mama'll be 'fraid, yes," he suggested with blinking eyes.

"She'll shut the house. Maybe she got Sylvie helpin' her this evenin'," Bobinôt responded reassuringly.

"No; she ent got Sylvie. Sylvie was helpin' her yistiday," piped Bibi.

Bobinôt arose and going across to the counter

purchased a can of shrimps, of which Calixta was very fond. Then he returned to his perch on the keg and sat stolidly holding the can of shrimps while the storm burst. It shook the wooden store and seemed to be ripping great furrows in the distant field. Bibi laid his little hand on his father's knee and was not afraid.

II

Calixta, at home, felt no uneasiness for their safety. She sat at a side window sewing furiously on a sewing machine. She was greatly occupied and did not notice the approaching storm. But she felt very warm and often stopped to mop her face on which the perspiration gathered in beads. She unfastened her white sacque at the throat. It began to grow dark, and suddenly realizing the situation she got up hurriedly and went about closing windows and doors.

Out on the small front gallery she had hung Bobinôt's Sunday clothes to air and she hastened out to gather them before the rain fell. As she stepped outside, Alcée Laballière rode in at the gate. She had not seen him very often since her marriage, and never alone. She stood there with Bobinôt's coat in her hands, and the big rain drops began to fall. Alcée rode his horse under the shelter of a side projection where the chickens had huddled and there were plows and a harrow piled up in the corner.

"May I come and wait on your gallery till the storm is over, Calixta?" he asked.

"Come 'long in, M'sieur Alcée."

His voice and her own startled her as if from a

trance, and she seized Bobinôt's vest. Alcée, mounting to the porch, grabbed the trousers and snatched Bibi's braided jacket that was about to be carried away by a sudden gust of wind. He expressed an intention to remain outside, but it was soon apparent that he might as well have been out in the open: the water beat in upon the boards in driving sheets, and he went inside, closing the door after him. It was even necessary to put something beneath the door to keep the water out.

"My! what a rain! It's good two years sence it rain' like that," exclaimed Calixta as she rolled up a piece of bagging and Alcée helped her to thrust it beneath the crack.

She was a little fuller of figure than five years before when she married; but she had lost nothing of her vivacity. Her blue eyes still retained their melting quality; and her yellow hair, dishevelled by the wind and rain, kinked more stubbornly than ever about her ears and temples.

The rain beat upon the low, shingled roof with a force and clatter that threatened to break an entrance and deluge them there. They were in the dining room—the sitting room—the general utility room. Adjoining was her bed room, with Bibi's couch along side her own. The door stood open, and the room with its white, monumental bed, its closed shutters, looked dim and mysterious.

Alcée flung himself into a rocker and Calixta nervously began to gather up from the floor the lengths of a cotton sheet which she had been sewing.

"If this keeps up, *Dieu sait* if the levees goin' to stan' it!" she exclaimed.

"What have you got to do with the levees?"

"I got enough to do! An' there's Bobinôt with Bibi out in that storm—if he only didn' left Friedheimer's!"

"Let us hope, Calixta, that Bobinôt's got sense enough to come in out of a cyclone."

She went and stood at the window with a greatly disturbed look on her face. She wiped the frame that was clouded with moisture. It was stiflingly hot. Alcée got up and joined her at the window, looking over her shoulder. The rain was coming down in sheets obscuring the view of far-off cabins and enveloping the distant wood in a gray mist. The playing of the lightning was incessant. A bolt struck a tall chinaberry tree at the edge of the field. It filled all visible space with a blinding glare and the crash seemed to invade the very boards they stood upon.

Calixta put her hands to her eyes, and with a cry, staggered backward. Alcée's arm encircled her, and for an instant he drew her close and spasmodically to him.

"Bonté!" she cried, releasing herself from his encircling arm and retreating from the window, "the house'll go next! If I only knew w'ere Bibi was!" She would not compose herself; she would not be seated. Alcée clasped her shoulders and looked into her face. The contact of her warm, palpitating body when he had unthinkingly drawn her into his arms, had aroused all the old-time infatuation and desire for her flesh.

"Calixta," he said, "don't be frightened. Nothing can happen. The house is too low to be struck, with so many tall trees standing about. There! aren't you going to be quiet? say, aren't you?" He pushed her hair back from her face that was warm and steaming. Her lips were as red and moist as pomegranate seed. Her white neck and a glimpse of her full, firm bosom disturbed him powerfully. As she glanced up at him the fear in her liquid blue eyes had given place to a drowsy gleam that unconsciously betrayed a sensuous desire. He looked down into her eyes and there was nothing for him to do but to gather her lips in a kiss. It reminded him of Assumption.

"Do you remember—in Assumption, Calixta?" he asked in a low voice broken by passion. Oh! she remembered; for in Assumption he had kissed her and kissed and kissed her; until his senses would well nigh fail, and to save her he would resort to a desperate flight. If she was not an immaculate dove in those days, she was still inviolate; a passionate creature whose very defenselessness had made her defense, against which his honor forbade him to prevail. Now—well, now—her lips seemed in a manner free to be tasted, as well as her round, white throat and her whiter breasts.

They did not heed the crashing torrents, and the roar of the elements made her laugh as she lay in his arms. She was a revelation in that dim, mysterious chamber; as white as the couch she lay upon. Her firm, elastic flesh that was knowing for the first time its birthright, was like a creamy lily that the sun invites to contribute its breath and perfume to the undying life of the world.

The generous abundance of her passion, without guile or trickery, was like a white flame which penetrated and found response in depths of his own sensuous nature that had never yet been reached.

When he touched her breasts they gave themselves up in quivering ecstasy, inviting his lips. Her mouth was a fountain of delight. And when he possessed her, they seemed to swoon together at the very borderland of life's mystery.

He stayed cushioned upon her, breathless, dazed, enervated, with his heart beating like a hammer upon her. With one hand she clasped his head, her lips lightly touching his forehead. The other hand stroked with a soothing rhythm his muscular shoulders.

The growl of the thunder was distant and passing away. The rain beat softly upon the shingles, inviting them to drowsiness and sleep. But they dared not yield.

The rain was over; and the sun was turning the glistening green world into a palace of gems. Calixta, on the gallery, watched Alcée ride away. He turned and smiled at her with a beaming face; and she lifted her pretty chin in the air and laughed aloud.

III

Bobinôt and Bibi, trudging home, stopped without at the cistern to make themselves presentable.

"My! Bibi, w'at will yo' mama say! You ought to be ashame'. You oughtn' put on those good pants. Look at 'em! An' that mud on yo' collar! How you got that mud on yo' collar, Bibi? I never saw such a boy!" Bibi was the picture of pathetic resignation. Bobinôt was the embodiment of serious solicitude as he strove to remove from his own person and his son's the signs of their tramp over heavy roads and through wet fields. He scraped the mud off Bibi's bare legs and feet with a stick and carefully removed all traces from his heavy brogans. Then, prepared for the worst—the meeting with an over-scrupulous housewife, they entered cautiously at the back door.

Calixta was preparing supper. She had set the table and was dripping coffee at the hearth. She sprang up as they came in.

"Oh, Bobinôt! You back! My! but I was uneasy. W'ere you been during the rain? An' Bibi? he ain't wet? he ain't hurt?" She had clasped Bibi and was kissing him effusively. Bobinôt's explanations and apologies which he had been composing all along the way, died on his lips as Calixta felt him to see if he were dry, and seemed to express nothing but satisfaction at their safe return.

"I brought you some shrimps, Calixta," offered Bobinôt, hauling the can from his ample side pocket and laying it on the table.

"Shrimps! Oh, Bobinôt! you too good fo' anything!" and she gave him a smacking kiss on the cheek that resounded. "*J'vous réponds,* we'll have a feas' to night! umph-umph!"

Bobinôt and Bibi began to relax and enjoy themselves, and when the three seated themselves at table they laughed much and so loud that anyone might have heard them as far away as Laballière's.

IV

Alcée Laballière wrote to his wife, Clarisse, that night. It was a loving letter, full of tender solicitude. He told her not to hurry back, but if she and the babies liked it at Biloxi, to stay a month longer. He was getting on nicely; and though he missed them, he was willing to bear the separation a while longer—realizing that their health and pleasure were the first things to be considered.

V

As for Clarisse, she was charmed upon receiving her husband's letter. She and the babies were doing well. The society was agreeable; many of her old friends and acquaintances were at the bay. And the first free breath since her marriage seemed to restore the pleasant liberty of her maiden days. Devoted as she was to her husband, their intimate conjugal life was something which she was more than willing to forego for a while.

So the storm passed and everyone was happy.

At Chênière Caminada

I

There was no clumsier looking fellow in church that Sunday morning than Antoine Bocaze—the one they called Tonie. But Tonie did not really care if he were clumsy or not. He felt that he could speak intelligibly to no woman save his mother; but since he had no desire to inflame the hearts of any of the island maidens, what difference did it make?

He knew there was no better fisherman on the Chênière Caminada than himself, if his face was too long and bronzed, his limbs too unmanageable and his eyes too earnest—almost too honest.

It was a midsummer day, with a lazy, scorching breeze blowing from the Gulf straight into the church windows. The ribbons on the young girls' hats fluttered like the wings of birds, and the old women clutched the flapping ends of the veils that covered their heads.

A few mosquitoes, floating through the blistering

air, with their nipping and humming fretted the people to a certain degree of attention and consequent devotion. The measured tones of the priest at the altar rose and fell like a song: "Credo in unum Deum patrem omnipotentem" he chanted. And then the people all looked at one another, suddenly electrified.

Some one was playing upon the organ whose notes no one on the whole island was able to awaken; whose tones had not been heard during the many months since a passing stranger had one day listlessly dragged his fingers across its idle keys. A long, sweet strain of music floated down from the loft and filled the church.

It seemed to most of them—it seemed to Tonie standing there beside his old mother—that some heavenly being must have descended upon the Church of Our Lady of Lourdes and chosen this celestial way of communicating with its people.

But it was no creature from a different sphere; it was only a young lady from Grand Isle. A rather pretty young person with blue eyes and nut-brown hair, who wore a dotted lawn of fine texture and fashionable make, and a white Leghorn sailor-hat.

Tonie saw her standing outside of the church after mass, receiving the priest's voluble praises and thanks for her graceful service.

She had come over to mass from Grand Isle in Baptiste Beaudelet's lugger, with a couple of young men, and two ladies who kept a pension over there. Tonie knew these two ladies—the widow Lebrun and her old mother—but he did not attempt to speak with them; he would not have known what to say. He stood aside gazing at the group, as others were doing, his serious eyes fixed earnestly upon the fair organist.

Tonie was late at dinner that day. His mother must have waited an hour for him, sitting patiently with her coarse hands folded in her lap, in that little still room with its "brick-painted" floor, its gaping chimney and homely furnishings.

He told her that he had been walking—walking he hardly knew where, and he did not know why. He must have tramped from one end of the island to the other; but he brought her no bit of news or gossip. He did not know if the Cotures had stopped for dinner with the Avendettes; whether old Pierre François was worse, or better, or dead, or if lame Philibert was drinking again this morning. He knew nothing; yet he had crossed the village, and passed every one of its small houses that stood close together in a long jagged line facing the sea; they were gray and battered by time and the rude buffets of the salt sea winds.

He knew nothing though the Cotures had all bade him "good day" as they filed into Avendette's, where a steaming plate of crab gumbo was waiting for each. He had heard some woman screaming, and others saying it was because old Pierre François had just passed away. But he did not remember this, nor did he recall the fact that lame Philibert had staggered against him when he stood absently watching a "fiddler" sidling across the sun-baked sand. He could tell his mother nothing of all this; but he said he had noticed that the wind was fair and must have driven Baptiste's boat, like a flying bird, across the water.

Well, that was something to talk about, and old

Ma'me Antoine, who was fat, leaned comfortably upon the table after she had helped Tonie to his courtbouillon, and remarked that she found Madame was getting old. Tonie thought that perhaps she was aging and her hair was getting whiter. He seemed glad to talk about her, and reminded his mother of old Madame's kindness and sympathy at the time his father and brothers had perished. It was when he was a little fellow, ten years before, during a squall in Barataria Bay.

Ma'me Antoine declared that she could never forget that sympathy, if she lived till Judgment Day; but all the same she was sorry to see that Madame Lebrun was also not so young or fresh as she used to be. Her chances of getting a husband were surely lessening every year; especially with the young girls around her, budding each spring like flowers to be plucked. The one who had played upon the organ was Mademoiselle Duvigné, Claire Duvigné, a great belle, the daughter of the famous lawyer who lived in New Orleans, on Rampart street. Ma'me Antoine had found that out during the ten minutes she and others had stopped after mass to gossip with the priest.

"Claire Duvigné," muttered Tonie, not even making a pretense to taste his courtbouillon, but picking little bits from the half loaf of crusty brown bread that lay beside his plate. "Claire Duvigné; that is a pretty name. Don't you think so, mother? I can't think of anyone on the Chênière who has so pretty a one, nor at Grand Isle, either, for that matter. And you say she lives on Rampart street?"

It appeared to him a matter of great importance

that he should have his mother repeat all that the priest had told her.

II

Early the following morning Tonie went out in search of lame Philibert, than whom there was no cleverer workman on the island when he could be caught sober.

Tonie had tried to work on his big lugger that lay bottom upward under the shed, but it had seemed impossible. His mind, his hands, his tools refused to do their office, and in sudden desperation he desisted. He found Philibert and set him to work in his own place under the shed. Then he got into his small boat with the red lateen-sail and went over to Grand Isle.

There was no one at hand to warn Tonie that he was acting the part of a fool. He had, singularly, never felt those premonitory symptoms of love which afflict the greater portion of mankind before they reach the age which he had attained. He did not at first recognize this powerful impulse that had, without warning, possessed itself of his entire being. He obeyed it without a struggle, as naturally as he would have obeyed the dictates of hunger and thirst.

Tonie left his boat at the wharf and proceeded at once to Mme. Lebrun's pension, which consisted of a group of plain, stoutly built cottages that stood in mid island, about half a mile from the sea.

The day was bright and beautiful with soft, velvety gusts of wind blowing from the water. From a cluster of orange trees a flock of doves ascended, and Tonie stopped to listen to the beating of their wings and follow their flight toward the water oaks whither he himself was moving.

He walked with a dragging, uncertain step through the yellow, fragrant camomile, his thoughts traveling before him. In his mind was always the vivid picture of the girl as it had stamped itself there yesterday, connected in some mystical way with that celestial music which had thrilled him and was vibrating yet in his soul.

But she did not look the same to-day. She was returning from the beach when Tonie first saw her, leaning upon the arm of one of the men who had accompanied her yesterday. She was dressed differently—in a dainty blue cotton gown. Her companion held a big white sunshade over them both. They had exchanged hats and were laughing with great abandonment.

Two young men walked behind them and were trying to engage her attention. She glanced at Tonie, who was leaning against a tree when the group passed by; but of course she did not know him. She was speaking English, a language which he hardly understood.

There were other young people gathered under the water oaks—girls who were, many of them, more beautiful than Mlle. Duvigné; but for Tonie they simply did not exist. His whole universe had suddenly become converted into a glamorous background for the person of Mlle. Duvigné, and the shadowy figures of men who were about her.

Tonie went to Mme. Lebrun and told her he would bring her oranges next day from the

Chênière. She was well pleased, and commissioned him to bring her other things from the stores there, which she could not procure at Grand Isle. She did not question his presence, knowing that these summer days were idle ones for the Chênière fishermen. Nor did she seem surprised when he told her that his boat was at the wharf, and would be there every day at her service. She knew his frugal habits, and supposed he wished to hire it, as others did. He intuitively felt that this could be the only way.

And that is how it happened that Tonie spent so little of his time at the Chênière Caminada that summer. Old Ma'me Antoine grumbled enough about it. She herself had been twice in her life to Grand Isle and once to Grand Terre, and each time had been more than glad to get back to the Chênière. And why Tonie should want to spend his days, and even his nights, away from home, was a thing she could not comprehend, especially as he would have to be away the whole winter; and meantime there was much work to be done at his own hearthside and in the company of his own mother. She did not know that Tonie had much, much more to do at Grand Isle than at the Chênière Caminada.

He had to see how Claire Duvigné sat upon the gallery in the big rocking chair that she kept in motion by the impetus of her slender, slippered foot; turning her head this way and that way to speak to the men who were always near her. He had to follow her lithe motions at tennis or croquet, that she often played with the children under the trees. Some days he wanted to see how she spread her bare, white arms, and walked out to meet the foam-crested waves. Even here there were men with her. And then at night, standing alone like a still shadow under the stars, did he not have to listen to her voice when she talked and laughed and sang? Did he not have to follow her slim figure whirling through the dance, in the arms of men who must have loved her and wanted her as he did. He did not dream that they could help it more than he could help it. But the days when she stepped into his boat, the one with the red lateen sail, and sat for hours within a few feet of him, were days that he would have given up for nothing else that he could think of.

III

There were always others in her company at such times, young people with jests and laughter on their lips. Only once she was alone.

She had foolishly brought a book with her, thinking she would want to read. But with the breath of the sea stinging her she could not read a line. She looked precisely as she had looked the day he first saw her, standing outside of the church at Chênière Caminada.

She laid the book down in her lap, and let her soft eyes sweep dreamily along the line of the horizon where the sky and water met. Then she looked straight at Tonie, and for the first time spoke directly to him.

She called him Tonie, as she had heard others do, and questioned him about his boat and his work. He trembled, and answered her vaguely and stupidly. She did not mind, but spoke to him anyhow, satisfied to talk herself when she found that he could not or would not. She spoke French, and talked about the Chênière Caminada, its people and its church. She talked of the day she had played upon the organ there, and complained of the instrument being woefully out of tune.

Tonie was perfectly at home in the familiar task of guiding his boat before the wind that bellied its taut, red sail. He did not seem clumsy and awkward as when he sat in church. The girl noticed that he appeared as strong as an ox.

As she looked at him and surprised one of his shifting glances, a glimmer of the truth began to dawn faintly upon her. She remembered how she had encountered him daily in her path, with his earnest, devouring eyes always seeking her out. She recalled—but there was no need to recall anything. There are women whose perception of passion is very keen; they are the women who most inspire it.

A feeling of complacency took possession of her with this conviction. There was some softness and sympathy mingled with it. She would have liked to lean over and pat his big, brown hand, and tell him she felt sorry and would have helped it if she could. With this belief he ceased to be an object of complete indifference in her eyes. She had thought, awhile before, of having him turn about and take her back home. But now it was really piquant to pose for an hour longer before a man—even a rough fisherman—to whom she felt herself to be an object of silent and consuming devotion. She could think of nothing more interesting to do on shore.

She was incapable of conceiving the full force and extent of his infatuation. She did not dream that under the rude, calm exterior before her a man's heart was beating clamorously, and his reason yielding to the savage instinct of his blood.

"I hear the Angelus ringing at Chênière, Tonie," she said. "I didn't know it was so late; let us go back to the island." There had been a long silence which her musical voice interrupted.

Tonie could now faintly hear the Angelus bell himself. A vision of the church came with it, the odor of incense and the sound of the organ. The girl before him was again that celestial being whom our Lady of Lourdes had once offered to his immortal vision.

It was growing dusk when they landed at the pier, and frogs had begun to croak among the reeds in the pools. There were two of Mlle. Duvigné's usual attendants anxiously awaiting her return. But she chose to let Tonie assist her out of the boat. The touch of her hand fired his blood again.

She said to him very low and half-laughing, "I have no money tonight, Tonie; take this instead," pressing into his palm a delicate silver chain, which she had worn twined about her bare wrist. It was purely a spirit of coquetry that prompted the action, and a touch of the sentimentality which most women possess. She had read in some romance of a young girl doing something like that.

As she walked away between her two attendants she fancied Tonie pressing the chain to his lips. But he was standing quite still and held it buried in his tightly-closed hand; wanting to hold as long as he might the warmth of the body that still penetrated the bauble when she thrust it into his hand.

He watched her retreating figure like a blotch against the fading sky. He was stirred by a terrible, an overmastering regret, that he had not clasped her in his arms when they were out there alone, and sprung with her into the sea. It was what he had vaguely meant to do when the sound of the Angelus had weakened and palsied his resolution. Now she was going from him, fading away into the mist with those figures on either side of her, leaving him alone. He resolved within himself that if ever again she were out there on the sea at his mercy, she would have to perish in his arms. He would go far, far out where the sound of no bell could reach him. There was some comfort for him in the thought.

But as it happened, Mlle. Duvigné never went out alone in the boat with Tonie again.

IV

It was one morning in January. Tonie had been collecting a bill from one of the fishmongers at the French Market, in New Orleans, and had turned his steps toward St. Philip street. The day was chilly; a keen wind was blowing. Tonie mechanically buttoned his rough, warm coat and crossed over into the sun.

There was perhaps not a more wretched-hearted being in the whole district, that morning, than he. For months the woman he so hopelessly loved had been lost to his sight. But all the more she dwelt in his thoughts, preying upon his mental and bodily forces until his unhappy condition became apparent to all who knew him. Before leaving his home for the winter fishing grounds he had opened his whole heart to his mother, and told her of the trouble that was killing him. She hardly expected that he would ever come back to her when he went away. She feared that he would not, for he had spoken wildly of the rest and peace that could only come to him with death.

That morning when Tonie had crossed St. Philip street he found himself accosted by Madame Lebrun and her mother. He had not noticed them approaching, and, moreover, their figures in winter garb appeared unfamiliar to him. He had never seen them elsewhere than at Grand Isle and the Chênière during the summer. They were glad to meet him, and shook his hand cordially. He stood as usual a little helplessly before them. A pulse in his throat was beating and almost choking him, so poignant were the recollections which their presence stirred up.

They were staying in the city this winter, they told him. They wanted to hear the opera as often as possible, and the island was really too dreary with everyone gone. Madame Lebrun had left her son there to keep order and superintend repairs, and so on.

"You are both well?" stammered Tonie.

"In perfect health, my dear Tonie," Madame Lebrun replied. She was wondering at his haggard eyes and thin, gaunt cheeks; but possessed too much tact to mention them.

"And—the young lady who used to go sailing—is she well?" he inquired lamely.

"You mean Mlle. Favette? She was married just after leaving Grand Isle."

"No; I mean the one you called Claire—Mamzelle Duvigné—is she well?"

Mother and daughter exclaimed together: "Impossible! You haven't heard? Why, Tonie," madame continued, "Mlle. Duvigné died three weeks ago! But that was something sad, I tell you . . . Her family heartbroken . . . Simply from a cold caught by standing in thin slippers, waiting for her carriage after the opera. . . . What a warning!"

The two were talking at once. Tonie kept looking from one to the other. He did not know what they were saying, after madame had told him, "Elle est morte."

As in a dream he finally heard that they said good-by to him, and sent their love to his mother.

He stood still in the middle of the banquette when they had left him, watching them go toward the market. He could not stir. Something had happened to him—he did not know what. He wondered if the news was killing him.

Some women passed by, laughing coarsely. He noticed how they laughed and tossed their heads. A mockingbird was singing in a cage which hung from a window above his head. He had not heard it before.

Just beneath the window was the entrance to a barroom. Tonie turned and plunged through its swinging doors. He asked the bartender for whisky. The man thought he was already drunk, but pushed the bottle toward him nevertheless. Tonie poured a great quantity of the fiery liquor into a glass and swallowed it at a draught. The rest of the day he spent among the fishermen and Barataria oystermen; and that night he slept soundly and peacefully until morning.

He did not know why it was so; he could not understand. But from that day he felt that he began to live again, to be once more a part of the moving world about him. He would ask himself over and over again why it was so, and stay bewildered before this truth that he could not answer or explain, and which he began to accept as a holy mystery.

One day in early spring Tonie sat with his mother upon a piece of drift-wood close to the sea.

He had returned that day to the Chênière Caminada. At first she thought he was like his former self again, for all his old strength and courage had returned. But she found that there was a new brightness in his face which had not been there before. It made her think of the Holy Ghost descending and bringing some kind of light to a man.

She knew that Mademoiselle Duvigné was dead, and all along had feared that this knowledge would be the death of Tonie. When she saw him come back to her like a new being, at once she dreaded that he did not know. All day the doubt had been fretting her, and she could bear the uncertainty no longer.

"You know, Tonie—that young lady whom you cared for—well, someone read it to me in the papers—she died last winter." She had tried to speak as cautiously as she could.

"Yes, I know she is dead. I am glad."

It was the first time he had said this in words, and it made his heart beat quicker.

Ma'me Antoine shuddered and drew aside from him. To her it was somehow like murder to say such a thing.

"What do you mean? Why are you glad?" she demanded, indignantly.

Tonie was sitting with his elbows on his knees. He wanted to answer his mother, but it would take time; he would have to think. He looked out across the water that glistened gem-like with the sun upon it, but there was nothing there to open his thought. He looked down into his open palm and began to pick at the callous flesh that was hard as a horse's hoof. Whilst he did this his ideas began to gather and take form.

"You see, while she lived I could never hope for anything," he began, slowly feeling his way. "Despair was the only thing for me. There were always men about her. She walked and sang and danced with them. I knew it all the time, even when I didn't see her. But I saw her often enough. I knew that some day one of them would please her and she would give herself to him—she would marry him. That thought haunted me like an evil spirit."

Tonie passed his hand across his forehead as if to sweep away anything of the horror that might have remained there.

"It kept me awake at night," he went on. "But that was not so bad; the worst torture was to sleep, for then I would dream that it was all true.

"Oh, I could see her married to one of them—his wife—coming year after year to Grand Isle and bringing her little children with her! I can't tell you all that I saw—all that was driving me mad! But now"—and Tonie clasped his hands together and smiled as he looked again across the water—"she is where she belongs; there is no difference up there; the curé has often told us there is no difference between men. It is with the soul that we approach each other there. Then she will know who has loved her best. That is why I am so contented. Who knows what may happen up there?"

Ma'me Antoine could not answer. She only took her son's big, rough hand and pressed it against her.

"And now, ma mère," he exclaimed, cheerfully, rising, "I shall go light the fire for your bread; it is a long time since I have done anything for you," and he stooped and pressed a warm kiss on her withered old cheek.

With misty eyes she watched him walk away in the direction of the big brick oven that stood open-mouthed under the lemon trees.

EDITH WHARTON

The Muse's Tragedy

Danyers afterwards liked to fancy that he had recognized Mrs. Anerton at once; but that, of course, was absurd, since he had seen no portrait of her—she affected a strict anonymity refusing even her photograph to the most privileged—and from Mrs. Memorall, whom he revered and cultivated as her friend, he had extracted but the one impressionist phrase: "Oh, well, she's like one of those old prints where the lines have the value of color."

He was almost certain, at all events, that he had been thinking of Mrs. Anerton as he sat over his breakfast in the empty hotel restaurant, and that, looking up on the approach of the lady who seated herself at the table near the window, he had said to himself, "*That might be she.*"

Ever since his Harvard days—he was still young enough to think of them as immensely remote—Danyers had dreamed of Mrs. Anerton, the Silvia of Vincent Rendle's immortal sonnet-cycle, the Mrs. A. of the *Life and Letters*. Her name was enshrined in some of the noblest English verse of the nineteenth century—and of all past or future centuries, as Danyers, from the stand-point of a maturer judgment, still believed. The first reading of certain poems—of the *Antinous,* the *Pia Tolomei,* the *Sonnets to Silvia,*—had been epochs in Danyers's growth, and the verse seemed to gain in mellowness, in amplitude, in meaning as one brought to its interpretation more experience of life, a finer emotional sense. Where, in his boyhood, he had felt only the perfect, the almost austere beauty of form, the subtle interplay of vowel-sounds, the rush and fulness of lyric emotion, he now thrilled to the close-packed significance of each line, the allusiveness of each word—his imagination lured hither and thither on fresh trails of thought, and perpetually spurred by the sense that, beyond what he had already discovered, more marvellous regions lay waiting to be explored. Danyers had written, at college, the prize essay on Rendle's poetry (it chanced to be the moment of the great man's death); he had fashioned the fugitive verse of his own storm-and-stress period on the forms which Rendle had first given to English metre; and when two years later the *Life and Letters* appeared, and the Silvia of the sonnets took substance as Mrs. A., he had included in his worship of Rendle the woman who had inspired not only such divine verse but such playful, tender, incomparable prose.

Danyers never forgot the day when Mrs. Memorall happened to mention that she knew Mrs. Anerton. He had known Mrs. Memorall for a year or more, and had somewhat contemptuously classified her as the kind of woman who runs cheap excursions to celebrities; when one afternoon she remarked, as she put a second lump of sugar in his tea:

"Is it right this time? You're almost as particular as Mary Anerton."

"Mary Anerton?"

"Yes, I never *can* remember how she likes her tea. Either it's lemon *with* sugar, or lemon without sugar, or cream without either, and whichever it is must be put into the cup before the tea is poured in; and if one hasn't remembered, one must begin all over again. I suppose it was Vincent Rendle's way of taking his tea and has become a sacred rite."

"Do you *know* Mrs. Anerton?" cried Danyers, disturbed by this careless familiarity with the habits of his divinity.

" 'And did I once see Shelley plain?' Mercy, yes! She and I were at school together—she's an American, you know. We were at a *pension* near Tours for nearly a year; then she went back to New York, and I didn't see her again till after her marriage. She and Anerton spent a winter in Rome while my husband was attached to our Legation there, and she used to be with us a great deal." Mrs. Memorall smiled reminiscently. "It was *the* winter."

"The winter they first met?"

"Precisely—but unluckily I left Rome just before the meeting took place. Wasn't it too bad? I might have been in the *Life and Letters*. You know he mentions that stupid Madame Vodki, at whose house he first saw her."

"And did you see much of her after that?"

"Not during Rendle's life. You know she has

lived in Europe almost entirely, and though I used to see her off and on when I went abroad, she was always so engrossed, so preoccupied, that one felt one wasn't wanted. The fact is, she cared only about his friends—she separated herself gradually from all her own people. Now, of course, it's different; she's desperately lonely; she's taken to writing to me now and then; and last year, when she heard I was going abroad, she asked me to meet her in Venice, and I spent a week with her there."

"And Rendle?"

Mrs. Memorall smiled and shook her head. "Oh, I never was allowed a peep at *him;* none of her old friends met him, except by accident. Ill-natured people say that was the reason she kept him so long. If one happened in while he was there, he was hustled into Anerton's study, and the husband mounted guard till the inopportune visitor had departed. Anerton, you know, was really much more ridiculous about it than his wife. Mary was too clever to lose her head, or at least to show she'd lost it—but Anerton couldn't conceal his pride in the conquest. I've seen Mary shiver when he spoke of Rendle as *our poet*. Rendle always had to have a certain seat at the dinner-table, away from the draught and not too near the fire, and a box of cigars that no one else was allowed to touch, and a writing-table of his own in Mary's sitting-room—and Anerton was always telling one of the great man's idiosyncrasies: how he never would cut the ends of his cigars, though Anerton himself had given him a gold cutter set with a star-sapphire, and how untidy his writing-table was, and how the house-maid had orders always to bring the waste-paper basket to her mistress before emptying it, lest some immortal verse should be thrown into the dust-bin."

"The Anertons never separated, did they?"

"Separated? Bless you, no. He never would have left Rendle! And besides, he was very fond of his wife."

"And she?"

"Oh, she saw he was the kind of man who was fated to make himself ridiculous, and she never interfered with his natural tendencies."

From Mrs. Memorall, Danyers further learned that Mrs. Anerton, whose husband had died some years before her poet, now divided her life between Rome, where she had a small apartment, and England, where she occasionally went to stay with those of her friends who had been Rendle's. She had been engaged, for some time after his death, in editing some juvenilia which he had bequeathed to her care; but that task being accomplished, she had been left without definite occupation, and Mrs. Memorall, on the occasion of their last meeting, had found her listless and out of spirits.

"She misses him too much—her life is too empty. I told her so—I told her she ought to marry."

"Oh!"

"Why not, pray? She's a young woman still—what many people would call young," Mrs. Memorall interjected, with a parenthetic glance at the mirror. "Why not accept the inevitable and begin over again? All the King's horses and all the

King's men won't bring Rendle to life—and besides, she didn't marry *him* when she had the chance."

Danyers winced slightly at this rude fingering of his idol. Was it possible that Mrs. Memorall did not see what an anti-climax such a marriage would have been? Fancy Rendle "making an honest woman" of Silvia; for so society would have viewed it! How such a reparation would have vulgarized their past—it would have been like "restoring" a masterpiece; and how exquisite must have been the perceptions of the woman who, in defiance of appearances, and perhaps of her own secret inclination, chose to go down to posterity as Silvia rather than as Mrs. Vincent Rendle!

Mrs. Memorall, from this day forth, acquired an interest in Danyers's eyes. She was like a volume of unindexed and discursive memoirs, through which he patiently plodded in the hope of finding embedded amid layers of dusty twaddle some precious allusion to the subject of his thought. When, some months later, he brought out his first slim volume, in which the remodelled college essay on Rendle figured among a dozen somewhat overstudied "appreciations," he offered a copy to Mrs. Memorall; who surprised him, the next time they met, with the announcement that she had sent the book to Mrs. Anerton.

Mrs. Anerton in due time wrote to thank her friend. Danyers was privileged to read the few lines in which, in terms that suggested the habit of "acknowledging" similar tributes, she spoke of the author's "feeling and insight," and was "so glad of the opportunity," etc. He went away disappointed, without clearly knowing what else he had expected.

The following spring, when he went abroad, Mrs. Memorall offered him letters to everybody, from the Archbishop of Canterbury to Louise Michel. She did not include Mrs. Anerton, however, and Danyers knew, from a previous conversation, that Silvia objected to people who "brought letters." He knew also that she travelled during the summer, and was unlikely to return to Rome before the term of his holiday should be reached, and the hope of meeting her was not included among his anticipations.

The lady whose entrance broke upon his solitary repast in the restaurant of the Hotel Villa d'Este had seated herself in such a way that her profile was detached against the window; and thus viewed, her domed forehead, small arched nose, and fastidious lip suggested a silhouette of Marie Antoinette. In the lady's dress and movements—in the very turn of her wrist as she poured out her coffee—Danyers thought he detected the same fastidiousness, the same air of tacitly excluding the obvious and unexceptional. Here was a woman who had been much bored and keenly interested. The waiter brought her a *Secolo,* and as she bent above it Danyers noticed that the hair rolled back from her forehead was turning gray; but her figure was straight and slender, and she had the invaluable gift of a girlish back.

The rush of Anglo-Saxon travel had not set toward the lakes, and with the exception of an Italian family or two, and a hump-backed youth with an *abbé,* Danyers and the lady had the marble halls of the Villa d'Este to themselves.

When he returned from his morning ramble among the hills he saw her sitting at one of the little tables at the edge of the lake. She was writing, and a heap of books and newspapers lay on the table at her side. That evening they met again in the garden. He had strolled out to smoke a last cigarette before dinner, and under the black vaulting of ilexes, near the steps leading down to the boat-landing, he found her leaning on the parapet above the lake. At the sound of his approach she turned and looked at him. She had thrown a black lace scarf over her head, and in this sombre setting her face seemed thin and unhappy. He remembered afterwards that her eyes, as they met his, expressed not so much sorrow as profound discontent.

To his surprise she stepped toward him with a detaining gesture.

"Mr. Lewis Danyers, I believe?"

He bowed.

"I am Mrs. Anerton. I saw your name on the visitors' list and wished to thank you for an essay on Mr. Rendle's poetry—or rather to tell you how much I appreciated it. The book was sent to me last winter by Mrs. Memorall."

She spoke in even melancholy tones, as though the habit of perfunctory utterance had robbed her voice of more spontaneous accents; but her smile was charming.

They sat down on a stone bench under the ilexes, and she told him how much pleasure his essay had given her. She thought it the best in the book—she was sure he had put more of himself into it than into any other; was she not right in conjecturing that he had been very deeply influenced by Mr. Rendle's poetry? *Pour comprendre il faut aimer*, and it seemed to her that, in some ways, he had penetrated the poet's inner meaning more completely than any other critic. There were certain problems, of course, that he had left untouched; certain aspects of that many-sided mind that he had perhaps failed to seize—

"But then you are young," she concluded gently, "and one could not wish you, as yet, the experience that a fuller understanding would imply."

II

She stayed a month at Villa d'Este, and Danyers was with her daily. She showed an unaffected pleasure in his society; a pleasure so obviously founded on their common veneration of Rendle, that the young man could enjoy it without fear of fatuity. At first he was merely one more grain of frankincense on the altar of her insatiable divinity; but gradually a more personal note crept into their intercourse. If she still liked him only because he appreciated Rendle, she at least perceptibly distinguished him from the herd of Rendle's appreciators.

Her attitude toward the great man's memory struck Danyers as perfect. She neither proclaimed nor disavowed her identity. She was frankly Silvia to those who knew and cared; but there was no trace of the Egeria in her pose. She spoke often of Rendle's books, but seldom of himself; there was no posthumous conjugality, no use of the possessive tense, in her abounding reminiscences. Of the master's intellectual life, of his habits of thought and work, she never wearied of talking. She knew the history of each poem; by what scene or episode each image had been evoked; how many times the words in a certain line had been transposed; how long a certain adjective had been sought, and what had at last suggested it; she could even explain that one impenetrable line, the torment of critics, the joy of detractors, the last line of *The Old Odysseus*.

Danyers felt that in talking of these things she was no mere echo of Rendle's thought. If her identity had appeared to be merged in his it was because they thought alike, not because he had thought for her. Posterity is apt to regard the women whom poets have sung as chance pegs on which they hung their garlands; but Mrs. Anerton's mind was like some fertile garden wherein, inevitably, Rendle's imagination had rooted itself and flowered. Danyers began to see how many threads of his complex mental tissue the poet had owed to the blending of her temperament with his; in a certain sense Silvia had herself created the *Sonnets to Silvia*.

To be the custodian of Rendle's inner self, the door, as it were, to the sanctuary, had at first seemed to Danyers so comprehensive a privilege that he had the sense, as his friendship with Mrs. Anerton advanced, of forcing his way into a life already crowded. What room was there, among such towering memories, for so small an actuality as his? Quite suddenly, after this, he discovered that Mrs. Memorall knew better: his fortunate friend was bored as well as lonely.

"You have had more than any other woman!" he had exclaimed to her one day; and her smile flashed a derisive light on his blunder. Fool that he was, not to have seen that she had not had enough! That she was young still—do years count?—tender, human, a woman; that the living have need of the living.

After that, when they climbed the alleys of the hanging park, resting in one of the little ruined temples, or watching, through a ripple of foliage, the remote blue flash of the lake, they did not always talk of Rendle or of literature. She encouraged Danyers to speak of himself; to confide his ambitions to her; she asked him the questions which are the wise woman's substitute for advice.

"You must write," she said, administering the most exquisite flattery that human lips could give.

Of course he meant to write—why not to do something great in his turn? His best, at least; with the resolve, at the outset, that his best should be *the* best. Nothing less seemed possible with that mandate in his ears. How she had divined him; lifted and disentangled his groping ambitions; laid the awakening touch on his spirit with her creative *Let there be light!*

It was his last day with her, and he was feeling very hopeless and happy.

"You ought to write a book about *him,*" she went on gently.

Danyers started; he was beginning to dislike Rendle's way of walking in unannounced.

"You ought to do it," she insisted. "A complete interpretation—a summing-up of his style, his purpose, his theory of life and art. No one else could do it as well."

He sat looking at her perplexedly. Suddenly—dared he guess?

"I couldn't do it without you," he faltered.

"I could help you—I would help you, of course."

They sat silent, both looking at the lake.

It was agreed, when they parted, that he should rejoin her six weeks later in Venice. There they were to talk about the book.

III

Lago d'Iseo, August 14th.

When I said good-by to you yesterday I promised to come back to Venice in a week: I was to give you your answer then. I was not honest in saying that; I didn't mean to go back to Venice or to see you again. I was running away from you—and I mean to keep on running! If *you* won't, *I* must. Somebody must save you from marrying a disappointed woman of—well, you say years don't count, and why should they, after all, since you are not to marry me?

That is what I dare not go back to say. *You are not to marry me*. We have had our month together in Venice (such a good month, was it not?) and now you are to go home and write a book—any book but the one we—didn't talk of!—and I am to stay here, attitudinizing among my memories like a sort of female Tithonus. The dreariness of this enforced immortality!

But you shall know the truth. I care for you, or at least for your love, enough to owe you that.

You thought it was because Vincent Rendle had loved me that there was so little hope for you. I had had what I wanted to the full; wasn't that what you said? It is just when a man begins to think he understands a woman that he may be sure he doesn't! It is because Vincent Rendle *didn't love me* that there is no hope for you. I never had what I wanted, and never, never, never will I stoop to wanting anything else.

Do you begin to understand? It was all a sham then, you say? No, it was all real as far as it went. You are young—you haven't learned, as you will later, the thousand imperceptible signs by which one gropes one's way through the labyrinth of human nature; but didn't it strike you, sometimes, that I never told you any foolish little anecdotes about him? His trick, for instance, of twirling a paper-knife round and round between his thumb and forefinger while he talked; his mania for saving the backs of notes; his greediness for wild strawberries, the little pungent Alpine ones; his childish delight in acrobats and jugglers; his way of always calling me *you—dear you,* every letter began—I never told you a word of all that, did I? Do you suppose I could have helped telling you, if he had loved me? These little things would have been mine, then, a part of my life—of our life—they would have slipped out in spite of me (it's only your unhappy woman who is always reticent and dignified). But there never was any "our life;" it was always "our lives" to the end. . . .

If you knew what a relief it is to tell some one at last, you would bear with me, you would let me hurt you! I shall never be quite so lonely again, now that some one knows.

Let me begin at the beginning. When I first met Vincent Rendle I was not twenty-five. That was twenty years ago. From that time until his death, five years ago, we were fast friends. He gave me fifteen years, perhaps the best fifteen years, of his life. The world, as you know, thinks that his greatest poems were written during those years; I am supposed to have "inspired" them, and in a sense I did. From the first, the intellectual sympathy between us was almost complete; my mind must have been to him (I fancy) like some perfectly tuned instrument on which he was never tired of playing. Someone told me of his once saying of me that I "always understood;" it is the only praise I ever heard of his giving me. I don't even know if he thought me pretty, though I hardly think my appearance could have been disagreeable to him, for he hated to be with ugly people. At all events he fell into the way of spending more and more of his time with me. He liked our house; our ways suited him. He was nervous, irritable; people bored him and yet he disliked solitude. He took sanctuary with us. When we travelled he went with us; in the winter he took rooms near us in Rome. In England or on the continent he was always with us for a good part of the year. In small ways I was able to help him in his work; he grew dependent on me. When we were apart he wrote to me continually—he liked to have me share in all he was doing or thinking; he was impatient for my criticism of every new book that interested him; I was a part of his intellectual life. The pity of it was that I wanted to be something more. I was a young woman and I was in love with him—not because he was Vincent Rendle, but just because he was himself!

People began to talk, of course—I was Vincent Rendle's Mrs. Anerton; when the *Sonnets to Silvia* appeared, it was whispered that I was Silvia. Wherever he went, I was invited; people made up to me in the hope of getting to know him; when I was in London my doorbell never stopped ringing. Elderly peeresses, aspiring hostesses, love-sick girls and struggling authors overwhelmed me with their assiduities. I hugged my success, for I knew what it meant—they thought that Rendle was in love with me! Do you know, at times, they almost made me think so too? Oh, there was no phase of folly I didn't go through. You can't imagine the excuses a woman will invent for a man's not telling her that he loves her—pitiable arguments that she would see through at a glance if any other woman used them! But all the while, deep down, I knew he had never cared. I should have known it if he had made love to me every day of his life. I could never guess whether he knew what people said about us—he listened so little to what people said; and cared still less, when he heard. He was always quite honest and straightforward with me; he treated me as one man treats another; and yet at times I felt he *must* see that with me it was different. If he did see, he made no sign. Perhaps he never noticed—I am sure he never meant to be cruel. He had never made love to me; it was no fault of his if I wanted more than he could give me. The *Sonnets to Silvia,* you say? But what are they? A cosmic philosophy, not a love-poem; addressed to Woman, not to a woman!

But then, the letters? Ah, the letters! Well, I'll make a clean breast of it. You have noticed the breaks in the letters here and there, just as they seem to be on the point of growing a little—warmer? The critics, you may remember, praised the editor for his commendable delicacy and good taste (so rare in these days!) in omitting from the correspondence all personal allusions, all those *détails intimes* which should be kept sacred from the public gaze. They referred, of course, to the asterisks in the letters to Mrs. A. Those letters I myself prepared for publication; that is to say, I copied them out for the editor, and every now and then I put in a line of asterisks to make it appear that something had been left out. You understand? The asterisks were a sham—*there was nothing to leave out.*

No one but a woman could understand what I went through during those years—the moments of revolt, when I felt I must break away from it all, fling the truth in his face and never see him again; the inevitable reaction, when not to see him seemed the one unendurable thing, and I trembled lest a look or word of mine should disturb the poise of our friendship; the silly days when I hugged the delusion that he *must* love me, since everybody thought he did; the long periods of numbness, when I didn't seem to care whether he loved me or not. Between these wretched days came others when our intellectual accord was so perfect that I forgot everything else in the joy of feeling myself lifted up on the wings of his thought. Sometimes, then, the heavens seemed to be opened. . . .

All this time he was so dear a friend! He had the genius of friendship, and he spent it all on me. Yes, you were right when you said that I have had more than any other woman. *Il faut de l'adresse pour aimer,* Pascal says; and I was so quiet, so cheerful, so frankly affectionate with him, that in all those years I am almost sure I never bored him. Could I have hoped as much if he had loved me?

You mustn't think of him, though, as having been tied to my skirts. He came and went as he pleased, and so did his fancies. There was a girl once (I am telling you everything), a lovely being who called his poetry "deep" and gave him *Lucile* on his birthday. He followed her to Switzerland one summer, and all the time that he was dangling after her (a little too conspicuously, I always thought, for a Great Man), he was writing to *me* about his theory of vowel-combinations—or was it his experiments in English hexameter? The letters were dated from the very places where I knew they went and sat by waterfalls together and he thought out adjectives for her hair. He talked to me about it quite frankly afterwards. She was perfectly beautiful and it had been a pure delight to watch her; but she *would* talk, and her mind, he said, was "all elbows." And yet, the next year, when her marriage was announced, he went away alone, quite suddenly . . . and it was just afterwards that he published *Love's Viaticum.* Men are queer!

After my husband died—I am putting things

crudely, you see—I had a return of hope. It was because he loved me, I argued, that he had never spoken; because he had always hoped some day to make me his wife; because he wanted to spare me the "reproach." Rubbish! I knew well enough, in my heart of hearts, that my one chance lay in the force of habit. He had grown used to me; he was no longer young; he dreaded new people and new ways; *il avait pris son pli*. Would it not be easier to marry me?

I don't believe he ever thought of it. He wrote me what people call "a beautiful letter;" he was kind, considerate, decently commiserating; then, after a few weeks, he slipped into his old way of coming in every afternoon, and our interminable talks began again just where they had left off. I heard later that people thought I had shown "such good taste" in not marrying him.

So we jogged on for five years longer. Perhaps they were the best years, for I had given up hoping. Then he died.

After his death—this is curious—there came to me a kind of mirage of love. All the books and articles written about him, all the reviews of the "Life," were full of discreet allusions to Silvia. I became again the Mrs. Anerton of the glorious days. Sentimental girls and dear lads like you turned pink when somebody whispered, "that was Silvia you were talking to." Idiots begged for my autograph—publishers urged me to write my reminiscences of him—critics consulted me about the reading of doubtful lines. And I knew that, to all these people, I was the woman Vincent Rendle had loved.

After a while that fire went out too and I was left

alone with my past. Alone—quite alone; for he had never really been with me. The intellectual union counted for nothing now. It had been soul to soul, but never hand in hand, and there were no little things to remember him by.

Then there set in a kind of Arctic winter. I crawled into myself as into a snow-hut. I hated my solitude and yet dreaded any one who disturbed it. That phase, of course, passed like the others. I took up life again, and began to read the papers and consider the cut of my gowns. But there was one question that I could not be rid of, that haunted me night and day. Why had he never loved me? Why had I been so much to him, and no more? Was I so ugly, so essentially unlovable, that though a man might cherish me as his mind's comrade, he could not care for me as a woman? I can't tell you how that question tortured me. It became an obsession.

My poor friend, do you begin to see? I had to find out what some other man thought of me. Don't be too hard on me! Listen first—consider. When I first met Vincent Rendle I was a young woman, who had married early and led the quietest kind of life; I had had no "experiences." From the hour of our first meeting to the day of his death I never looked at any other man, and never noticed whether any other man looked at me. When he died, five years ago, I knew the extent of my powers no more than a baby. Was it too late to find out? Should I never know *why?*

Forgive me—forgive me. You are so young; it will be an episode, a mere "document," to you so soon! And, besides, it wasn't as deliberate, as cold-blooded as these disjointed lines have made it appear. I didn't plan it, like a woman in a book.

Life is so much more complex than any rendering of it can be. I liked you from the first—I was drawn to you (you must have seen that)—I wanted you to like me; it was not a mere psychological experiment. And yet in a sense it was that, too—I must be honest. I had to have an answer to that question; it was a ghost that had to be laid.

At first I was afraid—oh, so much afraid—that you cared for me only because I was Silvia, that you loved me because you thought Rendle had loved me. I began to think there was no escaping my destiny.

How happy I was when I discovered that you were growing jealous of my past; that you actually hated Rendle! My heart beat like a girl's when you told me you meant to follow me to Venice.

After our parting at Villa d'Este my old doubts reasserted themselves. What did I know of your feeling for me, after all? Were you capable of analyzing it yourself? Was it not likely to be two-thirds vanity and curiosity, and one-third literary sentimentality? You might easily fancy that you cared for Mary Anerton when you were really in love with Silvia—the heart is such a hypocrite! Or you might be more calculating than I had supposed. Perhaps it was you who had been flattering *my* vanity in the hope (the pardonable hope!) of turning me, after a decent interval, into a pretty little essay with a margin.

When you arrived in Venice and we met again—do you remember the music on the lagoon, that evening, from my balcony?—I was so afraid you would begin to talk about the book—the book, you remember, was your ostensible reason for coming. You never spoke of it, and I soon saw your one fear was *I* might do so—might remind you of your object in being with me. Then I knew you cared for me! yes, at that moment really cared! We never mentioned the book once, did we, during that month in Venice?

I have read my letter over; and now I wish that I had said this to you instead of writing it. I could have felt my way then, watching your face and seeing if you understood. But, no, I could not go back to Venice; and I could not tell you (though I tried) while we were there together. I couldn't spoil that month—my one month. It was so good, for once in my life, to get away from literature . . . .

You will be angry with me at first—but, alas! not for long. What I have done would have been cruel if I had been a younger woman; as it is, the experiment will hurt no one but myself. And it will hurt me horribly (as much as, in your first anger, you may perhaps wish), because it has shown me, for the first time, all that I have missed . . . .

Souls Belated

Their railway-carriage had been full when the train left Bologna; but at the first station beyond Milan their only remaining companion—a courtly person who ate garlic out of a carpet-bag—had left his crumb-strewn seat with a bow.

Lydia's eye regretfully followed the shiny broadcloth of his retreating back till it lost itself in the cloud of touts and cab-drivers hanging about the station; then she glanced across at Gannett and caught the same regret in his look. They were both sorry to be alone.

"*Par-ten-za!*" shouted the guard. The train vibrated to a sudden slamming of doors; a waiter ran along the platform with a tray of fossilized sandwiches; a belated porter flung a bundle of shawls and band-boxes into a third-class carriage; the guard snapped out a brief *Partenza!* which indicated the purely ornamental nature of his first shout; and the train swung out of the station.

The direction of the road had changed, and a shaft of sunlight struck across the dusty red velvet seats into Lydia's corner. Gannett did not notice it. He had returned to his *Revue de Paris,* and she had to rise and lower the shade of the farther window. Against the vast horizon of their leisure such incidents stood out sharply.

Having lowered the shade, Lydia sat down, leaving the length of the carriage between herself and Gannett. At length he missed her and looked up.

"I moved out of the sun," she hastily explained.

He looked at her curiously: the sun was beating on her through the shade.

"Very well," he said pleasantly; adding, "You don't mind?" as he drew a cigarette-case from his pocket.

It was a refreshing touch, relieving the tension of her spirit with the suggestion that, after all, if he could *smoke*—! The relief was only momentary. Her experience of smokers was limited (her husband had disapproved of the use of tobacco) but she knew from hearsay that men sometimes smoked to get away from things; that a cigar might be the masculine equivalent of darkened windows and a headache. Gannett, after a puff or two, returned to his review.

It was just as she had foreseen; he feared to speak as much as she did. It was one of the misfortunes of their situation that they were never busy enough to necessitate, or even to justify, the postponement of unpleasant discussions. If they avoided a question it was obviously, unconcealably because the question was disagreeable. They had unlimited leisure and an accumulation of mental energy to devote to any subject that presented itself; new topics were in fact at a premium. Lydia sometimes had premonitions of a famine-stricken period when there would be nothing left to talk about, and she had already caught herself doling out piecemeal what, in the first prodigality of their confidences, she would have flung to him in a breath. Their silence therefore might simply mean that they had nothing to say; but it was another disadvantage of their position that it allowed infinite opportunity for the classification of minute differences. Lydia had learned to distinguish between real and factitious silences; and under Gannett's she now detected a hum of speech to which her own thoughts made breathless answer.

How could it be otherwise, with that thing between them? She glanced up at the rack overhead. The *thing* was there, in her dressing-bag, symbolically suspended over her head and his. He was thinking of it now, just as she was; they had been thinking of it in unison ever since they had entered the train. While the carriage had held other travellers they had screened her from his thoughts; but now that he and she were alone she knew exactly what was passing through his mind; she could almost hear him asking himself what he should say to her. . . .

The thing had come that morning, brought up to her in an innocent-looking envelope with the rest of their letters, as they were leaving the hotel at Bologna. As she tore it open, she and Gannett were laughing over some ineptitude of the local guide-book—they had been driven, of late, to make the most of such incidental humors of travel. Even when she had unfolded the document she took it for some unimportant business paper sent abroad for her signature, and her eye travelled inattentively over the curly *Whereases* of the preamble until a word arrested her:—Divorce. There it stood, an impassable barrier, between her husband's name and hers.

She had been prepared for it, of course, as healthy people are said to be prepared for death, in the sense of knowing it must come without in the least expecting that it will. She had known from the first that Tillotson meant to divorce her—but what did it matter? Nothing mattered, in those first days of supreme deliverance, but the fact that she was free; and not so much (she had begun to be aware) that freedom had released her from Tillotson as that it had given her to Gannett. This discovery had not been agreeable to her self-esteem. She had preferred to think that Tillotson had himself embodied all her reasons for leaving him; and those he represented had seemed cogent enough to stand in no need of reinforcement. Yet she had not left him till she met Gannett. It was her love for Gannett that had made life with Tillotson so poor and incomplete a business. If she had never, from the first, regarded her marriage as a full cancelling of her claims upon life, she had at least, for a number of years, accepted it as a provisional compensation,—she had made it "do." Existence in the commodious Tillotson mansion in Fifth Avenue—with Mrs. Tillotson senior commanding the approaches from the second-story front windows—had been reduced to a series of purely automatic acts. The moral atmosphere of the Tillotson interior was as carefully screened and curtained as the house itself: Mrs. Tillotson senior dreaded ideas as much as a draught in her back. Prudent people liked an even temperature; and to do anything unexpected was as foolish as going out in the rain. One of the chief advantages of being rich was that one need not be exposed to unforeseen contingencies: by the use of ordinary firmness and common sense one could make sure of doing exactly the same thing every day at the same hour. These doctrines, reverentially imbibed with his mother's milk, Tillotson (a model son who had never given his parents an hour's anxiety) complacently expounded to his wife, testifying to his sense of their importance by the regularity with which he wore goloshes on damp days, his punctuality at meals, and his elaborate precautions against burglars and contagious diseases. Lydia, coming from a smaller town, and entering New York life through the portals of the Tillotson mansion, had mechanically accepted this point of view as inseparable from having a front pew in church and a parterre box at the opera. All the people who came to the house revolved in the same small circle of prejudices. It was the kind of society in which, after dinner, the ladies compared the exorbitant charges of their children's teachers, and agreed that, even with the new duties on French clothes, it was cheaper in the end to get everything from Worth; while the husbands, over their cigars, lamented municipal corruption, and decided that the men to start a reform were those who had no private interests at stake.

To Lydia this view of life had become a matter of course, just as lumbering about in her mother-in-law's landau had come to seem the only possible means of locomotion, and listening every Sunday to a fashionable Presbyterian divine the inevitable atonement for having thought oneself bored on the other six days of the week. Before she met Gannett her life had seemed merely dull: his coming made it appear like one of those dismal Cruikshank prints in which the people are all ugly and all engaged in occupations that are either vulgar or stupid.

It was natural that Tillotson should be the chief sufferer from this readjustment of focus. Gannett's nearness had made her husband ridiculous, and a part of the ridicule had been reflected on herself. Her tolerance laid her open to a suspicion of obtuseness from which she must, at all costs, clear herself in Gannett's eyes.

She did not understand this until afterwards. At the time she fancied that she had merely reached the limits of endurance. In so large a charter of liberties as the mere act of leaving Tillotson seemed to confer, the small question of divorce or no divorce did not count. It was when she saw that she had left her husband only to be with Gannett that she perceived the significance of anything affecting their relations. Her husband, in casting her off, had virtually flung her at Gannett: it was thus that the world viewed it. The measure of alacrity with which Gannett would receive her would be the subject of curious speculation over afternoon-tea tables and in club corners. She knew what would be said—she had heard it so often of others! The recollection bathed her in misery. The men would probably back Gannett to "do the decent thing"; but the ladies' eye-brows would emphasize the worthlessness of such enforced fidelity; and after all, they would be right. She had put herself in a position where Gannett "owed" her something; where, as a gentleman, he was bound to "stand the damage." The idea of accepting such compensation had never crossed her mind; the so-called rehabilitation of such a marriage had always seemed to her the only real disgrace. What she dreaded was the necessity of having to explain herself; of having to combat his arguments; of calculating, in spite of herself, the exact measure of insistence with which he pressed them. She knew not whether she most shrank from his insisting too much or too little. In such a case the nicest sense of proportion might be at fault; and how easy to fall into the error of taking her resistance for a test of his sincerity! Whichever way she turned, an ironical implication confronted her: she had the exasperated sense of having walked into the trap of some stupid practical joke.

Beneath all these preoccupations lurked the dread of what he was thinking. Sooner or later, of course, he would have to speak; but that, in the meantime, he should think, even for a moment, that there was any use in speaking, seemed to her simply unendurable. Her sensitiveness on this point was aggravated by another fear, as yet barely on the level of consciousness; the fear of unwillingly involving Gannett in the trammels of her dependence. To look upon him as the instrument of her liberation; to resist in herself the least tendency to a wifely taking possession of his future; had seemed to Lydia the one way of maintaining the dignity of their relation. Her view had not changed, but she was aware of a growing inability to keep her thoughts fixed on the essential point—the point of parting with Gannett. It was easy to face as long as she kept it sufficiently far off: but what was this act of mental postponement but a gradual encroachment on his future? What was needful was the courage to recognize the moment when, by some word or look, their voluntary fellowship should be transformed into a bondage the more wearing that it was based on none of those common obligations which make the most imperfect marriage in some sort a centre of gravity.

When the porter, at the next station, threw the door open, Lydia drew back, making way for the hoped-for intruder; but none came, and the train took up its leisurely progress through the spring wheat-fields and budding copses. She now began to hope that Gannett would speak before the next station. She watched him furtively, half-disposed to return to the seat opposite his, but there was an artificiality about his absorption that restrained her. She had never before seen him read with so conspicuous an air of warding off interruption. What could he be thinking of? Why should he be afraid to speak? Or was it her answer that he dreaded?

The train paused for the passing of an express, and he put down his book and leaned out of the window. Presently he turned to her with a smile.

"There's a jolly old villa out here," he said.

His easy tone relieved her, and she smiled back at him as she crossed over to his corner.

Beyond the embankment, through the opening in a mossy wall, she caught sight of the villa, with its broken balustrades, its stagnant fountains, and the stone satyr closing the perspective of a dusky grass-walk.

"How should you like to live there?" he asked as the train moved on.

"There?"

"In some such place, I mean. One might do worse, don't you think so? There must be at least two centuries of solitude under those yew-trees. Shouldn't you like it?"

"I—I don't know," she faltered. She knew now that he meant to speak.

He lit another cigarette. "We shall have to live somewhere, you know," he said as he bent above the match.

Lydia tried to speak carelessly. "*Je n'en vois pas la nécessité!* Why not live everywhere, as we have been doing?"

"But we can't travel forever, can we?"

"Oh, forever's a long word," she objected, picking up the review he had thrown aside.

"For the rest of our lives then," he said, moving nearer.

She made a slight gesture which caused his hand to slip from hers.

"Why should we make plans? I thought you agreed with me that it's pleasanter to drift."

He looked at her hesitatingly. "It's been pleasant, certainly; but I suppose I shall have to get at my work again some day. You know I haven't written a line since—all this time," he hastily emended.

She flamed with sympathy and self-reproach. "Oh, if you mean *that*—if you want to write—of course we must settle down. How stupid of me not to have thought of it sooner! Where shall we go? Where do you think you could work best? We oughtn't to lose any more time."

He hesitated again. "I had thought of a villa in these parts. It's quiet; we shouldn't be bothered. Should you like it?"

"Of course I should like it." She paused and looked away. "But I thought—I remember your telling me once that your best work had been done in a crowd—in big cities. Why should you shut yourself up in a desert?"

Gannett, for a moment, made no reply. At length he said, avoiding her eye as carefully as she avoided his: "It might be different now; I can't tell, of course, till I try. A writer ought not to be dependent on his *milieu;* it's a mistake to humor oneself in that way; and I thought that just at first you might prefer to be—"

She faced him. "To be what?"

"Well—quiet. I mean—"

"What do you mean by 'at first'?" she interrupted.

He paused again. "I mean after we are married."

She thrust up her chin and turned toward the window. "Thank you!" she tossed back at him.

"Lydia!" he exclaimed blankly; and she felt in every fibre of her averted person that he had made the inconceivable, the unpardonable mistake of anticipating her acquiescence.

The train rattled on and he groped for a third cigarette. Lydia remained silent.

"I haven't offended you?" he ventured at length, in the tone of a man who feels his way.

She shook her head with a sigh. "I thought you

understood," she moaned. Their eyes met and she moved back to his side.

"Do you want to know how not to offend me? By taking it for granted, once for all, that you've said your say on this odious question and that I've said mine, and that we stand just where we did this morning before that—that hateful paper came to spoil everything between us!"

"To spoil everything between us? What on earth do you mean? Aren't you glad to be free?"

"I was free before."

"Not to marry me," he suggested.

"But I don't *want* to marry you!" she cried.

She saw that he turned pale. "I'm obtuse, I suppose," he said slowly. "I confess I don't see what you're driving at. Are you tired of the whole business? Or was I simply a—an excuse for getting away? Perhaps you didn't care to travel alone? Was that it? And now you want to chuck me?" His voice had grown harsh. "You owe me a straight answer, you know; don't be tender-hearted!"

Her eyes swam as she leaned to him. "Don't you see it's because I care—because I care so much? Oh, Ralph! Can't you see how it would humiliate me? Try to feel it as a woman would! Don't you see the misery of being made your wife in this way? If I'd known you as a girl—that would have been a real marriage! But now—this vulgar fraud upon society—and upon a society we despised and laughed at—this sneaking back into a position that we've voluntarily forfeited: don't you see what a cheap compromise it is? We neither of us believe in the abstract 'sacredness' of marriage; we both know that no ceremony is needed to consecrate our love for each other; what object can we have in marrying, except the secret fear of each that the other may escape, or the secret longing to work our way back gradually—oh, very gradually—into the esteem of the people whose conventional morality we have always ridiculed and hated? And the very fact that, after a decent interval, these same people would come and dine with us—the women who talk about the indissolubility of marriage, and who would let me die in a gutter to-day because I am 'leading a life of sin'—doesn't that disgust you more than their turning their backs on us now? I can stand being cut by them, but I couldn't stand their coming to call and asking what I meant to do about visiting that unfortunate Mrs. So-and-so!"

She paused, and Gannett maintained a perplexed silence.

"You judge things too theoretically," he said at length, slowly. "Life is made up of compromises."

"The life we ran away from—yes! If we had been willing to accept them"—she flushed—"we might have gone on meeting each other at Mrs. Tillotson's dinners."

He smiled slightly. "I didn't know that we ran away to found a new system of ethics. I supposed it was because we loved each other."

"Life is complex, of course; isn't it the very recognition of that fact that separates us from the people who see it *tout d'une pièce?* If *they* are right—if marriage is sacred in itself and the individual must always be sacrificed to the family—then there can be no real marriage between us, since our—our being together is a protest against the sacrifice of the individual to the family." She interrupted herself with a laugh. "You'll say now that I'm giving you a lecture on sociology! Of course one acts as one can—as one must, perhaps—pulled by all sorts of invisible threads; but at least one needn't pretend, for social advantages, to subscribe to a creed that ignores the complexity of human motives—that classifies people by arbitrary signs, and puts it in everybody's reach to be on Mrs. Tillotson's visiting-list. It may be necessary that the world should be ruled by conventions—but if we believed in them, why did we break through them? And if we don't believe in them, is it honest to take advantage of the protection they afford?"

Gannett hesitated. "One may believe in them or not; but as long as they do rule the world it is only by taking advantage of their protection that one can find a *modus vivendi.*"

"Do outlaws need a *modus vivendi?*"

He looked at her hopelessly. Nothing is more perplexing to man than the mental process of a woman who reasons her emotions.

She thought she had scored a point and followed it up passionately. "You do understand, don't you? You see how the very thought of the thing humiliates me! We are together to-day because we choose to be—don't let us look any farther than that!" She caught his hands. "*Promise* me you'll never speak of it again; promise me you'll never *think* of it even," she implored, with a tearful prodigality of italics.

Through what followed—his protests, his arguments, his final unconvinced submission to her wishes—she had a sense of his but half-discerning all that, for her, had made the moment so tumultuous. They had reached that memorable point in every heart-history when, for the first time, the man seems obtuse and the woman irrational. It was the abundance of his intentions that consoled her, on reflection, for what they lacked in quality. After all, it would have been worse, incalculably worse, to have detected any overreadiness to understand her.

II

When the train at night-fall brought them to their journey's end at the edge of one of the lakes, Lydia was glad that they were not, as usual, to pass from one solitude to another. Their wanderings during the year had indeed been like the flight of outlaws: through Sicily, Dalmatia, Transylvania and Southern Italy they had persisted in their tacit avoidance of their kind. Isolation, at first, had deepened the flavor of their happiness, as night intensifies the scent of certain flowers; but in the new phase on which they were entering, Lydia's chief wish was that they should be less abnormally exposed to the action of each other's thoughts.

She shrank, nevertheless, as the brightly-looming bulk of the fashionable Anglo-American hotel on the water's brink began to radiate toward their advancing boat its vivid suggestion of social order, visitors' lists, Church services, and the bland inquisition of the *table-d'hôte*. The mere fact that in a moment or two she must take her place on the hotel register as Mrs. Gannett seemed to weaken the springs of her resistance.

They had meant to stay for a night only, on their way to a lofty village among the glaciers of Monte Rosa; but after the first plunge into publicity, when they entered the dining-room, Lydia felt the relief of being lost in a crowd, of ceasing for a moment to be the centre of Gannett's scrutiny; and in his face she caught the reflection of her feeling. After dinner, when she went upstairs, he strolled into the smoking-room, and an hour or two later, sitting in the darkness of her window, she heard his voice below and saw him walking up and down the terrace with a companion cigar at his side. When he came up he told her he had been talking to the hotel chaplain—a very good sort of fellow.

"Queer little microcosms, these hotels! Most of these people live here all summer and then migrate to Italy or the Riviera. The English are the only people who can lead that kind of life with dignity—those soft-voiced old ladies in Shetland shawls somehow carry the British Empire under their caps. *Civis Romanus sum.* It's a curious study—there might be some good things to work up here."

He stood before her with the vivid preoccupied stare of the novelist on the trail of a "subject." With a relief that was half painful she noticed that, for the first time since they had been together, he was hardly aware of her presence.

"Do you think you could write here?"

"Here? I don't know." His stare dropped. "After being out of things so long one's first impressions are bound to be tremendously vivid, you know. I see a dozen threads already that one might follow—"

He broke off with a touch of embarrassment.

"Then follow them. We'll stay," she said with sudden decision.

"Stay here?" He glanced at her in surprise, and then, walking to the window, looked out upon the dusky slumber of the garden.

"Why not?" she said at length, in a tone of veiled irritation.

"The place is full of old cats in caps who gossip with the chaplain. Shall you like—I mean, it would be different if—"

She flamed up.

"Do you suppose I care? It's none of their business."

"Of course not; but you won't get them to think so."

"They may think what they please."

He looked at her doubtfully.

"It's for you to decide."

"We'll stay," she repeated.

Gannett, before they met, had made himself known as a successful writer of short stories and of a novel which had achieved the distinction of being widely discussed. The reviewers called him "promising," and Lydia now accused herself of having too long interfered with the fulfilment of his promise. There was a special irony in the fact, since his passionate assurances that only the stimulus of her companionship could bring out his latent faculty had almost given the dignity of a "vocation" to her course: there had been moments when she had felt unable to assume, before posterity, the responsibility of thwarting his career. And, after all, he had not written a line since they had been together: his first desire to write had come from renewed contact with the world! Was it all a mistake then? Must the most intelligent choice work more disastrously than the blundering combinations of chance? Or was there a still more humiliating answer to her perplexities? His sudden impulse of activity so exactly coincided with her own wish to withdraw, for a time, from the range of his observation, that she wondered if he too were not seeking sanctuary from intolerable problems.

"You must begin to-morrow!" she cried, hiding a tremor under the laugh with which she added, "I wonder if there's any ink in the inkstand?"

Whatever else they had at the Hotel Bellosguardo, they had, as Miss Pinsent said, "a certain tone." It was to Lady Susan Condit that they owed this inestimable benefit; an advantage ranking in Miss Pinsent's opinion above even the lawn tennis courts and the resident chaplain. It was the fact of Lady Susan's annual visit that made the hotel what it was. Miss Pinsent was certainly the last to underrate such a privilege:—"It's so important, my dear, forming as we do a little family, that there should be some one to give *the tone;* and no one could do it better than Lady Susan—an earl's daughter and a person of such determination. Dear Mrs. Ainger now—who really *ought,* you know, when Lady Susan's away—absolutely refuses to assert herself." Miss Pinsent sniffed derisively. "A bishop's niece!—my dear, I saw her once actually give in to some South Americans—and before us all. She gave up her seat at table to oblige them—such a lack of dignity! Lady Susan spoke to her very plainly about it afterwards."

Miss Pinsent glanced across the lake and adjusted her auburn front.

"But of course I don't deny that the stand Lady Susan takes is not always easy to live up to—for the rest of us, I mean. Monsieur Grossart, our good proprietor, finds it trying at times, I know—he has said as much, privately, to Mrs. Ainger and me. After all, the poor man is not to blame for wanting to fill his hotel, is he? And Lady Susan is so difficult—so very difficult—about new people. One might almost say that she disapproves of them beforehand, on principle. And yet she's had warnings—she very nearly made a dreadful mistake once with the Duchess of Levens, who dyed her hair and—well, swore and smoked. One would have thought that might have been a lesson to Lady Susan." Miss Pinsent resumed her knitting with a sigh. "There are exceptions, of course. She took at once to you and Mr. Gannett—it was quite remarkable, really. Oh, I don't mean that either—of course not! It was perfectly natural—we *all* thought you so charming and interesting from the first day—we knew at once that Mr. Gannett was intellectual, by the magazines you took in; but you know what I mean. Lady Susan is so very—well, I won't say prejudiced, as Mrs. Ainger does—but so prepared *not* to like new people, that her taking to you in that way was a surprise to us all, I confess."

Miss Pinsent sent a significant glance down the long laurustinus alley from the other end of which two people—a lady and gentleman—were strolling toward them through the smiling neglect of the garden.

"In this case, of course, it's very different; that I'm willing to admit. Their looks are against them; but, as Mrs. Ainger says, one can't exactly tell them so."

"She's very handsome," Lydia ventured, with her eyes on the lady, who showed, under the dome of a vivid sunshade, the hour-glass figure and superlative coloring of a Christmas chromo.

"That's the worst of it. She's too handsome."

"Well, after all, she can't help that."

"Other people manage to," said Miss Pinsent skeptically.

"But isn't it rather unfair of Lady Susan—considering that nothing is known about them?"

"But, my dear, that's the very thing that's against them. It's infinitely worse than any actual knowledge."

Lydia mentally agreed that, in the case of Mrs. Linton, it possibly might be.

"I wonder why they came here?" she mused.

"That's against them too. It's always a bad sign when loud people come to a quiet place. And they've brought van-loads of boxes—her maid told Mrs. Ainger's that they meant to stop indefinitely."

"And Lady Susan actually turned her back on her in the *salon?*"

"My dear, she said it was for our sakes: that makes it so unanswerable! But poor Grossart *is* in a way! The Lintons have taken his most expensive *suite,* you know—the yellow damask drawing-room above the portico—and they have champagne with every meal!"

They were silent as Mr. and Mrs. Linton sauntered by; the lady with tempestuous brows and challenging chin; the gentleman, a blond stripling, trailing after her, head downward, like a reluctant child dragged by his nurse.

"What does your husband think of them, my dear?" Miss Pinsent whispered as they passed out of earshot.

Lydia stooped to pick a violet in the border.

"He hasn't told me."

"Of your speaking to them, I mean. Would he approve of that? I know how very particular nice Americans are. I think your action might make a difference; it would certainly carry weight with Lady Susan."

"Dear Miss Pinsent, you flatter me!"

Lydia rose and gathered up her book and sunshade.

"Well, if you're asked for an opinion—if Lady Susan asks you for one—I think you ought to be prepared," Miss Pinsent admonished her as she moved away.

III

Lady Susan held her own. She ignored the Lintons, and her little family, as Miss Pinsent phrased it, followed suit. Even Mrs. Ainger agreed that it was obligatory. If Lady Susan owed it to the others not to speak to the Lintons, the others clearly owed it to Lady Susan to back her up. It was generally found expedient, at the Hotel Bellosguardo, to adopt this form of reasoning.

Whatever effect this combined action may have had upon the Lintons, it did not at least have that of driving them away. Monsieur Grossart, after a few days of suspense, had the satisfaction of seeing them settle down in his yellow damask *premier* with what looked like a permanent installation of palm-trees and silk sofa-cushions, and a gratifying continuance in the consumption of champagne. Mrs. Linton trailed her Doucet draperies up and down the garden with the same challenging air, while her husband, smoking innumerable cigarettes, dragged himself dejectedly in her wake; but neither of them, after the first encounter with Lady Susan, made any attempt to extend their acquaintance. They simply ignored their ignorers. As Miss Pinsent resentfully observed, they behaved exactly as though the hotel were empty.

It was therefore a matter of surprise, as well as of displeasure, to Lydia, to find, on glancing up one day from her seat in the garden, that the shadow which had fallen across her book was that of the enigmatic Mrs. Linton.

"I want to speak to you," that lady said, in a rich hard voice that seemed the audible expression of her gown and her complexion.

Lydia started. She certainly did not want to speak to Mrs. Linton.

"Shall I sit down here?" the latter continued, fixing her intensely-shaded eyes on Lydia's face, "or are you afraid of being seen with me?"

"Afraid?" Lydia colored. "Sit down, please. What is it that you wish to say?"

Mrs. Linton, with a smile, drew up a garden-chair and crossed one open-work ankle above the other.

"I want you to tell me what my husband said to your husband last night."

Lydia turned pale.

"My husband—to yours?" she faltered, staring at the other.

"Didn't you know they were closeted together for hours in the smoking-room after you went upstairs? My man didn't get to bed until nearly two o'clock and when he did I couldn't get a word out of him. When he wants to be aggravating I'll back him against anybody living!" Her teeth and eyes flashed persuasively upon Lydia. "But you'll tell me what they were talking about, won't you? I know I can trust you—you look so awfully kind. And it's for his own good. He's such a precious donkey and I'm so afraid he's got into some beastly scrape or other. If he'd only trust his own old woman! But they're always writing to him and setting him against me. And I've got nobody to turn to." She laid her hand on Lydia's with a rattle of bracelets. "You'll help me, won't you?"

Lydia drew back from the smiling fierceness of her brows.

"I'm sorry—but I don't think I understand. My husband has said nothing to me of—of yours."

The great black crescents above Mrs. Linton's eyes met angrily.

"I say—is that true?" she demanded.

Lydia rose from her seat.

"Oh, look here, I didn't mean that, you know—you mustn't take one up so! Can't you see how rattled I am?"

Lydia saw that, in fact, her beautiful mouth was quivering beneath softened eyes.

"I'm beside myself!" the splendid creature wailed, dropping into her seat.

"I'm so sorry," Lydia repeated, forcing herself to speak kindly; "but how can I help you?"

Mrs. Linton raised her head sharply.

"By finding out—there's a darling!"

"Finding what out?"

"What Trevenna told him."

"Trevenna—?" Lydia echoed in bewilderment.

Mrs. Linton clapped her hand to her mouth.

"Oh, Lord—there, it's out! What a fool I am! But I supposed of course you knew; I supposed everybody knew." She dried her eyes and bridled. "Didn't you know that he's Lord Trevenna? I'm Mrs. Cope."

Lydia recognized the names. They had figured in a flamboyant elopement which had thrilled fashionable London some six months earlier.

"Now you see how it is—you understand, don't you?" Mrs. Cope continued on a note of appeal. "I knew you would—that's the reason I came to you. I suppose *he* felt the same thing about your husband; he's not spoken to another soul in the place." Her face grew anxious again. "He's awfully sensitive, generally—he feels our position, he says—as if it wasn't *my* place to feel that! But when he does get talking there's no knowing what he'll say. I know he's been brooding over something lately, and I *must* find out what it is—it's to his interest that I should. I always tell him that I think only of his interest; if he'd only trust me! But he's been so odd lately—I can't think what he's plotting. You will help me, dear?"

Lydia, who had remained standing, looked away uncomfortably.

"If you mean by finding out what Lord Trevenna has told my husband, I'm afraid it's impossible."

"Why impossible?"

"Because I infer that it was told in confidence."

Mrs. Cope stared incredulously.

"Well, what of that? Your husband looks such a dear—any one can see he's awfully gone on you. What's to prevent your getting it out of him?"

Lydia flushed.

"I'm not a spy!" she exclaimed.

"A spy—a spy? How dare you?" Mrs. Cope flamed out. "Oh, I don't mean that either! Don't be angry with me—I'm so miserable." She essayed a softer note. "Do you call that spying—for one woman to help out another? I do need help so dreadfully! I'm at my wits' end with Trevenna, I am indeed. He's such a boy—a mere baby, you know; he's only two-and-twenty." She dropped her orbed lids. "He's younger than me—only fancy! a few months younger. I tell him he ought to listen to me as if I was his mother; oughtn't he now? But he won't, he won't! All his people are at him, you see—oh, I know *their* little game! Trying to get him away from me before I can get my divorce—that's what they're up to. At first he wouldn't listen to them; he used to toss their letters over to me to read; but now he reads them himself, and answers 'em too, I fancy; he's always shut up in his room, writing. If I only knew what his plan is I could stop him fast enough—he's such a simpleton. But he's dreadfully deep too—at times I can't make him out. But I know he's told your husband everything—I knew that last night the minute I laid eyes on him. And I *must* find out—you must help me—I've got no one else to turn to!"

She caught Lydia's fingers in a stormy pressure.

"Say you'll help me—you and your husband."

Lydia tried to free herself.

"What you ask is impossible; you must see that it is. No one could interfere in—in the way you ask."

Mrs. Cope's clutch tightened.

"You won't, then? You won't?"

"Certainly not. Let me go, please."

Mrs. Cope released her with a laugh.

"Oh, go by all means—pray don't let me detain you! Shall you go and tell Lady Susan Condit that there's a pair of us—or shall I save you the trouble of enlightening her?"

Lydia stood still in the middle of the path, seeing her antagonist through a mist of terror. Mrs. Cope was still laughing.

"Oh, I'm not spiteful by nature, my dear; but you're a little more than flesh and blood can stand! It's impossible, is it? Let you go, indeed! You're too good to be mixed up in my affairs, are you? Why, you little fool, the first day I laid eyes on you I saw that you and I were both in the same box—that's the reason I spoke to you."

She stepped nearer, her smile dilating on Lydia like a lamp through a fog.

"You can take your choice, you know; I always

play fair. If you'll tell I'll promise not to. Now then, which is it to be?"

Lydia, involuntarily, had begun to move away from the pelting storm of words; but at this she turned and sat down again.

"You may go," she said simply. "I shall stay here."

IV

She stayed there for a long time, in the hypnotized contemplation, not of Mrs. Cope's present, but of her own past. Gannett, early that morning, had gone off on a long walk—he had fallen into the habit of taking these mountain-tramps with various fellow-lodgers; but even had he been within reach she could not have gone to him just then. She had to deal with herself first. She was surprised to find how, in the last months, she had lost the habit of introspection. Since their coming to the Hotel Bellosguardo she and Gannett had tacitly avoided themselves and each other.

She was aroused by the whistle of the three o'clock steamboat as it neared the landing just beyond the hotel gates. Three o'clock! Then Gannett would soon be back—he had told her to expect him before four. She rose hurriedly, her face averted from the inquisitorial façade of the hotel. She could not see him just yet; she could not go indoors. She slipped through one of the overgrown garden-alleys and climbed a steep path to the hills.

It was dark when she opened their sitting-room door. Gannett was sitting on the window-ledge smoking a cigarette. Cigarettes were now his chief resource: he had not written a line during the two months they had spent at the Hotel Bellosguardo. In that respect, it had turned out not to be the right *milieu* after all.

He started up at Lydia's entrance.

"Where have you been? I was getting anxious."

She sat down in a chair near the door.

"Up the mountain," she said wearily.

"Alone?"

"Yes."

Gannett threw away his cigarette: the sound of her voice made him want to see her face.

"Shall we have a little light?" he suggested.

She made no answer and he lifted the globe from the lamp and put a match to the wick. Then he looked at her.

"Anything wrong? You look done up."

She sat glancing vaguely about the little sitting-room, dimly lit by the pallid-globed lamp, which left in twilight the outlines of the furniture, of his writing-table heaped with books and papers, of the tea-roses and jasmine drooping on the mantelpiece. How like home it had all grown—how like home!

"Lydia, what is wrong?" he repeated.

She moved away from him, feeling for her hat-pins and turning to lay her hat and sunshade on the table.

Suddenly she said: "That woman has been talking to me."

Gannett stared.

"That woman? What woman?"

"Mrs. Linton—Mrs. Cope."

He gave a start of annoyance, still, as she perceived, not grasping the full import of her words.

"The deuce! She told you—?"

"She told me everything."

Gannett looked at her anxiously.

"What impudence! I'm so sorry that you should have been exposed to this, dear."

"Exposed!" Lydia laughed.

Gannett's brow clouded and they looked away from each other.

"Do you know *why* she told me? She had the best of reasons. The first time she laid eyes on me she saw that we were both in the same box."

"Lydia!"

"So it was natural, of course, that she should turn to me in a difficulty."

"What difficulty?"

"It seems she has reason to think that Lord Trevenna's people are trying to get him away from her before she gets her divorce—"

"Well?"

"And she fancied he had been consulting with you last night as to—as to the best way of escaping from her."

Gannett stood up with an angry forehead.

"Well—what concern of yours was all this dirty business? Why should she go to you?"

"Don't you see? It's so simple. I was to wheedle his secret out of you."

"To oblige that woman?"

"Yes; or, if I was unwilling to oblige her, then to protect myself."

"To protect yourself? Against whom?"

"Against her telling every one in the hotel that she and I are in the same box."

"She threatened that?"

"She left me the choice of telling it myself or of doing it for me."

"The beast!"

There was a long silence. Lydia had seated herself on the sofa, beyond the radius of the lamp, and he leaned against the window. His next question surprised her.

"When did this happen? At what time, I mean?"

She looked at him vaguely.

"I don't know—after luncheon, I think. Yes, I remember; it must have been at about three o'clock."

He stepped into the middle of the room and as he approached the light she saw that his brow had cleared.

"Why do you ask?" she said.

"Because when I came in, at about half-past three, the mail was just being distributed, and Mrs. Cope was waiting as usual to pounce on her letters; you know she was always watching for the postman. She was standing so close to me that I couldn't help seeing a big official-looking envelope that was handed to her. She tore it open, gave one look at the inside, and rushed off upstairs like a whirlwind, with the director shouting after her that she had left all her other letters behind. I don't believe she ever thought of you again after that paper was put into her hand."

"Why?"

"Because she was too busy. I was sitting in the window, watching for you, when the five o'clock boat left, and who should go on board, bag and baggage, valet and maid, dressing-bags and poodle, but Mrs. Cope and Trevenna. Just an hour and a half to pack up in! And you should have seen her when they started. She was radiant—shaking hands with everybody—waving her handkerchief from the deck—distributing bows and smiles like an empress. If ever a woman got what she wanted just in the nick of time that woman did. She'll be Lady Trevenna within a week, I'll wager."

"You think she has her divorce?"

"I'm sure of it. And she must have got it just after her talk with you."

Lydia was silent.

At length she said, with a kind of reluctance, "She was horribly angry when she left me. It wouldn't have taken long to tell Lady Susan Condit."

"Lady Susan Condit has not been told."

"How do you know?"

"Because when I went downstairs half an hour ago I met Lady Susan on the way—"

He stopped, half smiling.

"Well?"

"And she stopped to ask if I thought you would act as patroness to a charity concert she is getting up."

In spite of themselves they both broke into a laugh. Lydia's ended in sobs and she sank down with her face hidden. Gannett bent over her, seeking her hands.

"That vile woman—I ought to have warned you to keep away from her; I can't forgive myself! But he spoke to me in confidence; and I never dreamed—well, it's all over now."

Lydia lifted her head.

"Not for me. It's only just beginning."

"What do you mean?"

She put him gently aside and moved in her turn to the window. Then she went on, with her face turned toward the shimmering blackness of the lake, "You see of course that it might happen again at any moment."

"What?"

"This—this risk of being found out. And we could hardly count again on such a lucky combination of chances, could we?"

He sat down with a groan.

Still keeping her face toward the darkness, she said, "I want you to go and tell Lady Susan—and the others."

Gannett, who had moved towards her, paused a few feet off.

"Why do you wish me to do this?" he said at length, with less surprise in his voice than she had been prepared for.

"Because I've behaved basely, abominably, since we came here: letting these people believe we were married—lying with every breath I drew—"

"Yes, I've felt that too," Gannett exclaimed with sudden energy.

The words shook her like a tempest: all her thoughts seemed to fall about her in ruins.

"You—you've felt so?"

"Of course I have." He spoke with low-voiced vehemence. "Do you suppose I like playing the sneak any better than you do? It's damnable."

He had dropped on the arm of a chair, and they stared at each other like blind people who suddenly see.

"But you have liked it here," she faltered.

"Oh, I've liked it—I've liked it." He moved impatiently. "Haven't you?"

"Yes," she burst out; "that's the worst of it—that's what I can't bear. I fancied it was for your sake that I insisted on staying—because you thought you could write here; and perhaps just at first that really was the reason. But afterwards I wanted to stay myself—I loved it." She broke into a laugh. "Oh, do you see the full derision of it? These people—the very prototypes of the bores you took me away from, with the same fenced-in view of life, the same keep-off-the-grass morality, the same little cautious virtues and the same little frightened vices—well, I've clung to them, I've delighted in them, I've done my best to please them. I've toadied Lady Susan, I've gossipped with Miss Pinsent, I've pretended to be shocked with Mrs. Ainger. Respectability! It was the one thing in life that I was sure I didn't care about, and it's grown so precious to me that I've stolen it because I couldn't get it in any other way."

She moved across the room and returned to his side with another laugh.

"I who used to fancy myself unconventional! I must have been born with a card-case in my hand. You should have seen me with that poor woman in the garden. She came to me for help, poor creature, because she fancied that, having 'sinned,' as they call it, I might feel some pity for others who had been tempted in the same way. Not I! She didn't know me. Lady Susan would have been kinder, because Lady Susan wouldn't have been afraid. I hated the woman—my one thought was not to be seen with her—I could have killed her for guessing my secret. The one thing that mattered to me at that moment was my standing with Lady Susan!"

Gannett did not speak.

"And you—you've felt it too!" she broke out accusingly. "You've enjoyed being with these people as much as I have; you've let the chaplain talk to you by the hour about 'The Reign of Law' and Professor Drummond. When they asked you to hand the plate in church I was watching you—*you wanted to accept*."

She stepped close, laying her hand on his arm.

"Do you know, I begin to see what marriage is for. It's to keep people away from each other. Sometimes I think that two people who love each other can be saved from madness only by the things that come between them—children, duties, visits, bores, relations—the things that protect married people from each other. We've been too close together—that has been our sin. We've seen the nakedness of each other's souls."

She sank again on the sofa, hiding her face in her hands.

Gannett stood above her perplexedly: he felt as though she were being swept away by some implacable current while he stood helpless on its bank.

At length he said, "Lydia, don't think me a brute—but don't you see yourself that it won't do?"

"Yes, I see it won't do," she said without raising her head.

His face cleared.

"Then we'll go to-morrow."

"Go—where?"

"To Paris; to be married."

For a long time she made no answer; then she asked slowly, "Would they have us here if we were married?"

"Have us here?"

"I mean Lady Susan—and the others."

"Have us here? Of course they would."

"Not if they knew—at least, not unless they could pretend not to know."

He made an impatient gesture.

"We shouldn't come back here, of course; and other people needn't know—no one need know."

She sighed. "Then it's only another form of deception and a meaner one. Don't you see that?"

"I see that we're not accountable to any Lady Susans on earth!"

"Then why are you ashamed of what we are doing here?"

"Because I'm sick of pretending that you're my wife when you're not—when you won't be."

She looked at him sadly.

"If I were your wife you'd have to go on pretending. You'd have to pretend that I'd never been—anything else. And our friends would have to pretend that they believed what you pretended."

Gannett pulled off the sofa-tassel and flung it away.

"You're impossible," he groaned.

"It's not I—it's our being together that's impossible. I only want you to see that marriage won't help it."

"What will help it then?"

She raised her head.

"My leaving you."

"Your leaving me?" He sat motionless, staring at the tassel which lay at the other end of the room. At length some impulse of retaliation for the pain she was inflicting made him say deliberately:

"And where would you go if you left me?"

"Oh!" she cried.

He was at her side in an instant.

"Lydia—Lydia—you know I didn't mean it; I couldn't mean it! But you've driven me out of my senses; I don't know what I'm saying. Can't you get out of this labyrinth of self-torture? It's destroying us both."

"That's why I must leave you."

"How easily you say it!" He drew her hands down and made her face him. "You're very scrupulous about yourself—and others. But have you thought of me? You have no right to leave me unless you've ceased to care—"

"It's because I care—"

"Then I have a right to be heard. If you love me you can't leave me."

Her eyes defied him.

"Why not?"

He dropped her hands and rose from her side.

"Can you?" he said sadly.

The hour was late and the lamp flickered and sank. She stood up with a shiver and turned toward the door of her room.

V

At daylight a sound in Lydia's room woke Gannett from a troubled sleep. He sat up and listened. She was moving about softly, as though fearful of disturbing him. He heard her push back one of the creaking shutters; then there was a moment's silence, which seemed to indicate that she was waiting to see if the noise had roused him.

Presently she began to move again. She had spent a sleepless night, probably, and was dressing to go down to the garden for a breath of air. Gannett rose also; but some undefinable instinct made his movements as cautious as hers. He stole to his window and looked out through the slats of the shutter.

It had rained in the night and the dawn was gray and lifeless. The cloud-muffled hills across the lake were reflected in its surface as in a tarnished mirror. In the garden, the birds were beginning to shake the drops from the motionless laurustinus-boughs.

An immense pity for Lydia filled Gannett's soul. Her seeming intellectual independence had blinded him for a time to the feminine cast of her mind. He had never thought of her as a woman who wept and clung: there was a lucidity in her intuitions that made them appear to be the result of reasoning. Now he saw the cruelty he had committed in detaching her from the normal conditions of life; he felt, too, the insight with which she had hit upon the real cause of their suffering. Their life was "impossible," as she had said—and its worst penalty was that it had made any other life impossible for them. Even had his love lessened, he was bound to her now by a hundred ties of pity and self-reproach; and she, poor child! must turn back to him as Latude returned to his cell . . .

A new sound startled him: it was the stealthy closing of Lydia's door. He crept to his own and heard her footsteps passing down the corridor. Then he went back to the window and looked out.

A minute or two later he saw her go down the steps of the porch and enter the garden. From his post of observation her face was invisible, but something about her appearance struck him. She wore a long travelling cloak and under its folds he detected the outline of a bag or bundle. He drew a deep breath and stood watching her.

She walked quickly down the laurustinus alley toward the gate; there she paused a moment, glancing about the little shady square. The stone benches under the trees were empty, and she seemed to gather resolution from the solitude about her, for she crossed the square to the steam-boat landing, and he saw her pause before the ticket-office at the head of the wharf. Now she was buying her ticket. Gannett turned his head a moment to look at the clock: the boat was due in five minutes. He had time to jump into his clothes and overtake her—

He made no attempt to move; an obscure reluctance restrained him. If any thought emerged from the tumult of his sensations, it was that he must let her go if she wished it. He had spoken last night of his rights: what were they? At the last issue, he and she were two separate beings, not made one by the miracle of common forbearances, duties, abnegations, but bound together in a *noyade* of passion that left them resisting yet clinging as they went down.

After buying her ticket, Lydia had stood for a

moment looking out across the lake; then he saw her seat herself on one of the benches near the landing. He and she, at that moment, were both listening for the same sound: the whistle of the boat as it rounded the nearest promontory. Gannett turned again to glance at the clock: the boat was due now.

Where would she go? What would her life be when she had left him? She had no near relations and few friends. There was money enough . . . but she asked so much of life, in ways so complex and immaterial. He thought of her as walking barefooted through a stony waste. No one would understand her—no one would pity her—and he, who did both, was powerless to come to her aid . . .

He saw that she had risen from the bench and walked toward the edge of the lake. She stood looking in the direction from which the steamboat was to come; then she turned to the ticket-office, doubtless to ask the cause of the delay. After that she went back to the bench and sat down with bent head. What was she thinking of?

The whistle sounded; she started up, and Gannett involuntarily made a movement toward the door. But he turned back and continued to watch her. She stood motionless, her eyes on the trail of smoke that preceded the appearance of the boat. Then the little craft rounded the point, a dead-white object on the leaden water: a minute later it was puffing and backing at the wharf.

The few passengers who were waiting—two or three peasants and a snuffy priest—were clustered near the ticket-office. Lydia stood apart under the trees.

The boat lay alongside now; the gang-plank was run out and the peasants went on board with their baskets of vegetables, followed by the priest. Still Lydia did not move. A bell began to ring querulously; there was a shriek of steam, and some one must have called to her that she would be late, for she started forward, as though in answer to a summons. She moved waveringly, and at the edge of the wharf she paused. Gannett saw a sailor beckon to her; the bell rang again and she stepped upon the gang-plank.

Half-way down the short incline to the deck she stopped again; then she turned and ran back to the land. The gang-plank was drawn in, the bell ceased to ring, and the boat backed out into the lake. Lydia, with slow steps, was walking toward the garden . . .

As she approached the hotel she looked up furtively and Gannett drew back into the room. He sat down beside a table; a Bradshaw lay at his elbow, and mechanically, without knowing what he did, he began looking out the trains to Paris . . .

The Other Two

I

Waythorn, on the drawing-room hearth, waited for his wife to come down to dinner.

It was their first night under his own roof, and he was surprised at his thrill of boyish agitation. He was not so old, to be sure—his glass gave him little more than the five-and-thirty years to which his wife confessed—but he had fancied himself already in the temperate zone; yet here he was listening for her step with a tender sense of all it symbolised, with some old trail of verse about the garlanded nuptial door-posts floating through his enjoyment of the pleasant room and the good dinner just beyond it.

They had been hastily recalled from their honeymoon by the illness of Lily Haskett, the child of Mrs. Waythorn's first marriage. The little girl, at Waythorn's desire, had been transferred to his house on the day of her mother's wedding, and the doctor, on their arrival, broke the news that she was ill with typhoid, but declared that all the symptoms were favourable. Lily could show twelve years of unblemished health, and the case promised to be a light one. The nurse spoke as reassuringly, and after a moment of alarm Mrs. Waythorn had adjusted herself to the situation. She was very fond of Lily—her affection for the child had perhaps been her decisive charm in Waythorn's eyes—but she had the perfectly balanced nerves which her little girl had inherited, and no woman ever wasted less tissue in unproductive worry. Waythorn was therefore quite prepared to see her come in presently, a little late because of a last look at Lily, but as serene and well-appointed as if her good-night kiss had been laid on the brow of health. Her composure was restful to him; it acted as ballast to his somewhat unstable sensibilities. As he pictured her bending over the child's bed he thought how soothing her presence must be in illness: her very step would prognosticate recovery.

His own life had been a gray one, from temperament rather than circumstance, and he had been drawn to her by the unperturbed gaiety which kept her fresh and elastic at an age when most women's activities are growing either slack or febrile. He knew what was said about her; for, popular as she was, there had always been a faint undercurrent of detraction. When she had appeared in New York, nine or ten years earlier, as the pretty Mrs. Haskett whom Gus Varick had unearthed somewhere—was it in Pittsburgh or Utica?—society, while promptly accepting her, had reserved the right to cast a doubt on its own indiscrimination. Enquiry, however, established her undoubted connection with a socially reigning family, and explained her recent divorce as the natural result of a runaway match at seventeen; and as nothing was known of Mr. Haskett it was easy to believe the worst of him.

Alice Haskett's remarriage with Gus Varick was a passport to the set whose recognition she coveted, and for a few years the Varicks were the most popular couple in town. Unfortunately the alliance was brief and stormy, and this time the husband had his champions. Still, even Varick's stanchest supporters admitted that he was not meant for matrimony, and Mrs. Varick's grievances were of a nature to bear the inspection of the New York courts. A New York divorce is in itself a diploma of virtue, and in the semi-widowhood of this second separation Mrs. Varick took on an air of sanctity, and was allowed to confide her wrongs to some of the most scrupulous ears in town. But when it was known that she was to marry Waythorn there was a momentary reaction. Her best friends would have preferred to see her remain in the rôle of the injured wife, which was as becoming to her as crape to a rosy complexion. True, a decent time had elapsed, and it was not even suggested that Waythorn had supplanted his predecessor. People shook their heads over him, however, and one grudging friend, to whom he affirmed that he took the step with his eyes open, replied oracularly: "Yes—and with your ears shut."

Waythorn could afford to smile at these innuendoes. In the Wall Street phrase, he had "discounted" them. He knew that society has not yet adapted itself to the consequences of divorce, and that till the adaptation takes place every woman who uses the freedom the law accords her must be her own social justification. Waythorn had an amused confidence in his wife's ability to justify herself. His expectations were fulfilled, and before the wedding took place Alice Varick's group had rallied openly to her support. She took it all imperturbably: she had a way of surmounting obstacles without seeming to be aware of them, and Waythorn looked back with wonder at the trivialities over which he had worn his nerves thin. He had the sense of having found refuge in a richer, warmer nature than his own, and his satisfaction, at the moment, was humourously summed up in the thought that his wife, when she had done all she could for Lily, would not be ashamed to come down and enjoy a good dinner.

The anticipation of such enjoyment was not, however, the sentiment expressed by Mrs. Waythorn's charming face when she presently joined him. Though she had put on her most engaging teagown she had neglected to assume the smile that went with it, and Waythorn thought he had never seen her look so nearly worried.

"What is it?" he asked. "Is anything wrong with Lily?"

"No; I've just been in and she's still sleeping." Mrs. Waythorn hesitated. "But something tiresome has happened."

He had taken her two hands, and now perceived that he was crushing a paper between them.

"This letter?"

"Yes—Mr. Haskett has written—I mean his lawyer has written."

Waythorn felt himself flush uncomfortably. He dropped his wife's hands.

"What about?"

"About seeing Lily. You know the courts—"

"Yes, yes," he interrupted nervously.

Nothing was known about Haskett in New York. He was vaguely supposed to have remained in the outer darkness from which his wife had been rescued, and Waythorn was one of the few who were aware that he had given up his business in Utica and followed her to New York in order to be near his little girl. In the days of his wooing, Waythorn had often met Lily on the doorstep, rosy and smiling, on her way "to see papa."

"I am so sorry," Mrs. Waythorn murmured.

He roused himself. "What does he want?"

"He wants to see her. You know she goes to him once a week."

"Well—he doesn't expect her to go to him now, does he?"

"No—he has heard of her illness; but he expects to come here."

"Here?"

Mrs. Waythorn reddened under his gaze. They looked away from each other.

"I'm afraid he has the right. . . . You'll see. . . ." She made a proffer of the letter.

Waythorn moved away with a gesture of refusal. He stood staring about the softly lighted room, which a moment before had seemed so full of bridal intimacy.

"I'm so sorry," she repeated. "If Lily could have been moved—"

"That's out of the question," he returned impatiently.

"I suppose so."

Her lip was beginning to tremble, and he felt himself a brute. "He must come, of course," he said. "When is—his day?"

"I'm afraid—to-morrow."

"Very well. Send a note in the morning."

The butler entered to announce dinner.

Waythorn turned to his wife. "Come—you must be tired. It's beastly, but try to forget about it," he said, drawing her hand through his arm.

"You're so good, dear. I'll try," she whispered back.

Her face cleared at once, and as she looked at him across the flowers, between the rosy candle-shades, he saw her lips waver back into a smile.

"How pretty everything is!" she sighed luxuriously.

He turned to the butler. "The champagne at once, please. Mrs. Waythorn is tired."

In a moment or two their eyes met above the sparkling glasses. Her own were quite clear and untroubled: he saw that she had obeyed his injunction and forgotten.

II

Waythorn, the next morning, went down town earlier than usual. Haskett was not likely to come till the afternoon, but the instinct of flight drove him forth. He meant to stay away all day—he had thoughts of dining at his club. As his door closed behind him he reflected that before he opened it again it would have admitted another man who had as much right to enter it as himself, and the thought filled him with a physical repugnance.

He caught the "elevated" at the employés' hour, and found himself crushed between two layers of pendulous humanity. At Eighth Street the man facing him wriggled out, and another took his place. Waythorn glanced up and saw that it was Gus Varick. The men were so close together that it was impossible to ignore the smile of recognition on Varick's handsome overblown face. And after all—why not? They had always been on good terms, and Varick had been divorced before Waythorn's attentions to his wife began. The two exchanged a word on the perennial grievance of the congested trains, and when a seat at their side was miraculously left empty the instinct of self-preservation made Waythorn slip into it after Varick.

The latter drew the stout man's breath of relief. "Lord—I was beginning to feel like a pressed flower." He leaned back, looking unconcernedly at Waythorn. "Sorry to hear that Sellers is knocked out again."

"Sellers?" echoed Waythorn, starting at his partner's name.

Varick looked surprised. "You didn't know he was laid up with the gout?"

"No. I've been away—I only got back last night." Waythorn felt himself reddening in anticipation of the other's smile.

"Ah—yes; to be sure. And Sellers's attack came on two days ago. I'm afraid he's pretty bad. Very awkward for me, as it happens, because he was just putting through a rather important thing for me."

"Ah?" Waythorn wondered vaguely since when Varick had been dealing in "important things."

Hitherto he had dabbled only in the shallow pools of speculation, with which Waythorn's office did not usually concern itself.

It occurred to him that Varick might be talking at random, to relieve the strain of their propinquity. That strain was becoming momentarily more apparent to Waythorn, and when, at Cortlandt Street, he caught sight of an acquaintance and had a sudden vision of the picture he and Varick must present to an initiated eye, he jumped up with a muttered excuse.

"I hope you'll find Sellers better," said Varick civilly, and he stammered back: "If I can be of any use to you—" and let the departing crowd sweep him to the platform.

At his office he heard that Sellers was in fact ill with the gout, and would probably not be able to leave the house for some weeks.

"I'm sorry it should have happened so, Mr. Waythorn," the senior clerk said with affable significance. "Mr. Sellers was very much upset at the idea of giving you such a lot of extra work just now."

"Oh, that's no matter," said Waythorn hastily. He secretly welcomed the pressure of additional business, and was glad to think that, when the day's work was over, he would have to call at his partner's on the way home.

He was late for luncheon, and turned in at the nearest restaurant instead of going to his club. The place was full, and the waiter hurried him to the back of the room to capture the only vacant table. In the cloud of cigar-smoke Waythorn did not at once distinguish his neighbours: but presently, looking about him, he saw Varick seated a few feet off. This time, luckily, they were too far apart for conversation, and Varick, who faced another way, had probably not even seen him; but there was an irony in their renewed nearness.

Varick was said to be fond of good living, and as Waythorn sat despatching his hurried luncheon he looked across half enviously at the other's leisurely degustation of his meal. When Waythorn first saw him he had been helping himself with critical deliberation to a bit of Camembert at the ideal point of liquefaction, and now, the cheese removed, he was just pouring his *café double* from its little two-storied earthen pot. He poured slowly, his ruddy profile bent above the task, and one beringed white hand steadying the lid of the coffee-pot; then he stretched his other hand to the decanter of cognac at his elbow, filled a liqueur-glass, took a tentative sip, and poured the brandy into his coffee-cup.

Waythorn watched him in a kind of fascination. What was he thinking of—only of the flavour of the coffee and the liqueur? Had the morning's meeting left no more trace in his thoughts than on his face? Had his wife so completely passed out of his life that even this odd encounter with her present husband, within a week after her remarriage, was no more than an incident in his day? And as Waythorn mused, another idea struck him: had Haskett ever met Varick as Varick and he had just met? The recollection of Haskett perturbed him, and he rose and left the restaurant, taking a circuitous way out to escape the placid irony of Varick's nod.

It was after seven when Waythorn reached

home. He thought the footman who opened the door looked at him oddly.

"How is Miss Lily?" he asked in haste.

"Doing very well, sir. A gentleman—"

"Tell Barlow to put off dinner for half an hour," Waythorn cut him off, hurrying upstairs.

He went straight to his room and dressed without seeing his wife. When he reached the drawing-room she was there, fresh and radiant. Lily's day had been good; the doctor was not coming back that evening.

At dinner Waythorn told her of Sellers's illness and of the resulting complications. She listened sympathetically, adjuring him not to let himself be over-worked, and asking vague feminine questions about the routine of the office. Then she gave him the chronicle of Lily's day; quoted the nurse and doctor, and told him who had called to inquire. He had never seen her more serene and unruffled. It struck him, with a curious pang, that she was very happy in being with him, so happy that she found a childish pleasure in rehearsing the trivial incidents of her day.

After dinner they went to the library, and the servant put the coffee and liqueurs on a low table before her and left the room. She looked singularly soft and girlish in her rosy pale dress, against the dark leather of one of his bachelor armchairs. A day earlier the contrast would have charmed him.

He turned away now, choosing a cigar with affected deliberation.

"Did Haskett come?" he asked, with his back to her.

"Oh, yes—he came."

"You didn't see him, of course?"

She hesitated a moment. "I let the nurse see him."

That was all. There was nothing more to ask. He swung round toward her, applying a match to his cigar. Well, the thing was over for a week, at any rate. He would try not to think of it. She looked up at him, a trifle rosier than usual, with a smile in her eyes.

"Ready for your coffee, dear?"

He leaned against the mantelpiece, watching her as she lifted the coffee-pot. The lamplight struck a gleam from her bracelets and tipped her soft hair with brightness. How light and slender she was, and how each gesture flowed into the next! She seemed a creature all compact of harmonies. As the thought of Haskett receded, Waythorn felt himself yielding again to the joy of possessorship. They were his, those white hands with their flitting motions, his the light haze of hair, the lips and eyes. . . .

She set down the coffee-pot, and reaching for the decanter of cognac, measured off a liqueur-glass and poured it into his cup.

Waythorn uttered a sudden exclamation.

"What is the matter?" she said, startled.

"Nothing; only—I don't take cognac in my coffee."

"Oh, how stupid of me," she cried.

Their eyes met, and she blushed a sudden agonised red.

III

Ten days later, Mr. Sellers, still house-bound, asked Waythorn to call on his way down town.

The senior partner, with his swaddled foot propped up by the fire, greeted his associate with an air of embarrassment.

"I'm sorry, my dear fellow; I've got to ask you to do an awkward thing for me."

Waythorn waited, and the other went on, after a pause apparently given to the arrangement of his phrases: "The fact is, when I was knocked out I had just gone into a rather complicated piece of business for—Gus Varick."

"Well?" said Waythorn, with an attempt to put him at his ease.

"Well—it's this way: Varick came to me the day before my attack. He had evidently had an inside tip from somebody, and had made about a hundred thousand. He came to me for advice, and I suggested his going in with Vanderlyn."

"Oh, the deuce!" Waythorn exclaimed. He saw in a flash what had happened. The investment was an alluring one, but required negotiation. He listened quietly while Sellers put the case before him, and, the statement ended, he said: "You think I ought to see Varick?"

"I'm afraid I can't as yet. The doctor is obdurate. And this thing can't wait. I hate to ask you, but no one else in the office knows the ins and outs of it."

Waythorn stood silent. He did not care a farthing for the success of Varick's venture, but the honour of the office was to be considered, and he could hardly refuse to oblige his partner.

"Very well," he said, "I'll do it."

That afternoon, apprised by telephone, Varick called at the office. Waythorn, waiting in his private room, wondered what the others thought of it. The newspapers, at the time of Mrs. Waythorn's marriage, had acquainted their readers with every detail of her previous matrimonial ventures, and Waythorn could fancy the clerks smiling behind Varick's back as he was ushered in.

Varick bore himself admirably. He was easy without being undignified, and Waythorn was conscious of cutting a much less impressive figure. Varick had no experience of business, and the talk prolonged itself for nearly an hour while Waythorn set forth with scrupulous precision the details of the proposed transaction.

"I'm awfully obliged to you," Varick said as he rose. "The fact is I'm not used to having much money to look after, and I don't want to make an ass of myself—" He smiled, and Waythorn could not help noticing that there was something pleasant about his smile. "It feels uncommonly queer to have enough cash to pay one's bills. I'd have sold my soul for it a few years ago!"

Waythorn winced at the allusion. He had heard it rumoured that a lack of funds had been one of the determining causes of the Varick separation, but it did not occur to him that Varick's words were intentional. It seemed more likely that the desire to keep clear of embarrassing topics had fatally drawn him into one. Waythorn did not wish to be outdone in civility.

"We'll do the best we can for you," he said. "I think this is a good thing you're in."

"Oh, I'm sure it's immense. It's awfully good of you—" Varick broke off, embarrassed. "I suppose the thing's settled now—but if—"

"If anything happens before Sellers is about, I'll see you again," said Waythorn quietly. He was glad, in the end, to appear the more self-possessed of the two.

The course of Lily's illness ran smooth, and as the days passed Waythorn grew used to the idea of Haskett's weekly visit. The first time the day came round, he stayed out late, and questioned his wife as to the visit on his return. She replied at once that Haskett had merely seen the nurse downstairs, as the doctor did not wish any one in the child's sick-room till after the crisis.

The following week Waythorn was again conscious of the recurrence of the day, but had forgotten it by the time he came home to dinner. The crisis of the disease came a few days later, with a rapid decline of fever, and the little girl was pronounced out of danger. In the rejoicing which ensued the thought of Haskett passed out of Waythorn's mind, and one afternoon, letting himself into the house with a latch-key, he went straight to his library without noticing a shabby hat and umbrella in the hall.

In the library he found a small effaced-looking man with a thinnish gray beard sitting on the edge of a chair. The stranger might have been a piano-tuner, or one of those mysteriously efficient persons who are summoned in emergencies to adjust some detail of the domestic machinery. He blinked at Waythorn through a pair of gold-rimmed spectacles and said mildly: "Mr. Waythorn, I presume? I am Lily's father."

Waythorn flushed. "Oh—" he stammered uncomfortably. He broke off, disliking to appear rude. Inwardly he was trying to adjust the actual Haskett to the image of him projected by his wife's reminiscences. Waythorn had been allowed to infer that Alice's first husband was a brute.

"I am sorry to intrude," said Haskett, with his over-the-counter politeness.

"Don't mention it," returned Waythorn, collecting himself. "I suppose the nurse has been told?"

"I presume so. I can wait," said Haskett. He had a resigned way of speaking, as though life had worn down his natural powers of resistance.

Waythorn stood on the threshold, nervously pulling off his gloves.

"I'm sorry you've been detained. I will send for the nurse," he said; and as he opened the door he added with an effort: "I'm glad we can give you a good report of Lily." He winced as the *we* slipped out, but Haskett seemed not to notice it.

"Thank you, Mr. Waythorn. It's been an anxious time for me."

"Ah, well, that's past. Soon she'll be able to go to you." Waythorn nodded and passed out.

In his own room he flung himself down with a groan. He hated the womanish sensibility which made him suffer so acutely from the grotesque chances of life. He had known when he married that his wife's former husbands were both living, and that amid the multiplied contacts of modern existence there were a thousand chances to one that he would run against one or the other, yet he found himself as much disturbed by his brief encounter with Haskett as though the law had not obligingly removed all difficulties in the way of their meeting.

Waythorn sprang up and began to pace the room nervously. He had not suffered half as much from his two meetings with Varick. It was Haskett's presence in his own house that made the situation so intolerable. He stood still, hearing steps in the passage.

"This way, please," he heard the nurse say. Haskett was being taken upstairs, then: not a corner of the house but was open to him. Waythorn dropped into another chair, staring vaguely ahead of him. On his dressing-table stood a photograph of Alice, taken when he had first known her. She was Alice Varick then—how fine and exquisite he had thought her! Those were Varick's pearls about her neck. At Waythorn's instance they had been returned before her marriage. Had Haskett ever given her any trinkets—and what had become of them, Waythorn wondered? He realised suddenly that he knew very little of Haskett's past or present situation; but from the man's appearance and manner of speech he could reconstruct with curious precision the surroundings of Alice's first marriage. And it startled him to think that she had, in the background of her life, a phase of existence so different from anything with which he had connected her. Varick, whatever his faults, was a gentleman, in the conventional, traditional sense of the term: the sense which at that moment seemed, oddly enough, to have most meaning to Waythorn. He and Varick had the same social habits, spoke the same language, understood the same allusions. But this other man . . . it was grotesquely uppermost in Waythorn's mind that Haskett had worn a made-up tie attached with an elastic. Why should that ridiculous detail symbolise the whole man? Waythorn was exasperated by his own paltriness, but the fact of the tie expanded, forced itself on him, became as it were the key to Alice's past. He could see her, as Mrs. Haskett, sitting in a "front parlour" furnished in plush, with a pianola, and a copy of "Ben Hur" on the centre-table. He could see her going to the theatre with Haskett—or perhaps even to a "Church Sociable"—she in a "picture hat" and Haskett in a black frock-coat, a little creased, with the made-up tie on an elastic. On the way home they would stop and look at the illuminated shop-windows, lingering over the photographs of New York actresses. On Sunday afternoons Haskett would take her for a walk, pushing Lily ahead of them in a white enamelled perambulator, and Waythorn had a vision of the people they would stop and talk to. He could fancy how pretty Alice must have looked, in a dress adroitly constructed from the hints of a New York fashion-paper, and how she must have looked down on the other women, chafing at her life, and secretly feeling that she belonged in a bigger place.

For the moment his foremost thought was one of wonder at the way in which she had shed the phase of existence which her marriage with Haskett implied. It was as if her whole aspect, every gesture, every inflection, every allusion, were a studied negation of that period of her life. If she had denied being married to Haskett she could hardly have stood more convicted of duplicity than in this obliteration of the self which had been his wife.

Waythorn started up, checking himself in the analysis of her motives. What right had he to create a fantastic effigy of her and then pass judgment on it? She had spoken vaguely of her first marriage as unhappy, had hinted, with becoming reticence, that Haskett had wrought havoc among her young illusions. . . . It was a pity for Waythorn's peace of mind that Haskett's very inoffensiveness shed a new light on the nature of those illusions. A man would rather think that his wife has been brutalised by her first husband than that the process has been reversed.

IV

"Mr. Waythorn, I don't like that French governess of Lily's."

Haskett, subdued and apologetic, stood before Waythorn in the library, revolving his shabby hat in his hand.

Waythorn, surprised in his armchair over the evening paper, stared back perplexedly at his visitor.

"You'll excuse my asking to see you," Haskett continued. "But this is my last visit, and I thought if I could have a word with you it would be a better way than writing to Mrs. Waythorn's lawyer."

Waythorn rose uneasily. He did not like the French governess either; but that was irrelevant.

"I am not so sure of that," he returned stiffly; "but since you wish it I will give your message to—my wife." He always hesitated over the possessive pronoun in addressing Hackett.

The latter sighed. "I don't know as that will help much. She didn't like it when I spoke to her."

Waythorn turned red. "When did you see her?" he asked.

"Not since the first day I came to see Lily—right after she was taken sick. I remarked to her then that I didn't like the governess."

Waythorn made no answer. He remembered distinctly that, after that first visit, he had asked his wife if she had seen Haskett. She had lied to him then, but she had respected his wishes since; and the incident cast a curious light on her character. He was sure she would not have seen Haskett that first day if she had divined that Waythorn would object, and the fact that she did not divine it was almost as disagreeable to the latter as the discovery that she had lied to him.

"I don't like the woman," Haskett was repeating with mild persistency. "She ain't straight, Mr. Waythorn—she'll teach the child to be underhand. I've noticed a change in Lily—she's too anxious to please—and she don't always tell the truth. She used to be the straightest child, Mr. Waythorn—" He broke off, his voice a little thick. "Not but what I want her to have a stylish education," he ended.

Waythorn was touched. "I'm sorry, Mr. Haskett; but frankly, I don't quite see what I can do."

Haskett hesitated. Then he laid his hat on the table, and advanced to the hearth-rug, on which Waythorn was standing. There was nothing aggressive in his manner, but he had the solemnity of a timid man resolved on a decisive measure.

"There's just one thing you can do, Mr. Waythorn," he said. "You can remind Mrs. Waythorn that, by the decree of the courts, I am entitled to have a voice in Lily's bringing up." He paused, and went on more deprecatingly: "I'm not the kind to talk about enforcing my rights, Mr. Waythorn. I don't know as I think a man is entitled to rights he hasn't known how to hold on to; but this business of the child is different. I've never let go there—and I never mean to."

The scene left Waythorn deeply shaken. Shamefacedly, in indirect ways, he had been finding out about Haskett; and all that he had learned was favourable. The little man, in order to be near his daughter, had sold out his share in a profitable business in Utica, and accepted a modest clerkship in a New York manufacturing house. He boarded in a shabby street and had few acquaintances. His passion for Lily filled his life. Waythorn felt that this exploration of Haskett was like groping about with a dark-lantern in his wife's past; but he saw now that there were recesses his lantern had not explored. He had never enquired into the exact circumstances of his wife's first matrimonial rupture. On the surface all had been fair. It was she who had obtained the divorce, and the court had given her the child. But Waythorn knew how many ambiguities such a verdict might cover. The mere fact that Haskett retained a right over his daughter implied an unsuspected compromise. Waythorn was an idealist. He always refused to recognise unpleasant contingencies till he found himself confronted with them, and then he saw them followed by a spectral train of consequences. His next days were thus haunted, and he determined to try to lay the ghosts by conjuring them up in his wife's presence.

When he repeated Haskett's request a flame of anger passed over her face; but she subdued it instantly and spoke with a slight quiver of outraged motherhood.

"It is very ungentlemanly of him," she said.

The word grated on Waythorn. "That is neither here nor there. It's a bare question of rights."

She murmured: "It's not as if he could ever be a help to Lily—"

Waythorn flushed. This was even less to his taste. "The question is," he repeated, "what authority has he over her?"

She looked downward, twisting herself a little in her seat. "I am willing to see him—I thought you objected," she faltered.

In a flash he understood that she knew the extent of Haskett's claims. Perhaps it was not the first time she had resisted them.

"My objecting has nothing to do with it," he said coldly; "if Haskett has a right to be consulted you must consult him."

She burst into tears, and he saw that she expected him to regard her as a victim.

Haskett did not abuse his rights. Waythorn had felt miserably sure that he would not. But the governess was dismissed, and from time to time the little man demanded an interview with Alice. After the first outburst she accepted the situation with her usual adaptability. Haskett had once reminded Waythorn of the piano-tuner, and Mrs. Waythorn, after a month or two, appeared to class him with that domestic familiar. Waythorn could not but respect the father's tenacity. At first he had tried to cultivate the suspicion that Haskett might be "up to" something, that he had an object in securing a foothold in the house. But in his heart Waythorn was sure of Haskett's single-mindedness; he even guessed in the latter a mild contempt for such advantages as his relation with the Waythorns might offer. Haskett's sincerity of purpose made him invulnerable, and his successor had to accept him as a lien on the property.

Mr. Sellers was sent to Europe to recover from his gout, and Varick's affairs hung on Waythorn's hands. The negotiations were prolonged and complicated; they necessitated frequent conferences between the two men, and the interests of the firm forbade Waythorn's suggesting that his client should transfer his business to another office.

Varick appeared well in the transaction. In moments of relaxation his coarse streak appeared, and Waythorn dreaded his geniality; but in the office he was concise and clear-headed, with a flattering deference to Waythorn's judgment. Their business relations being so affably established, it would have been absurd for the two men to ignore each other in society. The first time they met in a drawing-room, Varick took up their intercourse in the same easy key, and his hostess's grateful glance obliged Waythorn to respond to it. After that they ran across each other frequently, and one evening at a ball Waythorn, wandering through the remoter rooms, came upon Varick seated beside his wife. She coloured a little, and faltered in what she was saying; but Varick nodded to Waythorn without rising, and the latter strolled on.

In the carriage, on the way home, he broke out nervously: "I didn't know you spoke to Varick."

Her voice trembled a little. "It's the first time—he happened to be standing near me; I didn't know what to do. It's so awkward, meeting everywhere—and he said you had been very kind about some business."

"That's different," said Waythorn.

She paused a moment. "I'll do just as you wish," she returned pliantly. "I thought it would be less awkward to speak to him when we meet."

Her pliancy was beginning to sicken him. Had she really no will of her own—no theory about her relation to these men? She had accepted Haskett—did she mean to accept Varick? It was "less awkward," as she had said, and her instinct was to evade difficulties or to circumvent them. With sudden vividness Waythorn saw how the instinct had developed. She was "as easy as an old shoe"—a shoe that too many feet had worn. Her elasticity was the result of tension in too many different directions. Alice Haskett—Alice Varick—Alice Waythorn—she had been each in turn, and had left hanging to each name a little of her privacy, a little of her personality, a little of the inmost self where the unknown god abides.

"Yes—it's better to speak to Varick," said Waythorn wearily.

V

The winter wore on, and society took advantage of the Waythorns' acceptance of Varick. Harassed hostesses were grateful to them for bridging over a social difficulty, and Mrs. Waythorn was held up as a miracle of good taste. Some experimental spirits could not resist the diversion of throwing Varick and his former wife together, and there were those who thought he found a zest in the propinquity. But Mrs. Waythorn's conduct remained irreproachable. She neither avoided Varick nor sought him out. Even Waythorn could not but admit that she had discovered the solution of the newest social problem.

He had married her without giving much thought to that problem. He had fancied that a woman can shed her past like a man. But now he saw that Alice was bound to hers both by the circumstances which forced her into continued relation with it, and by the traces it had left on her nature. With grim irony Waythorn compared himself to a member of a syndicate. He held so many shares in his wife's personality and his predecessors were his partners in the business. If there had been any element of passion in the transaction he would have felt less deteriorated by it. The fact that Alice took her change of husbands like a change of weather reduced the situation to mediocrity. He could have forgiven her for blunders, for excesses; for resisting Haskett, for yielding to Varick; for anything but her acquiescence and her tact. She reminded him of a juggler tossing knives; but the knives were blunt and she knew they would never cut her.

And then, gradually, habit formed a protecting surface for his sensibilities. If he paid for each day's comfort with the small change of his illusions, he grew daily to value the comfort more and set less store upon the coin. He had drifted into a dulling propinquity with Haskett and Varick and he took refuge in the cheap revenge of satirising the situation. He even began to reckon up the advantages which accrued from it, to ask himself if it were not better to own a third of a wife who knew how to make a man happy than a whole one who had lacked opportunity to acquire the art. For it *was* an art, and made up, like all others, of concessions, eliminations and embellishments; of lights judiciously thrown and shadows skilfully softened. His wife knew exactly how to manage the lights, and he knew exactly to what training she owed her skill. He even tried to trace the source of his obligations, to discriminate between the influences which had combined to produce his domestic happiness: he perceived that Haskett's commonness had made Alice worship good breeding, while Varick's liberal construction of the marriage bond had taught her to value the conjugal virtues; so that he was directly indebted to his predecessors for the devotion which made his life easy if not inspiring.

From this phase he passed into that of complete acceptance. He ceased to satirise himself because time dulled the irony of the situation and the joke lost its humour with its sting. Even the sight of Haskett's hat on the hall table had ceased to touch the springs of epigram. The hat was often seen there now, for it had been decided that it was better for Lily's father to visit her than for the little girl to go to his boarding-house. Waythorn, having acquiesced in this arrangement, had been surprised to find how little difference it made. Haskett was never obtrusive, and the few visitors who met him on the stairs were unaware of his identity. Waythorn did not know how often he saw Alice, but with himself Haskett was seldom in contact.

One afternoon, however, he learned on entering that Lily's father was waiting to see him. In the library he found Haskett occupying a chair in his usual provisional way. Waythorn always felt grateful to him for not leaning back.

"I hope you'll excuse me, Mr. Waythorn," he said rising. "I wanted to see Mrs. Waythorn about Lily, and your man asked me to wait here till she came in."

"Of course," said Waythorn, remembering that a sudden leak had that morning given over the drawing-room to the plumbers.

He opened his cigar-case and held it out to his visitor, and Haskett's acceptance seemed to mark a fresh stage in their intercourse. The spring evening was chilly, and Waythorn invited his guest to draw up his chair to the fire. He meant to find an excuse to leave Haskett in a moment; but he was tired and cold, and after all the little man no longer jarred on him.

The two were enclosed in the intimacy of their blended cigar-smoke when the door opened and Varick walked into the room. Waythorn rose abruptly. It was the first time that Varick had come to the house, and the surprise of seeing him, combined with the singular inopportuneness of his arrival, gave a new edge to Waythorn's blunted sensibilities. He stared at his visitor without speaking.

Varick seemed too preoccupied to notice his host's embarrassment.

"My dear fellow," he exclaimed in his most expansive tone, "I must apologise for tumbling in on you in this way, but I was too late to catch you down town, and so I thought—"

He stopped short, catching sight of Haskett, and his sanguine colour deepened to a flush which spread vividly under his scant blond hair. But in a moment he recovered himself and nodded slightly. Haskett returned the bow in silence, and Waythorn was still groping for speech when the footman came in carrying a tea-table.

The intrusion offered a welcome vent to Waythorn's nerves. "What the deuce are you bringing this here for?" he said sharply.

"I beg your pardon, sir, but the plumbers are still in the drawing-room, and Mrs. Waythorn said she would have tea in the library." The footman's perfectly respectful tone implied a reflection on Waythorn's reasonableness.

"Oh, very well," said the latter resignedly, and the footman proceeded to open the folding tea-table and set out its complicated appointments. While this interminable process continued the three men stood motionless, watching it with a fascinated stare, till Waythorn, to break the silence, said to Varick: "Won't you have a cigar?"

He held out the case he had just tendered to Haskett, and Varick helped himself with a smile. Waythorn looked about for a match, and finding none, proffered a light from his own cigar. Haskett, in the background, held his ground mildly, examining his cigar-tip now and then, and stepping forward at the right moment to knock its ashes into the fire.

The footman at last withdrew, and Varick immediately began: "If I could just say half a word to you about this business—"

"Certainly," stammered Waythorn; "in the dining-room—"

But as he placed his hand on the door it opened from without, and his wife appeared on the threshold.

She came in fresh and smiling, in her street dress and hat, shedding a fragrance from the boa which she loosened in advancing.

"Shall we have tea in here, dear?" she began; and then she caught sight of Varick. Her smile deepened, veiling a slight tremor of surprise.

"Why, how do you do?" she said with a distinct note of pleasure.

As she shook hands with Varick she saw Haskett standing behind him. Her smile faded for a moment, but she recalled it quickly, with a scarcely perceptible side-glance at Waythorn.

"How do you do, Mr. Haskett?" she said, and shook hands with him a shade less cordially.

The three men stood awkwardly before her, till Varick, always the most self-possessed, dashed into an explanatory phrase.

"We—I had to see Waythorn a moment on business," he stammered, brick-red from chin to nape.

Haskett stepped forward with his air of mild obstinacy. "I am sorry to intrude; but you appointed five o'clock—" he directed his resigned glance to the time-piece on the mantel.

She swept aside their embarrassment with a charming gesture of hospitality.

"I'm so sorry—I'm always late; but the afternoon was so lovely." She stood drawing off her gloves, propitiatory and graceful, diffusing about her a sense of ease and familiarity in which the situation lost its grotesqueness. "But before talking business," she added brightly, "I'm sure every one wants a cup of tea."

She dropped into her low chair by the tea-table, and the two visitors, as if drawn by her smile, advanced to receive the cups she held out.

She glanced about for Waythorn, and he took the third cup with a laugh.

Roman Fever

From the table at which they had been lunching two American ladies of ripe but well-cared-for middle age moved across the lofty terrace of the Roman restaurant and, leaning on its parapet, looked first at each other, and then down on the outspread glories of the Palatine and the Forum, with the same expression of vague but benevolent approval.

As they leaned there a girlish voice echoed up gaily from the stairs leading to the court below. "Well, come along, then," it cried, not to them but to an invisible companion, "and let's leave the young things to their knitting"; and a voice as fresh laughed back: "Oh, look here, Babs, not actually *knitting*—" "Well, I mean figuratively," rejoined the first. "After all, we haven't left our poor parents much else to do. . . ." and at that point the turn of the stairs engulfed the dialogue.

The two ladies looked at each other again, this time with a tinge of smiling embarrassment, and the smaller and paler one shook her head and colored slightly.

"Barbara!" she murmured, sending an unheard rebuke after the mocking voice in the stairway.

The other lady, who was fuller, and higher in color, with a small determined nose supported by vigorous black eyebrows, gave a good-humored laugh. "That's what our daughters think of us!"

Her companion replied by a deprecating gesture. "Not of us individually. We must remember that. It's just the collective modern idea of Mothers. And you see—" Half-guiltily she drew from her handsomely mounted black handbag a twist of crimson silk run through by two fine knitting needles. "One never knows," she murmured. "The new system has certainly given us a good deal of time to kill; and sometimes I get tired just looking—even at this." Her gesture was now addressed to the stupendous scene at their feet.

The dark lady laughed again, and they both relapsed upon the view, contemplating it in silence, with a sort of diffused serenity which might have been borrowed from the spring effulgence of the Roman skies. The luncheon hour was long past, and the two had their end of the vast terrace to themselves. At its opposite extremity a few groups, detained by a lingering look at the outspread city, were gathering up guidebooks and fumbling for tips. The last of them scattered, and the two ladies were alone on the air washed height.

"Well, I don't see why we shouldn't just stay here," said Mrs. Slade, the lady of the high color and energetic brows. Two derelict basket chairs stood near, and she pushed them into the angle of the parapet, and settled herself in one, her gaze upon the Palatine. "After all, it's still the most beautiful view in the world."

"It always will be, to me," assented her friend Mrs. Ansley, with so slight a stress on the "me" that Mrs. Slade, though she noticed it, wondered if it were not merely accidental, like the random underlinings of old-fashioned letter writers.

"Grace Ansley was always old-fashioned," she thought; and added aloud, with a retrospective smile: "It's a view we've both been familiar with for a good many years. When we first met here we were younger than our girls are now. You remember?"

"Oh, yes, I remember," murmured Mrs. Ansley, with the same undefinable stress. "There's that headwaiter wondering," she interpolated. She was evidently far less sure than her companion of herself and of her rights in the world.

"I'll cure him of wondering," said Mrs. Slade, stretching her hand toward a bag as discreetly opulent-looking as Mrs. Ansley's. Signing to the headwaiter, she explained that she and her friend were old lovers of Rome, and would like to spend the end of the afternoon looking down on the view—that is, if it did not disturb the service? The headwaiter, bowing over her gratuity, assured her that the ladies were most welcome, and would be still more so if they would condescend to remain for dinner. A full-moon night, they would remember. . . .

Mrs. Slade's black brows drew together, as though references to the moon were out of place and even unwelcome. But she smiled away her frown as the headwaiter retreated. "Well, why not? We might do worse. There's no knowing, I suppose, when the girls will be back. Do you even know back from *where?* I don't!"

Mrs. Ansley again colored slightly. "I think those young Italian aviators we met at the Embassy invited them to fly to Tarquinia for tea. I suppose they'll want to wait and fly back by moonlight."

"Moonlight—moonlight! What a part it still plays. Do you suppose they're as sentimental as we were?"

"I've come to the conclusion that I don't in the least know what they are," said Mrs. Ansley. "And perhaps we didn't know much more about each other."

"No; perhaps we didn't."

Her friend gave her a shy glance. "I never should have supposed you were sentimental, Alida."

"Well, perhaps I wasn't." Mrs. Slade drew her lids together in retrospect; and for a few moments the two ladies, who had been intimate since childhood, reflected how little they knew each other. Each one, of course, had a label ready to attach to the other's name; Mrs. Delphin Slade, for instance, would have told herself, or anyone who asked her, that Mrs. Horace Ansley, twenty-five years ago, had been exquisitely lovely—no, you wouldn't believe it, would you? . . . though, of course, still charming, distinguished. . . . Well, as a girl she had been exquisite; far more beautiful than her daughter Barbara, though certainly Babs, according to the new standards at any rate, was more effective—had more *edge,* as they say. Funny where she got it, with those two nullities as parents. Yes; Horace Ansley was—well, just the duplicate of his wife. Museum specimens of old New York. Good-looking, irreproachable, exemplary. Mrs. Slade and Mrs. Ansley had lived opposite each other—actually as well as figuratively—for years. When the drawing-room curtains in No. 20 East 73rd Street were renewed, No. 23, across the way, was always aware of it. And of all the movings, buyings, travels, anniversaries, illnesses—the tame chronicle of an estimable pair. Little of it escaped Mrs. Slade. But she had grown bored with it by the time her husband made his big *coup* in Wall Street, and when they bought in upper Park Avenue had already begun to think: "I'd rather live opposite a speakeasy for a change; at least one might see it raided." The idea of seeing Grace raided was so amusing that (before the move) she launched it at a woman's lunch. It made a hit, and went the rounds—she sometimes wondered if it had crossed the street, and reached Mrs. Ansley. She hoped not, but didn't much mind. Those were the days when respectability was at a discount, and it did the irreproachable no harm to laugh at them a little.

A few years later, and not many months apart, both ladies lost their husbands. There was an appropriate exchange of wreaths and condolences, and a brief renewal of intimacy in the half-shadow of their mourning; and now, after another interval, they had run across each other in Rome, at the same hotel, each of them the modest appendage of a salient daughter. The similarity of their lot had again drawn them together, lending itself to mild jokes, and the mutual confession that, if in old days it must have been tiring to "keep up" with daughters, it was now, at times, a little dull not to.

No doubt, Mrs. Slade reflected, she felt her unemployment more than poor Grace ever would. It was a big drop from being the wife of Delphin Slade to being his widow. She had always regarded herself (with a certain conjugal pride) as his equal in social gifts, as contributing her full share to the making of the exceptional couple they were: but the difference after his death was irremediable. As the wife of the famous corporation lawyer, always with an international case or two on hand, every day brought its exciting and unexpected obligation: the impromptu entertaining of eminent colleagues from abroad, the hurried dashes on legal business to London, Paris or Rome, where the entertaining was so handsomely reciprocated; the amusement of hearing in her wake: "What, that handsome woman with the good clothes and the eyes is Mrs. Slade—*the* Slade's wife? Really? Generally the wives of celebrities are such frumps."

Yes; being *the* Slade's widow was a dullish business after that. In living up to such a husband all her faculties had been engaged; now she had only her daughter to live up to, for the son who seemed to have inherited his father's gifts had died suddenly in boyhood. She had fought through that agony because her husband was there, to be helped and to help; now, after the father's death, the thought of the boy had become unbearable. There was nothing left but to mother her daughter; and dear Jenny was such a perfect daughter that she needed no excessive mothering. "Now with Babs Ansley I don't know that I *should* be so quiet," Mrs. Slade sometimes half-enviously reflected; but Jenny, who was younger than her brilliant friend, was that rare accident, an extremely pretty girl who somehow made youth and prettiness seem as safe as their absence. It was all perplexing—and to Mrs. Slade a little boring. She wished that Jenny would fall in love—with the wrong man, even; that she might have to be watched, out-maneuvered, rescued. And instead, it was Jenny who watched her mother, kept her out of drafts, made sure that she had taken her tonic. . . .

Mrs. Ansley was much less articulate than her friend, and her mental portrait of Mrs. Slade was slighter, and drawn with fainter touches. "Alida Slade's awfully brilliant; but not as brilliant as she thinks," would have summed it up; though she would have added, for the enlightenment of strangers, that Mrs. Slade had been an extremely dashing girl; much more so than her daughter, who was pretty, of course, and clever in a way, but had none of her mother's—well, "vividness," someone had once called it. Mrs. Ansley would take up current words like this, and cite them in quotation marks, as unheard-of audacities. No; Jenny was not like her mother. Sometimes Mrs. Ansley thought Alida Slade was disappointed; on the whole she had had a sad life. Full of failures and mistakes; Mrs. Ansley had always been rather sorry for her. . . .

So these two ladies visualized each other, each through the wrong end of her little telescope.

II

For a long time they continued to sit side by side without speaking. It seemed as though, to both, there was a relief in laying down their somewhat futile activities in the presence of the vast Memento Mori which faced them. Mrs. Slade sat quite still, her eyes fixed on the golden slope of the Palace of the Caesars, and after a while Mrs. Ansley ceased to fidget with her bag, and she too sank into meditation. Like many intimate friends, the two ladies had never before had occasion to be silent together, and Mrs. Ansley was slightly embarrassed by what seemed, after so many years, a new stage in their intimacy, and one with which she did not yet know how to deal.

Suddenly the air was full of that deep clangor of bells which periodically covers Rome with a roof of silver. Mrs. Slade glanced at her wristwatch. "Five o'clock already," she said, as though surprised.

Mrs. Ansley suggested interrogatively: "There's bridge at the Embassy at five." For a long time Mrs. Slade did not answer. She appeared to be lost in contemplation, and Mrs. Ansley thought the remark had escaped her. But after a while she said, as if speaking out of a dream: "Bridge, did you say? Not unless you want to. . . . But I don't think I will, you know."

"Oh, no," Mrs. Ansley hastened to assure her. "I don't care to at all. It's so lovely here; and so full of old memories, as you say." She settled herself in her chair, and almost furtively drew forth her knitting. Mrs. Slade took sideway note of this activity, but her own beautifully cared-for hands remained motionless on her knee.

"I was just thinking," she said slowly, "what different things Rome stands for to each generation of travelers. To our grandmothers, Roman fever; to our mothers, sentimental dangers—how we used to be guarded!—to our daughters, no more dangers than the middle of Main Street. They don't know it—but how much they're missing!"

The long golden light was beginning to pale, and Mrs. Ansley lifted her knitting a little closer to her eyes. "Yes; how we were guarded!"

"I always used to think," Mrs. Slade continued, "that our mothers had a much more difficult job than our grandmothers. When Roman fever stalked the streets it must have been comparatively easy to gather in the girls at the danger hour; but when you and I were young, with such beauty calling us, and the spice of disobedience thrown in, and no worse risk than catching cold during the cool hour after sunset, the mothers used to be put to it to keep us in—didn't they?"

She turned again toward Mrs. Ansley, but the latter had reached a delicate point in her knitting. "One, two, three—slip two; yes, they must have been," she assented, without looking up.

Mrs. Slade's eyes rested on her with a deepened attention. "She can knit—in the face of *this!* How like her. . . ."

Mrs. Slade leaned back, brooding, her eyes ranging from the ruins which faced her to the long green hollow of the Forum, the fading glow of the church fronts beyond it, and the outlying immensity of the Colosseum. Suddenly she thought: "It's all very well to say that our girls have done away with sentiment and moonlight. But if Babs Ansley isn't out to catch that young aviator—the one who's a Marchese—then I don't know anything. And Jenny has no chance beside her. I know that too. I wonder if that's why Grace Ansley likes the two girls to go everywhere together? My poor Jenny as a foil—!" Mrs. Slade gave a hardly audible laugh, and at the sound Mrs. Ansley dropped her knitting.

"Yes—?"

"I—oh, nothing. I was only thinking how your Babs carries everything before her. That Campolieri boy is one of the best matches in Rome. Don't look so innocent, my dear—you know he is. And I was wondering, ever so respectfully, you understand . . . wondering how two such exemplary characters as you and Horace had managed to produce anything quite so dynamic." Mrs. Slade laughed again, with a touch of asperity.

Mrs. Ansley's hands lay inert across her needles. She looked straight out at the great accumulated wreckage of passion and splendor at her feet. But her small profile was almost expressionless. At length she said: "I think you overrate Babs, my dear."

Mrs. Slade's tone grew easier. "No, I don't. I appreciate her. And perhaps envy you. Oh, my girl's perfect; if I were a chronic invalid I'd—well, I think I'd rather be in Jenny's hands. There must be times . . . but there! I always wanted a brilliant daughter . . . and never quite understood why I got an angel instead."

Mrs. Ansley echoed her laugh in a faint murmur. "Babs is an angel too."

"Of course—of course! But she's got rainbow wings. Well, they're wandering by the sea with their young men; and here we sit . . . and it all brings back the past a little too acutely."

Mrs. Ansley had resumed her knitting. One might almost have imagined (if one had known her less well, Mrs. Slade reflected) that, for her also, too many memories rose from the lengthening shadows of those august ruins. But no; she was simply absorbed in her work. What was there for her to worry about? She knew that Babs would almost certainly come back engaged to the extremely eligible Campolieri. "And she'll sell the New York house, and settle down near them in Rome, and never be in their way . . . she's much too tactful. But she'll have an excellent cook, and just the right people in for bridge and cocktails . . . and a perfectly peaceful old age among her grandchildren."

Mrs. Slade broke off this prophetic flight with a recoil of self-disgust. There was no one of whom she had less right to think unkindly than of Grace Ansley. Would she never cure herself of envying her? Perhaps she had begun too long ago.

She stood up and leaned against the parapet, filling her troubled eyes with the tranquilizing magic of the hour. But instead of tranquilizing her the sight seemed to increase her exasperation. Her gaze turned toward the Colosseum. Already its golden flank was drowned in purple shadow, and above it the sky curved crystal clear, without light or color. It was the moment when afternoon and evening hang balanced in mid-heaven.

Mrs. Slade turned back and laid her hand on her

friend's arm. The gesture was so abrupt that Mrs. Ansley looked up, startled.

"The sun's set. You're not afraid, my dear?"

"Afraid—?"

"Of Roman fever or pneumonia? I remember how ill you were that winter. As a girl you had a very delicate throat, hadn't you?"

"Oh, we're all right up here. Down below, in the Forum, it does get deathly cold, all of a sudden . . . but not here."

"Ah, of course you know because you had to be so careful." Mrs. Slade turned back to the parapet. She thought: "I must make one more effort not to hate her." Aloud she said: "Whenever I look at the Forum from up here, I remember that story about a great-aunt of yours, wasn't she? A dreadfully wicked great-aunt?"

"Oh, yes; great-aunt Harriet. The one who was supposed to have sent her young sister out to the Forum after sunset to gather a night-blooming flower for her album. All our great-aunts and grandmothers used to have albums of dried flowers."

Mrs. Slade nodded. "But she really sent her because they were in love with the same man—"

"Well, that was the family tradition. They said Aunt Harriet confessed it years afterward. At any rate, the poor little sister caught the fever and died. Mother used to frighten us with the story when we were children."

"And you frightened *me* with it, that winter when you and I were here as girls. The winter I was engaged to Delphin."

Mrs. Ansley gave a faint laugh. "Oh, did I?

Really frightened you? I don't believe you're easily frightened."

"Not often; but I was then. I was easily frightened because I was too happy. I wonder if you know what that means?"

"I—yes . . ." Mrs. Ansley faltered.

"Well, I suppose that was why the story of your wicked aunt made such an impression on me. And I thought: 'There's no more Roman fever, but the Forum is deathly cold after sunset—especially after a hot day. And the Colosseum's even colder and damper'."

"The Colosseum—?"

"Yes. It wasn't easy to get in, after the gates were locked for the night. Far from easy. Still, in those days it could be managed; it *was* managed, often. Lovers met there who couldn't meet elsewhere. You knew that?"

"I—I dare say. I don't remember."

"You don't remember? You don't remember going to visit some ruins or other one evening, just after dark, and catching a bad chill? You were supposed to have gone to see the moon rise. People always said that expedition was what caused your illness."

There was a moment's silence; then Mrs. Ansley rejoined: "Did they? It was all so long ago."

"Yes. And you got well again—so it didn't matter. But I suppose it struck your friends—the reason given for your illness, I mean—because everybody knew you were so prudent on account of your throat, and your mother took such care of you. . . . You *had* been out late sight-seeing, hadn't you, that night?"

"Perhaps I had. The most prudent girls aren't always prudent. What made you think of it now?"

Mrs. Slade seemed to have no answer ready. But after a moment she broke out: "Because I simply can't bear it any longer—!"

Mrs. Ansley lifted her head quickly. Her eyes were wide and very pale. "Can't bear what?"

"Why—your not knowing that I've always known why you went."

"Why I went—?"

"Yes. You think I'm bluffing, don't you? Well, you went to meet the man I was engaged to—and I can repeat every word of the letter that took you there."

While Mrs. Slade spoke Mrs. Ansley had risen unsteadily to her feet. Her bag, her knitting and gloves, slid in a panic-stricken heap to the ground. She looked at Mrs. Slade as though she were looking at a ghost.

"No, no—don't," she faltered out.

"Why not? Listen, if you don't believe me. 'My one darling, things can't go on like this. I must see you alone. Come to the Colosseum immediately after dark tomorrow. There will be somebody to let you in. No one whom you need fear will suspect'—but perhaps you've forgotten what the letter said?"

Mrs. Ansley met the challenge with an unexpected composure. Steadying herself against the chair she looked at her friend, and replied: "No; I know it by heart too."

"And the signature? 'Only *your* D.S.' Was that it? I'm right, am I? That was the letter that took you out that evening after dark?"

Mrs. Ansley was still looking at her. It seemed to Mrs. Slade that a slow struggle was going on behind the voluntarily controlled mask of her small quiet face. "I shouldn't have thought she had herself so well in hand," Mrs. Slade reflected, almost resentfully. But at this moment Mrs. Ansley spoke. "I don't know how you knew. I burnt that letter at once."

"Yes; you would, naturally—you're so prudent!" The sneer was open now. "And if you burnt the letter you're wondering how on earth I know what was in it. That's it, isn't it?"

Mrs. Slade waited, but Mrs. Ansley did not speak.

"Well, my dear, I know what was in that letter because I wrote it!"

"You wrote it?"

"Yes."

The two women stood for a minute staring at each other in the last golden light. Then Mrs. Ansley dropped back into her chair. "Oh," she murmured, and covered her face with her hands.

Mrs. Slade waited nervously for another word or movement. None came, and at length she broke out: "I horrify you."

Mrs. Ansley's hands dropped to her knee. The face they uncovered was streaked with tears. "I wasn't thinking of you. I was thinking—it was the only letter I ever had from him!"

"And I wrote it. Yes; I wrote it! But I was the girl he was engaged to. Did you happen to remember that?"

Mrs. Ansley's head drooped again. "I'm not trying to excuse myself . . . I remembered. . . ."

"And still you went?"

"Still I went."

Mrs. Slade stood looking down on the small bowed figure at her side. The flame of her wrath had already sunk, and she wondered why she had ever thought there would be any satisfaction in inflicting so purposeless a wound on her friend. But she had to justify herself.

"You do understand? I'd found out—and I hated you, hated you. I knew you were in love with Delphin—and I was afraid; afraid of you, of your quiet ways, your sweetness . . . your . . . well, I wanted you out of the way, that's all. Just a few weeks; just till I was sure of him. So in a blind fury I wrote that letter . . . I don't know why I'm telling you now."

"I suppose," said Mrs. Ansley slowly, "it's because you've always gone on hating me."

"Perhaps. Or because I wanted to get the whole thing off my mind." She paused. "I'm glad you destroyed the letter. Of course I never thought you'd die."

Mrs. Ansley relapsed into silence, and Mrs. Slade, leaning above her, was conscious of a strange sense of isolation, of being cut off from the warm current of human communion. "You think me a monster!"

"I don't know. . . . It was the only letter I had, and you say he didn't write it?"

"Ah, how you care for him still!"

"I cared for that memory," said Mrs. Ansley.

Mrs. Slade continued to look down on her. She seemed physically reduced by the blow—as if, when she got up, the wind might scatter her like a puff of dust. Mrs. Slade's jealousy suddenly leapt up again at the sight. All these years the woman had been living on that letter. How she must have loved him, to treasure the mere memory of its ashes! The letter of the man her friend was engaged to. Wasn't it she who was the monster?

"You tried your best to get him away from me, didn't you? But you failed; and I kept him. That's all."

"Yes. That's all."

"I wish now I hadn't told you. I'd no idea you'd feel about it as you do; I thought you'd be amused. It all happened so long ago, as you say; and you must do me the justice to remember that I had no reason to think you'd ever taken it seriously. How could I, when you were married to Horace Ansley two months afterward? As soon as you could get out of bed your mother rushed you off to Florence and married you. People were rather surprised—they wondered at its being done so quickly; but I thought I knew. I had an idea you did it out of *pique*—to be able to say you'd got ahead of Delphin and me. Girls have such silly reasons for doing the most serious things. And your marrying so soon convinced me that you'd never really cared."

"Yes. I suppose it would," Mrs. Ansley assented.

The clear heaven overhead was emptied of all its gold. Dusk spread over it, abruptly darkening the Seven Hills. Here and there lights began to twinkle through the foliage at their feet. Steps were coming and going on the deserted terrace—waiters looking out of the doorway at the head of the stairs, then reappearing with trays and napkins and flasks of wine. Tables were moved, chairs straightened. A feeble string of electric lights flickered out. Some vases of faded flowers were carried away, and brought back replenished. A stout lady in a dust coat suddenly appeared, asking in broken Italian if anyone had seen the elastic band which held together her tattered Baedeker. She poked with her stick under the table at which she had lunched, the waiters assisting.

The corner where Mrs. Slade and Mrs. Ansley sat was still shadowy and deserted. For a long time neither of them spoke. At length Mrs. Slade began again: "I suppose I did it as a sort of joke—"

"A joke?"

"Well, girls are ferocious sometimes, you know. Girls in love especially. And I remember laughing to myself all that evening at the idea that you were waiting around there in the dark, dodging out of sight, listening for every sound, trying to get in—Of course I was upset when I heard you were so ill afterward."

Mrs. Ansley had not moved for a long time. But now she turned slowly toward her companion. "But I didn't wait. He'd arranged everything. He was there. We were let in at once," she said.

Mrs. Slade sprang up from her leaning position. "Delphin there? They let you in?—Ah, now you're lying!" she burst out with violence.

Mrs. Ansley's voice grew clearer, and full of surprise. "But of course he was there. Naturally he came—"

"Came? How did he know he'd find you there? You must be raving!"

Mrs. Ansley hesitated, as though reflecting. "But I answered the letter. I told him I'd be there. So he came."

Mrs. Slade flung her hands up to her face. "Oh, God—you answered! I never thought of your answering. . . ."

"It's odd you never thought of it, if you wrote the letter."

"Yes. I was blind with rage."

Mrs. Ansley rose, and drew her fur scarf about her. "It is cold here. We'd better go . . . I'm sorry for you," she said, as she clasped the fur about her throat.

The unexpected words sent a pang through Mrs. Slade. "Yes; we'd better go." She gathered up her bag and cloak. "I don't know why you should be sorry for me," she muttered.

Mrs. Ansley stood looking away from her toward the dusky secret mass of the Colosseum. "Well—because I didn't have to wait that night."

Mrs. Slade gave an unquiet laugh. "Yes; I was beaten there. But I oughtn't to begrudge it to you, I suppose. At the end of all these years. After all, I had everything; I had him for twenty-five years. And you had nothing but that one letter that he didn't write."

Mrs. Ansley was again silent. At length she turned toward the door of the terrace. She took a step, and turned back, facing her companion.

"I had Barbara," she said, and began to move ahead of Mrs. Slade toward the stairway.

WILLA CATHER

Paul's Case

A STUDY IN TEMPERAMENT

It was Paul's afternoon to appear before the faculty of the Pittsburgh High School to account for his various misdemeanors. He had been suspended a week ago, and his father had called at the Principal's office and confessed his perplexity about his son. Paul entered the faculty room suave and smiling. His clothes were a trifle outgrown, and the tan velvet on the collar of his open overcoat was frayed and worn; but for all that there was something of the dandy about him, and he wore an opal pin in his neatly knotted black four-in-hand, and a red carnation in his buttonhole. This latter adornment the faculty somehow felt was not properly significant of the contrite spirit befitting a boy under the ban of suspension.

Paul was tall for his age and very thin, with high, cramped shoulders and a narrow chest. His eyes were remarkable for a certain hysterical brilliancy, and he continually used them in a conscious, theatrical sort of way, peculiarly offensive in a boy. The pupils were abnormally large, as though he were addicted to belladonna, but there was a glassy glitter about them which that drug does not produce.

When questioned by the Principal as to why he was there Paul stated, politely enough, that he wanted to come back to school. This was a lie, but Paul was quite accustomed to lying; found it, indeed, indispensable for overcoming friction. His teachers were asked to state their respective charges against him, which they did with such a rancor and aggrievedness as evinced that this was not a usual case. Disorder and impertinence were among the offenses named, yet each of his instructors felt that it was scarcely possible to put into words the real cause of the trouble, which lay in a sort of hysterically defiant manner of the boy's; in the contempt which they all knew he felt for them, and which he seemingly made not the least effort to conceal. Once, when he had been making a synopsis of a paragraph at the blackboard, his English teacher had stepped to his side and attempted to guide his hand. Paul had started back with a shudder and thrust his hands violently behind him. The astonished woman could scarcely have been more hurt and embarrassed had he struck at her. The insult was so involuntary and definitely personal as to be unforgettable. In one way and another he had made all his teachers, men and women alike, conscious of the same feeling of physical aversion. In one class he habitually sat with his hand shading his eyes; in another he always looked out of the window during the recitation; in another he made a running commentary on the lecture, with humorous intention.

His teachers felt this afternoon that his whole

attitude was symbolized by his shrug and his flippantly red carnation flower, and they fell upon him without mercy, his English teacher leading the pack. He stood through it smiling, his pale lips parted over his white teeth. (His lips were continually twitching, and he had a habit of raising his eyebrows that was contemptuous and irritating to the last degree.) Older boys than Paul had broken down and shed tears under that baptism of fire, but his set smile did not once desert him, and his only sign of discomfort was the nervous trembling of the fingers that toyed with the buttons of his overcoat, and an occasional jerking of the other hand that held his hat. Paul was always smiling, always glancing about him, seeming to feel that people might be watching him and trying to detect something. This conscious expression, since it was as far as possible from boyish mirthfulness, was usually attributed to insolence or "smartness."

As the inquisition proceeded one of his instructors repeated an impertinent remark of the boy's, and the Principal asked him whether he thought that a courteous speech to have made a woman. Paul shrugged his shoulders slightly and his eyebrows twitched.

"I don't know," he replied. "I didn't mean to be polite or impolite, either. I guess it's a sort of way I have of saying things regardless."

The Principal, who was a sympathetic man, asked him whether he didn't think that a way it would be well to get rid of. Paul grinned and said he guessed so. When he was told that he could go he bowed gracefully and went out. His bow was but a repetition of the scandalous red carnation.

His teachers were in despair, and his drawing master voiced the feeling of them all when he declared there was something about the boy which none of them understood. He added: "I don't really believe that smile of his comes altogether from insolence; there's something sort of haunted about it. The boy is not strong, for one thing. I happen to know that he was born in Colorado, only a few months before his mother died out there of a long illness. There is something wrong about the fellow."

The drawing master had come to realize that, in looking at Paul, one saw only his white teeth and the forced animation of his eyes. One warm afternoon the boy had gone to sleep at his drawing board, and his master had noted with amazement what a white, blue-veined face it was; drawn and wrinkled like an old man's about the eyes, the lips twitching even in his sleep, and stiff with a nervous tension that drew them back from his teeth.

His teachers left the building dissatisfied and unhappy; humiliated to have felt so vindictive toward a mere boy, to have uttered this feeling in cutting terms, and to have set each other on, as it were, in the gruesome game of intemperate reproach. Some of them remembered having seen a miserable street cat set at bay by a ring of tormentors.

As for Paul, he ran down the hill whistling the "Soldiers' Chorus" from *Faust,* looking wildly behind him now and then to see whether some of his teachers were not there to writhe under his lightheartedness. As it was now late in the afternoon and Paul was on duty that evening as usher at

Carnegie Hall, he decided that he would not go home to supper. When he reached the concert hall the doors were not yet open and, as it was chilly outside, he decided to go up into the picture gallery—always deserted at this hour—where there were some of Raffelli's gay studies of Paris streets and an airy blue Venetian scene or two that always exhilarated him. He was delighted to find no one in the gallery but the old guard, who sat in one corner, a newspaper on his knee, a black patch over one eye and the other closed. Paul possessed himself of the place and walked confidently up and down, whistling under his breath. After a while he sat down before a blue Rico and lost himself. When he bethought him to look at his watch, it was after seven o'clock, and he rose with a start and ran downstairs, making a face at Augustus, peering out from the cast room, and an evil gesture at the Venus de Milo as he passed her on the stairway.

When Paul reached the ushers' dressing room half a dozen boys were there already, and he began excitedly to tumble into his uniform. It was one of the few that at all approached fitting, and Paul thought it very becoming—though he knew that the tight, straight coat accentuated his narrow chest, about which he was exceedingly sensitive. He was always considerably excited while he dressed, twanging all over to the tuning of the strings and the preliminary flourishes of the horns in the music room; but tonight he seemed quite beside himself, and he teased and plagued the boys until, telling him that he was crazy, they put him down on the floor and sat on him.

Somewhat calmed by his suppression, Paul

dashed out to the front of the house to seat the early comers. He was a model usher; gracious and smiling he ran up and down the aisles; nothing was too much trouble for him; he carried messages and brought programs as though it were his greatest pleasure in life, and all the people in his section thought him a charming boy, feeling that he remembered and admired them. As the house filled, he grew more and more vivacious and animated, and the color came to his cheeks and lips. It was very much as though this were a great reception and Paul were the host. Just as the musicians came out to take their places, his English teacher arrived with checks for the seats which a prominent manufacturer had taken for the season. She betrayed some embarrassment when she handed Paul the tickets, and a hauteur which subsequently made her feel very foolish. Paul was startled for a moment, and had the feeling of wanting to put her out; what business had she here among all these fine people and gay colors? He looked her over and decided that she was not appropriately dressed and must be a fool to sit downstairs in such togs. The tickets had probably been sent her out of kindness, he reflected as he put down a seat for her, and she had about as much right to sit there as he had.

When the symphony began Paul sank into one of the rear seats with a long sigh of relief, and lost himself, as he had done before the Rico. It was not that symphonies, as such, meant anything in particular to Paul, but the first sigh of the instruments seemed to free some hilarious and potent spirit within him; something that struggled there like the genie in the bottle found by the Arab fisherman. He felt a sudden zest of life; the lights danced before his eyes and the concert hall blazed into unimaginable splendor. When the soprano soloist came on Paul forgot even the nastiness of his teacher's being there and gave himself up to the peculiar stimulus such personages always had for him. The soloist chanced to be a German woman, by no means in her first youth, and the mother of many children; but she wore an elaborate gown and a tiara, and above all she had that indefinable air of achievement, that world-shine upon her, which, in Paul's eyes, made her a veritable queen of Romance.

After a concert was over Paul was always irritable and wretched until he got to sleep, and tonight he was even more than usually restless. He had the feeling of not being able to let down, of its being impossible to give up this delicious excitement which was the only thing that could be called living at all. During the last number he withdrew and, after hastily changing his clothes in the dressing room, slipped out to the side door where the soprano's carriage stood. Here he began pacing rapidly up and down the walk, waiting to see her come out.

Over yonder, the Schenley, in its vacant stretch, loomed big and square through the fine rain, the windows of its twelve stories glowing like those of a lighted cardboard house under a Christmas tree. All the actors and singers of the better class stayed there when they were in the city, and a number of the big manufacturers of the place lived there in the winter. Paul had often hung about the hotel, watching the people go in and out, longing to enter and leave schoolmasters and dull care behind him forever.

At last the singer came out, accompanied by the conductor, who helped her into her carriage and closed the door with a cordial *auf wiedersehen* which set Paul to wondering whether she were not an old sweetheart of his. Paul followed the carriage over to the hotel, walking so rapidly as not to be far from the entrance when the singer alighted, and disappeared behind the swinging glass doors that were opened by a Negro in a tall hat and a long coat. In the moment that the door was ajar it seemed to Paul that he, too, entered. He seemed to feel himself go after her up the steps, into the warm, lighted building, into an exotic, tropical world of shiny, glistening surfaces and basking ease. He reflected upon the mysterious dishes that were brought into the dining room, the green bottles in buckets of ice, as he had seen them in the supper party pictures of the *Sunday World* supplement. A quick gust of wind brought the rain down with sudden vehemence, and Paul was startled to find that he was still outside in the slush of the gravel driveway; that his boots were letting in the water and his scanty overcoat was clinging wet about him; that the lights in front of the concert hall were out and that the rain was driving in sheets between him and the orange glow of the windows above him. There it was, what he wanted—tangibly before him, like the fairy world of a Christmas pantomime—but mocking spirits stood guard at the doors, and, as the rain beat in his face,

Paul wondered whether he were destined always to shiver in the black night outside, looking up at it.

He turned and walked reluctantly toward the car tracks. The end had to come sometime; his father in his nightclothes at the top of the stairs, explanations that did not explain, hastily improvised fictions that were forever tripping him up, his upstairs room and its horrible yellow wallpaper, the creaking bureau with the greasy plush collarbox, and over his painted wooden bed the pictures of George Washington and John Calvin, and the framed motto, "Feed my Lambs," which had been worked in red worsted by his mother.

Half an hour later Paul alighted from his car and went slowly down one of the side streets off the main thoroughfare. It was a highly respectable street, where all the houses were exactly alike, and where businessmen of moderate means begot and reared large families of children, all of whom went to Sabbath school and learned the shorter catechism, and were interested in arithmetic; all of whom were as exactly alike as their homes, and of a piece with the monotony in which they lived. Paul never went up Cordelia Street without a shudder of loathing. His home was next to the house of the Cumberland minister. He approached it tonight with the nerveless sense of defeat, the hopeless feeling of sinking back forever into ugliness and commonness that he had always had when he came home. The moment he turned into Cordelia Street he felt the waters close above his head. After each of these orgies of living he experienced all the physical depression which follows a debauch; the loathing of respectable beds, of common food, of a house penetrated by kitchen odors; a shuddering repulsion for the flavorless, colorless mass of everyday existence; a morbid desire for cool things and soft lights and fresh flowers.

The nearer he approached the house, the more absolutely unequal Paul felt to the sight of it all: his ugly sleeping chamber; the cold bathroom with the grimy zinc tub, the cracked mirror, the dripping spiggots; his father, at the top of the stairs, his hairy legs sticking out from his nightshirt, his feet thrust into carpet slippers. He was so much later than usual that there would certainly be inquiries and reproaches. Paul stopped short before the door. He felt that he could not be accosted by his father tonight; that he could not toss again on that miserable bed. He would not go in. He would tell his father that he had no carfare and it was raining so hard he had gone home with one of the boys and stayed all night.

Meanwhile, he was wet and cold. He went around to the back of the house and tried one of the basement windows, found it open, raised it cautiously, and scrambled down the cellar wall to the floor. There he stood, holding his breath, terrified by the noise he had made, but the floor above him was silent, and there was no creak on the stairs. He found a soapbox, and carried it over to the soft ring of light that streamed from the furnace door, and sat down. He was horribly afraid of rats, so he did not try to sleep, but sat looking distrustfully at the dark, still terrified lest he might have awakened his father. In such reactions, after one of the experiences which made days and nights out of the dreary blanks of the calendar, when his senses were deadened, Paul's head was always singularly clear. Suppose his father had heard him getting in at the window and had come down and shot him for a burglar? Then, again, suppose his father had come down, pistol in hand, and he had cried out in time to save himself, and his father had been horrified to think how nearly he had killed him? Then, again, suppose a day should come when his father would remember that night, and wish there had been no warning cry to stay his hand? With this last supposition Paul entertained himself until daybreak.

The following Sunday was fine; the sodden November chill was broken by the last flash of autumnal summer. In the morning Paul had to go to church and Sabbath school, as always. On seasonable Sunday afternoons the burghers of Cordelia Street always sat out on their front stoops and talked to their neighbors on the next stoop, or called to those across the street in neighborly fashion. The men usually sat on gay cushions placed upon the steps that led down to the sidewalk, while the women, in their Sunday "waists," sat in rockers on the cramped porches, pretending to be greatly at their ease. The children played in the streets; there were so many of them that the place resembled the recreation grounds of a kindergarten. The men on the steps—all in their shirt sleeves, their vests unbuttoned—sat with their legs well apart, their stomachs comfortably protruding, and talked of the prices of things, or told anecdotes of the sagacity of their various chiefs and overlords. They occasionally looked over the multitude of squabbling children, listened affectionately to their high-pitched, nasal voices, smiling to see their own proclivities reproduced in their offspring, and interspersed their legends of the iron kings with remarks about their sons' progress at school, their grades in arithmetic, and the amounts they had saved in their toy banks.

On this last Sunday of November Paul sat all the afternoon on the lowest step of his stoop, staring into the street, while his sisters, in their rockers, were talking to the minister's daughters next door about how many shirtwaists they had made in the last week, and how many waffles someone had eaten at the last church supper. When the weather was warm, and his father was in a particularly jovial frame of mind, the girls made lemonade, which was always brought out in a red-glass pitcher, ornamented with forget-me-nots in blue enamel. This the girls thought very fine, and the neighbors always joked about the suspicious color of the pitcher.

Today Paul's father sat on the top step, talking to a young man who shifted a restless baby from knee to knee. He happened to be the young man who was daily held up to Paul as a model, and after whom it was his father's dearest hope that he would pattern. This young man was of a ruddy complexion, with a compressed, red mouth, and faded, nearsighted eyes, over which he wore thick spectacles, with gold bows that curved about his ears. He was clerk to one of the magnates of a great steel corporation, and was looked upon in Cordelia Street as a young man with a future. There was a story that, some five years ago—he was now barely twenty-six—he had been a trifle dissipated, but in order to curb his appetites and save the loss of time and strength that a sowing of wild oats might have entailed, he had taken his chief's advice, oft reiterated to his employees, and at twenty-one had married the first woman whom he could persuade to share his fortunes. She happened to be an angular schoolmistress, much older than he, who also wore thick glasses, and who had now borne him four children, all nearsighted, like herself.

The young man was relating how his chief, now cruising in the Mediterranean, kept in touch with all the details of the business, arranging his office hours on his yacht just as though he were at home, and "knocking off work enough to keep two stenographers busy." His father told, in turn, the plan his corporation was considering, of putting in an electric railway plant in Cairo. Paul snapped his teeth; he had an awful apprehension that they might spoil it all before he got there. Yet he rather liked to hear these legends of the iron kings that were told and retold on Sundays and holidays; these stories of palaces in Venice, yachts on the Mediterranean, and high play at Monte Carlo appealed to his fancy, and he was interested in the triumphs of these cash boys who had become famous, though he had no mind for the cash-boy stage.

After supper was over and he had helped to dry the dishes, Paul nervously asked his father whether he could go to George's to get some help in his geometry, and still more nervously asked for carfare. This latter request he had to repeat, as his father, on principle, did not like to hear requests for money, whether much or little. He asked Paul whether he could not go to some boy who lived nearer, and told him that he ought not to leave his schoolwork until Sunday; but he gave him the dime. He was not a poor man, but he had a worthy ambition to come up in the world. His only reason for allowing Paul to usher was that he thought a boy ought to be earning a little.

Paul bounded upstairs, scrubbed the greasy odor of the dishwater from his hands with the ill-smelling soap he hated, and then shook over his fingers a few drops of violet water from the bottle he kept hidden in his drawer. He left the house with his geometry conspicuously under his arm, and the moment he got out of Cordelia Street and boarded a downtown car, he shook off the lethargy of two deadening days and began to live again.

The leading juvenile of the permanent stock company which played at one of the downtown theaters was an acquaintance of Paul's, and the boy had been invited to drop in at the Sunday-night rehearsals whenever he could. For more than a year Paul had spent every available moment loitering about Charley Edwards's dressing room. He had won a place among Edwards's following not only because the young actor, who could not afford to employ a dresser, often found him useful, but because he recognized in Paul something akin to what churchmen term "vocation."

It was at the theater and at Carnegie Hall that Paul really lived; the rest was but a sleep and a forgetting. This was Paul's fairy tale, and it had for him all the allurement of a secret love. The moment he inhaled the gassy, painty, dusty odor behind the scenes, he breathed like a prisoner set free, and felt within him the possibility of doing or saying splendid, brilliant, poetic things. The moment the cracked orchestra beat out the overture from *Martha,* or jerked at the serenade from *Rigoletto,* all stupid and ugly things slid from him, and his senses were deliciously, yet delicately fired.

Perhaps it was because, in Paul's world, the natural nearly always wore the guise of ugliness, that a certain element of artificiality seemed to him necessary in beauty. Perhaps it was because his experience of life elsewhere was so full of Sabbath-school picnics, petty economies, wholesome advice as to how to succeed in life, and the inescapable odors of cooking, that he found this existence so alluring, these smartly clad men and women so attractive, that he was so moved by these starry apple orchards that bloomed perennially under the limelight.

It would be difficult to put it strongly enough how convincingly the stage entrance of that theater was for Paul the actual portal of Romance. Certainly none of the company ever suspected it, least of all Charley Edwards. It was very like the old stories that used to float about London of fabulously rich Jews, who had subterranean halls there, with palms, and fountains, and soft lamps and richly appareled women who never saw the disenchanting light of London day. So, in the midst of that smoke-palled city, enamored of figures and grimy toil, Paul had his secret temple, his wishing carpet, his bit of blue-and-white Mediterranean shore bathed in perpetual sunshine.

Several of Paul's teachers had a theory that his imagination had been perverted by garish fiction, but the truth was that he scarcely ever read at all. The books at home were not such as would either tempt or corrupt a youthful mind, and as for reading the novels that some of his friends urged upon him—well, he got what he wanted much more quickly from music; any sort of music, from an orchestra to a barrel organ. He needed only the spark, the indescribable thrill that made his imagination master of his senses, and he could make plots and pictures enough of his own. It was equally true that he was not stagestruck—not, at any rate, in the usual acceptation of that expression. He had no desire to become an actor, any more than he had to become a musician. He felt no necessity to do any of these things; what he wanted was to see, to be in the atmosphere, float on the wave of it, to be carried out, blue league after blue league, away from everything.

After a night behind the scenes Paul found the schoolroom more than ever repulsive; the bare floors and naked walls; the prosy men who never wore frock coats, or violets in their buttonholes; the women with their dull gowns, shrill voices, and pitiful seriousness about prepositions that govern the dative. He could not bear to have the other pupils think, for a moment, that he took these people seriously; he must convey to them that he considered it all trivial, and was there only by way of a jest, anyway. He had autographed pictures of all the members of the stock company which he showed his classmates, telling them the most incredible stories of his familiarity with these people, of his acquaintance with the soloists who came to Carnegie Hall, his suppers with them and the flowers he sent them. When these stories lost their effect, and his audience grew listless, he became desperate and would bid all the boys good-by, announcing that he was going to travel for a while; going to Naples, to Venice, to Egypt. Then, next Monday, he would slip back, conscious and nervously smiling; his sister was ill, and he should have to defer his voyage until spring.

Matters went steadily worse with Paul at school. In the itch to let his instructors know how heartily he despised them and their homilies, and how thoroughly he was appreciated elsewhere, he mentioned once or twice that he had no time to fool with theorems; adding—with a twitch of the eyebrows and a touch of that nervous bravado which so perplexed them—that he was helping the people down at the stock company; they were old friends of his.

The upshot of the matter was that the Principal went to Paul's father, and Paul was taken out of school and put to work. The manager at Carnegie Hall was told to get another usher in his stead; the doorkeeper at the theater was warned not to admit him to the house; and Charley Edwards remorsefully promised the boy's father not to see him again.

The members of the stock company were vastly amused when some of Paul's stories reached them—especially the women. They were hardworking women, most of them supporting indigent husbands or brothers, and they laughed rather bitterly at having stirred the boy to such fervid and florid inventions. They agreed with the faculty and with his father that Paul's was a bad case.

The eastbound train was plowing through a January snowstorm; the dull dawn was beginning to show gray when the engine whistled a mile out of Newark. Paul started up from the seat where he had lain curled in uneasy slumber, rubbed the breath-misted window glass with his hand, and peered out. The snow was whirling in curling eddies above the white bottom lands, and the drifts lay already deep in the fields and along the fences, while here and there the long dead grass and dried weed stalks protruded black above it. Lights shone from the scattered houses, and a gang of laborers who stood beside the track waved their lanterns.

Paul had slept very little, and he felt grimy and uncomfortable. He had made the all-night journey in a day coach, partly because he was ashamed, dressed as he was, to go into a Pullman, and partly because he was afraid of being seen there by some Pittsburgh businessman, who might have noticed him in Denny & Carson's office. When the whistle awoke him, he clutched quickly at his breast pocket, glancing about him with an uncertain smile. But the little, clay-bespattered Italians were still sleeping, the slatternly women across the aisle were in open-mouthed oblivion, and even the crumby, crying babies were for the nonce stilled. Paul settled back to struggle with his impatience as best he could.

When he arrived at the Jersey City station he hurried through his breakfast, manifestly ill at ease and keeping a sharp eye about him. After he reached the Twenty-third Street station, he consulted a cabman and had himself driven to a men's-furnishings establishment that was just opening for the day. He spent upward of two hours there, buying with endless reconsidering and great care. His new street suit he put on in the fitting room; the frock coat and dress clothes he had bundled into the cab with his linen. Then he drove to a hatter's and a shoe house. His next errand was at Tiffany's, where he selected his silver and a new scarf pin. He would not wait to have his silver marked, he said. Lastly, he stopped at a trunk shop on Broadway and had his purchases packed into various traveling bags.

It was a little after one o'clock when he drove up to the Waldorf, and after settling with the cabman, went into the office. He registered from Washington; said his mother and father had been abroad, and that he had come down to await the arrival of their steamer. He told his story plausibly and had no trouble, since he volunteered to pay for them in advance, in engaging his rooms; a sleeping room, sitting room, and bath.

Not once, but a hundred times, Paul had planned this entry into New York. He had gone over every detail of it with Charley Edwards, and in his scrapbook at home there were pages of description about New York hotels, cut from the Sunday papers. When he was shown to his sitting room on the eighth floor he saw at a glance that everything was as it should be; there was but one detail in his mental picture that the place did not realize, so he rang for the bellboy and sent him down for flowers.

He moved about nervously until the boy returned, putting away his new linen and fingering it delightedly as he did so. When the flowers came he put them hastily into water, and then tumbled into a hot bath. Presently he came out of his white bathroom, resplendent in his new silk underwear, and playing with the tassels of his red robe. The snow was whirling so fiercely outside his windows that he could scarcely see across the street, but within the air was deliciously soft and fragrant. He put the violets and jonquils on the taboret beside the couch, and threw himself down, with a long sigh, covering himself with a Roman blanket. He was thoroughly tired; he had been in such haste, he had stood up to such a strain, covered so much ground in the last twenty-four hours, that he wanted to think how it had all come about. Lulled by the sound of the wind, the warm air, and the cool fragrance of the flowers, he sank into deep, drowsy retrospection.

It had been wonderfully simple; when they had shut him out of the theater and concert hall, when they had taken away his bone, the whole thing was virtually determined. The rest was a mere matter of opportunity. The only thing that at all surprised him was his own courage—for he realized well enough that he had always been tormented by fear, a sort of apprehensive dread that, of late years, as the meshes of the lies he had told closed about him, had been pulling the muscles of his body tighter and tighter. Until now he could not remember the time when he had not been dreading something. Even when he was a little boy it was always there—behind him, or before, or on either side.

There had always been the shadowed corner, the dark place into which he dared not look, but from which something seemed always to be watching him—and Paul had done things that were not pretty to watch, he knew.

But now he had a curious sense of relief, as though he had at last thrown down the gauntlet to the thing in the corner.

Yet it was but a day since he had been sulking in the traces; but yesterday afternoon that he had been sent to the bank with Denny & Carson's deposit, as usual—but this time he was instructed to leave the book to be balanced. There was above two thousand dollars in checks, and nearly a thousand in the bank notes which he had taken from the book and quietly transferred to his pocket. At the bank he had made out a new deposit slip. His nerves had been steady enough to permit of his returning to the office, where he had finished his work and asked for a full day's holiday tomorrow, Saturday, giving a perfectly reasonable pretext. The bankbook, he knew, would not be returned before Monday or Tuesday, and his father would be out of town for the next week. From the time he slipped the bank notes into his pocket until he boarded the night train for New York, he had not known a moment's hesitation. It was not the first time Paul had steered through treacherous waters.

How astonishingly easy it had all been; here he was, the thing done; and this time there would be no awakening, no figure at the top of the stairs. He watched the snowflakes whirling by his window until he fell asleep.

When he awoke, it was three o'clock in the

afternoon. He bounded up with a start; half of one of his precious days gone already! He spent more than an hour in dressing, watching every stage of his toilet carefully in the mirror. Everything was quite perfect; he was exactly the kind of boy he had always wanted to be.

When he went downstairs Paul took a carriage and drove up Fifth Avenue toward the Park. The snow had somewhat abated; carriages and tradesmen's wagons were hurrying soundlessly to and fro in the winter twilight; boys in woolen mufflers were shoveling off the doorsteps; the avenue stages made fine spots of color against the white street. Here and there on the corners were stands, with whole flower gardens blooming under glass cases, against the sides of which the snowflakes stuck and melted; violets, roses, carnations, lilies of the valley—somehow vastly more lovely and alluring that they blossomed thus unnaturally in the snow. The Park itself was a wonderful stage winterpiece.

When he returned, the pause of the twilight had ceased and the tune of the streets had changed. The snow was falling faster, lights streamed from the hotels that reared their dozen stories fearlessly up into the storm, defying the raging Atlantic winds. A long, black stream of carriages poured down the avenue, intersected here and there by other streams, tending horizontally. There were a score of cabs about the entrance of his hotel, and his driver had to wait. Boys in livery were running in and out of the awning stretched across the sidewalk, up and down the red velvet carpet laid from the door to the street. Above, about, within it all was the rumble and roar, the hurry and toss of thousands of human beings as hot for pleasure as himself, and on every side of him towered the glaring affirmation of the omnipotence of wealth.

The boy set his teeth and drew his shoulders together in a spasm of realization; the plot of all dramas, the text of all romances, the nerve-stuff of all sensations was whirling about him like the snowflakes. He burnt like a faggot in a tempest.

When Paul went down to dinner the music of the orchestra came floating up the elevator shaft to greet him. His head whirled as he stepped into the thronged corridor, and he sank back into one of the chairs against the wall to get his breath. The lights, the chatter, the perfumes, the bewildering medley of color—he had, for a moment, the feeling of not being able to stand it. But only for a moment; these were his own people, he told himself. He went slowly about the corridors, through the writing rooms, smoking rooms, reception rooms, as though he were exploring the chambers of an enchanted palace, built and peopled for him alone.

When he reached the dining room he sat down at a table near a window. The flowers, the white linen, the many-colored wineglasses, the gay toilettes of the women, the low popping of corks, the undulating repetitions of the *Blue Danube* from the orchestra, all flooded Paul's dream with bewildering radiance. When the roseate tinge of his champagne was added—that cold, precious, bubbling stuff that creamed and foamed in his glass—Paul wondered that there were honest men in the world at all. This was what all the world was fighting for, he reflected; this was what all the struggle was about. He doubted the reality of his past. Had he ever known a place called Cordelia Street, a place where fagged-looking businessmen got on the early car; mere rivets in a machine they seemed to Paul,—sickening men, with combings of children's hair always hanging to their coats, and the smell of cooking in their clothes. Cordelia Street—Ah, that belonged to another time and country; had he not always been thus, had he not sat here night after night, from as far back as he could remember, looking pensively over just such shimmering textures and slowly twirling the stem of a glass like this one between his thumb and middle finger? He rather thought he had.

He was not in the least abashed or lonely. He had no especial desire to meet or to know any of these people; all he demanded was the right to look on and conjecture, to watch the pageant. The mere stage properties were all he contended for. Nor was he lonely later in the evening, in his lodge at the Metropolitan. He was now entirely rid of his nervous misgivings, of his forced aggressiveness, of the imperative desire to show himself different from his surroundings. He felt now that his surroundings explained him. Nobody questioned the purple; he had only to wear it passively. He had only to glance down at his attire to reassure himself that here it would be impossible for anyone to humiliate him.

He found it hard to leave his beautiful sitting room to go to bed that night, and sat long watching the raging storm from his turret window. When he went to sleep it was with the lights turned on in his bedroom; partly because of his old timidity, and partly so that, if he should wake in the night, there would be no wretched moment of doubt, no horrible suspicion of yellow wallpaper, or of Washington and Calvin above his bed.

Sunday morning the city was practically snowbound. Paul breakfasted late, and in the afternoon he fell in with a wild San Francisco boy, a freshman at Yale, who said he had run down for a "little flyer" over Sunday. The young man offered to show Paul the night side of the town, and the two boys went out together after dinner, not returning to the hotel until seven o'clock the next morning. They had started out in the confiding warmth of a champagne friendship, but their parting in the elevator was singularly cool. The freshman pulled himself together to make his train, and Paul went to bed. He awoke at two o'clock in the afternoon, very thirsty and dizzy, and rang for ice-water, coffee, and the Pittsburgh papers.

On the part of the hotel management, Paul excited no suspicion. There was this to be said for him, that he wore his spoils with dignity and in no way made himself conspicuous. Even under the glow of his wine he was never boisterous, though he found the stuff like a magician's wand for wonder-building. His chief greediness lay in his ears and eyes, and his excesses were not offensive ones. His dearest pleasures were the gray winter twilights in his sitting room; his quiet enjoyment of his flowers, his clothes, his wide divan, his cigarette, and his sense of power. He could not remember a time when he had felt so at peace with himself. The mere release from the necessity of petty lying, lying every day and every day, restored his self-respect. He had never lied for pleasure, even at school; but to be noticed and admired, to assert his difference from other Cordelia Street boys; and he felt a good deal more manly, more honest, even, now that he had no need for boastful pretensions, now that he could, as his actor friends used to say, "dress the part." It was characteristic that remorse did not occur to him. His golden days went by without a shadow, and he made each as perfect as he could.

On the eighth day after his arrival in New York he found the whole affair exploited in the Pittsburgh papers, exploited with a wealth of detail which indicated that local news of a sensational nature was at a low ebb. The firm of Denny & Carson announced that the boy's father had refunded the full amount of the theft and that they had no intention of prosecuting. The Cumberland minister had been interviewed, and expressed his hope of yet reclaiming the motherless lad, and his Sabbath-school teacher declared that she would spare no effort to that end. The rumor had reached Pittsburgh that the boy had been seen in a New York hotel, and his father had gone East to find him and bring him home.

Paul had just come in to dress for dinner; he sank into a chair, weak to the knees, and clasped his head in his hands. It was to be worse than jail, even; the tepid waters of Cordelia Street were to close over him finally and forever. The gray monotony stretched before him in hopeless, unrelieved years; Sabbath school, Young People's Meeting, the yellow-papered room, the damp dish-towels; it all rushed back upon him with a sickening vividness. He had the old feeling that the orchestra had suddenly stopped, the sinking sensation that the play was over. The sweat broke out on his face, and he sprang to his feet, looked about him with his white, conscious smile, and winked at himself in the mirror. With something of the old childish belief in miracles with which he had so often gone to class, all his lessons unlearned, Paul dressed and dashed whistling down the corridor to the elevator.

He had no sooner entered the dining room and caught the measure of the music than his remembrance was lightened by his old elastic power of claiming the moment, mounting with it, and finding it all-sufficient. The glare and glitter about him, the mere scenic accessories had again, and for the last time, their old potency. He would show himself that he was game, he would finish the thing splendidly. He doubted, more than ever, the existence of Cordelia Street, and for the first time he drank his wine recklessly. Was he not, after all, one of those fortunate beings born to the purple, was he not still himself and in his own place? He drummed a nervous accompaniment to the Pagliacci music and looked about him, telling himself over and over that it had paid.

He reflected drowsily, to the swell of the music and the chill sweetness of his wine, that he might have done it more wisely. He might have caught an outbound steamer and been well out of their clutches before now. But the other side of the world had seemed too far away and too uncertain then; he could not have waited for it; his need had been too sharp. If he had to choose over again, he would do the same thing tomorrow. He looked affectionately about the dining room, now gilded with a soft mist. Ah, it had paid indeed!

Paul was awakened next morning by a painful throbbing in his head and feet. He had thrown himself across the bed without undressing, and had slept with his shoes on. His limbs and hands were lead heavy, and his tongue and throat were parched and burnt. There came upon him one of those fateful attacks of clearheadedness that never occurred except when he was physically exhausted and his nerves hung loose. He lay still, closed his eyes, and let the tide of things wash over him.

His father was in New York; "stopping at some joint or other," he told himself. The memory of successive summers on the front stoop fell upon him like a weight of black water. He had not a hundred dollars left; and he knew now, more than ever, that money was everything, the wall that stood between all he loathed and all he wanted. The thing was winding itself up; he had thought of that on his first glorious day in New York, and had even provided a way to snap the thread. It lay on his dressing table now; he had got it out last night when he came blindly up from dinner, but the shiny metal hurt his eyes, and he disliked the looks of it.

He rose and moved about with a painful effort, succumbing now and again to attacks of nausea. It was the old depression exaggerated; all the world had become Cordelia Street. Yet somehow he was not afraid of anything, was absolutely calm; perhaps because he had looked into the dark corner at last and knew. It was bad enough, what he saw there, but somehow not so bad as his long fear of it had been. He saw everything clearly now. He had a feeling that he had made the best of it, that he had lived the sort of life he was meant to live, and for half an hour he sat staring at the revolver. But he told himself that was not the way, so he went downstairs and took a cab to the ferry.

When Paul arrived in Newark he got off the train and took another cab, directing the driver to follow the Pennsylvania tracks out of the town. The snow lay heavy on the roadways and had drifted deep in the open fields. Only here and there the dead grass or dried weed stalks projected, singularly black, above it. Once well into the country, Paul dismissed the carriage and walked, floundering along the tracks, his mind a medley of irrelevant things. He seemed to hold in his brain an actual picture of everything he had seen that morning. He remembered every feature of both his drivers, of the toothless old woman from whom he had bought the red flowers in his coat, the agent from whom he had got his ticket, and all of his fellow passengers on the ferry. His mind, unable to cope with vital matters near at hand, worked feverishly and deftly at sorting and grouping these images. They made for him a part of the ugliness of the world, of the ache in his head, and the bitter burning on his tongue. He stooped and put a handful of snow into his mouth as he walked, but that, too, seemed hot. When he reached a little hillside, where the tracks ran through a cut some twenty feet below him, he stopped and sat down.

The carnations in his coat were drooping with the cold, he noticed, their red glory all over. It occurred to him that all the flowers he had seen in the glass cases that first night must have gone the same way, long before this. It was only one splendid breath they had, in spite of their brave mockery at the winter outside the glass; and it was a losing game in the end, it seemed, this revolt against the homilies by which the world is run. Paul took one of the blossoms carefully from his coat and scooped a little hole in the snow, where he covered it up. Then he dozed awhile, from his weak condition, seemingly insensible to the cold.

The sound of an approaching train awoke him, and he started to his feet, remembering only his resolution, and afraid lest he should be too late. He stood watching the approaching locomotive, his teeth chattering, his lips drawn away from them in a frightened smile; once or twice he glanced nervously sidewise, as though he were being watched. When the right moment came, he jumped. As he fell, the folly of his haste occurred to him with merciless clearness, the vastness of what he had left undone. There flashed through his brain, clearer than ever before, the blue of Adriatic water, the yellow of Algerian sands.

He felt something strike his chest, and that his body was being thrown swiftly through the air, on and on, immeasurably far and fast, while his limbs were gently relaxed. Then, because the picture-making mechanism was crushed, the disturbing visions flashed into black, and Paul dropped back into the immense design of things.

The Sculptor's Funeral

A group of the townspeople stood on the station siding of a little Kansas town, awaiting the coming of the night train, which was already twenty minutes overdue. The snow had fallen thick over everything; in the pale starlight the line of bluffs across the wide, white meadows south of the town made soft, smoke-colored curves against the clear sky. The men on the siding stood first on one foot and then on the other, their hands thrust deep into their trousers pockets, their overcoats open, their shoulders screwed up with the cold; and they glanced from time to time toward the southeast, where the railroad track wound along the river shore. They conversed in low tones and moved about restlessly, seeming uncertain as to what was expected of them. There was but one of the company who looked as though he knew exactly why he was there; and he kept conspicuously apart; walking to the far end of the platform, returning to the station door, then pacing up the track again, his chin sunk in the high collar of his overcoat, his burly shoulders drooping forward, his gait heavy and dogged. Presently he was approached by a tall, spare, grizzled man clad in a faded Grand Army suit, who shuffled out from the group and advanced with a certain deference, craning his neck forward until his back made the angle of a jackknife three-quarters open.

"I reckon she's agoin' to be pretty late ag'in tonight, Jim," he remarked in a squeaky falsetto. "S'pose it's the snow?"

"I don't know," responded the other man with a shade of annoyance, speaking from out an astonishing cataract of red beard that grew fiercely and thickly in all directions.

The spare man shifted the quill toothpick he was chewing to the other side of his mouth. "It ain't likely that anybody from the East will come with the corpse, I s'pose," he went on reflectively.

"I don't know," responded the other, more curtly than before.

"It's too bad he didn't belong to some lodge or other. I like an order funeral myself. They seem more appropriate for people of some repytation," the spare man continued, with an ingratiating concession in his shrill voice, as he carefully placed his toothpick in his vest pocket. He always carried the flag at the G. A. R. funerals in the town.

The heavy man turned on his heel, without replying, and walked up the siding. The spare man shuffled back to the uneasy group. "Jim's ez full ez a tick, ez ushel," he commented commiseratingly.

Just then a distant whistle sounded, and there was a shuffling of feet on the platform. A number of lanky boys of all ages appeared as suddenly and slimily as eels wakened by the crack of thunder; some came from the waiting room, where they had been warming themselves by the red stove, or half-asleep on the slat benches; others uncoiled themselves from baggage trucks or slid out of express wagons. Two clambered down from the driver's seat of a hearse that stood backed up against the siding. They straightened their stooping shoulders and lifted their heads, and a flash of momentary animation kindled their dull eyes at that cold, vibrant scream, the world-wide call for men. It stirred them like the note of a trumpet; just as it had often stirred the man who was coming home tonight, in his boyhood.

The night express shot, red as a rocket, from out the eastward marsh lands and wound along the river shore under the long lines of shivering poplars that sentineled the meadows, the escaping steam hanging in gray masses against the pale sky and blotting out the Milky Way. In a moment the red glare from the headlight streamed up the snow-covered track before the siding and glittered on the wet, black rails. The burly man with the disheveled red beard walked swiftly up the platform toward the approaching train, uncovering his head as he went. The group of men behind him hesitated, glanced questioningly at one another, and awkwardly followed his example. The train stopped, and the crowd shuffled up to the express car just as the door was thrown open, the spare man in the G. A. R. suit thrusting his head forward with curiosity. The express messenger appeared in the doorway, accompanied by a young man in a long ulster and traveling cap.

"Are Mr. Merrick's friends here?" inquired the young man.

The group on the platform swayed and shuffled uneasily. Philip Phelps, the banker, responded with dignity: "We have come to take charge of the body. Mr. Merrick's father is very feeble and can't be about."

"Send the agent out here," growled the express messenger, "and tell the operator to lend a hand."

The coffin was got out of its rough box and down on the snowy platform. The townspeople drew back enough to make room for it and then formed a close semicircle about it, looking curiously at the palm leaf which lay across the black cover. No one said anything. The baggage man stood by his truck, waiting to get at the trunks. The engine panted heavily, and the fireman dodged in and out among the wheels with his yellow torch and long oilcan, snapping the spindle boxes. The young Bostonian, one of the dead sculptor's pupils who had come with the body, looked about him helplessly. He turned to the banker, the only one of that black, uneasy, stoop-shouldered group who seemed enough of an individual to be addressed.

"None of Mr. Merrick's brothers are here?" he asked uncertainly.

The man with the red beard for the first time stepped up and joined the group. "No, they have not come yet; the family is scattered. The body will be taken directly to the house." He stooped and took hold of one of the handles of the coffin.

"Take the long hill road up, Thompson—it will be easier on the horses," called the liveryman as the undertaker snapped the door of the hearse and prepared to mount to the driver's seat.

Laird, the red-bearded lawyer, turned again to the stranger: "We didn't know whether there would be anyone with him or not," he explained. "It's a long walk, so you'd better go up in the hack." He pointed to a single, battered conveyance, but the young man replied stiffly: "Thank you, but I think I will go up with the hearse. If you don't object," turning to the undertaker, "I'll ride with you."

They clambered up over the wheels and drove off in the starlight up the long, white hill toward the town. The lamps in the still village were shining from under the low, snow-burdened roofs; and beyond, on every side, the plains reached out into emptiness, peaceful and wide as the soft sky itself, and wrapped in a tangible, white silence.

When the hearse backed up to a wooden sidewalk before a naked, weatherbeaten frame house, the same composite, ill-defined group that had stood upon the station siding was huddled about the gate. The front yard was an icy swamp, and a couple of warped planks, extending from the sidewalk to the door, made a sort of rickety footbridge. The gate hung on one hinge and was opened wide with difficulty. Steavens, the young stranger, noticed that something black was tied to the knob of the front door.

The grating sound made by the casket, as it was drawn from the hearse, was answered by a scream from the house; the front door was wrenched open, and a tall, corpulent woman rushed out bareheaded into the snow and flung herself upon the coffin, shrieking: "My boy, my boy! And this is how you've come home to me!"

As Steavens turned away and closed his eyes with a shudder of unutterable repulsion, another woman, also tall, but flat and angular, dressed entirely in black, darted out of the house and caught Mrs. Merrick by the shoulders, crying sharply: "Come, come, Mother; you mustn't go on like this!" Her tone changed to one of obsequious solemnity as she turned to the banker: "The parlor is ready, Mr. Phelps."

The bearers carried the coffin along the narrow boards, while the undertaker ran ahead with the coffin-rests. They bore it into a large, unheated room that smelled of dampness and disuse and furniture polish, and set it down under a hanging lamp ornamented with jingling glass prisms and before a "Rogers group" of John Alden and Priscilla, wreathed with smilax. Henry Steavens stared about him with the sickening conviction that there had been some horrible mistake, and that he had somehow arrived at the wrong destination. He looked painfully about over the clover-green Brussels, the fat plush upholstery, among the hand-painted china plaques and panels, and vases, for some mark of identification, for something that might once conceivably have belonged to Harvey Merrick. It was not until he recognized his friend in the crayon portrait of a little boy in kilts and curls hanging above the piano that he felt willing to let any of these people approach the coffin.

"Take the lid off, Mr. Thompson; let me see my boy's face," wailed the elder woman between her sobs. This time Steavens looked fearfully, almost beseechingly into her face, red and swollen under its masses of strong, black, shiny hair. He flushed, dropped his eyes, and then, almost incredulously, looked again. There was a kind of power about her face—a kind of brutal handsomeness, even, but it was scarred and furrowed by violence, and so colored and coarsened by fiercer passions that grief seemed never to have laid a gentle finger there. The long nose was distended and knobbed at the end, and there were deep lines on either side of it; her heavy, black brows almost met across her forehead; her teeth were large and square and set far apart—teeth that could tear. She filled the room; the men were obliterated, seemed tossed about like twigs in an angry water, and even Steavens felt himself being drawn into the whirlpool.

The daughter—the tall, rawboned woman in crepe, with a mourning comb in her hair which curiously lengthened her long face—sat stiffly upon the sofa, her hands, conspicuous for their large knuckles, folded in her lap, her mouth and eyes drawn down, solemnly awaiting the opening of the coffin. Near the door stood a mulatto woman, evidently a servant in the house, with a timid bearing and an emaciated face pitifully sad and gentle. She was weeping silently, the corner of her calico apron lifted to her eyes, occasionally suppressing a long, quivering sob. Steavens walked over and stood beside her.

Feeble steps were heard on the stairs, and an old man, tall and frail, odorous of pipe smoke, with shaggy, unkept gray hair and a dingy beard, tobacco stained about the mouth, entered uncertainly. He went slowly up to the coffin and stood, rolling a blue cotton handkerchief between his hands, seeming so pained and embarrassed by his wife's orgy of grief that he had no consciousness of anything else.

"There, there, Annie, dear, don't take on so," he quavered timidly, putting out a shaking hand and awkwardly patting her elbow. She turned with a cry and sank upon his shoulder with such violence that he tottered a little. He did not even glance toward the coffin, but continued to look at her with a dull, frightened, appealing expression, as a spaniel looks at the whip. His sunken cheeks slowly reddened and burned with miserable shame. When his wife rushed from the room her daughter strode after her with set lips. The servant stole up to the coffin, bent over it for a moment, and then slipped away to the kitchen, leaving Steavens, the lawyer, and the father to themselves. The old man stood trembling and looking down at his dead son's face. The sculptor's splendid head seemed even more noble in its rigid stillness than in life. The dark hair had crept down upon the wide forehead; the face seemed strangely long, but in it there was not that beautiful and chaste repose which we expect to find in the faces of the dead. The brows were so drawn that there were two deep lines above the beaked nose, and the chin was thrust forward defiantly. It was as though the strain of life had been so sharp and bitter that death could not at once wholly relax the tension and smooth the countenance into perfect peace—as though he were still guarding something precious and holy, which might even yet be wrested from him.

The old man's lips were working under his stained beard. He turned to the lawyer with timid deference: "Phelps and the rest are comin' back to set up with Harve, ain't they?" he asked. "Thank 'ee, Jim, thank 'ee." He brushed the hair back gently from his son's forehead. "He was a good boy, Jim; always a good boy. He was ez gentle ez a child and the kindest of 'em all—only we didn't none of us ever onderstand him." The tears trickled slowly down his beard and dropped upon the sculptor's coat.

"Martin, Martin. Oh, Martin! come here," his wife wailed from the top of the stairs. The old man started timorously: "Yes, Annie, I'm coming." He turned away, hesitated, stood for a moment in miserable indecision; then he reached back and patted the dead man's hair softly, and stumbled from the room.

"Poor old man, I didn't think he had any tears left. Seems as if his eyes would have gone dry long ago. At his age nothing cuts very deep," remarked the lawyer.

Something in his tone made Steavens glance up. While the mother had been in the room the young man had scarcely seen anyone else; but now, from the moment he first glanced into Jim Laird's florid face and bloodshot eyes, he knew that he had found what he had been heartsick at not finding before—the feeling, the understanding, that must exist in someone, even here.

The man was red as his beard, with features

swollen and blurred by dissipation, and a hot, blazing blue eye. His face was strained—that of a man who is controlling himself with difficulty—and he kept plucking at his beard with a sort of fierce resentment. Steavens, sitting by the window, watched him turn down the glaring lamp, still its jangling pendants with an angry gesture, and then stand with his hands locked behind him, staring down into the master's face. He could not help wondering what link there could have been between the porcelain vessel and so sooty a lump of potter's clay.

From the kitchen an uproar was sounding; when the dining-room door opened the import of it was clear. The mother was abusing the maid for having forgotten to make the dressing for the chicken salad which had been prepared for the watchers. Steavens had never heard anything in the least like it; it was injured, emotional, dramatic abuse, unique and masterly in its excruciating cruelty, as violent and unrestrained as had been her grief of twenty minutes before. With a shudder of disgust the lawyer went into the dining room and closed the door into the kitchen.

"Poor Roxy's getting it now," he remarked when he came back. "The Merricks took her out of the poorhouse years ago; and if her loyalty would let her, I guess the poor old thing could tell tales that would curdle your blood. She's the mulatto woman who was standing in here a while ago, with her apron to her eyes. The old woman is a fury; there never was anybody like her for demonstrative piety and ingenious cruelty. She made Harvey's life a hell for him when he lived at home; he was so sick ashamed of it. I never could see how he kept himself so sweet."

"He was wonderful," said Steavens slowly, "wonderful; but until tonight I have never known how wonderful."

"That is the true and eternal wonder of it, anyway; that it can come even from such a dung heap as this," the lawyer cried, with a sweeping gesture which seemed to indicate much more than the four walls within which they stood.

"I think I'll see whether I can get a little air. The room is so close I am beginning to feel rather faint," murmured Steavens, struggling with one of the windows. The sash was stuck, however, and would not yield, so he sat down dejectedly and began pulling at his collar. The lawyer came over, loosened the sash with one blow of his red fist, and sent the window up a few inches. Steavens thanked him, but the nausea which had been gradually climbing into his throat for the last half-hour left him with but one desire—a desperate feeling that he must get away from this place with what was left of Harvey Merrick. Oh, he comprehended well enough now the quiet bitterness of the smile that he had seen so often on his master's lips!

He remembered that once, when Merrick returned from a visit home, he brought with him a singularly feeling and suggestive bas-relief of a thin, faded old woman, sitting and sewing something pinned to her knee; while a full-lipped, full-blooded little urchin, his trousers held up by a single gallows, stood beside her, impatiently twitching her gown to call her attention to a butterfly he had caught. Steavens, impressed by the tender and delicate modeling of the thin, tired face, had asked him if it were his mother. He remembered the dull flush that had burned up in the sculptor's face.

The lawyer was sitting in a rocking chair beside the coffin, his head thrown back and his eyes closed. Steavens looked at him earnestly, puzzled at the line of the chin, and wondering why a man should conceal a feature of such distinction under that disfiguring shock of beard. Suddenly, as though he felt the young sculptor's keen glance, he opened his eyes.

"Was he always a good deal of an oyster?" he asked abruptly. "He was terribly shy as a boy."

"Yes, he was an oyster, since you put it so," rejoined Steavens. "Although he could be very fond of people, he always gave one the impression of being detached. He disliked violent emotion; he was reflective, and rather distrustful of himself—except, of course, as regarded his work. He was surefooted enough there. He distrusted men pretty thoroughly and women even more, yet somehow without believing ill of them. He was determined, indeed, to believe the best, but he seemed afraid to investigate."

"A burnt dog dreads the fire," said the lawyer grimly, and closed his eyes.

Steavens went on and on, reconstructing that whole miserable boyhood. All this raw, biting ugliness had been the portion of the man whose tastes were refined beyond the limits of the reasonable—whose mind was an exhaustless gallery of beautiful impressions, and so sensitive that the mere shadow of a poplar leaf flickering against a sunny wall would be etched and held there forever. Surely, if ever a man had the magic word in his fingertips, it was Merrick. Whatever he touched, he revealed its holiest secret; liberated it from enchantment and restored it to its pristine loveliness, like the Arabian prince who fought the enchantress spell for spell. Upon whatever he had come in contact with, he had left a beautiful record of the experience—a sort of ethereal signature; a scent, a sound, a color that was his own.

Steavens understood now the real tragedy of his master's life; neither love nor wine, as many had conjectured, but a blow which had fallen earlier and cut deeper than these could have done—a shame not his, and yet so unescapably his, to hide in his heart from his very boyhood. And without—the frontier warfare; the yearning of a boy, cast ashore upon a desert of newness and ugliness and sordidness, for all that is chastened and old, and noble with traditions.

At eleven o'clock the tall, flat woman in black crepe entered, announced that the watchers were arriving, and asked them "to step into the dining room." As Steavens rose the lawyer said dryly: "You go on—it'll be a good experience for you, doubtless; as for me, I'm not equal to that crowd tonight; I've had twenty years of them."

As Steavens closed the door after him he glanced back at the lawyer, sitting by the coffin in the dim light, with his chin resting on his hand.

The same misty group that had stood before the door of the express car shuffled into the dining room. In the light of the kerosene lamp they separated and became individuals. The minister, a pale, feeble-looking man with white hair and blond chin-whiskers, took his seat beside a small side table and placed his Bible upon it. The Grand Army man sat down behind the stove and tilted his chair back comfortably against the wall, fishing his quill toothpick from his waistcoat pocket. The two bankers, Phelps and Elder, sat off in a corner behind the dinner table, where they could finish their discussion of the new usury law and its effect on chattel security loans. The real estate agent, an old man with a smiling, hypocritical face, soon joined them. The coal-and-lumber dealer and the cattle shipper sat on opposite sides of the hard coal-burner, their feet on the nickelwork. Steavens took a book from his pocket and began to read. The talk around him ranged through various topics of local interest while the house was quieting down. When it was clear that the members of the family were in bed the Grand Army man hitched his shoulders and, untangling his long legs, caught his heels on the rounds of his chair.

"S'pose there'll be a will, Phelps?" he queried in his weak falsetto.

The banker laughed disagreeably and began trimming his nails with a pearl-handled pocket-knife.

"There'll scarcely be any need for one, will there?" he queried in his turn.

The restless Grand Army man shifted his position again, getting his knees still nearer his chin. "Why, the ole man says Harve's done right well lately," he chirped.

The other banker spoke up. "I reckon he means

by that Harve ain't asked him to mortgage any more farms lately, so as he could go on with his education."

"Seems like my mind don't reach back to a time when Harve wasn't bein' edycated," tittered the Grand Army man.

There was a general chuckle. The minister took out his handkerchief and blew his nose sonorously. Banker Phelps closed his knife with a snap. "It's too bad the old man's sons didn't turn out better," he remarked with reflective authority. "They never hung together. He spent money enough on Harve to stock a dozen cattle farms and he might as well have poured it into Sand Creek. If Harve had stayed at home and helped nurse what little they had, and gone into stock on the old man's bottom farm, they might all have been well fixed. But the old man had to trust everything to tenants and was cheated right and left."

"Harve never could have handled stock none," interposed the cattleman. "He hadn't it in him to be sharp. Do you remember when he bought Sander's mules for eight-year-olds, when everybody in town knew that Sander's father-in-law give 'em to his wife for a wedding present eighteen years before, an' they was full-grown mules then."

Everyone chuckled, and the Grand Army man rubbed his knees with a spasm of childish delight.

"Harve never was much account for anything practical, and he shore was never fond of work," began the coal-and-lumber dealer. "I mind the last time he was home; the day he left, when the old man was out to the barn helpin' his hand hitch up to take Harve to the train, and Cal Moots was patchin' up the fence, Harve, he come out on the step and sings out, in his ladylike voice: "Cal Moots, Cal Moots! please come cord my trunk."

"That's Harve for you," approved the Grand Army man gleefully. "I kin hear him howlin' yet when he was a big feller in long pants and his mother used to whale him with a rawhide in the barn for lettin' the cows git foundered in the cornfield when he was drivin' 'em home from pasture. He killed a cow of mine that-a-way onc't—a pure Jersey and the best milker I had, an' the ole man had to put up for her. Harve, he was watchin' the sun set acros't the marshes when the anamile got away; he argued that sunset was oncommon fine."

"Where the old man made his mistake was in sending the boy East to school," said Phelps, stroking his goatee and speaking in a deliberate, judicial tone. "There was where he got his head full of traipsing to Paris and all such folly. What Harve needed, of all people, was a course in some first-class Kansas City business college."

The letters were swimming before Steavens's eyes. Was it possible that these men did not understand, that the palm on the coffin meant nothing to them? The very name of their town would have remained forever buried in the postal guide had it not been now and again mentioned in the world in connection with Harvey Merrick's. He remembered what his master had said to him on the day of his death, after the congestion of both lungs had shut off any probability of recovery, and the sculptor had asked his pupil to send his body home. "It's not a pleasant place to be lying while he world is moving and doing and bettering," he ad said with a feeble smile, "but it rather seems s though we ought to go back to the place we ame from in the end. The townspeople will come n for a look at me; and after they have had their ay I shan't have much to fear from the judgment f God. The wings of the Victory, in there"—with weak gesture toward his studio—"will not shel-er me."

The cattleman took up the comment. "Forty's oung for a Merrick to cash in; they usually hang n pretty well. Probably he helped it along with hisky."

"His mother's people were not long-lived, and Harvey never had a robust constitution," said the minister mildly. He would have liked to say more. He had been the boy's Sunday-school teacher, and ad been fond of him; but he felt that he was not in position to speak. His own sons had turned out adly, and it was not a year since one of them had made his last trip home in the express car, shot in a ambling house in the Black Hills.

"Nevertheless, there is no disputin' that Harve requently looked upon the wine when it was red, lso variegated, and it shore made an oncommon ool of him," moralized the cattleman.

Just then the door leading into the parlor rattled oudly, and everyone started involuntarily, looking elieved when only Jim Laird came out. His red ace was convulsed with anger, and the Grand Army man ducked his head when he saw the spark n his blue, bloodshot eye. They were all afraid of Jim; he was a drunkard, but he could twist the law o suit his client's needs as no other man in all western Kansas could do; and there were many who tried. The lawyer closed the door gently behind him, leaned back against it and folded his arms, cocking his head a little to one side. When he assumed this attitude in the courtroom, ears were always pricked up, as it usually foretold a flood of withering sarcasm.

"I've been with you gentlemen before," he began in a dry, even tone, "when you've sat by the coffins of boys born and raised in this town; and, if I remember rightly, you were never any too well satisfied when you checked them up. What's the matter, anyhow? Why is it that reputable young men are as scarce as millionaires in Sand City? It might almost seem to a stranger that there was some way something the matter with your progressive town. Why did Ruben Sayer, the brightest young lawyer you ever turned out, after he had come home from the university as straight as a die, take to drinking and forge a check and shoot himself? Why did Bill Merrit's son die of the shakes in a saloon in Omaha? Why was Mr. Thomas's son, here, shot in a gambling house? Why did young Adams burn his mill to beat the insurance companies and go to the pen?"

The lawyer paused and unfolded his arms, laying one clenched fist quietly on the table. "I'll tell you why. Because you drummed nothing but money and knavery into their ears from the time they wore knickerbockers; because you carped away at them as you've been carping here tonight, holding our friends Phelps and Elder up to them for their models, as our grandfathers held up George Washington and John Adams. But the boys, worse luck, were young and raw at the business you put them to; and how could they match coppers with such artists as Phelps and Elder? You wanted them to be successful rascals; they were only unsuccessful ones—that's all the difference. There was only one boy ever raised in this borderland between ruffianism and civilization who didn't come to grief, and you hated Harvey Merrick more for winning out than you hated all the other boys who got under the wheels. Lord, Lord, how you did hate him! Phelps, here, is fond of saying that he could buy and sell us all out any time he's a mind to; but he knew Harve wouldn't have given a tinker's damn for his bank and all his cattle farms put together; and a lack of appreciation, that way, goes hard with Phelps.

"Old Nimrod, here, thinks Harve drank too much; and this from such as Nimrod and me!

"Brother Elder says Harve was too free with the old man's money—fell short in filial consideration, maybe. Well, we can all remember the very tone in which brother Elder swore his own father was a liar, in the county court; and we all know that the old man came out of that partnership with his son as bare as a sheared lamb. But maybe I'm getting personal, and I'd better be driving ahead at what I want to say."

The lawyer paused a moment, squared his heavy shoulders, and went on: "Harvey Merrick and I went to school together, back East. We were dead in earnest, and we wanted you all to be proud of us some day. We meant to be great men. Even I, and I haven't lost my sense of humor, gentlemen, I meant to be a great man. I came back here to practice, and I found you didn't in the least want me to be a great man. You wanted me to be a shrewd lawyer—oh, yes! Our veteran here wanted me to get him an increase of pension, because he had dyspepsia; Phelps wanted a new county survey that would put the widow Wilson's little bottom farm inside his south line; Elder wanted to lend money at 5 per cent a month and get it collected; old Stark here wanted to wheedle old women up in Vermont into investing their annuities in real estate mortgages that are not worth the paper they are written on. Oh, you needed me hard enough, and you'll go on needing me; and that's why I'm not afraid to plug the truth home to you this once.

"Well, I came back here and became the damned shyster you wanted me to be. You pretend to have some sort of respect for me; and yet you'll stand up and throw mud at Harvey Merrick, whose soul you couldn't dirty and whose hands you couldn't tie. Oh, you're a discriminating lot of Christians! There have been times when the sight of Harvey's name in some Eastern paper has made me hang my head like a whipped dog; and, again, times when I liked to think of him off there in the world, away from all this hog wallow, doing his great work and climbing the big, clean upgrade he'd set for himself.

"And we? Now that we've fought and lied and sweated and stolen, and hated as only the disappointed strugglers in a bitter, dead little Western town know how to do, what have we got to show for it? Harvey Merrick wouldn't have given one sunset over your marshes for all you've got put together, and you know it. It's not for me to say why, in the inscrutable wisdom of God, a genius should ever have been called from this place of hatred and bitter waters; but I want this Boston man to know that the drivel he's been hearing here tonight is the only tribute any truly great man could ever have from such a lot of sick, side-tracked, burnt-dog, land-poor sharks as the here-present financiers of Sand City—upon which town may God have mercy!"

The lawyer thrust out his hand to Steavens as he passed him, caught up his overcoat in the hall, and had left the house before the Grand Army man had had time to lift his ducked head and crane his long neck about at his fellows.

Next day Jim Laird was drunk and unable to attend the funeral services. Steavens called twice at his office, but was compelled to start East without seeing him. He had a presentiment that he would hear from him again, and left his address on the lawyer's table; but if Laird found it, he never acknowledged it. The thing in him that Harvey Merrick had loved must have gone underground with Harvey Merrick's coffin; for it never spoke again, and Jim got the cold he died of driving across the Colorado mountains to defend one of Phelps's sons, who had got into trouble out there by cutting government timber.

A Wagner Matinee

I received one morning a letter, written in pale ink on glassy, blue-lined notepaper, and bearing the postmark of a little Nebraska village. This communication, worn and rubbed, looking as though it had been carried for some days in a coat pocket that was none too clean, was from my Uncle Howard and informed me that his wife had been left a small legacy by a bachelor relative who had recently died, and that it would be necessary for her to go to Boston to attend to the settling of the estate. He requested me to meet her at the station and render her whatever services might be necessary. On examining the date indicated as that of her arrival I found it no later than tomorrow. He had characteristically delayed writing until, had I been away from home for a day, I must have missed the good woman altogether.

The name of my Aunt Georgiana called up not alone her own figure, at once pathetic and grotesque, but opened before my feet a gulf of recollection so wide and deep that, as the letter dropped from my hand, I felt suddenly a stranger to all the present conditions of my existence, wholly ill at ease and out of place amid the familiar surroundings of my study. I became, in short, the gangling farm boy my aunt had known, scourged with chilblains and bashfulness, my hands cracked and sore from the corn husking. I felt the knuckles of my thumb tentatively, as though they were raw again. I sat again before her parlor organ, fumbling the scales with my stiff, red hands, while she, beside me, made canvas mittens for the huskers.

The next morning, after preparing my landlady somewhat, I set out for the station. When the train arrived I had some difficulty in finding my aunt. She was the last of the passengers to alight, and it was not until I got her into the carriage that she seemed really to recognize me. She had come all the way in a day coach; her linen duster had become black with soot, and her black bonnet gray with dust, during the journey. When we arrived at my boardinghouse the landlady put her to bed at once and I did not see her again until the next morning.

Whatever shock Mrs. Springer experienced at my aunt's appearance she considerately concealed. As for myself, I saw my aunt's misshapen figure with that feeling of awe and respect with which we behold explorers who have left their ears and fingers north of Franz Josef Land, or their health somewhere along the Upper Congo. My Aunt Georgiana had been a music teacher at the Boston Conservatory, somewhere back in the latter sixties. One summer, while visiting in the little village among the Green Mountains where her ancestors had dwelt for generations, she had kindled the callow fancy of the most idle and shiftless of all the village lads, and had conceived for this Howard Carpenter one of those extravagant passions which a handsome country boy of twenty-one sometimes inspires in an angular, spectacled woman of thirty. When she returned to her duties in Boston Howard followed her, and the upshot of this inexplicable infatuation was that she eloped with him, eluding the reproaches of her family and the criticisms of her friends by going with him to the Nebraska frontier. Carpenter, who, of course, had no money, had taken a homestead in Red Willow County, fifty miles from the railroad. There they had measured off their quarter section themselves by driving across the prairie in a wagon, to the wheel of which they had tied a red cotton handkerchief, and counting off its revolutions. They built a dugout in the red hillside, one of those cave dwellings whose inmates so often reverted to primitive conditions. Their water they got from the lagoons where the buffalo drank, and their slender stock of provisions was always at the mercy of bands of roving Indians. For thirty years my aunt had not been further than fifty miles from the homestead.

But Mrs. Springer knew nothing of all this, and must have been considerably shocked at what was left of my kinswoman. Beneath the soiled linen duster which, on her arrival, was the most conspicuous feature of her costume, she wore a black stuff dress, whose ornamentation showed that she had surrendered herself unquestioningly into the hands of a country dressmaker. My poor aunt's figure, however, would have presented astonishing difficulties to any dressmaker. Originally stooped, her shoulders were now almost bent together over her sunken chest. She wore no stays, and her gown, which trailed unevenly behind, rose in a sort of peak over her abdomen. She wore ill-fitting false teeth, and her skin was as yellow as a Mongolian's from constant exposure to a pitiless wind and to the alkaline water which hardens the most transparent cuticle into a sort of flexible leather.

I owed to this woman most of the good that ever came my way in my boyhood, and had a reverential affection for her. During the years when I was riding herd for my uncle, my aunt, after cooking the three meals—the first of which was ready at six o'clock in the morning—and putting the six children to bed, would often stand until midnight at her ironing board, with me at the kitchen table beside her, hearing me recite Latin declensions and conjugations, gently shaking me when my drowsy head sank down over a page of irregular verbs. It was to her, at her ironing or mending, that I read my first Shakespeare, and her old textbook on mythology was the first that ever came into my empty hands. She taught me my scales and exercises, too—on the little parlor organ, which her husband had bought her after fifteen years, during which she had not so much as seen any instrument, but an accordion that belonged to one of the Norwegian farmhands. She would sit beside me by the hour, darning and counting while I struggled with the "Joyous Farmer," but she seldom talked to me about music, and I understood why. She was a pious woman; she had the consolations of religion and, to her at least, her martyrdom was not wholly sordid. Once when I had been doggedly beating out some easy passages from an old score of *Euryanthe* I had found among her music books, she came up to me and, putting her hands over my eyes, gently drew my head back upon her shoulder, saying tremulously, "Don't love it so well, Clark, or it may be taken from you. Oh, dear boy, pray that whatever your sacrifice may be, it be not that."

When my aunt appeared on the morning after her arrival she was still in a semisomnambulant state. She seemed not to realize that she was in the city where she had spent her youth, the place longed for hungrily half a lifetime. She had been so wretchedly train-sick throughout the journey that she had no recollection of anything but her discomfort, and, to all intents and purposes, there were but a few hours of nightmare between the farm in Red Willow County and my study on Newbury Street. I had planned a little pleasure for her that afternoon, to repay her for some of the glorious moments she had given me when we used to milk together in the straw-thatched cowshed and she, because I was more than usually tired, or because her husband had spoken sharply to me, would tell me of the splendid performance of the *Huguenots* she had seen in Paris, in her youth. At two o'clock the Symphony Orchestra was to give a Wagner program, and I intended to take my aunt; though, as I conversed with her I grew doubtful about her enjoyment of it. Indeed, for her own sake, I could only wish her taste for such things quite dead, and the long struggle mercifully ended at last. I suggested our visiting the Conservatory and the

Common before lunch, but she seemed altogether too timid to wish to venture out. She questioned me absently about various changes in the city, but she was chiefly concerned that she had forgotten to leave instructions about feeding half-skimmed milk to a certain weakling calf, "old Maggie's calf, you know, Clark," she explained, evidently having forgotten how long I had been away. She was further troubled because she had neglected to tell her daughter about the freshly opened kit of mackerel in the cellar, which would spoil if it were not used directly.

I asked her whether she had ever heard any of the Wagnerian operas and found that she had not, though she was perfectly familiar with their respective situations, and had once possessed the piano score of *The Flying Dutchman*. I began to think it would have been best to get her back to Red Willow County without waking her, and regretted having suggested the concert.

From the time we entered the concert hall, however, she was a trifle less passive and inert, and for the first time seemed to perceive her surroundings. I had felt some trepidation lest she might become aware of the absurdities of her attire, or might experience some painful embarrassment at stepping suddenly into the world to which she had been dead for a quarter of a century. But, again, I found how superficially I had judged her. She sat looking about her with eyes as impersonal, almost as stony, as those with which the granite Rameses in a museum watches the froth and fret that ebbs and flows about his pedestal—separated from it by the lonely stretch of centuries. I have seen this same aloofness in old miners who drift into the Brown Hotel at Denver, their pockets full of bullion, their linen soiled, their haggard faces unshaven; standing in the thronged corridors as solitary as though they were still in a frozen camp on the Yukon, conscious that certain experiences have isolated them from their fellows by a gulf no haberdasher could bridge.

We sat at the extreme left of the first balcony, facing the arc of our own and the balcony above us, veritable hanging gardens, brilliant as tulip beds. The matinee audience was made up chiefly of women. One lost the contour of faces and figures—indeed, any effect of line whatever—and there was only the color of bodices past counting, the shimmer of fabrics soft and firm, silky and sheer: red, mauve, pink, blue, lilac, purple, ecru, rose, yellow, cream, and white, all the colors that an impressionist finds in a sunlit landscape, with here and there the dead shadow of a frock coat. My Aunt Georgiana regarded them as though they had been so many daubs of tube-paint on a palette.

When the musicians came out and took their places, she gave a little stir of anticipation and looked with quickening interest down over the rail at that invariable grouping, perhaps the first wholly familiar thing that had greeted her eye since she had left old Maggie and her weakling calf. I could feel how all those details sank into her soul, for I had not forgotten how they had sunk into mine when I came fresh from plowing forever and forever between green aisles of corn, where, as in a treadmill, one might walk from daybreak to dusk without perceiving a shadow of change. The clean profiles of the musicians, the gloss of their linen, the dull black of their coats, the beloved shapes of the instruments, the patches of yellow light thrown by the green-shaded lamps on the smooth, varnished bellies of the cellos and the bass viols in the rear, the restless, wind-tossed forest of fiddle necks and bows—I recalled how, in the first orchestra I had ever heard, those long bow strokes seemed to draw the heart out of me as a conjurer's stick reels out yards of paper ribbon from a hat.

The first number was the *Tannhauser* overture. When the horns drew out the first strain of the Pilgrim's chorus my Aunt Georgiana clutched my coat sleeve. Then it was I first realized that for her this broke a silence of thirty years; the inconceivable silence of the plains. With the battle between the two motives, with the frenzy of the Venusberg theme and its ripping of strings, there came to me an overwhelming sense of the waste and wear we are so powerless to combat; and I saw again the tall, naked house on the prairie, black and grim as a wooden fortress; the black pond where I had learned to swim, its margin pitted with sun-dried cattle tracks; the rain-gullied clay banks about the naked house, the four dwarf ash seedlings where the dishcloths were always hung to dry before the kitchen door. The world there was the flat world of the ancients; to the east, a cornfield that stretched to daybreak; to the west, a corral that reached to sunset; between, the conquests of peace, dearer bought than those of war.

The overture closed; my aunt released my coat sleeve, but she said nothing. She sat staring at the orchestra through a dullness of thirty years, through the films made little by little by each of the three hundred and sixty-five days in every one of them. What, I wondered, did she get from it? She had been a good pianist in her day I knew, and her musical education had been broader than that of most music teachers of a quarter of a century ago. She had often told me of Mozart's operas and Meyerbeer's, and I could remember hearing her sing, years ago, certain melodies of Verdi's. When I had fallen ill with a fever in her house she used to sit by my cot in the evening—when the cool, night wind blew in through the faded mosquito netting tacked over the window, and I lay watching a certain bright star that burned red above the cornfield—and sing "Home to our mountains, O, let us return!" in a way fit to break the heart of a Vermont boy near dead of homesickness already.

I watched her closely through the prelude to *Tristan and Isolde*, trying vainly to conjecture what that seething turmoil of strings and winds might mean to her, but she sat mutely staring at the violin bows that drove obliquely downward, like the pelting streaks of rain in a summer shower. Had this music any message for her? Had she enough left to at all comprehend this power which had kindled the world since she had left it? I was in a fever of curiosity, but Aunt Georgiana sat silent upon her peak in Darien. She preserved this utter immobility throughout the number from *The Flying Dutchman*, though her fingers worked mechanically upon her black dress, as though, of themselves, they were recalling the piano score they had once played. Poor old hands! They had been stretched and twisted into mere tentacles to hold and lift and knead with; the palms unduly swollen, the fingers bent and knotted—on one of them a thin, worn band that had once been a wedding ring. As I pressed and gently quieted one of those groping hands I remembered with quivering eyelids their services for me in other days.

Soon after the tenor began the "Prize Song," I heard a quick drawn breath and turned to my aunt. Her eyes were closed, but the tears were glistening on her cheeks, and I think, in a moment more, they were in my eyes as well. It never really died, then—the soul that can suffer so excruciatingly and so interminably; it withers to the outward eye only; like that strange moss which can lie on a dusty shelf half a century and yet, if placed in water, grows green again. She wept so throughout the development and elaboration of the melody.

During the intermission before the second half of the concert, I questioned my aunt and found that the "Prize Song" was not new to her. Some years before there had drifted to the farm in Red Willow County a young German, a tramp cowpuncher, who had sung the chorus at Bayreuth, when he was a boy, along with the other peasant boys and girls. Of a Sunday morning he used to sit on his gingham-sheeted bed in the hands' bedroom which opened off the kitchen, cleaning the leather of his boots and saddle, singing the "Prize Song," while my aunt went about her work in the kitchen. She had hovered about him until she had prevailed upon him to join the country church, though his sole fitness for this step, insofar as I could gather, lay in his boyish face and his possession of this divine melody. Shortly afterward he had gone to town on the Fourth of July, been drunk for several days, lost his money at a faro table, ridden a saddled Texan steer on a bet, and disappeared with a fractured collarbone. All this my aunt told me huskily, wanderingly, as though she were talking in the weak lapses of illness.

"Well, we have come to better things than the old *Trovatore* at any rate, Aunt Georgie?" I queried, with a well-meant effort at jocularity.

Her lip quivered and she hastily put her handkerchief up to her mouth. From behind it she murmured, "And you have been hearing this ever since you left me, Clark?" Her question was the gentlest and saddest of reproaches.

The second half of the program consisted of four numbers from the *Ring,* and closed with Siegfried's funeral march. My aunt wept quietly, but almost continuously, as a shallow vessel overflows in a rainstorm. From time to time her dim eyes looked up at the lights which studded the ceiling, burning softly under their dull glass globes; doubtless they were stars in truth to her. I was still perplexed as to what measure of musical comprehension was left to her, she who had heard nothing but the singing of gospel hymns at Methodist services in the square frame schoolhouse on Section Thirteen for so many years. I was wholly unable to gauge how much of it had been dissolved in soapsuds, or worked into bread, or milked into the bottom of a pail.

The deluge of sound poured on and on; I never knew what she found in the shining current of it; I never knew how far it bore her, or past what happy islands. From the trembling of her face I could well believe that before the last numbers she had been carried out where the myriad graves are, into the gray, nameless burying grounds of the sea; or into some world of death vaster yet, where, from the beginning of the world, hope has lain down with hope and dream with dream and, renouncing, slept.

The concert was over; the people filed out of the hall chattering and laughing, glad to relax and find the living level again, but my kinswoman made no effort to rise. The harpist slipped its green felt cover over his instrument; the flute players shook the water from their mouthpieces; the men of the orchestra went out one by one, leaving the stage to the chairs and music stands, empty as a winter cornfield.

I spoke to my aunt. She burst into tears and sobbed pleadingly. "I don't want to go, Clark, I don't want to go!"

I understood. For her, just outside the door of the concert hall, lay the black pond with the cattle-tracked bluffs; the tall, unpainted house, with weather-curled boards; naked as a tower, the crook-backed ash seedlings where the dishcloths hung to dry; the gaunt, molting turkeys picking up refuse about the kitchen door.

The Best Years

I

On a bright September morning in the year 1899 Miss Evangeline Knightly was driving through the beautiful Nebraska land which lies between the Platte River and the Kansas line. She drove slowly, for she loved the country, and she held the reins loosely in her gloved hand. She drove about a great deal and always wore leather gauntlets. Her hands were small, well shaped and very white, but they freckled in hot sunlight.

Miss Knightly was a charming person to meet—and an unusual type in a new country: oval face, small head delicately set (the oval chin tilting inward instead of the square chin thrust out), hazel eyes, a little blue, a little green, tiny dots of brown. . . . Somehow these splashes of colour made light—and warmth. When she laughed, her eyes positively glowed with humour, and in each oval cheek a roguish dimple came magically to the surface. Her laugh was delightful because it was intelligent, discriminating, not the physical spasm which seizes children when they are tickled, and growing boys and girls when they are embarrassed. When Miss Knightly laughed, it was apt to be because of some happy coincidence or droll mistake. The farmers along the road always felt flattered if they could make Miss Knightly laugh. Her voice had as many colours as her eyes—nearly always on the bright side, though it had a beautiful gravity for people who were in trouble.

It is only fair to say that in the community where she lived Miss Knightly was considered an intelligent young woman, but plain—distinctly plain. The standard of female beauty seems to be the same in all newly settled countries: Australia, New Zealand, the farming country along the Platte. It is, and was, the glowing, smiling calendar girl sent out to advertise agricultural implements. Colour was everything, modelling was nothing. A nose was a nose—any shape would do; a forehead was the place where the hair stopped, chin utterly negligible unless it happened to be more than two inches long.

Miss Knightly's old mare, Molly, took her time along the dusty, sunflower-bordered roads that morning, occasionally pausing long enough to snatch off a juicy, leafy sunflower top in her yellow teeth. This she munched as she ambled along. Although Molly had almost the slowest trot in the world, she really preferred walking. Sometimes she fell into a doze and stumbled. Miss Knightly also, when she was abroad on these long drives, preferred the leisurely pace. She loved the beautiful autumn country; loved to look at it, to breathe it. She was not a "dreamy" person, but she was thoughtful and very observing. She relished the morning; the great blue of the sky, smiling, cloudless,—and the land that lay level as far as the eye could see. The horizon was like a perfect circle, a great embrace, and within it lay the cornfields, still green, and the yellow wheat stubble, miles and miles of it, and the pasture lands where the white-faced cattle led lives of utter content. All their movements were deliberate and dignified. They grazed through all the morning; approached their metal water tank and drank. If the windmill had run too long and the tank had overflowed, the cattle trampled the overflow into deep mud and cooled their feet. Then they drifted off to graze again. Grazing was not merely eating, it was also a pastime, a form of reflection, perhaps meditation.

Miss Knightly was thinking, as Molly jogged along, that the barbed-wire fences, though ugly in themselves, had their advantages. They did not cut the country up into patterns as did the rail fences and stone walls of her native New England. They were, broadly regarded, invisible—did not impose themselves upon the eye. She seemed to be driving through a fineless land. On her left the Hereford cattle apparently wandered at will: the tall sunflowers hid the wire that kept them off the road. Far away, on the horizon line, a troop of colts were galloping, all in the same direction—purely for exercise, one would say. Between her and the horizon the white wheels of windmills told her where the farmhouses sat.

Miss Knightly was abroad this morning with a

special purpose—to visit country schools. She was the County Superintendent of Public Instruction. A grim title, that, to put upon a charming young woman. . . . Fortunately it was seldom used except on reports which she signed, and there it was usually printed. She was not even called "the Superintendent." A country schoolteacher said to her pupils: "I think Miss Knightly will come to see us this week. She was at Walnut Creek yesterday."

After she had driven westward through the pasture lands for an hour or so, Miss Knightly turned her mare north and very soon came into a rich farming district, where the fields were too valuable to be used for much grazing. Big red barns, rows of yellow straw stacks, green orchards, trim white farmhouses, fenced gardens.

Looking at her watch, Miss Knightly found that it was already after eleven o'clock. She touched Molly delicately with the whip and roused her to a jog trot. Presently they stopped before a little one-storey schoolhouse. All the windows were open. At the hitch-bar in the yard five horses were tethered—their saddles and bridles piled in an empty buckboard. There was a yard, but no fence—though on one side of the playground was a woven-wire fence covered with the vines of sturdy rambler roses—very pretty in the spring. It enclosed a cemetery—very few graves, very much sun and waving yellow grass, open to the singing from the schoolroom and the shouts of the boys playing ball at noon. The cemetery never depressed the children, and surely the school cast no gloom over the cemetery.

When Miss Knightly stopped before the door, a

boy ran out to hand her from the buggy and to take care of Molly. The little teacher stood on the doorstep, her face lost, as it were, in a wide smile of tremulous gladness.

Miss Knightly took her hand, held it for a moment and looked down into the child's face—she was scarcely more—and said in the very gentlest shade of her many-shaded voice, "Everything going well, Lesley?"

The teacher replied in happy little gasps. "Oh yes, Miss Knightly! It's all so much easier than it was last year. I have some such lovely children—and they're all *good!*"

Miss Knightly took her arm, and they went into the schoolroom. The pupils grinned a welcome to the visitor. The teacher asked the conventional question: What recitation would she like to hear? Whatever came next in the usual order, Miss Knightly said.

The class in geography came next. The children were "bounding" the States. When the North Atlantic States had been disposed of with more or less accuracy, the little teacher said they would now jump to the Middle West, to bring the lesson nearer home.

"Suppose we begin with Illinois. That is your State, Edward, so I will call on you."

A pale boy rose and came front of the class; a little fellow aged ten, maybe, who was plainly a newcomer—wore knee pants and stockings, instead of long trousers or blue overalls like the other boys. His hands were clenched at his sides, and he was evidently much frightened. Looking appealingly at the little teacher, he began in a high treble: "The State of Illinois is bounded on the north by Lake Michigan, on the east by Lake Michigan . . ." He felt he had gone astray, and language utterly failed. A quick shudder ran over him from head to foot, and an accident happened. His dark blue stockings grew darker still, and his knickerbockers very dark. He stood there as if nailed to the floor. The teacher went up to him and took his hand and led him to his desk.

"You're too tired, Edward," she said. "We're all tired, and it's almost noon. So you can all run out and play, while I talk to Miss Knightly and tell her how naughty you all are."

The children laughed (all but poor Edward), laughed heartily, as if they were suddenly relieved from some strain. Still laughing and punching each other they ran out into the sunshine.

Miss Knightly and the teacher (her name, by the way, was Lesley Ferguesson) sat down on a bench in the corner.

"I'm so sorry that happened, Miss Knightly. I oughtn't to have called on him. He's so new here, and he's a nervous little boy. I thought he'd like to speak up for his State. He seems homesick."

"My dear, I'm glad you did call on him, and I'm glad the poor little fellow had an accident,—if he doesn't get too much misery out of it. The way those children behaved astonished me. Not a wink, or grin, or even a look. Not a wink from the Haymaker boy. I watched him. His mother has no such delicacy. They have just the best kind of good manners. How do you do it, Lesley?"

Lesley gave a happy giggle and flushed as red as a poppy. "Oh, I don't do anything! You see they really *are* nice children. You remember last year I did have a little trouble—till they got used to me."

"But they all passed their finals, and one girl, who was older than her teacher, got a school."

"Hush, hush, ma'am! I'm afraid for the walls to hear it! Nobody knows our secret but my mother."

"I'm very well satisfied with the results of our crime, Lesley."

The girl blushed again. She loved to hear Miss Knightly speak her name, because she always sounded the *s* like a *z*, which made it seem gentler and more intimate. Nearly everyone else, even her mother, hissed the *s* as if it were spelled "Lessley." It was embarrassing to have such a queer name, but she respected it because her father had chosen it for her.

"Where are you going to stay all night, Miss Knightly?" she asked rather timidly.

"I think Mrs. Ericson expects me to stay with her."

"Mrs. Hunt, where I stay, would be awful glad to have you, but I know you'll be more comfortable at Mrs. Ericson's. She's a lovely housekeeper." Lesley resigned the faint hope that Miss Knightly would stay where she herself boarded, and broke out eagerly:

"Oh, Miss Knightly, have you seen any of our boys lately? Mother's too busy to write to me often."

"Hector looked in at my office last week. He came to the Court House with a telegram for the sheriff. He seemed well and happy."

"Did he? But Miss Knightly, I wish he hadn't taken that messenger job. I hate so for him to quit school."

"Now, I wouldn't worry about that, my dear. School isn't everything. He'll be getting good experience every day at the depot."

"Do you think so? I haven't seen him since he went to work."

"Why, how long has it been since you were home?"

"It's over a month now. Not since my school started. Father has been working all our horses on the farm. Maybe you can share my lunch with me?"

"I brought a lunch for the two of us, my dear. Call your favourite boy to go to my buggy and get my basket for us. After lunch I would like to hear the advanced arithmetic class."

While the pupils were doing their sums at the blackboard, Miss Knightly herself was doing a little figuring. This was Thursday. Tomorrow she would visit two schools, and she had planned to spend Friday night with a pleasant family on Farmers' Creek. But she could change her schedule and give this homesick child a visit with her family in the county seat. It would inconvenience her very little.

When the class in advanced arithmetic was dismissed, Miss Knightly made a joking little talk to the children and told them about a very bright little girl in Scotland who knew nearly a whole play of Shakespeare's by heart, but who wrote in her diary: "Nine times nine is the Devil"; which proved, she said, that there are two kinds of memory, and God is very good to anyone to whom he gives both kinds. Then she asked if the pupils might have a special recess of half an hour, as a present from her. They gave her a cheer and out they trooped, the boys to the ball ground, and the girls to the cemetery, to sit neatly on the headstones and discuss Miss Knightly.

During their recess the Superintendent disclosed her plan. "I've been wondering, Lesley, whether you wouldn't like to go back to town with me after school tomorrow. We could get into MacAlpin by seven o'clock, and you could have all of Saturday and Sunday at home. Then we would make an early start Monday morning, and I would drop you here at the schoolhouse at nine o'clock."

The little teacher caught her breath—she became quite pale for a moment.

"Oh Miss Knightly, could you? Could you?"

"Of course I can. I'll stop for you here at four o'clock tomorrow afternoon."

II

The dark secret between Lesley and Miss Knightly was that only this September had the girl reached the legal age for teachers, yet she had been teaching all last year when she was still under age!

Last summer, when the applicants for teachers' certificates took written examinations in the County Superintendent's offices at the Court House in MacAlpin, Lesley Ferguesson had appeared with some twenty-six girls and nine boys. She wrote all morning and all afternoon for two days. Miss Knightly found her paper one of the best in the lot. A week later, when all the papers were filed, Miss Knightly told Lesley she could certainly give her a school. The morning after she had thus notified Lesley, she found the girl herself waiting on the sidewalk in front of the house where Miss Knightly boarded.

"Could I walk over to the Court House with you, Miss Knightly? I ought to tell you something," she blurted out at once. "On that paper I didn't put down my real age. I put down sixteen, and I won't be fifteen until this September."

"But I checked you with the high-school records, Lesley."

"I know. I put it down wrong there, too. I didn't want to be the class baby, and I hoped I could get a school soon, to help out at home."

The County Superintendent thought she would long remember that walk to the Court House. She could see that the child had spent a bad night; and she had walked up from her home down by the depot, quite a mile away, probably without breakfast.

"If your age is wrong on both records, why do you tell me about it now?"

"Oh, Miss Knightly, I got to thinking about it last night, how if you did give me a school it might all come out, and mean people would say you knew about it and broke the law."

Miss Knightly was thoughtless enough to chuckle. "But, my dear, don't you see that if I didn't know about it until this moment, I am completely innocent?"

The child who was walking beside her stopped short and burst into sobs. Miss Knightly put her arm around those thin, eager, forward-reaching shoulders.

"Don't cry, dear. I was only joking. There's nothing very dreadful about it. You didn't give your age under oath, you know." The sobs didn't stop. "Listen, let me tell you something. That big Hatch boy put his age down as nineteen, and I know he was teaching down in Nemaha County four years ago. I can't always be sure about the age applicants put down. I have to use my judgment."

The girl lifted her pale, troubled face and murmured, "Judgment?"

"Yes. Some girls are older at thirteen than others are at eighteen. Your paper was one of the best handed in this year, and I am going to give you a school. Not a big one, but a nice one, in a nice part of the county. Now let's go into Ernie's coffee shop and have some more breakfast. You have a long walk home."

Of course, fourteen was rather young for a teacher in an ungraded school, where she was likely to have pupils of sixteen and eighteen in her classes. But Miss Knightly's "judgment" was justified by the fact that in June the school directors of the Wild Rose district asked to have "Miss Ferguesson" back for the following year.

III

At four o'clock on Friday afternoon Miss Knightly stopped at the Wild Rose schoolhouse to find the teacher waiting by the roadside, and the pupils already scattering across the fields, their tin lunch pails flashing back the sun. Lesley was standing almost in the road itself, her grey "telescope" bag at her feet. The moment old Molly stopped, she stowed her bag in the back of the buggy and climbed in beside Miss Knightly. Her smile was so eager and happy that her friend chuckled softly. "You still get a little homesick, don't you, Lesley?"

She didn't deny it. She gave a guilty laugh and murmured, "I do miss the boys."

The afternoon sun was behind them, throwing over the pastures and the harvested, resting fields that wonderful light, so yellow that it is actually orange. The three hours and the fourteen miles seemed not overlong. As the buggy neared the town of MacAlpin, Miss Knightly thought she could feel Lesley's heart beat. The girl had been silent a long while when she exclaimed:

"Look, there's the standpipe!"

The object of this emotion was a red sheet-iron tube which thrust its naked ugliness some eighty feet into the air and held the water supply for the town of MacAlpin. As it stood on a hill, it was the first thing one saw on approaching the town from the west. Old Molly, too, seemed to have spied this heartening landmark, for she quickened her trot without encouragement from the whip. From that point on, Lesley said not a word. There were two more low hills (very low), and then Miss Knightly turned off the main road and drove by a short cut through the baseball ground, to the south appendix of the town proper, the "depot settlement" where the Ferguessons lived.

Their house stood on a steep hillside—a storey-and-a-half frame house with a basement on the downhill side, faced with brick up to the first-floor level. When the buggy stopped before the yard gate, two little boys came running out of the front door. Miss Knightly's passenger vanished from her side—she didn't know just when Lesley alighted. Her attention was distracted by the appearance of the mother, with a third boy, still in kilts, trotting behind her.

Mrs. Ferguesson was not a person who could be overlooked. All the merchants in MacAlpin admitted that she was a fine figure of a woman. As she came down the little yard and out of the gate, the evening breeze ruffled her wavy auburn hair. Her quick step and alert, upright carriage gave one the impression that she got things done. Coming up to the buggy, she took Miss Knightly's hand.

"Why, it's Miss Knightly! And she's brought our girl along to visit us. That was mighty clever of you, Miss, and these boys will surely be a happy family. They do miss their sister." She spoke clearly, distinctly, but with a slight Missouri turn of speech.

By this time Lesley and her brothers had become telepathically one. Miss Knightly couldn't tell what the boys said to her, or whether they said anything, but they had her old canvas bag out of the buggy and up on the porch in no time at all. Lesley ran toward the front door, hurried back to thank Miss Knightly, and then disappeared, holding fast to the little chap in skirts. She had forgotten to ask at what time Miss Knightly would call for her on Monday, but her mother attended to that. When Mrs. Ferguesson followed the children through the hall and the little back parlour into the dining-room, Lesley turned to her and asked breathlessly, almost sharply:

"Where's Hector?"

"He's often late on Friday night, dear. He telephoned me from the depot and said not to wait supper for him—he'd get a sandwich at the lunch counter. Now how *are* you, my girl?" Mrs. Ferguesson put her hands on Lesley's shoulders and looked into her glowing eyes.

"Just fine, Mother. I like my school so much! And the scholars are nicer even than they were last year. I just love some of them."

At this the little boy in kilts (the fashion of the times, though he was four years old) caught his sister's skirt in his two hands and jerked it to get her attention. "No, no!" he said mournfully, "you don't love anybody but us!"

His mother laughed, and Lesley stooped and gave him the tight hug he wanted.

The family supper was over. Mrs. Ferguesson put on her apron. "Sit right down, Lesley, and talk to the children. No, I won't let you help me. You'll help me most by keeping them out of my way. I'll scramble you an egg and fry you some ham, so sit right down in your own place. I have some stewed plums for your dessert, and a beautiful angel cake I bought at the Methodist bake sale. Your father's gone to some political meeting, so we had supper early. You'll be a nice surprise for him when he gets home. He hadn't been gone half an hour when Miss Knightly drove up. Sit still, dear, it only bothers me if anybody tries to help me. I'll let you wash the dishes afterward, like we always do."

Lesley sat down at the half-cleared table; an oval-shaped table which could be extended by the insertion of "leaves" when Mrs. Ferguesson had company. The room was already dusky (twilights are short in a flat country), and one of the boys switched on the light which hung by a cord high above the table. A shallow china shade over the bulb threw a glaring white light down on the sister and the boys who stood about her chair. Lesley wrinkled up her brow, but it didn't occur to her that the light was too strong. She gave herself up to the feeling of being at home. It went all through her, that feeling, like getting into a warm bath when one is tired. She was safe from everything, was where she wanted to be, where she ought to be. A plant that has been washed out by a rain storm feels like that, when a kind gardener puts it gently back into its own earth with its own group.

The two older boys, Homer and Vincent, kept interrupting each other, trying to tell her things, but she didn't really listen to what they said. The little fellow stood close beside her chair, holding on to her skirt, fingering the glass buttons on her jacket. He was named Bryan, for his father's hero, but he didn't fit the name very well. He was a rather wistful and timid child.

Mrs. Ferguesson brought the ham and eggs and the warmed-up coffee. Then she sat down opposite her daughter to watch her enjoy her supper. "Now don't talk to her, boys. Let her eat in peace."

Vincent spoke up. "Can't I just tell her what happened to my lame pigeon?"

Mrs. Ferguesson merely shook her head. She had control in that household, sure enough!

Before Lesley had quite finished her supper she heard the front door open and shut. The boys started up, but the mother raised a warning finger.

They understood; a surprise. They were still as nice, and listened: A pause in the hall . . . he was hanging up his cap. Then he came in—the flower of the family.

For a moment he stood speechless in the doorway, the "incandescent" glaring full on his curly yellow hair and his amazed blue eyes. He was surprised indeed!

"Lesley!" he breathed, as if he were talking in his sleep.

She couldn't sit still. Without knowing that she got up and took a step, she had her arms around her brother. "It's me, Hector! Ain't I lucky? Miss Knightly brought me in."

"What time did you get here? You might have telephoned me, Mother."

"Dear, she ain't been here much more than half an hour."

"And Miss Knightly brought you in with old Molly, did she?" Oh, the lovely voice he had, that Hector!—warm, deliberate . . . it made the most commonplace remark full of meaning. He had to say merely that—and it told his appreciation of Miss Knightly's kindness, even a playful gratitude to Molly, her clumsy, fat, road-pounding old mare. He was tall for his age, was Hector, and he had the fair pink-cheeked complexion which Lesley should have had and didn't.

Mrs. Ferguesson rose. "Now let's all go into the parlour and talk. We'll come back and clear up afterward." With this she opened the folding doors, and they followed her and found comfortable chairs—there was even a home-made hassock for Bryan. There were real books in the sectional bookcases (old Ferg's fault), and there was a rea Brussels carpet in soft colours on the floor. Tha was Lesley's fault. Most of her savings from he first year's teaching had gone into that carpet. Sh had chosen it herself from the samples which Mar shall Field's travelling man brought to MacAlpin There were comfortable old-fashioned pictures o the walls—"Venice by Moonlight" and such. Les ley and Hector thought it a beautiful room.

Of course the room was pleasant because of th feeling the children had for one another, and be cause in Mrs. Ferguesson there was authority an organization. Here the family sat and talked unti Father came home. He was always treated a littl like company. His wife and his children had a dee respect for him and for experimental farming, an profound veneration for William Jennings Bryan Even little Bryan knew he was named for a grea man, and must some day stop being afraid of th dark.

James Grahame Ferguesson was a farmer. He spent most of his time on what he called an "ex- perimental farm." (The neighbours had other names for it—some of them amusing.) He was a loosely built man; had drooping shoulders carried with a forward thrust. He was a ready speaker, and usually made the Fourth of July speech in MacAlpin—spoke from a platform in the Court House grove, and even the farmers who joked about Ferguesson came to hear him. Alf Delaney declared: "I like to see anything done well—even talking. If old Ferg could shuck corn as fast as he can rustle the dictionary, I'd hire him, even if he is a Pop."

Old Ferg was not at all old—just turned forty—but he was fussy about the spelling of his name. He wrote it James Ferguesson. The merchants, even the local newspaper, simply would not spell it that way. They left letters out, or they put letters in. He complained about this repeatedly, and the result was that he was simply called "Ferg" to his face, and "old Ferg" to his back. His neighbours, both in town and in the country where he farmed, liked him because he gave them so much to talk about. He couldn't keep a hired man long at any wages. His habits were too unconventional. He rose early, saw to the chores like any other man, and went into the field for the morning. His lunch was a cold spread from his wife's kitchen, reinforced by hot tea. (The hired man was expected to bring his own lunch—outrageous!) After lunch Mr. Ferguesson took off his boots and lay down on the blue gingham sheets of a wide bed, and remained there until what he called "the cool of the afternoon." When that refreshing season arrived, he fed and watered his work horses, put the young gelding to his buckboard, and drove four miles to MacAlpin for his wife's hot supper. Mrs. Ferguesson, though not at all a meek woman or a stupid one, unquestioningly believed him when he told her that he did his best thinking in the afternoon. He hinted to her that he was working out in his head something that would benefit the farmers of the county more than all the corn and wheat they could raise even in a good year.

Sometimes Ferguesson did things she regretted—not because they were wrong, but because other people had mean tongues. When a fashion came in for giving names to farms which had hitherto been designated by figures (range, section, quarter, etc.), and his neighbours came out with "Lone Tree Farm," "Cold Spring Farm," etc., Ferguesson tacked on a cottonwood tree by his gate a neatly painted board inscribed: WIDE AWAKE FARM.

His neighbours, who could never get used to his afternoon siesta, were not long in converting this prophetic christening into "Hush-a-bye Farm." Mrs. Ferguesson overheard some of this joking on a Saturday night (she was marketing late after a lodge meeting on top of a busy day), and she didn't like it. On Sunday morning when he was dressing for church, she asked her husband why he ever gave the farm such a foolish name. He explained to her that the important crop on that farm was an idea. His farm was like an observatory where one watched the signs of the times and saw the great change that was coming for the benefit of all mankind. He even quoted Tennyson about looking into the future "far as human eye could see." It had been a long time since he had quoted any poetry to her. She sighed and dropped the matter.

On the whole, Ferg did himself a good turn when he put up that piece of nomenclature. People drove out of their way for miles to see it. They felt more kindly toward old Ferg because he wrote himself down such an ass. In a hard-working farming community a good joke is worth something. Ferguesson himself felt a gradual warming toward him among his neighbours. He ascribed it to the power of his oratory. It was really because he had made himself so absurd, but this he never guessed. Idealists are seldom afraid of ridicule—if they recognize it.

The Ferguesson children believed that their father was misunderstood by people of inferior intelligence, and that conviction gave them a "cause" which bound them together. They must do better than other children; better in school, and better on the playground. They must turn in a quarter of a dollar to help their mother out whenever they could. Experimental farming wasn't immediately remunerative.

Fortunately there was never any rent to pay. They owned their house down by the depot. When Mrs. Ferguesson's father died down in Missouri, she bought that place with what he left her. She knew that was the safe thing to do, her husband being a thinker. Her children were bound to her, and to that house, by the deepest, the most solemn loyalty. They never spoke of that covenant to each other, never even formulated it in their own minds—never. It was a consciousness they shared, and it gave them a family complexion.

On this Saturday of Lesley's surprise visit home, Father was with the family for breakfast. That was always a pleasant way to begin the day—especially on Saturday, when no one was in a hurry. He had grave good manners toward his wife and his children. He talked to them as if they were grown-up, reasonable beings—talked a trifle as if from a rostrum, perhaps,—and he never indulged in small-town gossip. He was much more likely to tell them what he had read in the *Omaha World-Herald* yesterday; news of the State capital and the national capital. Sometimes he told them what a grasping, selfish country England was. Very often he explained to them how the gold standard had kept the poor man down. The family seldom bothered him about petty matters—such as that Homer needed new shoes, or that the iceman's bill for the whole summer had come in for the third time. Mother would take care of that.

On this particular Saturday morning Ferguesson gave especial attention to Lesley. He asked her about her school, and had her name her pupils. "I think you are fortunate to have the Wild Rose school, Lesley," he said as he rose from the table. "The farmers up there are open-minded and prosperous. I have sometimes wished that I had settled up there, though there are certain advantages in living at the county seat. The educational opportunities are better. Your friendship with Miss Knightly has been a broadening influence."

He went out to hitch up the buckboard to drive to the farm, while his wife put up the lunch he was to take along with him, and Lesley went upstairs to make the beds.

"Upstairs" was a story in itself, a secret romance. No caller or neighbour had ever been allowed to go up there. All the children loved it—it was their very own world where there were no older people poking about to spoil things. And it was unique—not at all like other people's upstairs chambers. In her stuffy little bedroom out in the country Lesley had more than once cried for it.

Lesley and the boys liked space, not tight cubbyholes. Their upstairs was a long attic which ran the whole length of the house, from the front door downstairs to the kitchen at the back. Its great charm was that it was unlined. No plaster, no beaver-board lining; just the roof shingles, supported by long, unplaned, splintery rafters that sloped from the sharp roof-peak down to the floor of the attic. Bracing these long roof rafters were cross rafters on which one could hang things—a little personal washing, a curtain for tableaux, a rope swing for Bryan.

In this spacious, undivided loft were two brick chimneys, going up in neat little stair-steps from the plank floor to the shingle roof—and out of it to the stars! The chimneys were of red, unglazed brick, with lines of white mortar to hold them together.

Last year, after Lesley first got her school, Mrs. Ferguesson exerted her authority and partitioned off a little room over the kitchen end of the "up-stairs" for her daughter. Before that, all the children slept in this delightful attic. The three older boys occupied two wide beds, their sister her little single bed. Bryan, subject to croup, still slumbered downstairs near his mother, but he looked forward to his ascension as to a state of pure beatitude.

There was certainly room enough up there for widely scattered quarters, but the three beds stood in a row, as in a hospital ward. The children liked to be close enough together to share experiences.

Experiences were many. Perhaps the most exciting was when the driving, sleety snowstorms came on winter nights. The roof shingles were old and had curled under hot summer suns. In a driving snowstorm the frozen flakes sifted in through all those little cracks, sprinkled the beds and the children, melted on their faces, in their hair! That was delightful. The rest of you was snug and warm under blankets and comforters, with a hot brick at one's feet. The wind howled outside; sometimes the white light from the snow and the half-strangled moon came in through the single end window. Each child had his own dream-adventure. They did not exchange confidences; every "fellow" had a right to his own. They never told their love.

If they turned in early, they had a good while to enjoy the outside weather; they never went to sleep until after ten o'clock, for then came the sweetest morsel of the night. At that hour Number Seventeen, the westbound passenger, whistled in. The station and the engine house were perhaps an eighth of a mile down the hill, and from far away across the meadows the children could hear that whistle. Then came the heavy pants of the locomotive in the frosty air. Then a hissing—then silence: she was taking water.

On Saturdays the children were allowed to go down to the depot to see Seventeen come in. It was a fine sight on winter nights. Sometimes the great locomotive used to sweep in armoured in ice and snow, breathing fire like a dragon, its great red eye shooting a blinding beam along the white roadbed and shining wet rails. When it stopped, it panted like a great beast. After it was watered by the big hose from the overhead tank, it seemed to draw long deep breaths, ready to charge afresh over the great Western land.

Yes, they were grand old warriors, those towering locomotives of other days. They seemed to mean power, conquest, triumph—Jim Hill's dream. They set children's hearts beating from Chicago to Los Angeles. They were the awakeners of many a dream.

As she made the boys' beds that Saturday morning and put on clean sheets, Lesley was thinking she would give a great deal to sleep out here as she used to. But when she got her school last year, her mother had said she must have a room of her own. So a carpenter brought sheathing and "lined" the end of the long loft—the end over the kitchen; and Mrs. Ferguesson bought a little yellow washstand and a bowl and pitcher, and said with satisfaction: "Now you see, Lesley, if you were sick, we would have some place to take the doctor." To be sure, the doctor would have to be admitted through the kitchen, and then come up a dark winding stairway with two turns. (Mr. Ferguesson termed it "the turnpike." His old Scotch grandmother, he said, had always thus called a winding stairway.) And Lesley's room, when you got there, was very like a snug wooden box. It was possible, of course, to leave her door open into the long loft, where the wood was brown and the chimneys red and the weather always so close to one. Out there things were still wild and rough—it wasn't a bedroom or a chamber—it was a hall, in the old baronial sense, reminded her of the lines in their *Grimm's Fairy Tales* book:

> Return, return, thou youthful bride,
> This is a robbers' hall inside.

IV

When her daughter had put the attic to rights, Mrs. Ferguesson went uptown to do her Saturday marketing. Lesley slipped out through the kitchen door and sat down on the back porch. The front porch was kept neat and fit to receive callers, but the back porch was given over to the boys. It was a messy-looking place, to be sure. From the wooden ceiling hung two trapezes. At one corner four boxing gloves were piled in a broken chair. In the trampled, grassless back yard, two-by-fours, planted upright, supported a length of lead pipe on which Homer practised bar exercises. Lesley sat down on the porch floor, her feet on the ground, and sank into idleness and safety and perfect love.

The boys were much the dearest things in the world to her. To love them so much was just . . . happiness. To think about them was the most perfect form of happiness. Had they been actually present, swinging on the two trapezes, turning on the bar, she would have been too much excited, too actively happy to be perfectly happy. But sitting in the warm sun, with her feet on the good ground, even her mother away, she almost ceased to exist. The feeling of being at home was complete, absolute: it made her sleepy. And that feeling was not so much the sense of being protected by her father and mother as of being with, and being one with, her brothers. It was the clan feeling, which meant life or death for the blood, not for the individual. For some reason, or for no reason, back in the beginning, creatures wanted the blood to continue.

After the noonday dinner Mrs. Ferguesson thoughtfully confided to her daughter while they were washing the dishes:

"Lesley, I'm divided in my mind. I would so appreciate a quiet afternoon with you, but I've a sort of engagement with the P.E.O. A lady from Canada is to be there to talk to us, and I've promised to introduce her. And just when I want to have a quiet time with you."

Lesley gave a sigh of relief and thought how fortunate it is that circumstances do sometimes make up our mind for us. In that battered canvas bag upstairs there was a roll of arithmetic papers and "essays" which hung over her like a threat. Now she would have a still hour in their beautiful parlour to correct them; the shades drawn down, just enough light to read by, her father's unabridged at hand, and the boys playing bat and pitch in the back yard.

Lesley and her brothers were proud of their mother's good looks, and that she never allowed herself to become a household drudge, as so many of her neighbours did. She "managed," and the boys helped her to manage. For one thing, there were never any dreary tubs full of washing standing about, and there was no ironing day to make a hole in the week. They sent all the washing, even the sheets, to the town steam laundry. Hector, with his weekly wages as messenger boy, and Homer and Vincent with their stable jobs, paid for it. That simple expedient did away with the worst blight of the working man's home.

Mrs. Ferguesson was "public-spirited," and she was the friend of all good causes. The business men of the town agreed that she had a great deal of influence, and that her name added strength to any committee. She was generally spoken of as a very *practical* woman, with an emphasis which implied several things. She was a "joiner," too! She was a Royal Neighbor, and a Neighborly Neighbor, and a P.E.O., and an Eastern Star. She had even joined the Methodist Win-a-Couple, though she warned them that she could not attend their meetings, as she liked to spend some of her evenings at home.

Promptly at six thirty Monday morning Miss Knightly's old mare stopped in front of the Fergussons' house. The four boys were all on the front porch. James himself carried Lesley's bag down and put it into the buggy. He thanked the Superintendent very courteously for her kindness and kissed his daughter good-bye.

It had been at no trifling sacrifice that Miss Knightly was able to call for Lesley at six thirty. Customarily she started on her long drives at nine o'clock. This morning she had to give an extra half-dollar to the man who came to curry and harness her mare. She herself got no proper breakfast, but a cold sandwich and a cup of coffee at the station lunch counter—the only eating-place open at six o'clock. Most serious of all, she must push Molly a little on the road, to land her passenger at the Wild Rose schoolhouse at nine o'clock. Such small inconveniences do not sum up to an imposing total, but we assume them only for persons we really care for.

V

It was Christmas Eve. The town was busy with Christmas "exercises," and all the churches were lit up. Hector Ferguesson was going slowly up the hill which separated the depot settlement from the town proper. He walked at no messenger-boy pace tonight, crunching under his feet the snow which had fallen three days ago, melted, and then frozen hard. His hands were in the pockets of his new overcoat, which was so long that it almost touched the ground when he toiled up the steepest part of the hill. It was very heavy and not very warm. In those days there was a theory that in topcoats very little wool was necessary if they were woven tight enough and hard enough to "keep out the cold." A barricade was the idea. Hector carried the weight and clumsiness bravely, proudly. His new overcoat was a Christmas present from his sister. She had gone to the big town in the next county to shop for it, and bought it with her own money. He was thinking how kind Lesley was, and how hard she had worked for that money, and how much she had to put up with in the rough farmhouse where she boarded, out in the country. It was usually a poor housekeeper who was willing to keep a teacher, since they paid so little. Probably the amount Lesley spent for that coat would have kept her at a comfortable house all winter. When he grew up, and made lots of money (a brakeman—maybe an engineer), he would certainly be good to his sister.

Hector was a strange boy; a blend of the soft and the hard. In action he was practical, executive, like his mother. But in his mind, in his thoughts and plans, he was extravagant, often absurd. His mother suspected that he was "dreamy." Tonight, as he trailed up the frozen wooden sidewalk toward the town, he kept looking up at the stars, which were unusually bright, as they always seem over a stretch of snow. He was wondering if there were angels up there, watching the world on Christmas Eve. They came before, on the first Christmas Eve, he knew. Perhaps they kept the Anniversary. He thought about a beautiful coloured picture tacked up in Lesley's bedroom; two angels with white robes and long white wings flying toward a low hill in the early dawn before sunrise, and on that distant hill, against the soft daybreak light, were three tiny crosses. He never doubted angels looked like that. He was credulous and truthful by nature. There was that look in his blue eyes. He would get it knocked out of him, his mother knew. But she believed he would always keep some of it—enough to make him open-handed and open-hearted.

Tonight Hector had his leather satchel full of Christmas telegrams. After he had delivered them all, he would buy his presents for his mother and the children. The stores sold off their special Christmas things at a discount after eleven o'clock on Christmas Eve.

VI

Miss Knightly was in Lincoln, attending a convention of Superintendents of Public Instruction, when the long-to-be-remembered blizzard swept down over the prairie State. Travel and telephone service were discontinued. A Chicago passenger train was stalled for three days in a deep cut west of W—. There she lay, and the dining-car had much ado to feed the passengers.

Miss Knightly was snowbound in Lincoln. She

tarried there after the convention was dismissed and her fellow superintendents had gone home to their respective counties. She was caught by the storm because she had stayed over to see Julia Marlowe (then young and so fair!) in *The Love Chase*. She was not inconsolable to be delayed for some days. Why worry? She was staying at a small but very pleasant hotel, where the food was good and the beds were comfortable. She was New England born and bred, too conscientious to stay over in the city from mere self-indulgence, but quite willing to be lost to MacAlpin and X— County by the intervention of fate. She stayed, in fact, a week, greatly enjoying such luxuries as plenty of running water, hot baths, and steam heat. At that date MacAlpin houses, and even her office in the Court House, were heated by hard-coal stoves.

At last she was jogging home on a passenger train which left Lincoln at a convenient hour (it was two hours late, travel was still disorganized), when she was pleased to see Mr. Redman in conductor's uniform come into the car. Two of his boys had been her pupils when she taught in high school, before she was elected to a county office. Mr. Redman also seemed pleased, and after he had been through the train to punch tickets, he came back and sat down in the green plush seat opposite Miss Knightly and began to "tease."

"I hear there was a story going up at the Court House that you'd eloped. I was hoping you hadn't made a mistake."

"No. I thought it over and avoided the mistake. But what about you, Mr. Redman? You belong on the run west out of MacAlpin, don't you?"

"I don't know where I belong, Ma'm, and nobody else does. This is Jack Kelly's run, but he got his leg broke trying to help the train crew shovel the sleeping-car loose in that deep cut out of W—. The passengers were just freezing. This blizzard has upset everything. There's got to be better organization from higher up. This has taught us we just can't handle an emergency. Hard on stock, hard on people. A little neighbour of ours—why, you must know her, she was one of your teachers—Jim Ferguesson's little girl. She got pneumonia out there in the country and died out there."

Miss Knightly went so white that Redman without a word hurried to the end of the car and brought back a glass of water. He kept muttering that he was sorry . . . that he "always put his foot in it."

She did not disappoint him. She came back quickly. "That's all right, Mr. Redman. I'd rather hear it before I get home. Did she get lost in the storm? I don't understand."

Mr. Redman sat down and did the best he could to repair damages.

"No, Ma'm, little Lesley acted very sensible, didn't lose her head. You see, the storm struck us about three o'clock in the afternoon. The whole day it had been mild and soft, like spring. Then it came down instanter, like a thousand tons of snow dumped out of the sky. My wife was out in the back yard taking in some clothes she'd hung to dry. She hadn't even a shawl over her head. The suddenness of it confused her so (she couldn't see three feet before her), she wandered around in our back yard, couldn't find her way back to the house. Pretty soon our old dog—he's part shepherd—

came yappin' and whinin'. She dropped the clothes and held onto his hair, and he got her to the back porch. That's how bad it was in MacAlpin."

"And Lesley?" Miss Knightly murmured.

"Yes, Ma'm! I'm coming to that. Her scholars tell about how the schoolroom got a little dark, and they all looked out, and there was no graveyard, and no horses that some of them had rode to school on. The boys jumped up to run out and see after the horses, but Lesley stood with her back against the door and wouldn't let 'em go out. Told 'em it would be over in a few minutes. Well, you see it wasn't. Over four feet of snow fell in less'n an hour. About six o'clock some of the fathers of the children that lived aways off started out on horseback, but the horses waded belly-deep, and a wind come up and it turned cold.

"Ford Robertson is the nearest neighbour, you know,—scarcely more than across the road—eighth of a mile, maybe. As soon as he come in from his corral—the Herefords had all bunched up together, over a hundred of 'em, under the lee of a big haystack, and he knew they wouldn't freeze. As soon as he got in, the missus made him go over to the schoolhouse an' take a rope along an' herd 'em all over to her house, teacher an' all, with the boys leading their horses. That night Mrs. Robertson cooked nearly everything in the house for their supper, and she sent Ford upstairs to help Lesley make shakedown beds on the floor. Mrs. Robertson remembers when the big supper was ready and the children ate like wolves, Lesley didn't eat much—said she had a little headache. Next morning she was pretty sick. That day all the fathers came on horseback for the children.

Robertson got one of them to go for old Doctor Small, and he came down on his horse. Doctor said it was pneumonia, and there wasn't much he could do. She didn't seem to have strength to rally. She was out of her head when he got there. She was mostly unconscious for three days, and just slipped out. The funeral is tomorrow. The roads are open now. They were to bring her home today."

The train stopped at a station, and Mr. Redman went to attend to his duties. When he next came through the car Miss Knightly spoke to him. She had recovered herself. Her voice was steady, though very low and very soft when she asked him:

"Were any of her family out there with her when she was ill?"

"Why, yes, Mrs. Ferguesson was out there. That boy Hector got his mother through, before the roads were open. He'd stop at a farmhouse and explain the situation and borrow a team and get the farmer or one of his hands to give them a lift to the next farm, and there they'd get a lift a little further. Everybody knew about the school and the teacher by that time, and wanted to help, no matter how bad the roads were. You see, Miss Knightly, everything would have gone better if it hadn't come on so freezing cold, and if the snow hadn't been so darn soft when it first fell. That family are terrible broke up. We all are, down at the depot. She didn't recognize them when they got there, I heard."

VII

Twenty years after that historic blizzard Evangeline Knightly—now Mrs. Ralph Thorndike—

alighted from the fast eastbound passenger at the MacAlpin station. No one at the station knew who she was except the station master, and he was not quite sure. She looked older, but she also looked more prosperous, more worldly. When she approached him at his office door and asked, "Isn't this Mr. Beardsley?" he recognized her voice and speech.

"That's who. And it's my guess this is, or used to be, Miss Knightly. I've been here almost forever. No ambition. But you left us a long time ago. You're looking fine, Ma'm, if I may say so."

She thanked him and asked him to recommend a hotel where she could stay for a day or two.

He scratched his head. "Well, the Plummer House ain't no Waldorf-Astoria, but the travelling men give a good report of it. The Bishop always stays there when he comes to town. You like me to telephone for an otto [automobile] to take you up? Lord, when you left here there wasn't an otto in the town!"

Mrs. Thorndike smiled. "Not many in the world, I think. And can you tell me, Mr. Beardsley, where the Ferguessons live?"

"The depot Ferguessons? Oh, they live uptown now. Ferg built right west of the Court House, right next to where the Donaldsons used to live. You'll find lots of changes. Some's come up, and some's come down. We used to laugh at Ferg and tell him politics didn't bring in the bacon. But he's got it on us now. The Democrats are sure grand job-givers. Throw 'em round for value received. I still vote the Republican ticket. Too old to change. Anyhow, all those new jobs don't affect the railroads much. They can't put a college professor on to run trains. Now I'll telephone for an otto for you."

Miss Knightly, after going to Denver, had married a very successful young architect, from New England, like herself, and now she was on her way back to Brunswick, Maine, to revisit the scenes of her childhood. Although she had never been in MacAlpin since she left it fifteen years ago, she faithfully read the MacAlpin *Messenger* and knew the important changes in the town.

After she had settled her room at the hotel, and unpacked her toilet articles, she took a cardboard box she had brought with her in the sleeping-car, and went out on a personal errand. She came back to the hotel late for lunch—had a tray sent up to her room, and at four o'clock went to the office in the Court House which used to be her office. This was the autumn of the year, and she had a great desire to drive out among the country schools and see how much fifteen years had changed the land, the pupils, the teachers.

When she introduced herself to the present incumbent, she was cordially received. The young Superintendent seemed a wide-awake, breezy girl, with bobbed blond hair and crimson lips. Her name was Wanda Bliss.

Mrs. Thorndike explained that her stay would not be long enough to let her visit all the country schools, but she would like Miss Bliss's advice as to which were the most interesting.

"Oh, I can run you around to nearly all of them in a day, in my car!"

Mrs. Thorndike thanked her warmly. She liked young people who were not in the least afraid of life or luck or responsibility. In her own youth there were very few like that. The teachers, and many of the pupils out in the country schools, were eager—but anxious. She laughed and told Miss Bliss that she meant to hire a buggy, if there was such a thing left in MacAlpin, and drive out into the country alone.

"I get you. You want to put on an old-home act. You might phone around to any farmers you used to know. Some of them still keep horses for haying."

Mrs. Thorndike got a list of the country teachers and the districts in which they taught. A few of them had been pupils in the schools she used to visit. Those she was determined to see.

The following morning she made the call she had stopped off at MacAlpin to make. She rang the doorbell at the house pointed out to her, and through the open window heard a voice call: "Come in, come in, please. I can't answer the bell."

Mrs. Thorndike opened the door into a shining oak hall with a shining oak stairway.

"Come right through, please. I'm in the back parlour. I sprained my ankle and can't walk yet."

The visitor followed the voice and found Mrs. Ferguesson sitting in a spring rocker, her bandaged right foot resting on a low stool.

"Come in, Ma'm. I have a bad sprain, and the little girl who does for me is downtown marketing. Maybe you came to see Mr. Ferguesson, but his office is—" here she broke off and looked up sharply—intently—at her guest. When the guest smiled, she broke out: "Miss Knightly! *Are* you Miss Knightly? Can it be?"

"They call me Mrs. Thorndike now, but I'm Evangeline Knightly just the same." She put out her hand, and Mrs. Ferguesson seized it with both her own.

"It's too good to be true!" she gasped with tears in her voice, "just too good to be true. The things we dream about that way don't happen." She held fast to Mrs. Thorndike's hand as if she were afraid she might vanish. "When did you come to town, and why didn't they let me know!"

"I came only yesterday, Mrs. Ferguesson, and I wanted to slip in on you just like this, with no one else around."

"Mr. Ferguesson must have known. But his mind is always off on some trail, and he never brings me any news when I'm laid up like this. Dear me! It's a long time." She pressed the visitor's hand again before she released it. "Get yourself a comfortable chair, dear, and sit down by me. I do hate to be helpless like this. It wouldn't have happened but for those slippery front stairs. Mr. Ferguesson just wouldn't put a carpet on them, because he says folks don't carpet hardwood stairs, and I tried to answer the doorbell in a hurry, and this is what come of it. I'm not naturally a clumsy woman on my feet."

Mrs. Thorndike noticed an aggrieved tone in her talk which had never been there in the old days when she had so much to be aggrieved about. She brought a chair and sat down close to Mrs. Ferguesson, facing her. The good woman had not changed much, she thought. There was a little grey in her crinkly auburn hair, and there were lines about her mouth which used not to be there, but her eyes had all the old fire.

"How comfortably you are fixed here, Mrs. Ferguesson! I'm so glad to find you like this."

"Yes, we're comfortable—now that they're all gone! It's mostly his taste. He took great interest." She spoke rather absently, and kept looking out through the polished hall toward the front door, as if she were expecting someone. It seemed a shame that anyone naturally so energetic should be enduring this foolish antiquated method of treating a sprain. The chief change in her, Mrs. Thorndike thought, was that she had grown softer. She reached for the visitor's hand again and held it fast. Tears came to her eyes.

Mrs. Thorndike ventured that she had found the town much changed for the better.

Yes, Mrs. Ferguesson supposed it was.

Then Mrs. Thorndike began in earnest. "How wonderful it is that all your sons have turned out so well! I take the MacAlpin paper chiefly to keep track of the Ferguesson boys. You and Mr. Ferguesson must be very proud."

"Yes'm, we are. We are thankful."

"Even the Denver papers have long articles about Hector and Homer and their great sheep ranches in Wyoming. And Vincent has become such a celebrated chemist, and is helping to destroy all the irreducible elements that I learned when I went to school. And Bryan is with Marshall Field!"

Mrs. Ferguesson nodded and pressed her hand,

but she still kept looking down the hall toward the front door. Suddenly she turned with all herself to Mrs. Thorndike and with a storm of tears cried out from her heart: "Oh, Miss Knightly, talk to me about my Lesley! Seems so many have forgot her, but I know you haven't."

"No, Mrs. Ferguesson, I never forget her. Yesterday morning I took a box of roses that I brought with me from my own garden down to where she sleeps. I was glad to find a little seat there, so that I could stay for a long while and think about her."

"Oh, I wish I could have gone with you, Miss Knightly! (I can't call you anything else.) I wish we could have gone together. I can't help feeling she knows. *Anyhow,* we know! And there's nothing in all my life so precious to me to remember and think about as my Lesley. I'm no soft woman, either. The boys will tell you that. They'll tell you they got on because I always had a firm hand over them. They're all true to Lesley, my boys. Every time they come home they go down there. They feel it like I do, as if it had happened yesterday. Their father feels it, too, when he's not taken up with his abstractions. Anyhow, I don't think men feel things like women and boys. My boys have stayed boys. I do believe they feel as bad as I do about moving up here. We have four nice bedrooms upstairs to make them comfortable, should they all come home at once, and they're polite about us and tell us how well fixed we are. But Miss Knightly, I know at the bottom of their hearts they wish they was back in the old house down by the depot, sleeping in the attic."

Mrs. Thorndike stroked her hand. "I looked for

the old house as I was coming up from the station. I made the driver stop."

"Ain't it dreadful, what's been done to it? If I'd foreseen, I'd never have let Mr. Ferguesson sell it. It was in my name. I'd have kept it to go back to and remember sometimes. Folks in middle age make a mistake when they think they can better themselves. They can't, not if they have any heart. And the other kind don't matter—they aren't real people—just poor put-ons, that try to be like the advertisements. Father even took me to California one winter. I was miserable all the time. And there were plenty more like me—miserable underneath. The women lined up in cafeterias, carrying their little trays—like convicts, seemed to me—and running to beauty shops to get their poor old hands manicured. And the old men, Miss Knightly, I pitied them most of all! Old bent-backed farmers, standing round in their shirt-sleeves, in plazas and alleyways, pitching horseshoes like they used to do at home. I tell you, people are happiest where they've had their children and struggled along and been real folks, and not tourists. What do you think about all this running around, Miss Knightly? You're an educated woman, I never had much schooling."

"I don't think schooling gives people any wisdom, Mrs. Ferguesson. I guess only life does that."

"Well, this I know: our best years are when we're working hardest and going right ahead when we can hardly see our way out. Times I was a good deal perplexed. But I always had one comfort. I did own our own house. I never had to worry about the rent. Don't it seem strange to you, though, tha all our boys are so practical, and their father such a dreamer?''

Mrs. Thorndike murmured that some people think boys are most likely to take after their mother.

Mrs. Ferguesson smiled absently and shook her head. Presently she came out with: "It's a comfort to me up here, on a still night I can still hear the trains whistle in. Sometimes, when I can't sleep, I lie and listen for them. And I can almost think I am down there, with my children up in the loft. We were very happy." She looked up at her guest and smiled bravely. "I suppose you go away tonight?"

Mrs. Thorndike explained her plan to spend a day in the country.

"You're going out to visit the little schools? Why, God bless you, dear! You're still our Miss Knightly! But you'd better take a car, so you can get up to the Wild Rose school and back in one day. Do go there! The teacher is Mandy Perkins—she was one of her little scholars. You'll like Mandy, an' she loved Lesley. You must get Bud Sullivan to drive you. Engage him right now—the telephone's there in the hall, and the garage is 306. He'll creep along for you, if you tell him. He does for me. I often go out to the Wild Rose school, and over to see dear Mrs. Robertson, who ain't so young as she was then. I can't go with Mr. Ferguesson. He drives so fast it's no satisfaction. And then he's not always mindful. He's had some accidents. When he gets to thinking, he's just as likely to run down a cow as not. He's had to pay for one. You know cows will cross the road right in front of a car. Maybe their grandchildren calves will be more modern-minded."

Mrs. Thorndike did not see her old friend again, but she wrote her a long letter from Wiscasset, Maine, which Mrs. Fergusson sent to her son Hector, marked, "To be returned, but first pass on to your brothers."

CHRONOLOGIES AND BIBLIOGRAPHIES

Sarah Orne Jewett: Chronology

1849—born in South Berwick, Maine in the house that had been purchased in 1820 by her grandfather; the family continued to live in this home during her father's lifetime (he was a country doctor)
1868—published her first short story, "Jenny Garrow's Lovers," in *The Flag of Our Union,* a Boston periodical
1873—published the first of her Maine stories, "The Shore House," in the *Atlantic Monthly*
1877—published *Deephaven* at the suggestion of W. D. Howells, who felt she ought to publish a collection of the Maine stories
1878—published *Play Days: A Book of Stories for Children;* her father, Dr. Jewett, died—giving her (according to her own account) the greatest sorrow she was ever to know
1881—established her friendship with Annie Addams Fields, widow of the influential publisher and editor of the *Atlantic Monthly,* James Fields; began to spend three months each winter away from Maine, visiting Mrs. Fields in Boston
1882—made her first trip to Europe
1886—published *The White Heron and Other Stories*
1896—published *The Country of the Pointed Firs,* her greatest work
1902—had a serious accident, falling from a carriage and injuring her neck and spine; met Willa Cather and became friendly with this young author, whose work she encouraged
1909—died in the family home in South Berwick, Maine

NOTE: Not all of Jewett's publications have been included in this list.

Sarah Orne Jewett: Bibliography *(In chronological order)*

F. O. Matthiessen, *Sarah Orne Jewett* (Boston and New York: Houghton Mifflin, 1929).

Edward M. Chapman, "The New England of Sarah Orne Jewett," *Yale Review,* n.s., 3: 157-172.

A. M. Buchan, *"Our Dear Sarah": An Essay On Sarah Orne Jewett,* Washington University Studies, No. 24 (St. Louis: Washington University Press, 1953).

Eleanor M. Smith, "The Literary Relationship of Sarah Orne Jewett and Willa Cather," *New England Quarterly,* 29: 472-492.

Warner Berthoff, "The Art of Jewett's *Pointed Firs,*" *New England Quarterly,* 32: 31-53.

Mary Ellen Chase, "Sarah Orne Jewett as a Social Historian," in *The World of Dunnet Landing,* ed., David Bonnell Green (Lincoln: University of Nebraska Press, 1962).

James Ellis, "The World of Dreams: Sexual Symbolism in 'A White Heron'," *Naussau Review,* 3, iii: 3-9.

Kate Chopin: Chronology

1851—born in St. Louis
1855—father died in a railroad crash
1870—married Oscar Chopin; moved to New Orleans
1879—moved to Cloutierville
1883—Oscar Chopin died suddenly
1884—returned to live in St. Louis
1889—published her first short story, "Wiser than a God"
1890—published *At Fault,* her first novel
1894—published *Bayou Folk,* her first collection of short stories
1897—published *A Night in Acadie,* her second collection of short stories
1899—published *The Awakening*
1904—died in St. Louis

NOTE: Not all of Chopin's work is cited here; Per Seyersted has collected her complete works in *The Complete Works of Kate Chopin* (Baton Rouge: Louisiana State Press, 1969).

***Kate Chopin: Bibliography** (In chronological order)*

Daniel S. Rankin, *Kate Chopin and Her Creole Stories* (Philadelphia: University of Pennsylvania Press, 1932).

Joan Zlotnick, "A Woman's Will: Kate Chopin on Selfhood, Wifehood, and Motherhood," *Markham Review*, 3: no pages.

Marie Fletcher, "The Southern Women in the Fiction of Kate Chopin," *Louisiana History*, 7: 117-132.

Per Seyersted, *Kate Chopin: A Critical Biography* (Baton Rouge: Louisiana State University Press, 1969).

Robert Arner, "Landscape Symbolism in Kate Chopin's 'At Fault'," *Louisiana Studies*, 9: 142-153.

———, "Kate Chopin's Realism: 'At the 'Cadian Ball' and 'The Storm' " *Markham Review*, 2: no pages.

Carolyn Forrey, "The New Woman Revisited," *Women's Studies*, 2: 37-56.

Cynthia Griffin Wolff, "Thanatos and Eros: Kate Chopin's *The Awakening*," *American Quarterly*, 25: 449-471.

———, "Kate Chopin and the Fiction of Limits: Désirée's Baby," The *Southern Literary Journal*, 10, ii: 123-134.

Edith Wharton: Chronology

1862—born in New York City

1886—married Edward Robbins Wharton

1899—published *The Greater Inclination*, her first volume of short stories

1905—published *The House of Mirth*, her first great novel

1907—met Morton Fullerton

1911—published *Ethan Frome*

1913—published *The Custom of the Country*, having taken up permanent residence in France; divorced Edward Wharton

1914-1918—active in Paris homefront activities during World War I
1916—made a Chevalier in the French Legion of Honor
1917—published *Summer*
1920—published *The Age of Innocence*
1921—awarded the Pulitzer Prize for novels
1923—awarded an Honorary Doctor of Letters from Yale University, the first ever awarded by Yale to a woman; made her last visit to America
1937—died in Paris

NOTE: Not all of Wharton's fiction is listed here; she continued to write after 1921, but her best work was written prior to that date.

***Edith Wharton: Bibliography** (In chronological order)*

Blake Nevius, *Edith Wharton, A Study of Her Fiction* (Berkeley and Los Angeles: University of California Press, 1953).
Millicent Bell, *Edith Wharton and Henry James* (New York: Braziller, 1965).
Louis Auchincloss, *Edith Wharton, A Woman in Her Time* (New York: Viking Press, 1971).
Gary H. Lindberg, *Edith Wharton and the Novel of Manners* (Charlottesville: University of Virginia Press, 1975).
R. W. B. Lewis, *Edith Wharton: A Biography* (New York: Harper & Row, 1975).
Cynthia Griffin Wolff, *A Feast of Words: The Triumph of Edith Wharton* (New York: Oxford University Press, 1977).

Willa Cather: Chronology

1873—born in Virginia
1883—moved with family to Red Cloud, Nebraska
1891-1895—attended the University of Nebraska
1896-1901—worked in Pittsburgh, serving as newspaperwoman on the *Home Monthly* and on the *Daily*

Leader, wrote drama criticism, and taught English and Latin in the Pittsburgh high schools
1903—published *April Twilights,* a slender book of poetry
1905—published *The Troll Garden,* a book of short stories; went to work for *McClure's Magazine* in New York, soon becoming managing editor
1912—published *Alexander's Bridge,* her first novel; resigned from *McClure's* and lived thereafter on the profits from her writing
1913—published *O Pioneers!*
1915—published *The Song of the Lark*
1918—published *My Ántonia*
1923—published *A Lost Lady;* won the Pulitzer Prize for novels
1925—published *The Professor's House*
1927—published *Death Comes for the Archbishop*
1931—published *Shadows on the Rock*
1947—died

NOTE: Not all Cather's publications have been included in this selective list; it is true, however, that her best work was done before 1932.

Willa Cather: Bibliography *(In chronological order)*

E. K. Brown and Leon Edel, *Willa Cather: A Critical Biography* (New York: Knopf, 1953).

Edith Lewis, *Willa Cather Living* (New York: Knopf, 1953).

John H. Randall, *The Landscape and the Looking Glass: Willa Cather's Search for Value* (Boston: Houghton Mifflin, 1960).

Mildred R. Bennett, *The World of Willa Cather* (Lincoln: University of Nebraska Press, 1961).

David Daiches, *Willa Cather: A Critical Introduction* (New York: Collier, 1962).

James Schroeter, ed., *Willa Cather and Her Critics* (Ithaca N.Y.: Cornell University Press, 1967).

Western American Literature (Spring 1972), an entire special issue on Cather.

Virginia Faulkner and Bernice Slote, eds., *The Art of Willa Cather* (Lincoln: University of Nebraska Press, 1974).